THE BIN LADEN PLOT

ALSO BY RICK CAMPBELL

THE
BIN LADEN
PLOT

RICK
CAMPBELL

ST. MARTIN'S
PRESS
NEW YORK

First published in the United States by St. Martin's Press, an imprint of St. Martin's Publishing Group.

THE BIN LADEN PLOT. Copyright © 2024 by Rick Campbell. All rights reserved. Printed in the United States of America. For information, address St. Martin's Publishing Group, 120 Broadway, New York, NY 10271.

www.stmartins.com

Library of Congress Cataloging-in-Publication Data

Names: Campbell, Rick (Navy Commander) author.
Title: The Bin Laden plot / Rick Campbell.
Description: First edition. | New York : St. Martin's Press, 2024. | Series: Trident deception series ; 7
Identifiers: LCCN 2023056222 | ISBN 9781250277107 (hardcover) | ISBN 9781250277114 (e-book)
Subjects: LCSH: United States. Navy—Fiction. | Marines—Fiction. | Assassins—Fiction. | Hacking—Fiction. | Corruption—Fiction. | LCGFT: Thrillers (Fiction) | Novels.
Classification: LCC PS3603.A48223 B56 2024 | DDC 813/.6—dc23/eng/20231211
LC record available at https://lccn.loc.gov/2023056222

Our books may be purchased in bulk for promotional, educational, or business use. Please contact your local bookseller or the Macmillan Corporate and Premium Sales Department at 1-800-221-7945, extension 5442, or by email at MacmillanSpecialMarkets@macmillan.com.

First Edition: 2024

10 9 8 7 6 5 4 3 2 1

CHARACTERS

UNITED STATES ADMINISTRATION
Kevin Hardison—chief of staff
Marcy Perini—secretary of state
Tom Glass—secretary of defense
Nova Conover—secretary of homeland security
Thom Parham—national security advisor
Glen McGlothin (Captain)—senior military advisor

CENTRAL INTELLIGENCE AGENCY
Christine O'Connor—director (DCIA)
Monroe Bryant—deputy director (DDCIA)
PJ Rolow—deputy director for operations (DDO)
Tracey McFarland—deputy director for analysis (DDA)
Becky Rock—deputy director for support (DDS)
Jake Harrison—paramilitary operations officer
Khalila Dufour—specialized skills officer, National Clandestine Service
Asad Durrani—collection management officer
Nizar Mussan—paramilitary operations officer (Bluestone Security)
Marzouq Ashour—specialized skills officer (Salmiya, Kuwait)

OFFICE OF NAVAL INTELLIGENCE
Elizabeth Gherlone—supervisor
Sara Inman—torpedo expert

OTHER U.S. GOVERNMENT AGENCIES

BRENDA VERBECK—secretary of the Navy

JOHN RODGAARD—director of National Intelligence

BILL GUISEWHITE—director of the Federal Bureau of Investigation

USS *MICHIGAN* (OHIO CLASS GUIDED MISSILE SUBMARINE)— BLUE CREW

MURRAY WILSON (Captain)—Commanding Officer

TOM MONTGOMERY (Lieutenant Commander)—Executive Officer

RYAN JESCOVITCH (Lieutenant)—Weapons Officer

BRIAN RESOR (Lieutenant)—Officer of the Deck

BRITTANY KERN (Lieutenant)—Officer of the Deck

KAREN BASS (Lieutenant)—Officer of the Deck

JIM MOORE (Sonar Technician Chief)—Sonar Division Chief

ANDREW BUBB (Sonar Technician Second Class)—Narrowband Operator

USS *MICHIGAN*—SEAL DETACHMENT

JON PETERS (Commander)—SEAL Team Commander

TRACEY NOVIELLO (Lieutenant)—SEAL Platoon Officer-in-Charge

RUSS BURKHARDT (Special Warfare Operator Senior Chief)—SEAL
   Platoon Leading Chief Petty Officer

JOHN SHEAKOSKI (Special Warfare Operator First Class)

MICHAEL KELLER (Special Warfare Operator Second Class)

KURT HACKER (Special Warfare Operator First Class)

JOHN PICKERING (Special Warfare Operator Second Class)

DAVE NAREHOOD (Special Warfare Operator First Class)

RICH MEYER (Special Warfare Operator Second Class)

USS *JIMMY CARTER* (SEAWOLF CLASS FAST ATTACK SUBMARINE)

DENNIS GALLAGHER (Commander)—Commanding Officer

USS *STETHEM* (ARLEIGH BURKE CLASS DESTROYER)
RICHARD WORTMAN (Petty Officer Second Class)
JAY NEAL (Seaman)

OTHER MILITARY CHARACTERS
JOE SITES (Admiral)—Chief of Naval Operations (CNO)
ANDY HOSKINS (Captain)—secretary of the Navy's military aide
JASON JOHNSON (Cryptologic Technician Chief)—Pentagon watch-
stander

KUWAITI CHARACTERS
AYMAN ABOUD—Persian rug dealer
BASIM IQBAL—Kuwait Security Service agent
MALIK AL-RASHIDI—Director, Kuwait Security Service

OTHER CHARACTERS
LONNIE MIXELL (alias Mitch Larson)—former Navy SEAL
GARY NAGLE—former Navy SEAL
JOHN MCNEIL—former Navy SEAL / secretary of the Navy protective
agent
GRETCHEN MCNEIL—John McNeil's wife
ANGIE HARRISON—Jake Harrison's wife
MADELINE (MADDY) HARRISON—Jake Harrison's daughter
BRIAN HUMM—*Alvin* operations officer
KEN HILLSLEY—*Alvin* pilot
CAROLINE RICE—Fairfax County, Virginia, detective
ADELLE MURPHY—housekeeping supervisor at the Intercontinental Hotel
CAITLIN JOHNSON—gymnastics coach

1
USS *STETHEM*

In the Strait of Hormuz, the thirty-mile-wide opening to the strategically important Persian Gulf, USS *Stethem* cruised through the warm water, her navigation lights revealing the presence of the U.S. warship twelve miles off the coast, hugging the edge of Iranian territorial waters. To the south, white masthead lights announced the passage of numerous merchant ships transiting the busy choke point.

Hours earlier, after being battered by a storm as the destroyer passed through the Gulf of Oman, *Stethem* had entered the Strait, where the narrow waterway turned sharply southwest. The sun had recently set, and an outward calm had returned to the warship. In the darkness, the topside decks were deserted aside from two men on the fantail taking a smoke break, the occasional red glow from the ends of their cigarettes faintly illuminating their faces.

Petty Officer Second Class Richard Wortman, leaning against the hangar bulkhead on the helicopter deck, took another puff of his cigarette while his newfound friend rattled on about his girlfriend back home. Seaman Jay Neal, who happened to be from a town less than an hour from Wortman's, was a new addition to the crew, having reported aboard just before *Stethem*'s departure for its Gulf deployment several weeks ago.

Wortman's gaze shifted from the masthead lights in the distance to the bluish-green trail behind the destroyer, created by bioluminescent algae disturbed by the ship's passage. It was times like this that reaffirmed his decision to join the Navy. He replayed an old recruiting slogan in his mind—*It's not just a job, it's an adventure.* He reflected on the challenge of learning how to operate and maintain complex weapon systems, the excitement of foreign port visits, and the tranquility of cruising the Gulf aboard a warship as the sun set over the Middle East. Things your average corn-fed midwestern kid would never experience.

Neal pointed to starboard. "Hey, that's pretty cool. What is it?"

Wortman spotted a second bioluminescent trail in the distance, narrow and moving swiftly through the water, curving toward *Stethem*. It took a few seconds to realize what it was.

"Torpedo in the water!"

No one besides Neal could hear him from the helicopter deck, but he reacted instinctively, calling out the warning. He grabbed Neal by the arm and pulled him toward the nearest watertight door on the starboard side of the ship.

The bridge lookout or sonar technicians on watch must have detected the torpedo at about the same time, because Wortman heard the roar of the ship's four gas turbine engines spring to life, followed by a surge as the ship's twin shafts accelerated, churning the water behind them. An announcement came over the ship's intercom, ordering *Stethem*'s crew to General Quarters and battle stations.

It was all happening too fast—and too late.

The luminescent trail closed on *Stethem* while Wortman and Neal were still topside, culminating in a muffled explosion that bucked the destroyer's deck upward, launching both men several feet in the air. When Wortman landed on the deck, sharp pain sliced through his right leg.

After the upward buckling, the destroyer's midships sagged into the bubble void created by the explosion, putting additional stress on the ship's keel. The most devastating effect of the torpedo explosion followed: the water-jet plume, traveling upward as the bubble collapsed, shearing through the already weakened keel, tearing through steel bulkheads and decks.

Seawater from the plume fell onto Wortman like rain. As he pushed himself to his feet, pain shot through his right leg again. He looked down, spotting a six-inch-long gash in his thigh, bleeding profusely. He had landed against a metal stanchion plate, slicing into his thigh. He looked for Neal, but he was nowhere to be found. He must have been launched overboard when the ship lurched upward.

Wortman ripped his shirt off and tied it around his thigh to stem the bleeding. With a hand on the railing, he pulled himself up and resumed his trek toward the watertight door and his battle station. But he stopped after his first step. Not far ahead, a crack had opened in the destroyer, splitting the ship in half, and the deck began slanting down toward the opening. The keel had been broken and water was flooding into the ship. It took only a moment for Wortman to realize what was about to happen.

Stethem was going to the bottom.

He held on to the topside railing as the deck angle steepened. The ship's engines went dead, then the lighting in the forward half of the ship flickered and extinguished, followed by darkness aft. The ship then sheared completely in half. Both halves remained afloat for the moment, their tilt steadily increasing as the bow and stern rose in the air.

Crew members began streaming topside. In the darkness, with their ship and surrounding water lit only by a half-moon, he could barely see them. But he heard their frantic shouts, followed by splashes as they jumped into the water.

Wortman's feet started slipping on the deck as the stern pitched upward. He realized he must have stood frozen where he was, a hand on the railing, as he took in the scene and what it portended for his future. He searched for a life preserver or other flotation device nearby, but none could be located in the weak moonlight. The deck angle steepened, forcing Wortman to grab onto the railing with both hands, and the stern began descending into the water. He was running out of time.

He'd have to jump overboard—a twenty-foot drop. He glanced over the side to ensure he wouldn't land on any flotsam, then lifted his right leg over the railing. Holding his breath, he flipped himself over the side and plunged into the dark water.

After orienting himself, spotting the shimmering moon on the ocean's surface, he swam toward the light. He finally broke the surface and gasped for air, treading water as he assessed his predicament. The stern continued its descent, accompanied by loud metallic groans as air trapped within its compartments compressed and bulkheads deformed. He knew it was a sound he would never forget; *Stethem*'s death throes as it descended into the ocean depth.

Wortman suddenly realized his proximity to the ship was a threat to his survival. Once the stern completely slipped into the water, its submergence would supposedly create a swirling vortex, sucking any nearby debris—and sailors—deep beneath the surface. It was occasionally a topic of debate among shipmates, whether the vortex pulling sailors to their doom was fact or fiction, but he figured it was better to not take the chance.

He started swimming away, deciding to keep going until he no longer heard the sounds of *Stethem*'s demise. While he swam, pain shot through his right leg with each kick, but he slowly pulled away from the stern.

As he kept swimming, his arms and legs began to chill. He was losing too much blood. He felt light-headed and stopped to catch his breath. He scanned the area for other crew members, and more important, a flotation device of some sort—anything to hang on to until a rescue effort arrived. He spotted nothing.

While he treaded water, his arms and legs tired, and he soon had difficulty keeping his head above the waves. He called for help, but his shouts were weak and he received no response.

The metallic groans from the sinking stern faded and a calm returned to the sea, punctured only by the sporadic voices of shipmates in the distance. After discerning which sound was closest, he swam toward it. But his muscles were already fatigued, and he didn't get far before he stopped. The choppy waves began to pass over his head, and he struggled to keep his face above water.

When the next wave passed, he didn't resurface. He stroked upward, but his kick and arm stroke didn't have much power. He spotted the white, wavering moon on the water's surface, and it seemed to be getting smaller. Panic set in and he redoubled his efforts. The size of the moon stabilized. But it wasn't getting any bigger, and he was running out of oxygen.

Despite his best efforts, the moon began shrinking again. Terror tore through his mind as he stroked furiously upward, hoping by some miracle he'd make it back to the surface. But then the movement of his arms and legs slowed as his muscles tired even further. As he stared at the surface, a darkness slowly converged on the glittering moon, and a peaceful warmth and calm spread throughout his body.

For some reason, his thoughts drifted to the day he told his parents he was joining the Navy, continuing his family's proud heritage of naval service, dating all the way back to World War II. As his thoughts faded away, the last image in Wortman's mind was the proud look on his father's face as he congratulated his son.

WASHINGTON, D.C.

It was just after 4 p.m. when a black Lincoln Navigator turned onto West Executive Avenue, headed toward the White House. In the back seat, CIA director Christine O'Connor contemplated the information contained in a folder inside the black leather satchel on her lap. She'd been the director for only a few months and was still learning about the myriad programs the CIA was involved in. The agency had tentacles in almost every facet of the U.S. government.

The district's buildings glided past her window until the SUV stopped in front of black steel bars blocking the entrance to the White House. After the gate guards checked her driver's identification and completed a security sweep of the vehicle, the gate slid aside and the vehicle pulled forward, grinding to a halt beneath the curved overhang of the West Wing portico.

Standing at the entrance between two Marines in dress blues was Kevin Hardison, the president's chief of staff, whom Christine had worked with when she was the president's national security advisor.

He greeted her, then asked, "Are you up to speed on the program?"

"I am. But I know only half of the story."

"That's fine. SecNav will have the lead during this afternoon's briefing, considering the situation and its complexities. Everyone's assembling in the Situation Room. We'll begin when the SecNav and CNO arrive." He cast a glance toward the street. Another black SUV was approaching the White House.

Christine left Hardison at the West Wing entrance and entered the White House, proceeding past her former corner office and down toward the Situation Room in the basement. She left her cell phone outside the room and entered to find the expected collection of White House staff and cabinet members seated around the table: Secretary of Defense Tom Glass, Secretary of State Marcy Perini, Captain Glen McGlothin—the president's senior military advisor—and finally, Christine's successor in the White House—Thom Parham—the president's national security advisor.

Secretary of the Navy Brenda Verbeck arrived, followed by Chief of Naval Operations Admiral Joe Sites. They took their seats beside Glass, while Christine sat beside Parham, chatting with him while waiting for the meeting to commence. An information specialist approached Verbeck, informing her that her brief was loaded, handing her the remote control as the wide-screen display on the far wall flickered to life. The title slide of her presentation appeared, containing a single, innocuous line: USS *Stethem* Incident. Hardison and the president entered the Situation Room a moment later.

The president took his seat at the head of the table and cast his gaze toward Verbeck, an attractive and articulate woman in her late forties, a rising star in the administration and one of the leading contenders for secretary of defense if Tom Glass moved on.

"What have you got, Brenda?"

"Good morning, Mr. President." She pressed the remote control, advancing her brief to the next slide, displaying a map of the Persian Gulf annotated with the location of the incident. "As you're aware, USS *Stethem*, an Arleigh Burke class destroyer on deployment in the Persian Gulf, was sunk four hours ago by a torpedo attack. Twenty-four crew members are reported missing and feared dead. Search efforts are continuing, but the odds that there are additional survivors are slim."

Verbeck advanced the brief to the next slide, showing a satellite view of the Persian Gulf at the time of the attack, then zoomed in until the distinct bioluminescent trail of the torpedo intercepting *Stethem* could be seen.

"At the time of the attack, *Stethem* was operating in international waters just outside the twelve-nautical-mile limit from Iran. The most obvious scenario is that *Stethem* was sunk by an Iranian submarine. Iran has denied the attack, of course."

"Did we have any indication of pending military engagement by Iran?" the president asked.

"No, sir. Only the standard indignant verbiage regarding the presence of American warships in the Gulf. The lack of ratcheting tensions between our two countries, although that is certainly not the case now, indicates there may be another potential scenario."

Secretary Verbeck's brief shifted to the next slide, showing a schematic of an unmanned undersea vehicle.

"We currently have a small fleet of large-diameter UUVs, called Scorpions, operating in the Persian Gulf. Their primary mission is surveillance, operating near the coast to intercept short-range electronic communications, which Iran and other countries have been using to thwart our satellite collection efforts. Due to the sensitive capabilities of these UUVs and the desire to keep their existence secret, they're managed as a black program in concert with the CIA, which analyzes the information obtained."

The brief advanced to another slide, which displayed a map of the Persian Gulf, divided into sectors.

"It turns out that the UUV assigned to the area where *Stethem* was operating has failed to report in. Every attempt to force it to report its location and status has failed."

"The Iranians may have also destroyed our UUV?" the president asked.

Verbeck shifted uncomfortably in her chair. "No, Mr. President. The situation could be far more serious. Unknown to anyone outside the program, even the CIA"—she glanced briefly at Christine—"these UUVs are weaponized." She clicked the remote control, advancing her brief to the next slide, showing a front view of the vehicle, which revealed two round portals in the bow. "Each Scorpion carries two torpedoes."

The president's gaze shifted slowly from the display to Verbeck. "Are you saying that one of our UUVs went renegade and sank *Stethem*?"

"It's a possibility, sir. Nothing is certain, but the data is aligning that way. The UUV failed to report in several hours before the *Stethem* attack, and there was a previous concern that these UUVs were being rushed into service with insufficient testing."

The president turned to the Chief of Naval Operations, who cleared his throat before speaking.

"Due to the crucial need for consistent electronic surveillance in the Middle East, Fifth Fleet submitted an Urgent Operational Need request. UONs enable the rapid fielding of new technology with limited testing. What Secretary Verbeck is alluding to is that the testing in this case may not have detected latent defects in the Scorpion's artificial intelligence and attack protocol. Another possibility is that this UUV was hacked and a virus was inserted. We think that's unlikely, however, due to the strict secrecy of this program—we doubt Iran or any other country is aware of the existence of these vehicles—which means the problem is most likely internal."

"How do you recommend we proceed?" the president asked, turning back to Verbeck.

"I propose a dual response: one public and one internal," she replied. "Publicly, we keep what might have happened regarding our UUV confidential, hinting instead that Iran is the likely culprit. Tell the press we're evaluating the situation and what our response might be. Internally, we need to locate and destroy this UUV quickly. Assuming it sank *Stethem*, it still carries another torpedo, and who knows what else it might attack."

"What assets do we have available?"

Verbeck advanced her brief a few slides, stopping on the U.S. order of battle in the Persian Gulf, then deferred to the CNO, who answered the president.

"We have several surface ships in the Gulf, but no carrier strike group at the moment. As far as submarines go, *Michigan* is the closest asset. Submarines are the most capable platform for hunting down the UUV, so I recommend we assign *Michigan* to the task. The BLUE crew is aboard, so Captain Murray Wilson is in command. If you recall, he was the officer we assigned to track down the Russian submarine *Kazan*."

"Yes, of course," the president replied. "*Michigan* sounds like an excellent choice."

"One more thing, Mr. President," Verbeck interjected. "Due to these UUVs being a black program directly under the SecNav's purview, I'd like to personally oversee the operation to locate and destroy our UUV. I think it's prudent to minimize the number of personnel who are made aware of the Scorpion program and its potential shortcomings."

The president looked to the CNO, who announced, "That can be arranged."

"I concur," the president replied. "Move quickly on this. We already have two dozen missing and likely dead sailors. If our UUV was truly responsible, we don't need more blood on our hands."

3

ARLINGTON, VIRGINIA

Brenda Verbeck's SUV rolled to a stop at the base of the Pentagon's Mall Entrance, where she was escorted up the steps by two protective agents, one on each side, then into the massive military complex covering thirty-four acres, designed in a fashion that would enthrall a cribbage player: five sides, five stories, five rings, with a five-acre courtyard in the middle. As Verbeck stepped into the building, she reflected on the Pentagon's unusual concentration of power—not at its center but along its perimeter: a mile-long pentagonal corridor labeled the E-Ring, where the main offices of the Department of Defense were located.

Verbeck entered the reception area adjacent to her office, taking no heed this morning of one of the perks of her position: a suite offering splendid views of the Robert E. Lee memorial and surrounding Arlington National Cemetery. She passed her military aide, Captain Andy Hoskins, seated at his desk. Their eyes locked briefly, then he followed her into her office. After closing the door, he took a seat beside Verbeck at her conference table.

"How did the brief go?" he asked.

"As well as I had hoped."

"Did everyone buy the renegade UUV story?"

"Hook, line, and sinker," Verbeck replied. "The administration is concerned about the potential negative publicity, so they're reacting quickly, before evidence from the attack is analyzed."

"Excellent," Hoskins replied. "Were you put directly in charge of the mission to hunt down the UUV?"

"Exactly as planned. The CNO will make the necessary arrangements, so I'll have direct authority over the effort, bypassing the combatant commanders."

"What assets are assigned?"

"A submarine. USS *Michigan*, already in the Persian Gulf. We'll need to send orders to her right away."

"I'll draft a Commanding Officer's Eyes Only message, providing the necessary direction."

"I have a better idea," Verbeck replied. "I want to minimize the number of individuals who are exposed to the details. If we transmit a message, someone at the communications center has to upload and review it before sending, and then it has to be received by the submarine. Who knows how many people will read it. Instead, I'd like to deliver the orders to *Michigan*'s captain personally. Can that be arranged?"

"Certainly. Fifth Fleet Command is located in Bahrain, and I can direct the submarine to meet us there. I'll arrange your transportation—a flight first thing in the morning." After a short hesitation, he asked, "I assume I'll be coming with you?"

"Of course."

Verbeck placed a hand inside his thigh, sliding it upward as she leaned toward Hoskins, engaging him in a passionate kiss.

"I appreciate everything you've done so far," she said after she pulled back, "keeping this issue under wraps. No one can learn the truth. Aside from you, is anyone else aware of the transaction?"

"One other person—the cryptologic technician here in the Pentagon who reviewed the information upon receipt. The data has been deleted from our servers; it never went to the CIA."

"How do we keep the cryptologic technician from talking?"

"I had him sign a nondisclosure agreement, reminding him he'd lose his security clearance if he revealed the contents of the UUV transmission to anyone."

"Do you have the agreement?"

Hoskins pulled the NDA from his notepad.

"If I may," Verbeck said, holding her hand out. "I'd like to keep this close hold."

"Understandable." Hoskins handed it to Verbeck. "I'll send the message directing *Michigan* to meet us in Bahrain, then make our travel arrangements. Afterward . . . are you available tonight?"

"How about eight o'clock?" she replied as she leaned in for another kiss.

After Hoskins departed her office, closing the door behind him, Verbeck moved to her desk, placing the NDA before her. She picked up the phone and dialed.

When her call was answered, she said, "This is Brenda. I need a favor."

"What kind of favor?"

"Your kind."

"What do you need?"

"I have some loose ends I need tied up."

"I'd rather not get involved."

"You have some loose ends to tie up yourself. You've left them dangling for far too long. Why not take care of them as well?"

There was silence for a moment before Verbeck received a response.

"I agree. But there's a complication. One of my loose ends is assigned to your protective detail. However, it could be considered an opportunity. I could arrange his death while he's assigned to you for an event, or do you prefer it be done during a quieter, off-duty moment?"

Brenda considered the question, and it didn't take long for her to decide on the former option.

"Definitely while on duty. Can you make it look like I was the intended victim? The agent will go down a hero, and I'll get some welcome publicity. SecNav is my stepping stone to SecDef, and the more publicity I can get, the better."

"I'll see what I can arrange. How many loose ends do you have?"

"Two."

"Who?"

Verbeck skimmed the NDA agreement, locating the person's name. "Jason Lee Johnson. He's a Navy cryptologic technician here at the Pentagon."

"And the second?"

"Captain Andrew Howard Hoskins, my military aide."

4

CALVERTON, MARYLAND

Seated at a desk in his hotel room a block from the Capital Beltway, Lonnie Mixell studied the four surveillance videos on his laptop computer screen, searching for any indication that tonight's endeavor had been tipped to the authorities. At first, the shipment to the Middle East had seemed straightforward—almost childishly simplistic—until he had discerned its contents. Given the sensitivity of the matter, he had taken precautions, installing surveillance cameras at the loadout location a few weeks ago, which he had monitored daily. Thus far, there was no indication anything was awry.

He had taken additional precautions, changing his appearance. His hair was dyed brown and he wore blue contact lenses. The changes wouldn't fool computerized facial recognition algorithms, but it should prevent any law enforcement officials he happened to run into from recognizing him as one of the most wanted men by Interpol and America's FBI. The man who, a few months ago, had almost enabled the destruction of the twenty largest cities in the United States and the assassination of the nation's president.

A notification appeared on his computer display, indicating he had received an encrypted transmission. He clicked on the note, which launched a portal to a secure messaging site.

Looking for more work?

As a matter of fact, he was. The current job would wrap up sometime tomorrow, once the containers were loaded aboard the ship, and the ten-million-dollar payment would last only so long.

Mixell responded: "Activity?"

Snap a few pictures.

"How many?" Mixell typed, wondering how many pictures—
assassinations—were being requested.

Five.

"Location?"

All in the United States. Four in the D.C. area. One on West Coast.

"Rate?"

$1M each.

"Due date?"

No hard dates, but ASAP.

Mixell pondered the request. A million each could be plenty or woe-
fully inadequate, depending on the targets.

"Names and details?"

Five names scrolled down the screen, accompanied by a short description of each man's current job and background. Three of the targets
were retired Navy SEALs, and he knew each one. The other two were
active-duty Navy: one officer and one enlisted, and he had never heard
of either.

He typed: "What's the connection?"

Their relationship is not your concern.

Mixell's eyes went back to the names on the list. The fourth was the
most problematic, while the fifth sparked Mixell's curiosity.

The fourth man was Johnathon Patrick McNeil, a former Navy
SEAL commander who had retired recently and was now working as
a government protective agent, currently assigned to the secretary of
the Navy. Additionally, it was specified that he be killed in her vicinity.
Make it look like she was the target.

Mixell typed his response: "The scenario specified for the fourth
man will cost you double. But the fifth man, I'll do for free."

You two have a history?

"You could call it that."

We have a contract.

Mixell's gaze returned to the last name on the computer display, then
smiled at the irony.

Jake Edward Harrison was already on his list.

5

USS *MICHIGAN*

"Dive, make your depth eight-zero feet."

The Diving Officer, the senior of three watchstanders seated before the submarine's Ship Control Panel, acknowledged the Officer of the Deck's order, then executed it.

"Ten up," he ordered the Lee Helm, who adjusted the stern planes until the submarine achieved a ten-degree up angle.

"Full rise, fairwater planes," he ordered the Helm, who tilted the control surfaces protruding from both sides of the submarine's sail to maximum rise.

Slowly, the eighteen-thousand-ton submarine rose toward the surface.

Peering through the periscope with its optics shifted upward, Lieutenant Brian Resor, on watch as *Michigan*'s Officer of the Deck, searched for evidence of ships that had evaded detection by Sonar: sailboats, trawlers with their nets out and engines off, or close contacts blending in with farther ones.

Aside from the Diving Officer's reports, it was silent in the Control Room. There would be no conversation until the periscope broke the surface and Resor called out *No close contacts* or *Emergency Deep*. Like the rest of the watchstanders in Control, Resor knew the ascent to periscope depth was hazardous. A few years earlier, transiting these same waters, USS *Hartford* had collided with USS *New Orleans* while *Hartford* rose toward the surface, almost ripping the sail from the top of the submarine.

Sitting on the starboard side of the Conn in the Captain's chair, Captain Murray Wilson monitored his submarine's ascent. Less than twenty-four hours ago, *Stethem* had been sunk in the Strait, most likely by an Iranian submarine. For the next few minutes, *Michigan* would be vulnerable. It was traveling slowly as it ascended, plus the hull expanded slightly as the water pressure decreased; the submarine's decks adjusted accordingly, emitting hull pops that could be detected miles away.

The Diving Officer called out the submarine's depth in ten-foot increments, and Resor gradually rotated his wrist, tilting the scope optics down toward the horizon. The scope broke the surface of the water and Resor began his circular sweeps, searching for nearby threat contacts— quiet warships or deep-draft merchants bearing down on them.

After assessing a half dozen distant ships on the horizon, Resor called out the report everyone in Control was hoping for.

"No close contacts!"

Conversation in the Control Room resumed, and now that the antenna built into the top of the periscope had broached the surface, Radio's expected report over the Control Room speakers broke the subdued discussions. "Conn, Radio. In sync with the broadcast. Receiving message traffic."

The Quartermaster followed with his report, "GPS fix received."

After the usual two-minute duration, Radio confirmed that *Michigan* had received the latest batch of naval messages. "Conn, Radio. Download complete."

They had accomplished the two objectives for their trip to periscope depth—copy the message broadcast and obtain a navigation fix—so Resor ordered *Michigan* back to the safety of the ocean depths.

"All stations, Conn. Going deep. Helm, ahead two-thirds. Dive, make your depth two hundred feet."

Michigan tilted downward, leaving periscope depth behind.

"Scope's under," Resor announced, then lowered the scope into its well.

As *Michigan* leveled off at two hundred feet, a radioman entered the Control Room, message board in hand. He delivered the clipboard to Captain Wilson, who reviewed the messages, then handed the board to Resor.

"Change in plans," Wilson said. "Someone decided we're due for a port call. Only for a few hours, though, but enough time to load fresh food. Have the Navigator plot our course to Bahrain."

LANHAM, MARYLAND

As darkness crept across the Eastern Seaboard, Lonnie Mixell stood in the misting rain not far from a large warehouse, his SIG Sauer P226 in a shoulder holster beneath his gray windbreaker. It was late in the day, and the encroaching night added a layer of secrecy to the overcast skies, reducing what prying eyes far above might discern.

The transportation hub of Snyder Industries was immense. The warehouse of interest, one of several dozen in this complex, stretched into the distance, perforated by loadout platforms every thirty feet. Backed up against each of the ten nearest platforms was an eighteen-wheeler transporting a CONEX shipping container, its rear doors open. A steady stream of forklifts moved back and forth, loading long, rectangular metal containers into the awaiting CONEX boxes.

A black Rolls-Royce Phantom turned the corner of an adjacent warehouse and angled toward Mixell, gliding to a halt nearby. The driver emerged into the misty rain and hurried to the back door, opened it, then gestured for Mixell to enter. It was dark inside the Phantom's privacy suite, but Mixell spotted the figure of a man seated on the far side.

Mixell slid into the back seat, and the heavy door thudded shut. The lights in the rear suite illuminated, dim at first, growing slowly brighter until the cabin was fully illuminated. Beside Mixell sat an older gentleman, impeccably dressed in a dark gray three-piece suit and burgundy tie. The man pressed a button on his door console, and an electrochromic glass panel behind the front seats switched from transparent to fully opaque, isolating the rear cabin in privacy. Dan Snyder, CEO of Snyder Industries, turned toward Mixell.

"Mr. Larson, I presume?" he asked.

Not only had Mixell altered his appearance for this venture, he was also traveling under a new alias: Mitch Larson.

Snyder continued, "I wanted to meet the man to whom I have entrusted so much. You come highly recommended by your previous business associates," he said, "despite your shortcomings."

Mixell did his best not to show his displeasure at Snyder's insult—*his shortcomings*.

"What might those be?"

Mixell assumed Snyder was referring to the U.S. Navy hunting down the submarine *Kazan* before it destroyed twenty of America's largest cities. Or perhaps the discovery of the missile launcher as Air Force One was taking off. Neither of those plots had been guaranteed to succeed; the obstacles were numerous and difficult, but each plot had been thwarted only moments away from success.

"Your failure to deliver," Snyder answered. "In this venture, you don't get points for running a good race. The only thing that matters is if you cross the finish line. Anything less will be viewed unfavorably."

Mixell surveyed Snyder. He wore shined oxford shoes and a fifty-thousand-dollar Desmond Merrion suit with a jacket pocket square that matched his tie, complemented by manicured fingernails and trimmed eyebrows. Mixell suppressed a laugh. Snyder was trying to play tough guy. A pampered billionaire who had probably never had a callus on his hand or blister on his foot and had likely never made a meal for himself in his life. A man whose attempt to intimidate him was probably derived from watching Mafia movies.

He had no idea about the type of men Mixell had sat beside. Men like the leader of al-Qaeda, whose ruthless nature was hidden beneath a veneer of pleasant questions, not tough-guy theatrics. Mixell decided to play along.

"Will be viewed unfavorably? Could you explain?"

"I'll spell it out for you, Mr. Larson. No one can discover what I've agreed to ship, and it *must* be delivered to my clients."

"Then I've got nothing to worry about."

"For my education," Snyder said, "could you provide an overview of your arrangements?"

"Certainly. Tonight, all ten shipping containers will arrive at the Port of Baltimore, where they'll be loaded aboard a merchant ship first thing in the morning. By this time tomorrow, they'll be at sea, on their way to your requested destination."

"How long before they arrive?"

"A few weeks."

"How have you ensured that what's inside these containers won't be discovered by customs inspectors?"

Mixell was quite familiar with the measures required to smuggle highly sensitive equipment into and out of various countries. After all, only a few months ago, he had shipped prohibited Russian military equipment into the United States.

"The necessary precautions have been taken and bribes made so that no one will discover what is being shipped. From tonight on, that is. What occurred up to this point and who knows about it, however, is your concern."

"I understand," Snyder replied. "I assure you that no one on my side can put all the pieces together."

"That's very comforting," Mixell replied.

Snyder nodded. "Then I'll leave you to your work." He extended his hand.

"It's a pleasure working for you," Mixell said as they shook.

Mixell stepped from the Phantom and closed the door, then the vehicle sped from the complex.

He returned his attention to tonight's task. One by one, the shipping containers were filled, the doors closed and sealed, and the trucks pulled away from the loading docks. As the last of the eighteen-wheelers vanished into the darkness, Mixell's thoughts shifted from his current task to his next.

Five men to kill.

NSA BAHRAIN

As the sun climbed into a clear blue sky above the Persian Gulf, Secretary of the Navy Brenda Verbeck peered out her window aboard the C-32 executive transport, the military version of Boeing's 757. The C-32, normally used by the vice president and designated Air Force Two when he was aboard, lacked the official moniker for this trip, since only Verbeck and her military aide, Captain Andy Hoskins, seated beside her, were passengers on this flight.

Sixteen hours earlier, Verbeck and Hoskins had departed Joint Base Andrews near Washington, D.C., stopping in Frankfurt, Germany, for a quick refueling before continuing toward their destination in the Gulf. As the aircraft descended, Verbeck examined the Kingdom of Bahrain, an archipelago nation comprising fifty natural islands and thirty-three artificial ones—a country designated by the U.S. as a major non-NATO ally.

Bahrain Island, where they would soon land, was the largest island by far, making up over eighty percent of the country's landmass. Located on the northern tip of the island was Naval Support Activity Bahrain, home to U.S. Naval Forces Central Command and the United States Fifth Fleet, an area advertised as the busiest 152 acres in the world, hosting 78 military commands.

As the C-32's landing wheels were deployed, Verbeck's thoughts returned to the reason for her trip.

That pompous ass, Dan Snyder.

He thought he could arrange a secret deal with Iran. With him, it was always about making the next buck, and in this case, the next billion. As a kid, he would hoard his allowance, saving it for the annual summer trip to Aunt Kay's, knowing they'd stop by the Phantom Fireworks store on the way back. Upon returning home, where it was illegal to buy fireworks, he'd sell his stash to the neighborhood kids at a tenfold markup. Dan had probably invented the term *shipping and handling charges apply.*

The C-32 touched down at NSA Bahrain, and after having been met by representatives from U.S. Naval Forces Command and Fifth Fleet, Verbeck and Hoskins were in the back seat of a Navy sedan, on their way to the pier where USS *Michigan* was tied up, skipping the normal perfunctory greetings with the base's senior officers. For this trip, speed was of the essence.

If Wilson was as good as advertised, the UUV problem would be quickly resolved. However, there was a wrinkle in the situation that she hadn't discussed while briefing the president, and the issue was on the verge of spiraling out of control. If that happened, she would end up in an untenable position with no good options. She already knew the choice she would make—one that made her decision to eliminate her military aide pale in comparison. She prayed that it didn't come to that.

The sedan stopped beside *Michigan*'s brow, a walkway extending from the submarine's deck to the pier, where they were greeted by *Michigan*'s Executive Officer, Lieutenant Commander Tom Montgomery. He escorted them topside, then down the nearest hatch as the submarine's shipwide intercom announced, *Secretary of the Navy, arriving.*

They entered the submarine's Wardroom, where a table covered with a white tablecloth was laden with drinks, pastries, and fruit. Two place settings awaited them, as did the submarine's Supply Officer and chief culinary specialist. Following introductions, Verbeck and Hoskins were offered a hot breakfast in addition to the continental offerings. Verbeck declined, as did Hoskins, since the fruit and freshly baked pastries were more than enough.

Both selected a few items, then took their seats, and Captain Murray Wilson entered a moment later, introducing himself before settling into his chair at the head of the table.

Wilson, sporting a full head of gray hair, was much older than Verbeck expected. Then she recalled Hoskins's brief during the flight. Wilson was a mustang, a term for an officer who was prior-enlisted, plus he was a captain. *Michigan* was a special warfare submarine carrying two platoons of SEALs and 154 Tomahawk cruise missiles, one of only four submarines commanded by an officer with the rank of captain—not to be confused with the Captain of a warship, who could be of any rank—whereas all other submarines were skippered by commanders. His seniority, plus the extra time Wilson had spent as an enlisted reactor controls technician, added fifteen years to the age of a typical submarine skipper.

Wilson engaged in small talk while his visitors ate, then cleared the Wardroom of other personnel once they finished.

"Secretary, I understand you'd like to talk with me privately."

Although *Michigan*'s mission would become apparent to its crew, Verbeck preferred the details of her conversation with Wilson be confidential. Depending on how things evolved, credible deniability regarding what she had directed Wilson to do was essential. His orders, which Hoskins carried in a locked courier satchel, were vague, with the details conveyed verbally.

"That's correct, Captain," Verbeck replied. She glanced at the satchel on the table beside Captain Hoskins, and he took his cue.

He unlocked it and retrieved an orange folder marked *Top Secret*, which he handed to Wilson.

Wilson pulled out his orders and quickly read them, then looked up in surprise. "One of our own UUVs may have sunk *Stethem*?"

"That's the scenario we're looking at," Verbeck replied. "Your mission is to locate and destroy it before it does more harm."

"Assuming it actually sank *Stethem*. That's still conjecture at this point, correct?"

"It is. But we're not taking any chances. We'd rather destroy a good UUV than let a bad one roam the Gulf."

"Are there any other UUVs in the Gulf?"

"There are, but none in your assigned operating area." She turned to Hoskins, who delved into the details.

"In addition to your orders, there's an appendix in your folder containing the UUV's characteristics: operating speeds, depths, and acoustic frequencies for your sonar search plan, and its armament."

Wilson perused the appendix, then looked up. "Two torpedoes per UUV. I assume it still carries the second; only one was fired at *Stethem*?"

"ONI is still in the preliminary stage of the investigation, but initial reports indicate a single-torpedo attack."

"What type of torpedo?"

Verbeck's eyes met Hoskins's briefly, then she looked back toward Wilson. *Michigan*'s Captain had homed in on the first and potentially fatal flaw in their *UUV-may-have-sunk-Stethem* ruse. Once a detailed examination of *Stethem*, resting on the ocean floor, was conducted, it would become apparent that it had not been sunk by the UUV, which carried lightweight torpedoes, incapable of inflicting the extent of damage *Stethem* had sustained. By then, however, if Wilson moved quickly enough, the UUV would be a mangled wreck on the bottom of the ocean.

Hoskins answered truthfully, "MK 54 MOD 1 lightweight torpedoes."

Wilson seemed pleased that the UUV carried a lightweight and not a MK 48 heavyweight torpedo, and moved on to his next question. "I see the UUV is battery powered. How does it recharge?"

The second problematic issue.

This time, Hoskins lied. "It has solar panels on top, which it uses to recharge its battery. It surfaces during the day when required."

"How often does it recharge its battery, and how long does it take?"

"The charging interval and time are variable. The interval is dependent on its operating parameters, and the charging time is determined primarily by how depleted its battery is when commencing the recharge."

Wilson examined the appendix a while longer, then looked up, seemingly satisfied with the information provided.

Verbeck added, "One important detail not included in your orders is that you'll be communicating directly with my office—either myself or Captain Hoskins—on this matter. There's a sheet in the folder with the applicable communication details for message traffic or videocons. I understand *Michigan* has the latest Radio Room updates, so data bandwidth shouldn't be an issue."

Wilson nodded. "Videocons won't be a problem."

"That's all I have for you," Verbeck said. "Any other questions?"

"Not at the moment."

Verbeck stood, as did Wilson, and she shook his hand. "Good luck,

Captain. But I believe a more appropriate phrase in the Submarine Force is—*Good hunting!*"

Wilson smiled. "Indeed, it is."

Wilson escorted them topside, then saluted as they departed.

As Verbeck and her aide walked off the brow toward their awaiting sedan, Hoskins asked quietly, "Do you think he believed everything we told him?"

Verbeck replied, "The only thing that matters is that he destroys the UUV before it mates for a recharge."

Hoskins cast a concerned look her way. "If it mates, we're done. We'll have to come clean."

"Of course," Verbeck replied. "That would force our hand."

This time, it was Verbeck who lied. This was what she had been worried about. Hoskins didn't have the stomach to see this issue to the end. Fortunately, in a few days, she wouldn't have to worry about him.

WASHINGTON, D.C.

It was almost midnight when a group of weary passengers emerged from the Mount Vernon Square metro station. After a short ride on the Yellow Line from the Pentagon, Navy Chief Cryptologic Technician Jason Johnson stepped off the rising escalator. He turned right onto a nearby street, leaving behind the brightly lit exterior of the Walter E. Washington Convention Center, headed toward a sleepy row of townhomes in a dimly lit portion of the city a few blocks away.

Johnson had just finished his evening shift at the Pentagon, monitoring intelligence data from a black program of UUVs in the Persian Gulf. It was late, but he was hungry, and he contemplated a stop at Full Yum Carryout, a few blocks from his home. As he passed the 7th and N Streets Park on his right, he paid little attention to a man wearing a dirty gray sweatshirt slouched on a bench beneath the trees, sipping from a bottle inside a crumpled brown paper bag.

Lonnie Mixell locked his eyes onto Johnson for only a few seconds, long enough to verify who he was, before looking away. It wasn't hard to spot Johnson; he wore the Service Khaki uniform that Navy chiefs were required to wear at the Pentagon. He had also arrived at the expected time, emerging from the metro station shortly after his evening shift in the five-sided building. After Johnson pulled a fair distance away, Mixell stood and followed, leaving the bottle of water inside the brown paper bag behind.

Mixell closed on Johnson, adjusting his pace to reach the Navy chief at a predetermined point near a dark alley on the right. The man seemed oblivious to his impending doom, trudging along until Mixell was only ten steps behind. Johnson's sixth sense must have kicked in, because he cast a glance over his shoulder, spotting the drunk from the park moving briskly toward him. He picked up his pace, matching that of the drunk, who was probably approaching to beg for money. Mixell sped up, continuing to close on his prey.

Johnson glanced behind him again, surprised to find the drunk only five paces behind. He slowed and veered toward the street, hoping the man would pass by without engaging. Mixell reached behind his back, pulling his sweatshirt up with one hand and retrieving his P226 with the other, aiming it at Johnson when he stopped a few feet away.

"Into the alley," he said, gesturing with his pistol toward a dark opening on the right.

Johnson held his hands up before him in a supplicating manner. "If it's money you want . . ." He fumbled for his wallet.

Mixell motioned with the gun again. "Into the alley."

Johnson eyed the darkness as he pulled out his wallet and opened it. "I'll give you whatever you want—money, credit cards. Just let me go."

Mixell waved his gun again. "Now!"

"All right, all right!"

The Navy chief moved slowly into the alley. Mixell sensed the man's mind was going in several directions at once, wondering what Mixell wanted, what he might do to him, and whether there was a way to ensure his safety.

He turned suddenly toward Mixell, his features silhouetted by a streetlight farther down the alley. "Look, mister. I'll give you all the money I've got on me, plus I can get you more. Just don't kill me. I've got a wife and kids."

"I don't want your money," Mixell replied. "It's information I want."

Since reading the five names on his hit list, Mixell had wondered about the connection. That the three SEALs had something in common was obvious, although he hadn't yet determined what that was. The other two men worked in the Pentagon, so they seemed connected. But what was the relationship between the Pentagon guys and the SEALs?

While researching his targets, it hadn't taken long to figure out that Johnson worked in a black, off-the-books program. He'd start there.

"What's your job in the Pentagon?"

"How do you know I work there?"

"Just answer the question!"

"I review overseas intelligence data."

"What kind of data?"

"Communications, primarily."

"From who and where?"

Johnson hesitated. "That's classified."

Mixell raised his pistol, aiming it at Johnson's head. "We can either end this conversation now, or you can start talking."

"CENTCOM, Persian Gulf area," Johnson said. "Mostly Iran."

Mixell cursed silently under his breath. It was now clear why he'd been offered this assignment—it was related to the shipment en route. That damn Snyder guy. He said he had everything on his side under wraps, but that clearly wasn't the case. The Navy, at least, had been tipped off.

"Has anything of special interest been collected? A shipment from the U.S. to Iran, perhaps?"

Johnson nodded. "One of the UUV data dumps contained discussions about a high-priority shipment to Iran, due in the next few weeks. I flagged it for further research by the CIA, but it must have been something sensitive, because I was directed to delete the information from our servers and sign a nondisclosure agreement."

"Who directed you to do this?"

"Captain Andy Hoskins."

The reason Johnson and Hoskins were on the list suddenly became apparent. Both were aware of the shipment to Iran, and the two *loose ends* were being taken care of. That was good news, but it raised another question. This wasn't Snyder's work. Someone else, far more ruthless, was pulling the strings.

"Is there anyone else who's aware of this shipment?"

"Not that I know of."

Mixell contemplated what he had learned about the Navy chief and Captain Hoskins, then pivoted to the other three men.

"Have you ever interfaced with Navy SEALs, or have they come up in any context with regard to this shipment?"

"No."

"Have you ever come across the names Gary Nagle, John McNeil, or Jake Harrison?"

"Not that I recall."

"Based on our discussion, is there anything else I might be interested in?"

Johnson shook his head.

"Thanks, Chief. You've been somewhat helpful."

The Navy chief glanced at Mixell's pistol. "You're going to let me go now?"

"Yes. But just one more thing. Turn around."

"What for?"

Mixell pressed his pistol against Johnson's head. "I said *turn around*!"

Johnson turned around, standing tensely while Mixell slid his pistol under the waistband of his jeans, then pulled out a knife with a six-inch blade. He stepped closer, then clamped one hand around Johnson's mouth as he reached around with his other and drove the knife deep into the man's chest, just below the sternum, severing his aorta.

Mixell held him as he bled out until his body went limp. He released Johnson, letting him collapse onto the ground.

He took Johnson's wallet, hoping the murder would be interpreted as a mugging gone bad, then cleaned his knife on the Navy chief's uniform.

After sliding the knife back into its sheath, Mixell emerged onto N Street NW. There was no one within eyesight. As he walked to his car, not far away, his thoughts had already turned to the next man on the list.

BURKE, VIRGINIA

In the early-morning light, a blue Chevy Tahoe with stolen license plates turned onto Marquand Drive, a dead-end road in a quiet suburban neighborhood of single-family homes. Halfway down the street, where it bent ninety degrees to the left, the SUV stopped beside the curb, far enough down the road to provide an unobstructed view of the blue-and-white house in the cul-de-sac at the end of the street.

Mixell left the engine running as he lowered the driver's side window, then pulled the blanket from the passenger seat, revealing a Steyr SSG 69 rifle with an attached Kahles ZF 95 Riflescope. He didn't need such precise firepower from this range, but it was his favorite long-range weapon.

The man living in the blue-and-white house was a former Navy SEAL and one of the five men on Mixell's to-do list. A man he had served with and had once considered a brother; someone he would previously have given his life for. That, of course, was before he'd been forsaken by his so-called brethren.

Mixell's thoughts drifted momentarily to his childhood and the friendships he had developed. Almost ten percent of his hometown population were Russian immigrants, and his mother had become good friends with two other Russian women, getting together often for tea and social activities. As a result, Mixell had become good friends with two other second-generation Russians: Jake Harrison and Christine O'Connor.

Christine, who went by Chris until she left for college, was a tomboy growing up, hanging out with the guys all the way through high school. She was fast and strong, more than capable of holding her own during the rowdy outdoor games, at least until the boys hit puberty, when they gained a significant strength and speed advantage. By then, however, their focus was less on roughhouse games and more on girls, and as Chris developed into a young woman, the guys began to look at her in a different light. Mixell had to admit he'd been quite jealous when Chris had chosen Jake over himself.

Jake Harrison. His former best friend, the man who betrayed him.

While a Navy SEAL in Afghanistan, Mixell had killed an unarmed prisoner, a man who had strapped a bomb to a ten-year-old boy and sent him toward American troops. Harrison had witnessed the murder first-hand, choosing *duty* over his commitment to his fellow SEALs, and had reported the incident to their commanding officer.

Mixell's recollection of the issue was selective, however, choosing to glaze over an important fact: the prisoner Mixell killed hadn't been his first. It was his third. The first time, Harrison had pulled him aside, asking him what the hell he'd been thinking. Mixell explained that he'd been caught up in the heat of the moment—another SEAL had been killed in the engagement.

The second time, the prisoner had also deserved it. Moments earlier, he had killed an entire Afghan family, including women and children, because the father had been discovered aiding the Americans. Mixell had reached for his pistol as he approached the man, who had placed his hands in front of his face as if they could somehow ward off the impending bullet. Mixell shot through the man's palm, putting a bullet in his head. Afterward, Harrison pulled him into an adjacent room and slammed him against the wall, hoping to knock some sense into him.

He could tell that Harrison had been prepared for a fight—Mixell was the same size as he was and just as strong, plus Mixell had a reputation for being a hothead. But as Harrison pressed his friend's back against the wall, he offered no resistance. During the one-way conversation, he displayed neither anger nor remorse as he listened to Harrison's heated words.

After Harrison explained he would have no choice but to report future incidents, Mixell's response had been short.

I got it, buddy.

Of course, Harrison's words were all for show, Mixell had thought. There was no way Harrison—or any other SEAL, for that matter—

would turn him in. SEALs were a tight-knit fraternity, men who had one another's backs. The despicable terrorists were simply getting what they deserved, and Mixell was saving the military and civil justice system a ton of money and effort.

But he had gotten it wrong. He could still recall the shock and visceral anger that overcame him when he learned that Harrison had reported what he'd done to their commanding officer. After months in the brig followed by a court-martial, he'd been sentenced to fifteen years in prison, getting out after eight.

While incarcerated, Mixell had made a mental revenge list, which included Harrison and the country that had turned its back on him after he'd fought valiantly for it, risking his life countless times. He would repay America for what it had done to him.

The front door of the blue-and-white house opened, pulling Mixell from his reverie. Gary Nagle emerged, heading toward the car in the driveway.

As Nagle pulled the keys from his pocket, Mixell brought the rifle to his shoulder and an eye to the scope, centering the crosshairs on the man's head. When Nagle reached the car door and stopped to insert the key, it was all too easy.

Mixell pulled the trigger, and Nagle's head jerked as the round drilled into his skull and exited the other side, accompanied by a pink puff of blood and gray matter spraying over the top of the car.

Nagle slumped onto the driveway, then Mixell returned the rifle to the passenger's seat and did a U-turn with the Tahoe, heading back down Marquand Drive.

Two down, three to go.

10

USS *MICHIGAN*

"Helm, ahead two-thirds. Sonar, Conn. Commence sonar search, all sectors."

Captain Murray Wilson stood on the Conn as Lieutenant Brittany Kern, the submarine's Officer of the Deck, standing beside him, slowed *Michigan* from ahead flank to ten knots, extending the sonar's search range. After departing NSA Bahrain, *Michigan* had headed east at maximum speed for the last fifteen hours and was now entering the UUV's operating area.

Wilson had put the transit time to good use. Using the UUV information Verbeck's aide had provided, *Michigan*'s crew had developed a sonar search plan based on the acoustic tonals the vehicle emitted, along with the various speeds and depths at which the submersible was programmed to operate. However, it would be a challenge to detect the small vehicle.

The UUV was battery powered with a direct-drive motor propulsion— no engine, spinning steam turbine, or reduction gears—also lacking any oil, hydraulic, or water pumps that were the acoustic bane of larger, manned submarines. The submersible was quiet indeed. If it weren't for the small size of the UUV's operating area, *Michigan*'s chance of detecting the vehicle would have been almost nil.

Wilson looked up at the red digital display of the submarine's course, speed, and depth above the Quartermaster's stand. Traveling at ahead flank, *Michigan*'s acoustic sensors had been blunted by the flow noise past the sonar hydrophones at high speed. But the submarine had coasted down to ten knots several minutes earlier, long enough for Sonar to complete its initial long-range search.

Lieutenant Kern called out to the microphone in the overhead, "Sonar, Conn. Report all contacts."

"Conn, Sonar. Hold no contacts of interest. All contacts correlate to merchants."

Wilson examined the contact solutions being generated on the nearest combat control console. Every contact was traveling at a relatively high speed—twenty knots or more.

Merchant ships weren't high-speed vessels, but they usually didn't dawdle as they traveled from port to port, typically transiting at twenty knots. The UUV, on the other hand, usually traveled slowly, just fast enough to maintain steerage and depth control as it traveled near the surface with an antenna lifted above the water to collect electromagnetic signals.

Wilson settled into the Captain's chair on the Conn, waiting while Sonar continued its search.

The small UUV was going to be a challenge to find, indeed.

11

NATIONAL HARBOR, MARYLAND

Located along the Potomac River on 350 acres is the National Harbor waterfront complex, comprising over two hundred shops, forty restaurants, and eight hotels, along with multiple entertainment venues such as the MGM resort with Las Vegas–style gambling. A centerpiece of National Harbor is the Gaylord National Resort and Convention Center, which contains a nineteen-story, glass-encased lush garden atrium and over a half million square feet of event space, including several fifty-thousand-square-foot ballrooms.

The Gaylord is also home to the Navy League's annual Sea-Air-Space Global Maritime Exposition, the world's largest maritime and defense technology gathering, bringing together the key decision-makers in the U.S. defense industry and military for three days of exhibits, policy discussions, and speeches, along with fifteen thousand attendees. Traditional keynote speakers each year include the Chief of Naval Operations, Commandants of the U.S. Marine Corps and Coast Guard, high-ranking congressmen, and of course, the secretary of the Navy.

Across Waterfront Street from the Gaylord is the Hampton Inn, where several of the rooms on the southeast side of the building have a clear view of the side entrance to the Gaylord, which has a service loop used for dropping off and picking up dignitaries.

Seated beside an open window in his hotel room on the second floor, Mixell examined the weapon on the table before him: the Steyr SSG 69 rifle, outfitted this time with a ten-round box magazine and propped up by an integrated folding bipod. He placed the rifle against his shoulder and an eye against the attached scope, peering through the center crack of the room's drawn curtains, studying the men and women entering and leaving the Gaylord's side entrance.

According to the Sea-Air-Space Exposition schedule, the secretary of the Navy's speech should be wrapping up any moment. In concert with his thoughts, a black Lincoln Navigator pulled into the service loop, stopping beside the entrance.

Mixell would have a small window of opportunity when Secretary Verbeck emerged from the Gaylord, accompanied by a pair of protective agents, McNeil being one of them. It was a short walk from the building to the vehicle—only about forty feet—leaving Mixell with scant time to identify his target, obtain a clear shot, and shoot. Plus, he needed to kill McNeil when he was less than a foot away from Verbeck, to make it look like the assassin had missed, accidentally killing her protective agent instead.

Additionally, he had only a fifty-fifty chance McNeil would be on Mixell's side of the secretary as he escorted her from the building to the SUV. If he accompanied her on the other side, getting a clear shot would be notably more difficult.

The side doors opened and Secretary Verbeck emerged from the Gaylord, accompanied by McNeil and another agent. McNeil was on the secretary's far side, walking directly beside her, and Mixell cursed his bad luck. He had no offset angle; Verbeck was squarely between Mixell and McNeil. The former SEAL was several inches taller than Verbeck, but Mixell could barely see the top of his head. If only Verbeck had worn shorter heels.

He followed their progression toward the SUV, with the crosshair centered on Verbeck, hoping for separation between the two. But McNeil remained steady by her side. With Verbeck in his scope, Mixell's eye—and thoughts—were focused on the attractive and wealthy woman.

During his discussion with Chief Johnson a few days earlier, Mixell had learned that Johnson and Captain Hoskins were connected via the UUV program, and Mixell had concluded that Hoskins was either shielding Verbeck from the UUV issue or working as her minion. It hadn't taken much research to determine it was the latter. It turned out that Verbeck's maiden name was Snyder. She was Dan Snyder's sister.

She was covering her brother's tracks, ordering the deletion of the communications intercepted by the UUV and the elimination of the two men who knew about it. For some reason, Mixell's thoughts shifted to his former soul mate, whom Harrison had killed. Technically, it was Mixell's bullet that had done her in. But the cowardly Harrison had hidden behind Trish and pulled her in front of him when he fired. It was his fault she was dead.

Until today, he hadn't thought about a replacement. But Brenda Verbeck—a beautiful, conniving, and ruthless woman—what more could a man want?

His thoughts returned to the task at hand. He was running out of time. Only ten more feet to go.

There was only one way this was going to work out. When Verbeck reached the SUV, one of the protective agents would move forward and open the door for her. Based on the orientation of the two men beside Verbeck, Mixell concluded it would be McNeil. If so, there would be a clear shot, but only for a second or two.

Mixell shifted the crosshair to just forward of Verbeck's face. As they reached the vehicle, he let out a slow breath and increased his index finger's pressure on the trigger.

One of the agents moved ahead to open the SUV door. It was McNeil.

Mixell took the shot.

He heard the slap of the round as it impacted McNeil's head, dropping him instantly. The other agent shoved Verbeck into the SUV and jumped in after her, then the vehicle peeled away, doing a one-eighty around the service loop before speeding toward the National Harbor exit. The scene outside the Gaylord was pandemonium, as those nearby either ran to McNeil's aid or scattered in various directions.

Mixell left the rifle behind. He hadn't bothered wearing gloves and was certain that DNA evidence would link him to the crime. But that's what he wanted; he was leaving his calling card. He stepped from his hotel room and headed to the attached parking garage, where his car was parked near the exit.

12

LANGLEY, VIRGINIA

Christine O'Connor stepped from the elevator on the ground floor of the CIA headquarters in Langley, accompanied by two protective agents as she headed to her awaiting car. After she slid into the back seat and the SUV pulled away, she mulled the stunning news, which had filled the country's television and radio broadcasts—yesterday's assassination attempt against Secretary of the Navy Brenda Verbeck.

What the public didn't know was that the likely perpetrator had been identified. Lonnie Mixell had been spotted on a surveillance camera exiting one of the National Harbor parking garages moments after the assassination attempt. Clearly, the former Navy SEAL had not been killed a few months ago.

Jake Harrison had put three bullets into Mixell that night, the third being a suspected fatal shot that sent Mixell slumping onto the side of his boat before slipping beneath the dark surface of the Potomac River. Although Mixell's body hadn't been recovered, that hadn't been surprising considering the Potomac was the fourth-largest river on the East Coast, with thousands of small bays and coves along its banks as it emptied into the Chesapeake Bay. Painfully obvious this morning, the CIA's conclusion regarding Mixell's fate had been overly optimistic.

Her thoughts remained on Mixell, a childhood playmate and one of her two best friends growing up, the other being Jake Harrison, whom she had dated for a decade beginning in high school. As kids, the three of them had been almost inseparable. Even in high school, they had stuck together, with Mixell's various girlfriends tagging along as fourth wheels.

As Christine's SUV pulled onto the George Washington Memorial

Parkway, her thoughts shifted to the pending White House meeting, where the CIA would most likely assist the FBI's search for Mixell, due to the agency's previous success tracking him down and thwarting his attacks on the country's largest cities and the president himself. She would have egg on her face this morning, though. The CIA's erroneous conclusion that Mixell had been killed would call into question the veracity of previous and future CIA analyses.

Christine was the last to arrive at the White House for the meeting and stopped outside the Situation Room, where she pulled a laptop computer from her satchel for inspection by security personnel, who verified it had no camera or wireless capability. Once cleared, she entered the conference room and took one of two empty seats at the table, leaving the chair at one end for the president, then connected her laptop to the audiovisual cable on the conference room table.

Once her presentation was ready to display, she took note of the attendance, which included Secretary of Homeland Security Nova Conover, FBI Director Bill Guisewhite, Director of National Intelligence John Rodgaard, and Thom Parham, the president's national security advisor. Given Mixell's previous ties to al-Qaeda and its international implications, Secretary of State Marcy Perini was also present.

Hardison contacted the president's secretary, informing her they were ready for the president, who arrived a moment later. All stood as he entered, returning to their seats after the president settled into his chair.

"What's the status?" he asked.

Hardison replied, "Director Guisewhite has the lead on the investigation and will brief you on what we know."

After the president nodded his concurrence, Guisewhite began.

"Good morning, Mr. President. As you're aware, there was an attempt on Secretary Verbeck's life yesterday following her keynote speech at the Sea-Air-Space Exposition at National Harbor, with the attempt occurring as she exited the Gaylord convention center. A sniper was positioned in a hotel room across from the Gaylord, but the bullet missed Verbeck, killing one of her protective agents instead. John McNeil was his name, a recently retired Navy SEAL."

Christine looked up suddenly from her computer. John McNeil had been the commanding officer of the SEAL detachment aboard USS

Michigan, a man she had worked with several times. She'd been so focused on the news that Mixell had survived that she hadn't bothered to
ask the name of the slain agent.

"How is Brenda doing?" the president asked.

"She's at home, recovering from the ordeal," Guisewhite replied.
"She's quite shaken over the close call and death of her protective agent."

"Do we have a motive? Why would someone target her?"

"We don't have anything solid at the moment. However, she's been
pushing aggressive anti-terrorist policies, focused not only on the roles
our Navy can fulfill but on methods the military overall can implement
in our war against terror. I don't think it's any secret that she'd like to
be the next secretary of defense, and in that position, she'd be quite
influential and could reshape the military's role, intensifying America's
effort in this area.

"We'll update you if we identify anything more concrete regarding the motive or those behind the assassination attempt. What we do
know, however, is who the likely assassin is: Leonard Mixell, nickname
Lonnie, who has gone by multiple aliases in the recent past. I presume
you recall the details of his court-martial while a Navy SEAL and subsequent imprisonment, and his assassination of United Nations Ambassador Marshall Hill, followed by his role in the *Kazan* and Air Force
One plots."

The president nodded. "Of course. I also recall that he is supposedly
dead."

He leveled his gaze at Christine, who leaned back slightly under his
scrutiny. She knew the issue would arise this morning. Unfortunately,
the criticism was warranted.

Guisewhite continued, thankfully capturing the president's attention
again. "Unlike Mixell's assassination of Ambassador Hill, we don't have
video of the event. We did, however, capture Mixell on camera shortly
afterward."

The director activated a video clip on his laptop. The display at the front
of the Situation Room energized, showing a car pulling up to the automated exit gate in a parking garage. The video zoomed in on Mixell's face
and froze.

"As you can see, Mixell is alive and almost assuredly responsible for the attempt on Secretary Verbeck's life. Mixell has changed the color of his hair and eyes but has otherwise not altered his appearance. In the past, he used temporary mouth implants to alter his cheek and jaw structure, but Mixell is apparently aware that this no longer fools our facial recognition algorithms.

"As for where Mixell is now or what he's been up to, all we know is that he was at National Harbor yesterday afternoon. There have been no database hits or sightings of Mixell since he was reported killed several months ago. He's clearly been lying low while his wounds healed and using an alias or perhaps multiple ones.

"Not only is Mixell alive and well, but it appears he's employed again. Whether he continues to do the bidding of al-Qaeda under new leadership—we've confirmed the death of Ayman al-Zawahiri from our drone strike a few months ago—or is employed by others is unclear."

"What do we know about al-Qaeda's new leadership," the president asked, "now that Zawahiri is dead?"

Guisewhite glanced at Christine, who took over.

She pressed the video switch on the conference table, shifting control of the wall display from Guisewhite's computer to hers, then pulled up the first slide of her brief, a head-and-shoulder portrait of an Arab man.

"The heir apparent to al-Qaeda was Osama bin Laden's son Hamza, the only child by Osama's eldest wife, Khairiah Saber. However, Hamza was killed by a U.S. counterterrorism operation in 2019. That left Zawahiri in charge and al-Qaeda looking for a new successor, for which there are four leading contenders."

Christine went quickly though the list, one slide per man:

Saif al-Adel: al-Qaeda's number two, a longtime head of its military council and well respected within the global al-Qaeda network.

Abd al-Rahman al-Maghribi: a shura council member married to one of Zawahiri's daughters and head of al-Qaeda's media operations.

Yasin al-Suri: head of al-Qaeda's organization in Iran, in charge of facilitating the transfer of money and personnel in and out of the country.

Abu Hamza al-Khalidi: a central link between al-Qaeda's global affiliates and al-Qaeda's leadership; one of a new generation of leaders being groomed by al-Qaeda and currently the head of al-Qaeda's military council, having taken over from Saif al-Adel.

"Our assessment is that the new leader of al-Qaeda is likely Saif al-Adel. His relationships with jihadi cells throughout the Middle East put him in a position to solidify the somewhat fractured al-Qaeda organization and pursue additional attacks against the United States, similar to 9/11."

Christine shifted her eyes to Guisewhite, who picked up where he had left off.

"We don't have much to go on yet, Mr. President. But since Mixell has resurfaced and due to his recent ties to al-Qaeda, we'll work with the CIA again to track him down as soon as possible. This concludes my brief."

The president didn't immediately respond. Instead, his eyes canvassed each person at the table. This was the second meeting in the White House Situation Room in only a few days, with the attempted assassination coming on the heels of *Stethem*'s sinking. It had not been a good week for the administration.

Finally, the president spoke. "I want a full-court press on this. Find Mixell before he does any more damage, and figure out who's pulling the strings."

13

LANGLEY, VIRGINIA

The setting sun, hovering just above the treetops, cast long shadows through the bomb-resistant and soundproof windows as Christine O'Connor entered her spacious seventh-floor office. The reddish-orange sunset was a pleasant scene, but one that didn't match her mood. She had left the White House only thirty minutes earlier and was still contemplating the best way to track Mixell down. The CIA's error—misclassifying him as deceased—accompanied by the president's subtle admonishment, had stung. Next time, they had better get it right.

Regarding next time, Christine wanted to get to Mixell first, before any of the domestic law enforcement or intelligence agencies did. The situation had turned personal, starting with Mixell's attempt to kill Harrison. As kids, they had been best friends, often invoking the Three Musketeers' motto—*All for one, and one for all*—throughout their childhood. But after Harrison helped send Mixell to prison and Christine's recent effort to thwart Mixell's plans, it was now two against one.

Upon reaching her desk, she directed her secretary, "Have the DD, DDO, and DDA meet me in my office."

Monroe Bryant and PJ Rolow arrived shortly thereafter, joining Christine at her conference table. While they waited for Tracey McFarland to arrive, Christine evaluated the two men seated beside her. In the several months she had been CIA director, her initial assessments hadn't changed.

In his late fifties, Deputy Director Monroe Bryant was the quintessential government bureaucrat, one Christine found easy to read. In Bryant's mind, Christine and the other CIA directors who rolled through Langley learned just enough to be dangerous, making well-intentioned but often damaging decisions. His self-ordained job was to manage the issues that captured her attention, ensuring she did no harm. Christine was also convinced that Bryant ensured that certain sensitive issues never rose to her level.

On the other hand, Deputy Director for Operations Patrick Rolow, who went by PJ, was unreadable. He was a man of average height and weight, blending into the background of almost any setting. That anonymity was due primarily to his experience as a field officer, spending fifteen years in the Middle East before a rapid rise through the management layers in the Directorate of Operations. In his late forties, he was one of the youngest DDOs in the history of the agency.

Even their offices reflected the men. Bryant had filled his office with mahogany furniture and Italian leather chairs, while Rolow's office was Spartan; standard CIA furniture sprinkled with several photos from his time as a field agent.

Tracey McFarland arrived and joined them at the conference table. The deputy director for analysis was as competent as they came, someone Christine had learned she could depend on for quick and accurate analysis. Aside from the Mixell issue, that is, but that wasn't entirely McFarland's fault. She had relied heavily on Jake Harrison's eyewitness account of what happened that night in Alexandria.

"How'd it go?" she asked Christine after she took her seat.

"As expected," Christine replied. "The president wasn't pleased that Mixell is still alive."

"Does the FBI have any leads?"

"Nothing we didn't already know—Mixell was spotted departing National Harbor after the assassination attempt. Due to Mixell's previous ties to al-Qaeda, we'll be assisting the FBI again." She turned to Rolow. "Same arrangement as before?"

The DDO nodded. "I'll establish a team from the National Resources Division," he said, referring to the CIA's domestic division, which handled issues the CIA pursued in tandem with the FBI or other domestic agencies. "I'll also put Khalila on it, in case there are any leads to al-Qaeda again."

"She's fully recovered?" Christine asked, referring to the wounds Khalila had received while engaging Mixell that night with Harrison.

"She was cleared last week," Rolow replied.

"What about Harrison?"

"He's no longer an employee."

"*Rehire* him," Christine said firmly. "Or do I have to do it myself again?"

During their previous effort to track down Mixell, Harrison had initially turned down the CIA's offer of employment due to a catch-22. Christine knew Harrison would agree to join the CIA and help track down Mixell, but he couldn't be told Mixell was the person of interest. The situation was classified, and Harrison, who had recently retired from the Navy, no longer had a security clearance. Christine had decided to bend the rules, informing him that Mixell was out of prison and a lead suspect in a case they were working on.

But now that Harrison had left the CIA, they were back where they started; Harrison wasn't allowed to know Mixell had survived and was the main suspect in the secretary of the Navy's assassination attempt.

"I don't make the rules," Rolow said, "but you can bend them again, if you desire."

"Fine," Christine said. "I'll talk with Harrison."

She turned to McFarland. "When it comes to tracking someone down on U.S. soil, the FBI and other domestic agencies have access to more surveillance systems and analysis resources than we do. They're going to discover information about Mixell faster than we can, and I'd rather not play catch-up or even be purposefully left in the dark."

Prior to becoming CIA director, Christine had been well aware that relations between the CIA and FBI were strained, with difficulties dating back to former FBI director J. Edgar Hoover and former CIA directors Allen Dulles and Richard Helms. The tension stemmed partly from bureaucratic rivalry created by overlapping responsibilities for counterintelligence activities and from conflict caused by decidedly different cultures and agendas. Succinctly put, the CIA played offense while the FBI played defense. Add in each agency's concerted efforts to protect their sources, and information sharing between the two organizations was often a casualty.

When it came to Mixell, Christine was determined to ensure all relevant information was provided to the CIA, and there was only one way to do that.

She asked McFarland, "Do we have the ability to tap into domestic data collection systems?"

McFarland glanced at Rolow and Bryant, then replied, "You mean, do we have the ability to infiltrate the surveillance and data systems of domestic law enforcement and sister intelligence agencies?"

Christine nodded. "And the answer is . . . ?"

McFarland leaned forward. "That depends on who's asking."

Christine contemplated McFarland's response. She had answered the question.

"Do it," Christine said. "If anyone learns anything about Mixell, I want us to know as soon as possible."

After the meeting ended, the three deputy directors departed Christine's office, heading down the corridor toward their own offices. After Mc-Farland stepped into hers and closed the door, Bryant turned to Rolow.

"I didn't care much for our new director at first, but she's starting to grow on me."

"I told you," Rolow said. "Christine is a wolf in sheep's clothing. The president knew what he was doing when he nominated her for director."

"However," Bryant said, "she's still more loyal to the president than to the agency."

"I agree," Rolow replied, then lowered his voice. "There are some things that must remain between the two of us."

14

SILVERDALE, WASHINGTON

Angie Harrison fluffed a couch pillow, then stepped back and examined it with a critical eye. She straightened a corner, then surveyed the couch and the rest of the living room again. After ensuring everything was in its place, she stopped in the foyer and inspected herself in the mirror. For this afternoon's visit, she had picked out a pair of capris and a shirt that accentuated her figure.

Looking out the dining room window, she searched for a sign of the expected guest. But there were no cars on the long road approaching their house in the countryside. That wasn't unexpected, however. Christine O'Connor was supposed to call when her meeting at the nearby Naval Undersea Warfare Center had ended and she was on her way, and there had been no word thus far. Angie checked her watch. She should be calling anytime now.

Angie entered the kitchen and stopped by the sink, looking out the window. A light mist was falling from a gray overcast sky, but that hadn't stopped Jake from working in the backyard.

They were both so predictable.

Several months ago, they had both spent the hours before Christine's previous visit the same way: Jake working in the yard to take his mind off Christine, while Angie worried how she would measure up to the woman Jake had dated for ten years and proposed to twice. Angie had met Christine for the first time four months ago, and it was obvious that Jake's former flame was a beautiful, accomplished, and powerful woman, while she was . . .

Angie caught a partial reflection of her face in the kitchen window. She was attractive, no doubt. She turned heads when she entered a room, and she could have dated almost any man she wanted in high school and college. But she still felt inferior to Christine. The woman who had spent three years as the president's national security advisor and was now the director of the CIA was in a different league from someone who was a member of an elementary school's parent-teacher association.

The phone rang, and Angie let the answering machine pick up. It was Christine, letting them know she would arrive in fifteen minutes. After she hung up, Angie took a deep breath, then opened the back door and yelled to Jake, letting him know Christine was almost there.

She returned to the living room and waited, checking over her shoulder occasionally to see if Jake had come in from the yard, until she spotted a black SUV with two men in the front seats approaching. The vehicle pulled into the driveway and stopped. Christine stepped from the vehicle and walked to the front door, accompanied by one of her protective agents holding an umbrella over her, shielding her from the misty rain.

Angie glanced over her shoulder again. There was no sign of Jake. *Damn him. Leaving her alone to greet Christine again.*

She waited for the doorbell to ring, then after one last glance in the mirror and a rearrangement of a wayward lock of hair, she opened the door.

"Director O'Connor, it's a pleasure to see you again." Angie forced the words out.

"Please, call me Christine," the CIA director said as she entered the foyer.

The protective agent, after a quick look inside, returned to the SUV.

"Thank you again for accommodating my visit on such short notice," Christine said as she accompanied Angie through the living room and into the kitchen. "During my last visit, I forgot to mention what a lovely home you have."

Angie was sure Christine didn't mean it. Her home was nice, but it surely didn't measure up to the luxurious homes and mansions Christine would have visited during her career in Washington. But at least Christine was trying to be nice. They stopped at the kitchen window, looking out over the backyard. Jake was edging a flower bed with a straight-edge shovel, cutting back the intruding grass.

"That's so like him," Christine said. "Trying to take his mind off things."

"Yeah," Angie said as she was hit with a twinge of jealousy. Christine knew Jake as well as she did, and maybe even better.

Angie opened the back door. "Jake! Christine's here!"

Harrison looked up, then stowed the shovel in a nearby barn before trudging toward the house in the light rain. Angie disappeared into an adjacent laundry room, returning with a towel she tossed to her husband as he entered.

"Hi, Chris," he said as he dried his face and hair.

"Hi, Jake," Christine replied, then smiled warmly.

Jake didn't return the smile. He gestured toward the kitchen table, and all three took their seats. Harrison draped the towel around his neck.

"What's so important *this* time?" he asked.

Under the table, Angie placed her hand on Jake's thigh and squeezed it gently, showing her appreciation. Prior to Christine's arrival, they had discussed her pending visit and potential reasons why—most likely another CIA job offer. Angie had pointed out that Jake had agreed years ago to take a safer job after retiring from the Navy, one where he didn't put his life on the line every time he went to work. Jake had loved being a SEAL, but it was time now to think of Angie and their twelve-year-old daughter, Madeline, and the impact on them if anything happened to him. His first responsibility was to his wife and daughter now, not his country. He had already served it well.

Following Jake's retirement, Angie had looked forward to the end of sleepless nights, lying awake wondering if she and Maddy would ever see him again. But then Jake took the CIA job, and a few weeks later, she had received the call she had always dreaded. Jake was in a hospital in critical condition, and they didn't know if he was going to make it. She had left Maddy with a friend and flown to Virginia, joining Jake in his hospital room after his surgery. He'd been lucky. Although Mixell's first bullet had been the most painful, shattering a shoulder blade, the second one had almost killed him, narrowly missing his heart.

Jake's wounds had finished healing and he had quit the CIA, finally putting the high-risk jobs behind them. Upon learning of Christine's visit today, Jake had agreed to decline another job offer if she presented it—there was no reason for him to return to the CIA.

Christine's response, however, changed everything.

"Lonnie is alive."

A cold shiver ran down Angie's spine. Jake's body tensed, but his facial expression remained unchanged. She imagined that the same thoughts going through her mind were going through his.

Mixell had a vengeful streak and wouldn't stop until he paid Jake back for betraying him. She ought to know—she had dated Mixell for a year. That's how she'd met Jake. The two men were still best friends back then. But her relationship with Mixell didn't last; he had anger management issues.

"Also," Christine said, "John McNeil is dead."

"I heard," Harrison replied. "I'm planning to attend his funeral. But what does that have to do with Mixell?"

"Lonnie was the sniper who tried to assassinate the secretary of the Navy. He missed and killed McNeil instead."

Harrison's face hardened at the news. "That bastard. But I'm surprised he missed—he's an excellent marksman. How far away was he?"

"I don't know the details, other than he was in a hotel across the street. You can look into things if you'd like, once you return to Langley."

"Is that a job offer?"

"It is."

Angie exchanged looks with Jake. Now that they had learned Mixell was still alive, she already knew what the answer would be. But Jake said, "I'll have to think about it."

The front door opened, then slammed shut, followed by the sound of someone running through the house.

"I'm home!" a young girl called out. "I'll be upstairs getting ready for gymnastics!"

"That must be Madeline," Christine said. "How old is she now? Twelve?"

Angie nodded. Christine had been keeping tabs. But when had she learned Maddy's age? After Angie and Jake married, he supposedly hadn't kept in touch with Christine. Then Angie recalled that Jake had run into Christine several times over the last few years while on various missions, saving her life twice.

However, things hadn't gone quite the same during his last SEAL mission, even though he'd run into Christine again. Jake's SEAL team had been escorting the Russian president from his Crimean summer home during a military coup, with Christine accompanying them. She'd been visiting the Russian president at the time, no doubt taking *international relations* to a new level. During their escape, Christine and the Russian president had slid toward a cliff overhanging a raging river a hundred feet below. Jake had managed to grab ahold of them, one in each hand. His grip on both began to slip, and he'd been forced to make a decision—he could save only one of them. He had let go of Christine.

She had survived the fall but had been none too pleased about Jake's decision. The next time she saw him, she punched him in the face. They seemed to have worked things out, but the scenario atop the cliff brought Angie comfort. Not because Christine had almost met her demise but because Jake had been forced to choose and he had let Christine go.

There was the sound of feet pounding on the wood floor again, and Maddy burst into the kitchen as she asked, "Have you seen my purple leo?"

She stopped suddenly and examined the stranger at the kitchen table. When she realized who she was, her eyes grew big. But not because Christine was the CIA director—Madeline had no idea—it was because Christine had been a collegiate national champion on the beam.

Harrison made the introduction. "Maddy, I'd like you to meet Miss O'Connor."

Madeline shook Christine's hand as words tumbled from her mouth. About how much she'd heard about her, that she was a gymnast too, what level she had attained, and which skills were the most difficult for her.

"The beam is my weakest event," Madeline said. "I have trouble with the back handsprings. But Dad says if I work hard, I might become a national champion, like you."

"There's no substitute for hard work," Christine said. "It all starts there."

Angie checked the clock on the wall. "Your leo is hanging in the laundry room. Better finish getting ready for practice. Miss Young will be here in a few minutes."

Madeline collected her leotard, then either because she was excited to meet Christine or wanted to impress her, she exited the kitchen via a back walkover, keeping her legs straight and feet pointed as they passed overhead.

After Madeline disappeared from sight, Christine smiled. "She's adorable."

Jake and Angie talked with Christine for a few minutes more until they heard a car pull up and honk. Madeline yelled goodbye as she bounded down the stairs, the front door slamming shut a few seconds later.

"Well," Christine said as she stood, "I should be going now too."

Harrison and Angie walked Christine to the front door, where she shook Angie's hand. Then she turned to Jake.

"This time, we're going to put Mixell away for good, one way or another." She extended a hand. "Let me know what your decision is."

Jake took Christine's hand. "It was a pleasure seeing you again, Miss O'Connor."

Christine offered a wry smile at Jake's formal goodbye, then departed.

When he closed the door, Angie leaned against the foyer wall, tears in her eyes.

"I know you have to take this job," she said. "Lonnie will eventually come after you, and the sooner he's back behind bars or dead, the better. But be more careful this time. Maddy and I can't afford to lose you."

"I can take care of myself," he replied.

"Tell that to the two bullets they cut out of you."

"They weren't the first."

Tears fell down Angie's cheeks.

Jake wiped the tears away. "Nothing's going to happen to me. We'll find Lonnie and either kill him or put him in prison again, and this time he won't get out. I'll be safe. You and Maddy will be safe. I promise."

"Okay," Angie said, forcing a smile. "But I'm still worried. Not just about Lonnie but about Christine."

"You have nothing to worry about. During my last stint at Langley, I barely saw her. She was at three meetings the entire time I was there, and we barely spoke. It's not like I'll be working in the field with her."

"It could be different this time," Angie replied, "and working closely with her could rekindle your feelings toward her."

"You know I love you more than—" Harrison halted, regretting his poorly chosen words. When they had discussed Christine before, he had insisted he no longer had feelings for her.

Angie felt the heat rise in her neck and face. "You said there was nothing left between you. But you still love her, don't you?"

Harrison tried to salvage what he could. "Chris is nothing more than a friend now. The only woman I love and care about is you."

She poked her finger into his chest. "I know that deep in your heart, there will always be a special place for that woman."

Harrison pulled Angie close and kissed her, then held her for a while, caressing her back.

Then he slid his hands down and grabbed her butt. "And I know that deep inside *you*, there will always be a special place for *me*."

Angie rolled her eyes. "You have a one-track mind. And don't change the subject!"

"Interested?" Harrison asked.

She eyed his wet shirt and the specks of dirt clinging to his skin. "You're filthy."

"I'm jumping into the shower. Care to join me?"

"Maybe," Angie said, reaching behind and pulling Harrison's hands from her butt. "But you'll have to catch me first."

She bolted from the foyer. Harrison started after her, catching her as she reached the stairs. He snagged a foot, tripping her onto the steps. She turned onto her back, screaming in mock fear as Harrison dragged her toward him.

15

LANGLEY, VIRGINIA

Dark clouds rolling in from the west were accompanied by a brisk morning wind as Jake Harrison's car stopped at the main entrance to the George Bush Center for Intelligence. One of the armed security guards verified he was on the day's visitor list, then waved his car through. After pulling into the parking garage, Harrison entered the lobby of the CIA headquarters and took the elevator to the seventh floor. After informing the director's secretary he had arrived, he was asked to wait in a conference room down the hall.

Three others soon arrived: CIA Director Christine O'Connor, Deputy Director Monroe Bryant, and Deputy Director for Operations PJ Rolow.

"Welcome back, Jake," Christine said as she took her seat at the head of the table.

Bryant and Rolow likewise welcomed him back to the agency. The conference room door opened again, and two women entered. The first was Deputy Director for Analysis Tracey McFarland, carrying two manila folders. The second was an attractive six-foot-tall Middle Eastern woman with straight black hair falling across her shoulders, wearing a formfitting shirt and short skirt emphasizing her long, lean legs. Harrison's eyes narrowed when he spotted his former partner.

Khalila had been one of two agents assigned to assist him during his first stint in the CIA, with Khalila accompanying him whenever leads to the whereabouts of Lonnie Mixell took him to the Middle East. According to Rolow, Khalila's contacts in the region and linguistic skills were the best the agency had to offer.

McFarland greeted Harrison after taking her seat, but Khalila said nothing after settling into her chair. She folded her arms across her chest, projecting a *why-am-I-here* attitude, much like she'd done the first time they met. Harrison also wondered why she was here, considering he had decided he would never work with her again if he had anything to say about it. Then he remembered he hadn't voiced his concerns to anyone, instead making a pact with Khalila after she had almost put a bullet into him.

Months ago in Sochi, it had taken Harrison a moment to realize that Khalila had her pistol aimed at him and not the perpetrator they had run down. He recalled the indecision in her eyes as she debated whether to kill him—*her own partner*! It was then that he realized there was something critical about Khalila that she and Rolow were hiding, something they didn't want discovered. He had learned too much during their trip to Syria, where it had become apparent that she had a special status in the Arab world.

During those few seconds in Sochi, with Khalila's finger on the pistol trigger, the warning from his other partner, Pat Kendall, had echoed in his mind.

The DDO and DD kept Khalila at the farm for two training cycles, trying to figure out what to do with her, then didn't send her on any meaningful missions for years. That means either they don't trust her or she's too valuable to risk except in extreme circumstances. Now that Khalila has been released into the field, she's lost more partners than socks, each one dead in suspicious circumstances.

After Khalila almost killed him, there was no doubt in his mind what had happened to her previous partners—the ones who had learned too much about her.

The conversation after their encounter in Sochi had been short and the agreement shorter. Harrison would not reveal anything he had learned, or would learn, about her, and she wouldn't kill him. As a corollary to the agreement, Harrison had decided he would never work with Khalila again. With his departure from the agency shortly thereafter, once Mixell had supposedly been killed, he hadn't relayed his thoughts to Rolow.

After a bit of small talk, Christine got down to business.

"Your primary goal is to track down Mixell. We know he tried to kill the secretary of the Navy, but we're concerned about what else he's up to. He doesn't fit the lone-assassin-for-hire profile. The attempted murder of Brenda Verbeck is likely tied to something bigger. We need to find out what that is."

Christine turned to McFarland, who handed Harrison one of the two folders she had brought to the meeting.

McFarland walked Harrison through the material. "Here's a summary of what we've got regarding the SecNav's attempted assassination. You'll find a photo of Mixell as he's leaving the parking garage about a minute after the attempt, plus a report showing Mixell's DNA on the rifle used to kill McNeil, which he left behind in the hotel room."

She pushed the second folder across the table. "In addition to McNeil, another former SEAL, Gary Nagle, was murdered a few days ago. There's speculation within the directorate that the two SEAL killings are related and that McNeil was the real target and not the SecNav. It's conjecture at this point, but since the first SEAL was killed nearby in Burke, we want you to see what you can figure out. Based on your military record, it appears you worked with both men, correct?"

Harrison nodded. "We were on the same SEAL team a while back."

"While we search for additional relationships and leads," McFarland said, "we'd like you and Khalila to check in on both investigations."

Harrison glanced at his former partner before shifting his eyes to Rolow, then asked the question that had been on his mind since Khalila walked into the room. "Why Khalila? I don't need a translator or a partner with Middle East contacts."

Rolow replied, "Mixell's two previous plots were funded by Middle Eastern terrorist organizations. Since Mixell is implicated, we thought it prudent that Khalila be involved from the outset. Besides, she's one of the best field officers we've got."

Harrison couldn't disagree. He'd seen Khalila in action, watching her leap over a ten-foot-tall wall with catlike dexterity. She was an expert marksman and even more proficient with knives, which she had wielded on several occasions during their previous assignment. None of that mattered, however, if he couldn't trust her. Not wanting to have that conversation in front of Khalila, he acquiesced.

"Sounds like a plan."

"Besides," Rolow added, "you two did a great job tracking Mixell down before. Why mess with a winning formula? I'd also like to point out that Mixell got away. I'd say your job isn't finished."

"I understand," Harrison replied. There was no one more motivated to find Mixell and put him behind bars than he was.

Christine interjected, changing the subject. "John McNeil's funeral is at Arlington this afternoon. Are you planning to attend?"

"I am," Harrison replied. "His widow gave me a call. She wants to speak with me afterward."

"I'll be attending as well," Christine replied. "I'll see you there."

She looked to Bryant and Rolow in case they had anything else to discuss.

No other issues were raised, so Rolow said, "You know the drill, Jake, same as before. You're being assigned to the special operations group within the special activities center. Pick up your ID and check out a weapon and any other gear you need. I'll leave it to you and Khalila, but I'd start with Nagle. Find out what you can before you attend McNeil's funeral. Any questions so far?"

"Not at the moment."

"Well, then," Rolow said, "we'll let you and Khalila get reacquainted."

The four senior officials left the conference room, leaving Harrison and Khalila behind.

Harrison turned to his former—and present—partner, searching for the right words to begin. She spoke first.

"I'll contact local law enforcement and have them meet us in Burke. Get your gear and I'll pick you up at the entrance."

Without waiting for a response, she headed toward the door.

So much for getting reacquainted.

16

BURKE, VIRGINIA

It had been a quiet ride to Burke, Virginia, only a half-hour drive from Langley. Khalila had just pulled her sleek blue BMW M8 coupe off I-495 onto Braddock Road, ten minutes from their destination. At the beginning of their trip, as Khalila waited outside the CIA entrance, Harrison had tossed a backpack filled with his new gear into the back seat of her car, then slid into the passenger seat. As she peeled away from Langley and accelerated onto the George Washington Memorial Parkway, a simple thought had flashed through his mind.

Fast cars and fast women.

Khalila's M8 was fast, and so was she. While chasing the Russian attempting to evade them in Sochi, Khalila had almost kept up with Harrison. Whether she was *fast* in the proverbial sense, Harrison didn't know. Their interactions thus far had been purely professional, with a distance between them created by her cold personality and ruthless behavior. By the end of their first stint together, Harrison had concluded Khalila was a sociopath, a label she hadn't disagreed with.

Harrison's first attempt at conversation during their trip to Burke, shortly after they pulled onto the parkway, had been short.

You look well, he'd said.

Khalila had also been wounded in the firefight with Mixell, but her injuries were worse than his, and she had almost died on the operating table. Even two months later, during his last day at the agency when both had been awarded the CIA Intelligence Star for saving the president's life, she hadn't looked well. She had lost a good bit of weight from her already lean build. Today, however, she looked fully recovered, back to her previous physical condition, and her personality hadn't changed either. Her response to Harrison's attempt to begin a conversation had been abrupt.

You too.

They were a few minutes from their destination when Khalila spoke again.

"You're not happy about working with me again." It was more of a statement than a question.

"Why would I? You almost put a bullet in my head."

"We made an agreement. As long as you keep whatever you learn about me to yourself, you have nothing to worry about. Besides, I took two bullets for you when Mixell had you pinned down. I saved your life and nearly lost mine. I think I've proven that I can be trusted."

Harrison mentally added a caveat to Khalila's words.

I think I've proven that I can be trusted—in certain circumstances.

"Fair enough," Harrison replied, temporarily ignoring the qualification he had appended to Khalila's statement. "I'll concede that you can be trusted. But you need to concede the same—that you can trust me as well."

There was no response from Khalila, but she seemed to be contemplating his proposal.

Harrison continued, "As part of our bargain, I've agreed to keep whatever I've learned about you to myself. So why don't you tell me your real name and why the Syrians deferred to you?"

Khalila laughed. "Not a chance."

"You already told me your first name." Harrison recalled the moment after their encounter with Mixell, when Khalila was bleeding out on the warehouse floor as Harrison applied pressure to her wounds.

She looked away, but not before Harrison caught a sly smile on her face.

"You lied?" he asked. "You were practically on your deathbed and you still couldn't be honest with me?"

Khalila didn't answer, keeping her eyes fixed on the road instead. Harrison decided to press the issue anyway.

"Telling me your real name would be a nice token of trust. What harm can come from that? I figure you're somewhere between Arabian royalty and the FBI's most wanted. Or perhaps you could just tell me which end of the spectrum you're on."

"I have to admit, you're persistent," Khalila answered. "But my real name is something you will never learn. There's a common saying when revealing classified information to someone unauthorized to receive it—*I could tell you, but then I'd have to kill you*. Let's not complicate our relationship any further. Let me be clear—if you ever learn who I am, our agreement is void."

"Really?" Harrison asked. "You just made a case about how you can be trusted, and now you're adding a disclaimer."

"My trust is conditional. I'm not the one who makes the rules."

"Then who does?" Harrison asked, his thoughts already focused on the one person who could. "The DDO?"

Khalila didn't respond, but Harrison noticed her grip on the steering wheel tighten.

"I suggest we move on from this topic," she said. "Here's the situation. As long as you don't learn who I am, you can trust me completely. If you do, our agreement is void, and you've been forewarned."

She extended her right hand. "Deal?"

Harrison recalled the original agreement they had struck in Sochi, when he extended his hand and Khalila ignored it, simply nodding before departing. At least their relationship was making progress, however slight. He didn't like Khalila's caveat—*If you learn who I am, our agreement is void*—but decided the arrangement was suitable for the time being.

He shook her hand. "Deal."

Khalila turned in to a neighborhood of single-family homes, then onto Marquand Drive. After a few houses, the road curved sharply to the left, leading to a cul-de-sac a few houses later. Up ahead, a woman waited in the driver's seat of a gray sedan parked beside the curb. Khalila stopped behind the vehicle.

Harrison and Khalila emerged from their car as the woman stepped from hers. She was a plainclothes detective who showed them her badge.

"Detective Caroline Rice," she said as they shook hands and Harrison and Khalila introduced themselves.

Rice filled them in on the details: the victim's name along with his current and former occupations, date and time of his murder, plus other specifics, including the bullet size and entry location in Nagle's head. No cartridge case was found.

Harrison assimilated the information and surveyed the neighborhood, concluding that the assassin had likely been positioned down the street behind them, probably at the bend in the road. It was a fairly upscale neighborhood, but he noted a few houses with security company placards in the front yard. He turned to Rice.

"I'd check with the residents to see if they've got any security cameras that might have captured the event. My guess is the perpetrator fired from a car parked at the curve in the road."

"We're one step ahead of you," Rice replied, "and you're right on both counts. We were able to collect video from a doorbell camera down the street."

She retrieved a cell phone from her jacket pocket and pulled up a short video clip, which she showed to Harrison and Khalila. A man was parked across the street, lifting a rifle to his shoulder as he placed his eye to the scope. The video was grainy and provided only a side view of the man's face, but Harrison immediately recognized him.

"It's Lonnie Mixell."

17

ARLINGTON, VIRGINIA

On the western side of the Pentagon, Christine O'Connor walked along the outer-ring hallway, headed toward an office between corridors four and five. A series of briefings on programs the CIA was involved in had just wrapped up, and Christine had decided to see how Secretary Verbeck was doing following her close call at National Harbor.

Christine stepped into the secretary of the Navy's reception area, where she was greeted by Navy Captain Andy Hoskins, who disappeared into an adjoining office, returning a few seconds later, holding the door open for Christine.

"The secretary will see you now."

Christine entered Verbeck's office as the secretary of the Navy, seated at her desk, rose to greet her, motioning toward a nearby conference table. Both women took their seats as Brenda welcomed the CIA director.

"Thank you for taking time out of your busy day to stop by. What can I do for you?"

"Actually," Christine replied, "I was wondering what I could do for you. It must have been terrifying for you outside the Gaylord."

"It was. Everything happened so fast. At first, I was just shocked at what happened to John McNeil, hearing the rifle shot and watching him fall to the ground. Then I was shoved into the SUV and evacuated to safety. It wasn't until later that I realized how lucky I'd been. I have to admit, there were a few minutes where my hands were shaking uncontrollably."

"That's perfectly understandable."

"Do you know who's responsible? I haven't been briefed. I've been avoiding the issue, trying to focus on other things."

"We do. He's a former SEAL named Lonnie Mixell, the same man responsible for the *Kazan* plot and the attempt on the president's life a few months ago."

"I thought Mixell was killed."

"So did we, until we spotted him on a surveillance camera at National Harbor, moments after the assassination attempt."

"Is he working alone, or are there others?"

"We suspect he's working alone. We also think there's something else going on. Whatever he's into has bigger implications."

"I hope you track him down quickly, then."

"We're working on it. The agency is assisting the FBI with all resources available. If you'd like to be informed of what we learn along the way, I can keep you up to date and also pass the request to Directors Guisewhite and Rodgaard," she said, referring to the directors of the FBI and National Intelligence.

"No, that's quite all right," Brenda replied. "I'd rather not become consumed with the investigation details. I trust you'll track Mixell down."

Christine agreed. "It's only a matter of time."

"By the way," Brenda said, "my husband had impressive things to say about you during your time at Ice Station Nautilus."

Brenda's statement caught Christine off guard, then she made the connection. Brenda's husband was Vance Verbeck, the technical director of the Navy's Arctic Submarine Laboratory, who had been the officer in charge of Ice Station Nautilus, established during their search for American and Russian submarines that had collided and sunk beneath the polar ice cap.

"You're married to Vance," Christine replied. "I should have realized sooner; Verbeck isn't a common surname."

Brenda leaned slightly toward Christine. "Is it true you killed two Russian Spetsnaz?"

Christine nodded. "I had help: an ice pick and a lot of vodka."

She recalled the deadly encounter, particularly the struggle with the second Spetsnaz. He'd had a choke hold on her, cutting off her airway as she was pinned against the wall, while she had driven an ice pick through his neck. It had been a race against time; whether she would run out of oxygen first or he ran out of blood.

Brenda must have noticed the distant look in Christine's eyes as she recalled the encounter. "I'm sorry I brought it up. It must have been traumatic."

Christine nodded, then forced a smile. "I did what I had to."

"I understand," Brenda replied. "I've been there myself a few times."

It seemed like a good time to bring their visit to a close, so Christine reiterated her offer as she stood. "Let me know if there's anything I can do to help in this matter."

"Absolutely," Brenda replied. "I won't hesitate to call."

18

ARLINGTON, VIRGINIA

The morning's dark clouds to the west had moved over the city, and a light rain was falling from an overcast sky as a sentry waved Khalila's car into Arlington National Cemetery. He saluted Harrison as he passed by, since the former SEAL was now wearing a Service Dress Blue uniform. Following their trip to Nagle's murder scene, Khalila had stopped by Harrison's room at the Intercontinental in D.C., waiting in the car while he changed into his Navy uniform for this afternoon's funeral. Khalila had stopped by her town house as well, also changing into something more appropriate: a black business suit paired with a white blouse.

Khalila was continuing down Eisenhower Drive past the Tomb of the Unknowns, headed toward McNeil's burial site, when Harrison spotted a black SUV in the distance and a woman standing among the grave sites not far away. Based on the location, Harrison had a fair idea of who it was, and since they were thirty minutes early, he decided to swing by.

"Take a left up there," he said to Khalila. He pointed to the SUV. "I think that's Christine."

"On a first-name basis with the director?" Khalila asked. "It's obvious there's something going on with you two. What's the deal?"

Harrison considered filling Khalila in, but it was a long backstory and he decided otherwise, repeating Khalila's earlier response when he had asked about her name.

"I could tell you, but then I'd have to kill you."

Khalila smiled. "Fair enough."

She turned left on Patton Drive as directed, then stopped behind the SUV. The woman standing among the graves was definitely Christine.

As Harrison opened the car door, Khalila retrieved an umbrella from the side pocket of her door. "Take this."

It was Harrison's turn to smile. "I'm a former SEAL. A little rain isn't going to bother me."

Harrison headed across the wet grass toward Christine, who stood before headstone 1851. DANIEL O'CONNOR was engraved on the front, and Harrison didn't look, but he knew TATYANA O'CONNOR was inscribed on the back. He had still been dating Christine when her mother died and had been with her at Tatyana's funeral.

That Christine had grown up without a father had always been a sensitive subject, and he wondered if her tomboy persona as a kid was compensation for the lack of a male influence at home. Her father had been killed in action while Tatyana was pregnant, and Tatyana had never remarried, dying from cancer when Christine was in her early twenties. In accordance with policy at Arlington National Cemetery, she'd been buried atop Daniel in the same grave, her name inscribed on the back of the headstone.

Harrison stopped beside Christine, and with neither saying a word, she instinctively moved closer and placed her umbrella over both of them. There was something natural about being with Christine. He wanted to put his arm around her, pulling her close to comfort her, but didn't want to send the wrong signal. He knew she was still in love with him. It had become apparent aboard USS *Michigan*, when she had asked him a simple question.

How's home?

He had seen the disappointment in her eyes when he'd replied, *It's good*.

It had been a truthful answer. He loved Angie and wasn't about to leave her. Christine had let her opportunity slip by—they had dated for over a decade when he had finally given up and moved on to Angie. A month after he proposed to Angie, Christine had called, letting him know she was ready to settle down. She hadn't heard the news.

However, he wondered what his decision would have been if Christine had called before he'd proposed. He would never admit it to Angie, but he shared a bond with Christine, one that would probably never be broken.

"I thought you might be here early," Harrison said. "Do you stop by often?"

"Not as often as I should."

"Your parents would have been proud of you. It's a shame neither one lived to see what you've accomplished."

"I wonder sometimes. Professionally, yes. I'm sure they'd be proud. But my personal life leaves a lot to be desired. I'm in my forties, unmarried, no kids—"

Harrison cut her off. "You could have almost any man you want. You're beautiful, intelligent, accomplished. If you made yourself available, there'd be men lining up to date you."

"You know how it is, Jake. I never seem to make time in my life for men. There's always something more important. I kept you waiting too long, and then my marriage to Dave didn't last, which was primarily my fault. Marriage takes work, and my heart wasn't in it."

"It's a different time in your life now, Chris. Make it a priority."

"That's what Joan keeps telling me. You remember Joan, from college?"

Harrison nodded. Joan was on Christine's gymnastics team and a political science major as well.

She continued, "Joan ended up in D.C. too. Only she's married with kids."

"It's not too late," Harrison said. "You just need to decide what you want."

"I *know* what I want," Christine said tersely. "The problem is, I can't *have* it."

An awkward silence followed. This was the most direct Christine had been concerning her feelings toward him since they had reconnected a few years ago. Assuming, of course, he was interpreting things correctly.

Christine seemed to regret her words. She looked down quickly, then checked her watch. "We should probably get going."

Harrison accompanied Christine to the road, where she said, "Thanks for stopping by," before heading toward her SUV.

Harrison returned to Khalila's car, and they were soon at McNeil and Nagle's burial site. After parking beside the curb, they made their way to the grave site, where Harrison greeted several active duty and retired SEALs who had gathered for the funeral. Christine arrived shortly thereafter, taking a seat in the family and dignitary section, covered by a canopy protecting them from the rain. As the ceremony time drew near,

Harrison stood beside Khalila, beneath her umbrella, along one side of the graves.

While they waited for the funeral to begin, Christine's gaze eventually settled on Harrison for a few seconds before flitting to Khalila. He felt Khalila move closer, pressing her body against his as her umbrella shielded them from the rain. He caught a flicker of jealousy in Christine's eyes before she turned away.

He wondered about the timing of Khalila's movement. He turned to his partner, who was looking at him. Then she smirked.

"Stop it," Harrison whispered.

"So touchy," Khalila replied softly. "I just wanted to get a bead on this thing between you and the director. Now I know." She pressed her body more firmly against him. "But don't confuse my curiosity for affection. As you've noted, I don't get attached to my partners."

She eased up, returning to a normal stance beside him.

A movement in the distance caught Harrison's attention. A horse-drawn limber and caisson carrying two flag-draped caskets was working its way toward the grave site. Following closely behind was a procession of cars carrying McNeil's and Nagle's families.

The limber and caisson pulled to a halt beside a twelve-member honor guard serving as the casket teams, and McNeil's and Nagle's families emerged from their sedans and stood alongside the road as the caskets were removed from the caisson. The chaplain led the procession to the grave site, where the caskets were placed atop metal supports above the graves while the family members took their seats beneath the canopy alongside the grave site.

The casket teams lifted the American flags from both coffins and held them stretched taut above each casket as the chaplain began the committal service. After the chaplain read the scripture, the Officer-in-Charge of the ceremony signaled the firing detail, and military personnel saluted as a seven-member rifle team fired three volleys. After the last round, a bugler sounded taps.

As the final note faded, the chaplain offered the benediction, then the casket team folded the American flags they had held over each casket, which were presented to the widows. Gretchen McNeil accepted the flag with tears streaming down her cheeks, as did Nagle's widow.

The SEALs in attendance approached the graves and pounded their metal warfare insignias into the top of each coffin. After they stepped back, visitors formed a line, offering their condolences to the widows and their families. Harrison waited, since Gretchen had mentioned during their short phone conversation that she wanted to talk with him afterward.

The line of mourners wound down, and when there was no one left, he approached the grieving families, offering condolences first to Nagle's widow, then to Gretchen. John McNeil's wife stood and hugged him tightly, holding him close for a moment.

"John truly respected you, Jake. I know he felt fortunate to have you under his command." She stepped back and wiped the tears from her eyes, then reached for her purse. "The day he was killed, he knew something bad was going to happen. He found out the night before that Nagle had been killed. He spent most of the night going through storage boxes."

Gretchen pulled an envelope from her purse. "When he left the next morning, he handed this to me on the way out the door. He said to give it to you if anything happened to him."

She handed Harrison the sealed envelope, which had *JAKE* scribbled on the front. Gretchen hugged him again, whispering into his ear this time.

"Find whoever did this, and make him pay."

She stepped back and joined the rest of her family as they departed the grave site.

After everyone except Harrison and Khalila had departed, he opened the envelope. Inside was a computer flash drive, plus an index card with a short note written on the back.

3rd floor desk. Find him.

"Do you have a laptop with you?" Harrison asked Khalila.

"I do, but we need to have the flash drive screened for viruses first."

"How long will that take?"

"Depends on the priority."

"This is high priority. I'd like to see what's on the drive *now*."

Khalila hesitated a moment, then replied, "Okay. Let's see what we've got."

After they returned to her car, Khalila reached behind her seat and pulled a laptop from its case. After turning it on and gaining access with her fingerprint, she inserted the flash drive and examined its contents: a single file containing several gigabytes of data. When Khalila tried to open the file, a display popped up, asking for the password.

"It's encrypted," she said. "I'll have Analysis break it."

19

POTOMAC, MARYLAND

Dusk was giving way to darkness, streetlights flickering on, as a silver Ford Mustang followed a blue Prius as it turned onto Highland Farm Road in Potomac, Maryland, in an affluent neighborhood of twenty-thousand-square-foot mansions. A few houses after the turn, the Prius pulled into the driveway of an eight-bedroom house brightly lit in the distance, stopping at the closed metal gate. The Mustang passed by as Captain Andy Hoskins lowered the window of his Prius and spoke into the intercom box, announcing his presence. The gate slid slowly aside and the Prius pulled up the driveway as the Mustang disappeared around the bend.

Mixell drove on for a while, pulling his Mustang to the side of the road near a break in the trees where there was a clear view of Hoskins's destination: Secretary of the Navy Brenda Verbeck's estate. The Prius stopped beneath a portico, where Hoskins, carrying a briefcase, was met at the door by a servant, and the front door closed after he stepped inside the mansion.

A light flicked on in an upstairs room, which Hoskins entered while Brenda Verbeck waited by the doorway. He placed his briefcase on a conference table, then stopped beside Verbeck, placing his hands on her waist as he gently kissed her neck. They disappeared from view, and a moment later, a faint light lit the master bedroom at the back corner of the house.

A twisted scenario indeed, Mixell thought.

Verbeck was having an affair with the man she had contracted to kill. But perhaps he had gotten it wrong and someone else had targeted the Pentagon Navy chief and captain. After considering the possible scenarios,

Mixell's conviction returned; his assessment was likely correct. What he'd gotten wrong was underestimating how conniving and ruthless Verbeck was. A woman truly to be admired.

With his eyes on the bedroom widows, Mixell reviewed the relevant details he had gleaned thus far. Hoskins had been divorced for about a year, with custody of his daughter on weekends. Verbeck, on the other hand, was a married woman, whose husband worked and lived in San Diego. Whether Brenda and her husband were estranged or she was simply taking advantage of their separation, Mixell didn't know.

It looked like there was no more to learn tonight about Hoskins's travels, so Mixell started his car and headed down the road.

Shortly after Mixell returned to his hotel room, his phone vibrated, followed by a notification sliding onto the screen.

An encrypted message.

He launched the application and typed in his password followed by his thumbprint, and a message appeared on screen.

You were spotted at National Harbor and identified. You shouldn't have been so sloppy.

Mixell typed, "I wasn't sloppy. I prefer they know who was behind the attempted assassination."

But I also know who you are now, instead of a faceless For Hire on the dark web.

"Is that supposed to be some sort of threat?"

No. It means there's the potential for future work.

"What kind of work?"

Finish your current assignment, then we'll talk. How long until the other two men are eliminated?

"No definitive timeline yet. I'm working on the plan for the Pentagon captain. The fifth man on the list is on the other side of the country, so I'll deal with him last."

The fifth man has been rehired by the CIA. He's in your neck of the woods now.

Mixell considered the new information, then grinned. Harrison had been rehired to track him down. A new message appeared on his phone.

Don't let authorities discover you're behind the other four deaths. My client doesn't want these killings connected.

"Preventing the authorities from connecting the dots is going to be difficult. You've got two men at the Pentagon, plus three retired Navy SEALs. It won't take a rocket scientist to make the connections. I've already linked the Pentagon men. But what's the connection between the three SEALs?"

None of your concern.

"Not even a hint?"

Focus on your assignment. Complete it as soon as possible.

The secure connection terminated and the messages disappeared from Mixell's phone.

He put the phone down and focused on the remaining two men on his list. Hoskins was next, and his thoughts soon shifted to Jake Harrison. Mixell envisioned several possible scenarios, searching for the one that would inflict the most emotional and physical pain.

One scenario in particular was immensely appealing.

He was saving Harrison for last. When it happened, he would savor every moment.

20

USS *MICHIGAN*

"Conn, Sonar. Hold a new contact on the towed array, designated Sierra eight-five, ambiguous bearings three-one-five and zero-four-five. High-frequency tonal detection only. Analyzing."

Lieutenant Brian Resor, on watch as the submarine's Officer of the Deck, acknowledged Sonar's report via the microphone mounted above the Conn.

"Sonar, Conn. Aye."

Finally, something noteworthy to investigate.

They had been at it for days, scouring *Michigan*'s operating area for sign of the small and elusive UUV. It was like searching for a needle in a haystack. Sonar had identified hundreds of contacts, each subsequently classified as a merchant ship or other surface craft. This contact, however, seemed promising. Sonar had picked up Sierra eight-five only via high-frequency tonals, which traveled short distances compared to the lower frequency and broadband noise normally emitted by surface ships.

In concert with Resor's thoughts, Sonar made the report he'd been hoping for.

"Conn, Sonar. Sierra eight-five is classified submerged. Tonals correlate to the target of interest."

Resor acknowledged, then pulled the 27-MC microphone from its holder and pressed the button for the Captain's stateroom. "Captain, Officer of the Deck. Hold a new submerged contact on the towed array. Tonals match the target of interest."

Captain Wilson acknowledged and entered the Control Room a moment later. Stepping onto the Conn, he examined the contact frequencies on the display. Satisfied the contact was the UUV, he gave the order everyone aboard had been waiting for since they departed Bahrain.

"Man Battle Stations Torpedo."

The Chief of the Watch, stationed at the Ballast Control Panel on the port side of Control, twisted a lever on his panel, and the *gong, gong, gong* of the submarine's General Emergency alarm reverberated throughout the ship. As the alarm faded, the Chief of the Watch picked up his 1-MC microphone, repeating the Captain's order over the shipwide announcing system.

Crew members streamed into Control, taking their seats at dormant consoles, bringing them to life as they donned sound-powered phone headsets. Sonar technicians passed through Control on their way to the Sonar Room while supervisors gathered behind their respective stations and other personnel throughout the ship reported to their battle stations.

Three minutes after the order, the Chief of the Watch reported, "Officer of the Deck, Battle Stations are manned."

Resor acknowledged and passed the report to Wilson, who announced, "This is the Captain. I have the Conn. Lieutenant Resor retains the Deck."

Wilson would manage the tactical situation and control the submarine's movements, while Resor monitored the navigation picture and handled routine ship evolutions.

"Designate Sierra eight-five as Master one," Wilson said. "Track Master one."

The process from this point was straightforward: develop a firing solution for the target, proceed to Firing Point Procedures, and shoot. What was not entirely straightforward was what the UUV would do in response or even before Wilson sent their torpedo on its way.

The UUV clearly had the ability to track and identify targets of interest, and a submarine in its waterspace would definitely meet that criterion unless it was informed a friendly unit was passing through. Based on what happened to *Stethem*, that safety feature could not be relied upon. If the UUV detected *Michigan*, it could easily attack it.

Wilson assumed the UUV would attack *Michigan* at some point, either before or after Wilson launched a torpedo. Regarding that endeavor, the first step was to determine which of the towed array bearings was the real contact and which was the false one.

Michigan's towed array detected contacts at longer ranges than the submarine's other acoustic sensors. However, the array was an assembly of hydrophones connected in a straight line, which meant it could not determine which side of the submarine the sound arrived from, resulting in two potential bearings to the contact—one on each side of the array. The way to resolve that question was to maneuver and evaluate what happened to the contacts on each side of the array. The correct bearing would remain relatively constant, while the false bearing would shift to a wildly different bearing to maintain the same relative position on the other side of the array.

"Helm, left twenty degrees rudder. Steady course two-seven-zero."

After completing the ninety-degree turn, Wilson waited for the towed array to stabilize, its snaking motion gradually dissipating. After a few minutes, the array straightened out and Sonar made the awaited report.

"Conn, Sonar. Bearing ambiguity has been resolved. Master one is to the northwest."

Lieutenant Commander Tom Montgomery, the submarine's Executive Officer and in charge of the Fire Control Tracking Party, announced, "Set maximum speed to five knots."

Although the UUV was capable of high-speed, short-duration bursts, it normally traveled at very low speed to extend the time between battery recharges. According to the specifications provided by Secretary Verbeck, the UUV normally transited at three to five knots, depending on the ocean current—just enough to maintain steerageway.

Montgomery stopped briefly behind each of the combat control consoles, examining the target solution on each one, eventually tapping one of the fire control technicians, who pressed a button on his console, sending an updated target solution to the torpedo.

Montgomery announced, "I have a firing solution."

Wilson called out, "Firing Point Procedures, Master one, tube One."

Lieutenant Ryan Jescovitch, *Michigan*'s Weapons Officer, acknowledged Wilson's order and relayed it to the fire control technician at the Weapon Launch Console, who sent the engagement presets to the torpedo.

Montgomery stopped briefly behind each of the combat control consoles, examining the target solution on each one, verifying that the best target solution had been promoted to Master.

"Solution ready!" he announced.

"Weapon ready!" Jescovitch called out, verifying that the torpedo presets matched those in combat control and that the target's solution—its course, speed, and range—had been sent to the torpedo in tube One.

"Ship ready!" Resor reported, ensuring the counterfire corridor from the UUV had been identified and that *Michigan*'s torpedo countermeasures were ready to deploy.

Wilson was about to order the torpedo launch when a report from Sonar came across the Control Room speakers.

"Conn, Sonar. Hold a new contact on the towed array, designated Sierra eight-six, ambiguous bearings three-five-five and one-eight-five, classified submerged. Analyzing."

Wilson examined the sonar display on the Conn. The new contact was moving much faster than the UUV. If it was submerged, it was likely a submarine. But *Michigan* was the only U.S. submarine in this waterspace, which meant they had detected a foreign submarine. Firing a torpedo in this situation was perilous since the torpedo could lock on to the submarine instead of the UUV.

The issue was—modern torpedoes were artificially intelligent weapons, which had pros and cons. After launch, they would analyze the returns from the sonar in their noses, sorting through what could be a submarine or surface ship, or a decoy. Reassuring in its capability, the torpedo's independent nature was also disconcerting. It could not distinguish between friend and foe, and there was always the possibility that the torpedo, while searching for its intended target, could lock on to the wrong one, or even the submarine that fired it.

There were safeguards to prevent that, plus a guidance wire attached to the torpedoes fired by U.S. submarines. Over the thin copper wire, the submarine's crew could send new commands after the torpedo was launched, changing its course, depth, or other search parameters. But if the guidance wire broke, the torpedo would be on its own, deciding which target to attack.

Additionally, a torpedo launched in another submarine's vicinity would almost assuredly prompt a counterfire, which was something Wilson wanted to avoid. That was two strikes—*Michigan*'s torpedo might sink the wrong target, and the foreign submarine, target or not, would likely counterfire. Wilson didn't need a third strike to make his decision.

"Check Fire," Wilson announced, canceling the firing order. "Designate Sierra eight-six as Master two. Track Master one and Master two."

Inside the Sonar Room, the sonar technicians were starting to sort things out. Based on the tonal frequencies and strength, along with the lack of a broadband trace, they had already determined the new contact was submerged.

Sonar Chief Jim Moore tapped the Narrowband Operator seated before him, Petty Officer Andrew Bubb, on the shoulder. "I need a classification."

Moore had lots of experience tracking foreign submarines, in both shore-based trainers and at sea, but the frequencies weren't making sense; they didn't match anything they expected to see in the Persian Gulf.

Bubb completed his analysis and looked up from his display, a confused expression on his face. "The closest match I've got is a Seawolf class."

"That can't be right," Moore replied. "Seawolfs are U.S. submarines, and *Michigan* is the only American submarine authorized in this waterspace."

"I know," Bubb said. "But look." He gestured toward his display. "A few of the frequencies are off, but the propulsion-related tonals are definitely Seawolf."

Moore leaned forward, examining the frequencies over Bubb's shoulder. He was right. Even without the automated classification algorithm flashing on the screen—SEAWOLF—Moore would have made the same call.

He relayed the information to the Sonar Coordinator beside him, who announced Master two's classification over the sound-powered phones.

In the Control Room, Lieutenant Commander Montgomery, who was examining a display over a fire control technician's shoulder, suddenly stood erect, a perplexed look on his face as he turned to Wilson.

"Sonar reports Master two is classified Seawolf."

"That can't be right," Wilson replied.

After Montgomery verified the report had been correctly understood, Wilson went to the Sonar shack. He opened the door and poked his head in.

"What the hell is going on in here? A Seawolf can't possibly be in our waterspace."

"I know, Captain," Moore replied with an exasperated look on his face. "But that's what the tonals indicate. Whatever's out there has definitely got a Seawolf propulsion system."

Wilson considered the information for a minute, then returned to the Conn. As he evaluated the best path forward, a report by his Executive Officer caught him by surprise.

"Captain, the solutions for Master one and Master two are converging."

Wilson stepped from the Conn, stopping behind one of the combat control consoles, which displayed the solutions for both contacts. Master two had slowed to a few knots faster than the UUV, and the contacts were angling toward each other. A moment later, the two contacts steadied up on the same course, with Master two closing slowly from behind until both contacts blended into a single trace on the display.

"Conn, Sonar. Detecting mechanical transients on a bearing to Masters one and two. Sounds similar to torpedo outer doors opening."

Wilson considered whether the sounds were the precursor to a torpedo launch. Given that the submarine had slowed to five knots, it was unlikely it was preparing to fire; submarine crews typically prosecuted contacts at medium speed, maneuvering quickly to help their tracking algorithms develop a target solution and to enable rapid acceleration to ahead flank if the target counterfired.

There was no indication that either contact had detected them, and given that their tracks overlaid upon each other, Wilson drew the most logical conclusion. Master two was a mother ship retrieving the UUV, opening doors in its hull to do so.

However, Secretary Verbeck hadn't mentioned anything about a mother ship. The UUV was supposedly completely independent, recharging itself via solar panels while languishing near the surface. Now that Wilson thought about it, something had to launch the UUV and retrieve it for periodic maintenance. Perhaps Verbeck had simply failed to mention those additional details. But if a mother ship could retrieve the defective UUV, why not just order it to do so and keep the UUV aboard, solving the renegade UUV problem?

Other things weren't adding up either. If Master two was a mother ship, why did it have Seawolf tonals? As far as he knew, Seawolf submarines didn't have the necessary modifications to launch and retrieve UUVs of this size.

These were critical questions that needed answers. A discussion with Secretary Verbeck and her aide would be required.

"Attention in Control," he announced. When everyone focused on him, he continued. "Master two has been classified as a Seawolf. We're supposed to be the only U.S. submarine in this waterspace, but this wouldn't be the first time two submarines have been routed through the same water. Master two also appears to be a mother ship for the UUV, which doesn't correlate to known Seawolf capabilities. Whatever Master two is, we're not authorized to sink it, since our mission is to destroy the UUV only. We're going to break off from this engagement and figure out what's going on.

"Secure from Battle Stations Torpedo."

After the announcement went out, Wilson ordered Lieutenant Resor to station the Section Tracking Party, keeping tabs on the UUV and its mother ship.

As the crew transitioned to its normal watch stations, Wilson directed his Communicator, "Prepare for a secure VTC with the secretary of the Navy. I'll take it in my stateroom."

After the Communicator acknowledged, Wilson turned to the Officer of the Deck.

"Make preparations to come to periscope depth."

ARLINGTON, VIRGINIA

In a secure conference room in the Pentagon basement, Brenda Verbeck paced back and forth before the front row of chairs. In a few minutes, their videoconference with Captain Wilson would begin. The only other person in the room was her senior military aide, Captain Andy Hoskins, seated in one of the chairs facing the display screen and camera.

"I was afraid this would happen," Verbeck said as she kept pacing, casting a sideways glance at her aide.

During their trip to Bahrain, Hoskins had already voiced his opinion: *if it comes to that, we'll have to come clean.* That, however, wasn't something Verbeck was willing to do. Moments earlier, while they waited for the videoconference to commence, their conversation had become heated, until Hoskins had finally agreed.

At the appointed time, the display energized, revealing a video of Captain Wilson seated at his stateroom desk. It appeared that no one else was present, per Verbeck's direction when she had replied to *Michigan's* communication request. Verbeck took her seat beside Hoskins.

"Good afternoon, Secretary Verbeck," Wilson began. "How do you copy?"

Verbeck turned to Hoskins, not understanding the question.

Hoskins replied, "Hold you Lima-Charlie." He leaned toward Verbeck and translated. "Loud and Clear."

It was odd, using radio lingo for a videoconference, but old habits were hard to break.

"Same here," Wilson replied. "Thank you for the short-notice communication request, but we've run into a complication. It appears the UUV we've been directed to sink has mated with a mother ship of some sort, which raises a number of questions. I'm hoping you can shed light on the matter and provide updated orders."

"Of course," Verbeck replied. "There is indeed a UUV mother ship. That's something we didn't discuss because we were hopeful you'd locate and sink the UUV before its retrieval. The reason we didn't mention the mother ship is because its existence is even more sensitive than the weaponized UUVs. It's a full-size, automated submarine, built primarily with components already fabricated when the Seawolf submarine program was unexpectedly canceled after the Cold War ended. Three more Seawolf submarines had been under construction in various stages, including their reactor plants, and the parts were put into storage for use as spares for the three operational Seawolfs.

"When the idea for a fully automated mother ship was devised, an economical solution was to build one with already-paid-for and fabricated components. For the most part, the mother ship resembles a Seawolf submarine."

"That explains its sonar signature," Wilson replied.

Verbeck continued, "The mother ship extracts the data collected from each UUV after mating, as a backup to what they've transmitted while operating on their own. It also recharges the UUVs; they don't have built-in solar panels. You were misled on that aspect because we didn't want to divulge the existence of the mother ship unless it was absolutely necessary.

"As you can imagine, a fully automated mother ship containing a nuclear reactor is a sensitive subject we'd rather not reveal to the public. Safeguards have been put in place, of course, keeping the submarine away from land in case of a severe casualty. But that's the least of our worries now that the UUV has mated with it."

"Why is that?" Wilson asked.

"We suspect the UUV has been infected with a virus, corrupting its artificial intelligence. Now that it has mated with the mother ship, it too is likely infected, and it will now transmit the virus to every UUV it mates with. The situation is now far more severe. Instead of sinking a single UUV, your task has become more involved and more urgent. You'll also need to sink the mother ship before it infects more UUVs."

"I understand," Wilson replied. "How long before the mother ship retrieves the next vehicle?"

"Seven days," Verbeck replied. "Are you still tracking the UUV and mother ship?"

"We aren't," Wilson replied. "There's a sharp thermocline here in the Gulf, and we lost both contacts coming up to periscope depth."

Wilson went on to explain what a thermocline was—a thin layer of water where the temperature transitioned rapidly between the warm surface heated by the sun and the cold water beneath. Submarines used thermoclines to their advantage because the rapid temperature change bent sound waves as they traveled through the layer, reflecting the sound back toward its source like light reflecting off a window. Depending on the frequency and angle of the sound wave, some tonals didn't make it through.

"Will it be difficult to regain contact?"

"That depends on if they've altered their course or speed while we're at periscope depth, and whether they've separated. Do you know how long it takes before the UUV de-mates from the mother ship?"

Verbeck turned to Hoskins again.

"About an hour. It depends on how depleted the UUV battery is."

"Then we'll need to end this videocon soon so I can get *Michigan* below the thermocline again."

"I understand," Verbeck replied. "Do you have any more questions?"

"I do. Is the mother ship weaponized?"

There was a tense moment in the conference room before Hoskins answered.

"Yes."

"What weapons does it carry?"

"MK 48 ADCAP, MOD 7."

Wilson appeared to be evaluating the revised scenario. Instead of dealing with a UUV carrying a single lightweight torpedo, he now faced an automated, full-size submarine carrying heavyweight torpedoes, with warheads over six times more powerful than those built into lightweight torpedoes.

"How many torpedoes?"

"A full torpedo room's worth," Hoskins replied. "A *Seawolf* torpedo room."

Wilson nodded solemnly. A Seawolf torpedo room carried fifty torpedoes, twice that of other U.S. fast-attack submarines and three times what *Michigan* carried.

"I understand," he replied. "Is there anything else I need to know?"

"Not that I can think of," Verbeck replied. She looked to Hoskins, who shook his head.

"Thank you for your time, Secretary Verbeck. We'll destroy the UUV and mother ship as soon as possible."

"Thank *you*, Captain. I appreciate your assistance in this matter."

The secure videocon terminated, and the display went black.

There was silence in the conference room until Hoskins spoke. "This has gotten out of hand. If he sinks that submarine—"

Verbeck cut him off. "Wilson will be to blame, not us. He has no official direction to sink that submarine aside from the verbal order I just gave him—he has nothing in writing. He'll just be an overzealous captain who exceeded his authority. What matters is that the UUV and the information it collected is destroyed."

Hoskins didn't reply, but his face was tight. He had agreed to lend his assistance in the matter, but his resolve was wavering.

Verbeck considered the tenuous relationship with her military aide. His demise couldn't come fast enough. What was taking so long?

22

DICKERSON, MARYLAND

Sitting atop a large boulder beside the mountain trail, Lonnie Mixell aimed his binoculars through an opening in the trees, surveying the parking lot at the foot of Sugarloaf Mountain. Aside from his car, there was one other vehicle, with a woman and young girl inside, the woman with a phone to her ear. Another car pulled into the lot and parked. Navy Captain Andy Hoskins stepped from the vehicle with a water bottle in one hand, which he placed in a fanny pack he clipped around his waist.

Clearly a weekend warrior.

It was warm this morning, already eighty degrees, and Mixell wore only shorts and a T-shirt. His P226 pistol was in his backpack beside him, but he wouldn't need it today. He put his binoculars away and loosened the laces of his right shoe, then slid down to the ground with his back against the boulder. It'd be about ten minutes before Hoskins made his way up the trail.

From his backpack, Mixell pulled out a small container and unscrewed the base, revealing a ring inside with a sharp metal point the size of a tack and covered by a transparent plastic sheath. Mixell slid the ring onto his right hand, then rotated it until the metal point faced in toward his palm.

The metal tip was coated with a poison that would paralyze the heart, simulating a heart attack within minutes. It was also coated with a numbing agent, so the victim wouldn't feel the puncture and suspect anything until it was too late.

As expected, Hoskins appeared on the trail ten minutes later, still a fair bit away, partially visible through the foliage. What wasn't expected, however, was that he was accompanied by a young girl about ten years old.

The girl in the car with the woman.

Mixell connected the dots. Hoskins was divorced and his wife had custody of their daughter. This was his weekend with her, and he had decided to take her hiking with him this time. The woman and girl had been waiting in the parking lot for Hoskins to arrive.

Mixell chastised himself for his inadequate reconnaissance and assessment, not accounting for the possibility that Hoskins's daughter would accompany him on his next hike. He analyzed the issue quickly, deciding he would kill only Hoskins and not his daughter. He killed people who deserved to be killed, with *deserved* meeting a broad definition that included those he'd been *paid* to kill and those he *wanted* to kill. But innocent kids were typically off-limits.

He'd have to be careful, poisoning only Hoskins and not the girl. The situation wasn't ideal. He preferred that the girl not be with her dad when he dropped dead, but he had other issues to attend to and couldn't let this opportunity go to waste.

Hoskins and his daughter emerged from the foliage and spotted him leaning against the boulder, the laces of his right shoe loosened.

"Are you okay?" Hoskins asked.

"Sprained my ankle," Mixell replied. "I sure could use a hand."

"I'll help," the daughter said as she moved eagerly toward him.

"Thanks, sweetie, but I'm too heavy. I'll need your dad's help." He shifted his gaze to Hoskins. "If you could help me down the mountain, I'd really appreciate it."

"No problem," Hoskins replied as he stepped toward Mixell.

As the man approached, Mixell reached into the palm of his right hand and removed the plastic sheath from the poisoned tack. He extended his right hand and Hoskins gripped it, pulling Mixell to his feet. Hoskins seemed not to notice the tack penetrating his palm; the numbing agent worked as advertised.

"Thanks," Mixell said, gingerly putting weight onto his right ankle. "Wow," he said. "It feels much better now." He took a tentative step. "You know what? I think I can make it back down by myself."

"You sure?" Hoskins asked.

Mixell took another few steps, putting more weight on his right foot. "Yeah, I can make it. I just needed to rest for a while."

"I'd be happy to help you down," Hoskins offered again.

Mixell preferred he not be around once the toxin took effect, not wanting to be associated with Hoskins's death.

"Thanks, but I'll be all right. Why don't you enjoy the hike with your daughter?"

"All right," Hoskins said as Mixell grabbed his backpack and started down the mountain. "But be careful!"

Mixell waved his appreciation as he kept moving, then carefully slid the plastic sheath back onto the ring's tack, concealing the action with his body.

A few minutes later, as Mixell worked his way down the trail, he heard a young girl's faint scream from farther up the mountain.

He smiled.

That leaves Harrison.

23

POTOMAC, MARYLAND

On the second floor of her residence, Brenda Verbeck closed the door to the study and approached Dan Snyder, who had his back to her as he examined one of the oil paintings on the wall. While not up to Snyder's standards—only paintings worth ten million dollars or more would grace the walls of *his* mansion—the six-figure abstract painting complemented the study's décor quite well.

As usual, Snyder was dressed to impress, wearing one of his expensive Desmond Merrion suits. Brenda stopped behind him and, when he seemed not to notice, cleared her throat.

When he turned around, she slapped him across the face.

Snyder's eyes widened, and he took a step back when he noticed the fury on his sister's face.

"How dare you put me in this situation!" she said.

"What situation?"

"You know damn well what I'm talking about! Did you think your deal with Iran would go unnoticed?"

Snyder opened his mouth to deny any knowledge of what she was talking about, then decided otherwise. "How did you find out?"

"Because you're sloppy. Your business associates thought they were clever, using point-to-point communications to defeat satellite intercepts, but we have assets covering those transmissions as well. You're lucky the intercept was made by a black program under my cognizance and that the senior man in charge had more allegiance to me than to the Navy."

It took a moment for Snyder to process Brenda's statement—about a man who had more allegiance to her than the Navy. "You're having another affair?"

"And you're a saint?"

Snyder offered no response.

"I've put my reputation and career on the line for you, and you're not even my favorite brother!"

Snyder remained silent, waiting for Brenda's fury to run its course. But then he keyed on Brenda's use of the past tense—*had more allegiance*—when referring to the man who helped her cover his tracks.

"This man who helped you conceal the information. Why did you refer to him in the past tense?"

Snyder's question inflamed her. "Everything I've done, I've done for you!" she said as she poked him in the chest, her face turning red. "If the wrong people discover what I've done, I'll be in jail for the rest of my life!"

"What have you done?"

"I've cleaned up most of the loose ends."

"How, exactly, have you taken care of these loose ends?"

"I have contacts. I didn't get to where I am without forging alliances with powerful people. The problem has been taken care of. You just need to stay out of trouble from now on."

"What about Larson? Have you taken care of him?"

"Who's Larson?"

"He's the man I hired to ship the equipment, although it's probably not his real name. I don't think he's a man you want to mess with, though."

Brenda considered the new information, concluding he shouldn't be a problem. "I'll trust that he's the type of man whose silence you buy along with his services."

Snyder nodded. "I got that impression."

Brenda folded her arms across her chest, the color of her face slowly returning to normal.

"What now?" Snyder asked.

"There are data archives on a submarine and UUV that contain the intercepted data. Once those are destroyed, you'll be in the clear."

She chose not to explain how those files would be destroyed. The less her brother knew, the better.

24

LANGLEY, VIRGINIA

The morning mist had begun to lift as Harrison was waved through the main gate at Langley. As he approached the parking garage, his cell phone vibrated. It was Khalila.

"Heads up," she said when Harrison answered. "We've been directed to attend a meeting in the director's conference room at 8 a.m."

"What's the topic?"

"The meeting invite doesn't say, but I'm sure it's about the file on McNeil's flash drive. When I stopped by Analysis this morning to check on the decryption status, the tech told me the file activated a trip wire of some sort when it was decrypted. He said McFarland got called back into the office last night."

Harrison checked his watch: 7:55 a.m.

"I just pulled into the parking garage. I'll meet you on the seventh floor."

He joined Khalila as he stepped from the elevator, and the pair headed toward the director's office. When they entered the adjoining conference room, Harrison immediately registered the tension in the air.

Christine was seated at the head of the table, flanked by Bryant and Rolow on one side and McFarland on the other. The DDA had her laptop computer open, with several thick folders stacked beside it. She looked exhausted, as if she'd been up all night.

No greetings or smiles were offered.

"Have a seat," Christine said.

After they settled into their chairs, Bryant asked Khalila, "Where did you get this file?"

Khalila turned to Harrison, who answered, "From John McNeil's widow. What is it?"

"It's a video of the Abbottabad raid, during which Osama bin Laden was killed. A raid that both you and McNeil participated in. Apparently, you've been keeping secrets," Bryant replied in an accusatory tone.

"As I should have," Harrison countered. "I'm not allowed to share those details with anyone not read into the program."

"It was a CIA-led operation," Bryant replied with attitude. "A reasonable person would assume that the people around this table, aside from Khalila, are authorized access to that information."

"Until thirty seconds ago, my participation in that operation wasn't relevant. Now that it is, what would you like to know?"

There was a short silence as Harrison stared Bryant down.

McFarland replied instead. "We want to know how this highly classified and sensitive video was floating around in the public domain."

"You'd have to ask John McNeil. He gave the flash drive containing the video to his wife the morning he was killed. He put it in an envelope with my name on it, then told his wife to give it to me if anything happened to him."

"Was there anything else in the envelope?" McFarland asked.

"A note in McNeil's handwriting, which said—*3rd floor desk. Find him.*"

Bryant and Rolow exchanged looks, then Rolow spoke next.

"Khalila, have you accessed this file and watched the video?"

"I have not. The file was encrypted."

"Have you made a copy of this file?"

"No."

"You may leave."

Khalila rose from her chair as Harrison intervened. "Khalila is my partner, assigned to track down Mixell. It appears that whatever Mixell is involved in, and the reason he killed McNeil, may have had something to do with the Abbottabad raid. Khalila should be privy to all relevant information."

"She's not read into the program," Rolow replied.

"Then read her in."

There was a strained silence in the conference room until McFarland spoke. "The CIA is the original classification authority for this operation. We can authorize Khalila access to the information." She pulled a form from one of her folders. "I brought a nondisclosure agreement for this program, just in case." She looked to Christine for direction.

"Read her in," Christine said.

Khalila dropped back into her chair as McFarland pushed the agreement across the table to Khalila, who read and signed it. As McFarland retrieved the document, she said, "Like the other Top Secret, SCI programs, you cannot disclose protected information to unauthorized personnel." She slid a sheet of paper, containing the names of those read into the program, to Khalila.

After Khalila reviewed the list, McFarland asked Christine, "Shall I play the video now?"

Christine nodded.

McFarland activated a display at the front of the conference room with a remote control, then clicked on a computer file. A video began playing.

Harrison realized they were watching a video of the Abbottabad raid from a night vision camera built into a SEAL's gear, most likely Commander McNeil's. He was aboard the second of two stealth Black Hawk helicopters speeding just above the treetops in the darkness. Both helicopters hugged the hilly ground, hoping to avoid detection by Pakistani military radar during their approach to Abbottabad.

Bin Laden's compound came into view: a three-story concrete structure surrounded by a stone wall. The lead helicopter, barely audible, slowed to a hover inside the compound walls and began its descent. Harrison watched from a distance what he had experienced firsthand—he'd been aboard the lead Black Hawk.

The helicopter got caught in a vortex ring state, an airflow condition that prevented the rotor downwash from diffusing. The pilot lost control of the helicopter and its tail grazed the compound wall, damaging the tail rotor. The helicopter tilted to one side and the pilot performed an emergency landing, burying the Black Hawk's nose in the ground to prevent it from tipping over. Harrison recalled those perilous seconds as the helicopter's main rotor churned into the dirt as the aircraft tilted. But the vehicle held together as the rotor ground to a halt.

McNeil's helicopter landed nearby and the other SEALs joined those from the first Black Hawk, who had egressed from the damaged helicopter without injuries. After clearing the smaller building inside the compound, SEAL breachers—demolition experts—placed explosives on the main building's doors, gaining access. McNeil entered the house after several SEAL fire teams entered the building, with each unit assigned to clear and control a specific floor.

The video moved through each level of the house, recording the greenish images. By the time the video reached the third floor, they had passed four motionless persons lying on the floor—three men and one woman—each with several bloodstains, plus several groups of women and children sequestered along the walls.

On the third floor was another group of women and children with a SEAL watching over them, and a tall man lying supine on the ground, with several gunshot wounds to his head and torso. His face was a bloody mess, making visual identification impossible.

Normal lighting flicked on, illuminating the room in yellow, incandescent light.

The video abruptly ended.

McFarland shifted her gaze to Harrison. "This video raises several questions. The first issue is that this video isn't in our archives; there's no record of it even being recorded. It appears that McNeil took it upon himself to record the raid, then never turned the video in.

"The second issue is—why did he want his wife to give this to you if something happened to him?" She stared at Harrison, waiting for a response.

"I don't know. There isn't anything on the video that I wasn't already aware of, and I assume it's the same for you."

McFarland replied, "Correct. Which makes this a puzzling issue. What about McNeil's note. Do you have it?"

Harrison pulled it from his back pocket and tossed the index card across the table to McFarland. She read the message aloud, confirming Harrison's earlier report.

"3rd floor desk. Find him."

McFarland picked the note up with tweezers and placed it into a small plastic bag she pulled from one of her folders. Then she rewound the video to when McNeil reached the third floor.

"Let's take a look at the desk."

The video began playing again, culminating with the view of Osama bin Laden's body on the floor. The lights flicked on for a few seconds before the video ended.

"There it is," McFarland said, backing the video up to just before it ended. Against the back wall of the room was a desk crowded with various items: a computer tower, display, keyboard, several thumb drives, a handheld radio-transceiver, a cup holding several pens and pencils, three stacks of manila folders, and a few books standing beside each other.

Harrison and the others stared at the image, trying to make sense of McNeil's message.

Find who?

And how would the desk help them?

They spent several minutes staring at the desk's contents, postulating what McNeil's message meant. They made no appreciable headway until, while watching the video again, McFarland spotted something.

"There," she said, pointing at the dark computer display. There's a reflection on the screen."

Harrison looked closer. It was an image of two men, visible for a few seconds before the video ended. The reflection was blurry due to the camera movement, making it difficult to determine who they were.

McFarland enhanced the image with an editing program on her computer. The two men came into focus. One was a SEAL, escorting a tall, hooded man with his hands tied behind him toward the stairs.

There was a tense silence in the room as Harrison waited for the inevitable question, which came from McFarland.

"Bin Laden was supposedly the only male on the third level. If that's him on the floor, who's the guy in the hood?"

25

WASHINGTON, D.C.

Christine O'Connor eyed Jake Harrison, seated at the other end of the conference table. He had not yet answered the question—*Who was the man wearing the hood?*

She had known Harrison for most of her life, and it was clear that he was evaluating how to respond. Finally, he answered.

"He was the senior al-Qaeda courier."

McFarland looked at her computer display. "You're saying that Abu Ahmed al-Kuwaiti, who was reportedly killed during the raid, was captured instead?"

"That's my understanding," Harrison replied. "I never saw the hooded man's face. He was escorted from the compound and loaded aboard the Chinook with bin Laden's body."

Rolow interjected, "Why is there no record in our files about a prisoner? It was our operation, damn it!"

"That's because JSOC," Harrison replied, referring to the Joint Special Operations Command, which planned and conducted the mission, "took custody of the prisoner, and every member of the assault team was instructed to not mention him in our after-action reports."

"Who gave this instruction?"

"John McNeil."

"And now that McNeil is dead, we can't ask who gave *him* the order. How convenient."

McFarland resumed the questioning. "Why did JSOC take custody of the courier and keep that a secret from the CIA?"

"JSOC took custody because he was classified as an enemy combatant. As far as the secrecy, I suspect it was to prevent al-Qaeda from learning we had taken their lead courier prisoner, so they wouldn't immediately change their communication protocols."

"That doesn't make sense," McFarland replied. "The only way we would have benefited is if JSOC provided what they learned from the courier to us, so we could exploit it. To my knowledge, no information regarding al-Qaeda communication protocols was ever provided to the agency as a result of the Abbottabad raid. If they had the courier and extracted this information, what did they do with it?"

"I have a better question," Rolow said. "Where *is* the courier?" He directed his gaze toward Harrison.

"I don't know."

Christine asked, "Why would McNeil want you to track down this courier?"

That really wasn't the question she wanted to ask—she was working her way to it. She had always wondered why the goal of the Abbottabad raid was to kill bin Laden instead of apprehending him. He was the mastermind of al-Qaeda, a gold mine of information if captured. Of course, letting the world know you had bin Laden in custody would have been unwise, setting American citizens up for innumerable hostage situations until bin Laden was freed. There was only one logical conclusion.

"What if the man on the floor is the courier and the captured man is Osama bin Laden?"

There was a heavy silence in the conference room until Harrison spoke.

"That thought has crossed my mind."

"Why is that?" Christine asked.

"The SEALs on the first and second floors were issued strict orders to remain on their floors after the compound was secured, and not venture up to the third floor. It's understandable to some degree. Each team was assigned to a floor—to neutralize or disarm all threats, contain and control any noncombatants, and, once the compound was secure, strip the area of anything that might be of intelligence value: documents, computers, thumb drives, phones, and other electronic gear. We didn't have extra time to tour the compound and gawk at bin Laden's body.

"As a result, only the SEALs on the third floor knew the identity of the second man. By the time he descended, he had already been hooded. Once we landed in Afghanistan, he was taken to a separate hangar and I never saw him again.

"Regarding the dead man on the third floor, a positive ID couldn't be made in the compound. He took two bullets to the face, leaving a gory mess, which made it difficult to verify his identity via facial recognition. Even when he was cleaned up afterward, we couldn't achieve one hundred percent identification visually. We had to rely on DNA analysis."

McFarland examined the files on her computer.

"I have the photos," she said. "Want to take a look?"

Christine nodded.

McFarland paged through three sets of photographs: bin Laden on his bedroom floor after being killed; in an aircraft hangar at a military base in Afghanistan after he'd been cleaned up, which were the most recognizable and gruesome; and those taken prior to the burial at sea before a shroud was placed around his body. There was extensive facial damage from the two bullet wounds—one bullet had blown out his left eye and a large part of his frontal bone, and the other had collapsed a good portion of the right side of his face.

McFarland broke the silence after viewing the macabre pictures. "I have to agree with Harrison. Based on these photos, positive visual ID wouldn't have been possible. Regarding DNA analysis, how many times have we dealt with screwups using DNA identification?"

"We're not talking about a screwup here," Rolow replied. "If the dead man on the third floor wasn't bin Laden, we're talking about a deliberate cover-up to ensure the public didn't learn that bin Laden was taken alive. They could have either faked the DNA results or taken a sample from an alive-and-well bin Laden and submitted it for analysis."

"Then there's the burial at sea," Christine said. "No body to dig up for further analysis. There's no way to prove bin Laden was actually killed, in case conspiracy theories circulate and take hold."

"You mean, there's no way to prove the body *wasn't* bin Laden's," Rolow replied.

"Exactly."

"I have the video of bin Laden's burial at sea. Want to take a look?"

There was a murmured consensus, so McFarland activated another video file, and the clip began playing on the conference room display. The video appeared to have been taken from Vulture's Row, high atop an aircraft carrier's island superstructure, looking down at the carrier's flight deck, and McFarland provided details as the video progressed.

Osama bin Laden's body had been flown to the aircraft carrier USS *Carl Vinson* for burial at sea. Within twenty-four hours of his death, Muslim religious rites were performed: the body was washed and wrapped in a white shroud, and prayers were offered in Arabic. Bin Laden's body was then placed in a black plastic bag along with three hundred pounds of aircraft tie-down chains to ensure the bag sank, then taken topside for burial. At the edge of the carrier deck, the body was placed on a flat board, which was tilted upward, and the body slid into the northern Arabian Sea.

After the video clip ended and the display went black, Christine pondered the burial-at-sea decision, which ensured the body could not be inspected later if anyone doubted bin Laden was killed. Was it possible he had been taken alive, with the CIA kept in the dark? If so, who was pulling the strings and how far up did the deception go?

"Here are my thoughts," Christine said. "A four-pronged plan to run this to ground. First, track down the SEALs on the third floor and have a conversation with them. Find out who they took prisoner." Looking at Harrison, she asked, "Who were the SEALs on the third floor?"

He provided the names, which McFarland verified matched the mission report. "Checks."

"Second, identify and interview every agency member who participated in Operation Neptune Spear. Piece together what we know. I don't believe any of us were in our current position during the Abbottabad raid, so we're at a disadvantage and need to get up to speed." She looked at Bryant Monroe.

"That's correct. I became deputy director four years afterward, and PJ and Tracey assumed their positions only a few years ago."

"Third," Christine said, "I'll discuss this matter with the president. I'll see what he knows or if he has any guidance on how to proceed.

"Finally"—Christine turned to McFarland—"I suppose we have the ability to infiltrate the JSOC data archives?"

McFarland smiled. "Depends on who's asking . . ."

"Tunnel into the JSOC files. Find every bit of information on the Abbottabad raid and the prisoner they took custody of."

"You got it," McFarland replied.

26

WASHINGTON, D.C.

Christine's Lincoln Navigator approached the White House, coasting to a stop beneath the West Wing's north portico, offering protection from dark gray clouds that threatened to open in a downpour at any moment. After emerging from the SUV, she left her protective agents behind and entered the West Wing, on her way to an impromptu meeting with the president.

She was a few minutes early and decided to stop by the corner office occupied by Kevin Hardison, the president's chief of staff and Christine's White House nemesis during her three years as the president's national security advisor.

While she was serving as NSA, Hardison had been a thorn in her side. She and Hardison had frequently found themselves supporting opposite positions on critical issues, and it hadn't helped that she was a member of the opposite political party from the president and the rest of his staff and cabinet. Nevertheless, she had won more than her fair share of those debates, swaying the president to her side, much to Hardison's chagrin, and the animosity between them had steadily grown over the years.

Hardison looked up from his computer when Christine appeared in his doorway.

"Afternoon, Christine," he said in a surprisingly pleasant tone as he rose from his desk. "I see you're here for a meeting with the president. Anything I can help you with?"

For the time being, Christine had decided to keep the Osama bin Laden issue between her and the president and had requested a private meeting. Hardison had no doubt noticed his exclusion.

"Nothing at the moment," she replied. "But thanks for offering."

"Not a problem," he said as he approached. "I'll walk you to the Oval Office."

Hardison's offer caught Christine by surprise. Since her transition to CIA director, Hardison's demeanor had turned surprisingly cordial. The hostility toward her when she was on the president's staff had been nothing personal, apparently.

As they strode down the seventy-foot-long hallway, side by side, Christine decided to probe where she stood with him—whether their previous adversarial relationship had truly been put behind them.

She began by inquiring about her replacement on the president's staff. "How's Thom Parham doing?"

Hardison wasted no time getting a barb in. "He's top-notch, as opposed to the previous NSA."

Christine wasn't fazed by the comment. It was Hardison's way of saying *good morning*.

He returned the query. "How are things going in Langley?"

"Quite well, especially since I no longer have to deal with an overbearing, type A chief of staff."

Hardison offered no reply, but Christine noticed a small grin on his face.

"So," Christine said, "you miss me, don't you?"

Without breaking stride, Hardison replied, "Like a bad rash."

After a few more steps down the hallway, he added, "Yeah, I miss you. Working with you was much more entertaining, I'll admit. Parham is far too reasonable for my taste."

Christine offered a smile of her own. It felt like she had never left the president's staff.

When they reached the Oval Office, Hardison said, "Don't be a stranger," before heading back to his office.

Christine knocked on the Oval Office door and, after an acknowledgment, entered to find the president seated behind his desk, framed by tall colonnade windows overlooking the South Lawn and Rose Garden. The president stood and greeted her as she entered, motioning toward the two couches atop the oval carpet. It felt odd being treated as a guest instead of a White House staffer.

It felt even odder briefing the president on such a sensitive issue from a sofa instead of a chair before his desk, as she'd done countless times over the last three years.

"If it's okay with you, Mr. President, I'd prefer to brief you at your desk."

He smiled. "Of course. Like old times."

He returned to his seat, while Christine took the middle chair facing his desk.

"So, all settled in at Langley?"

"Mostly. And as I mentioned during our last meeting, things are quite a bit more interesting across the river. There's still a lot to learn, but I'm getting the swing of things."

"That's good to hear," the president replied. "So, why the urgent meeting today?"

"An issue has come to my attention that you might be able to shed light on. A *very* sensitive issue."

Her words piqued the president's interest. "What might that be?"

Christine decided to skip the details on how they had obtained Mc-Neil's flash drive, and got straight to the point.

"We've obtained a previously unknown video of the Abbottabad raid where we killed Osama bin Laden. The video is unusual in that it reveals a second man on the third floor of the house, who was taken prisoner. Until yesterday, we had no record of this individual surviving the raid—we don't know who he is because he had a hood over his head—and we were also unaware he had been taken prisoner, apparently by JSOC."

"That's interesting," the president said. "But why is this an urgent matter? The Abbottabad raid was over a decade ago."

Christine summed up the issue succinctly. "Two men on the third floor. One man dead. One man prisoner. Which one was bin Laden?"

The president's eyes widened in understanding. "I thought we verified bin Laden was dead by both visual and DNA analysis."

"The visual identification wasn't one hundred percent positive due to the extensive damage caused by two bullet wounds in the man's face. Regarding the DNA analysis, if bin Laden was captured instead of killed, the DNA match could easily have been faked to convince the world he was dead."

The president considered the scenario Christine had painted, then replied, "It certainly sounds plausible. If we actually captured bin Laden, there would have been many reasons to keep that a secret."

"That's why I'm here, Mr. President. Can you shed light on this matter?"

The president didn't immediately reply, eyeing Christine carefully instead. Finally, he answered, "You mean, am I aware that Osama bin Laden is alive, and if so, am I willing to reveal that knowledge to an individual from the opposite party of my administration?"

Christine was taken aback by the president's directness. While she was his NSA, there had been several discussions about former political appointees using sensitive information as weapons against a subsequent administration of the opposite political party. Regarding herself, until this moment, the fact that she was a member of the opposite party from the president had never been an issue, at least not with him. She had relied on his backing and confidence in her numerous times over the years. Now, however, the president himself had brought it up.

"You're concerned about my political affiliation after all these years?"

"I'm not," the president said as he leaned back in his chair. "I'm just properly phrasing your question."

Christine realized the president had made an important point. If bin Laden had been captured alive, there were many good reasons to create the subterfuge that he'd been killed. There were also reasons to *maintain* that deception. If she pursued this matter, where would the trail lead, and whose careers and lives would be put at risk?

She was momentarily at a loss for words, searching for a way to express the question she desperately wanted to ask. She decided to be direct.

"Was Osama bin Laden captured alive?"

An uneasy silence followed, magnified by the room's bombproof windows, insulating them from the sound outside. The dark skies over Washington had opened up, bringing the Rose Garden outside the Oval Office to life; the red, pink, and white flowers bobbed up and down as fat drops of rain splattered on their petals. But there was no sound in the room, not even from the rain pelting the Oval Office windows, the patter attenuated by the windows' triple-paned design.

Finally, the president responded, "Not that I'm aware of."

Christine tried to gauge the honesty of the president's response, something she had never had to do during her three years as his national security advisor.

The president seemed to sense Christine's concern. He leaned forward. "I'm telling you the truth, Christine. Nothing of this sort was mentioned by the previous administration—nothing about bin Laden at all. If Osama was captured alive—and is still alive—then it's a secret being kept from me as well. However, when it comes to the inner secrets of government bureaucracy, nothing would surprise me."

He pressed a button on his phone, and his secretary answered.

"Have the chief of staff see me right away," the president said.

Hardison arrived a moment later, and the president gestured to a chair beside Christine.

The president explained the issue, then gave Hardison his instructions. "Search the classified files turned over by the previous administrations, all the way back to bin Laden's death. Also contact your previous counterparts over the years and see what they know."

Turning back to Christine, he said, "We'll look into it on our end. As for you, follow the trail wherever it leads, but keep it quiet."

"Yes, Mr. President."

The meeting ended, and Christine rose and excused herself. As she departed the Oval Office, she noticed the president and Hardison exchanging concerned looks.

27

LANGLEY, VIRGINIA

It had been a long day, and it was about to get longer.

As Harrison and Khalila rode the elevator to the seventh floor of the Original Headquarters Building, they discussed the next step in their search for Mixell. They had spent the day at the National Counterterrorism Center in McLean, Virginia, a logistical hub staffed by fourteen government agencies, including the CIA and FBI, which coordinated the collation and dissemination of terrorist-related information within the U.S. intelligence community. Working on the main floor among sixty other analysts, with supervisors observing from glass-enclosed offices on the second floor, they had reviewed the cases being investigated, searching for potential links to Mixell. They had found nothing thus far.

A half hour earlier at McLean, messages had appeared on his and Khalila's computers—a meeting had been scheduled for 5 p.m. today at Langley, with their attendance required. As they stepped from the elevator and headed down the hallway, Khalila spoke.

"Thank you for what you did the other day, insisting I be authorized access to the Neptune Spear program. When Rolow directed me to leave, you could have done nothing and have been rid of me. Why did you do it?"

"Because my goal is to track Mixell down as soon as possible. He killed McNeil, so he's probably involved with Neptune Spear in some way. If so, I suspect those leads will take me to the Middle East. As Rolow pointed out, when it comes to the linguistic skills and contacts in the region, you're the best the agency has to offer. In that regard, it was a logical decision to include you."

"And in other regards?"

Harrison eyed her for a moment, wondering why he needed to explain the obvious. Upon his return to the agency, Khalila had proffered a deal: he could trust her as long as he didn't learn her true identity. They had shaken on it, but Harrison had reservations. There was no telling what situation he might be in when he discovered her real identity, nor could he predict her response.

"The inability to completely trust you is a problem," he replied. "Conditional trust, as you put it, doesn't really work."

"Trust is an overblown commodity," Khalila replied.

"What's more important?"

"Competence. Putting your trust in an incompetent partner will get you killed."

"You don't get it," Harrison replied. "Both elements are required for a team to function properly."

Khalila stopped suddenly, and Harrison turned to face his partner, as did Khalila. She stepped closer, stopping only a few inches from his face. At six feet tall, Khalila was only two inches shorter than he was, and her eyes bored into his.

"Oh, I *do* get it. I just disagree. I know for a fact that complete trust is not an essential element."

"How do you know that?"

Her lips pursed momentarily, then she replied, "None of your business."

She continued toward the conference room, bumping into him on purpose as she passed.

Harrison shook his head. He was beginning to regret the olive branch he had extended by requesting Khalila be read into the program. It had been an attempt to establish the trust between them that he considered essential. Then he realized he'd gotten it all wrong. Khalila already trusted him. It was *he* who didn't trust *her*, and his effort had reinforced the wrong side of the issue.

Khalila was already seated when he entered the conference room, and Christine, Bryant, Rolow, and McFarland arrived a moment later. After Christine took her seat, McFarland energized the display.

"We were able to penetrate the JSOC firewall and locate their Operation Neptune Spear files. On the screen is a summary of the critical findings."

McFarland worked her way down the list. "As McNeil's video and Jake indicated, the JSOC files confirm that a prisoner was indeed taken from bin Laden's compound in Abbottabad. However, the captive's identity is never mentioned. What we do know is that he was sent from the base in Afghanistan to Kuwait, where he was turned over to Kuwaiti intelligence officials for detention and interrogation."

Christine asked, "Why would JSOC turn their prisoner over to Kuwait?"

The DDO replied, "Two reasons. The first is because the *transfer* is a ruse. To get around U.S. laws and regulations, the standard practice is to transfer a detainee to another country with less stringent restrictions on interrogation methods. In reality, the prisoner remains under U.S. control and is interrogated by American personnel, but more effective methods of extracting information can be employed.

"Kuwait was chosen because their government owes the United States a significant debt of gratitude for liberating their country after Saddam Hussein's invasion. Managing this issue for us would be partial payback."

"Why would the JSOC files go silent on this prisoner?" Christine asked. "No identity or specific location."

McFarland replied, "That information is likely hidden under another code name operation, to prevent what we're trying to do—locate that information. It's undoubtedly in the JSOC files somewhere, but without knowing the name of the operation or the individual, there's no way to quickly identify which one of the over one hundred million files in the JSOC directory contains that information. We'd have to search every file.

"We could automate the process with programmed spiders, but searching every file would likely be detected by a cyber watchdog. Plus, it's possible the information is kept offline in segregated storage or only in paper files if deemed sensitive enough."

"How do you recommend we proceed?" Christine asked.

"I think we should hold off on this discussion until after the next few slides," McFarland replied. She waited for concurrence, and Christine nodded her agreement.

McFarland's presentation moved to the next slide. It was a single-page dossier of a Navy SEAL: a picture of the man's face in the top-right corner, with the rest of the slide filled with personal information, training, and assignment details. On the bottom of the slide, large red letters were printed.

DECEASED

"We were hoping to discover the identity of the third-floor prisoner by interviewing the SEALs on the third floor. However, we ran into an unexpected issue."

McFarland flipped through the next few slides, each one containing a dossier of a SEAL assigned to the third floor of bin Laden's house in Abbottabad. On the bottom of each slide, in bold red letters, was DECEASED.

"It turns out that every member of the third-floor SEAL team is dead." She went through the details of each death: mission in Afghanistan, helicopter crash during a training exercise, car accident, et cetera.

"We were surprised that every SEAL assigned to the third floor is deceased but were stunned when we attempted to contact the other assault team members." McFarland flipped through another twenty slides, each one annotated with DECEASED on the bottom, stopping on McNeil's slide. "It turns out that McNeil and Nagle were two of only three surviving men who entered the compound at Abbottabad. Now that they're dead, there's only one man left alive."

McFarland advanced her brief to the next slide, which had a familiar picture and name.

Jake Edward Harrison.

Heads turned toward Harrison as he digested the information.

He'd been aware that several of the SEALs who participated in the bin Laden raid had died, but he hadn't kept track of everyone. Until McFarland flipped through her slides, he hadn't realized that he was the only member of the assault team still alive. Considering the odds of the entire team, sans one, meeting their demise, it left only one logical conclusion.

Someone was systematically killing every member of the assault team.

McNeil had put the pieces together and believed it was related to what the video revealed—that a man on the third floor had been taken captive, with the event being a closely held secret. That led to a second conclusion.

Osama bin Laden had been taken alive.

It seems the others around the table had reached the same conclusions. They eyed each other, waiting for someone to say aloud what each was thinking.

McFarland broke the silence, offering a more nuanced assessment. "Analysis has identified two primary scenarios. The first scenario is that Osama bin Laden was captured instead of killed. In an effort to keep that knowledge secret, the men who know he was taken alive or could piece things together are being silenced.

"The second scenario is that bin Laden was, in fact, killed, and al-Qaeda has learned the identities of the SEALs who participated in the Abbottabad raid and is arranging their deaths."

McFarland turned to Christine, awaiting her questions or direction.

"Any comments?" Christine asked.

Rolow replied, "The implications of bin Laden being captured are far worse than al-Qaeda exacting revenge. If he was taken alive, we'd be dealing with a rogue U.S. organization covering its tracks, operating outside the law, willing to murder anyone who threatens to expose what they've done."

Christine asked McFarland, "Any thoughts on how to proceed, from an Analysis perspective?"

"The first step should be to determine whether bin Laden was killed or taken captive. Once that's determined, we'll know which scenario we're dealing with. I recommend a two-pronged approach. The first is to prove bin Laden was indeed the man killed on the third floor."

"How do we do that?" Bryant asked. "The body was buried at sea."

"It was, but what isn't well known was that a sonic beacon was included in the plastic bag with the tie-down chains, so his body could be located and retrieved later if desired. The beacon has enough battery power to transmit for twenty years, maybe longer. With the necessary support, the body can be located and a DNA sample taken. That will determine whether the man we buried was bin Laden."

"How deep is the water where he was buried?" Christine asked.

McFarland looked up USS *Carl Vinson*'s reported location at the time of bin Laden's burial, then pulled up a bathymetric chart of the Arabian Sea. "Just over nine thousand feet."

"Does the agency have a deep-submergence vessel that can go that deep?" Christine asked.

Rolow shook his head.

"Then we're going to need assistance, which complicates things. We'll need to disguise the reason we need a DSV, or at least minimize the number of people who know. If we're truly dealing with a bin-Laden-is-alive scenario, we'll need to prevent the organization responsible from being alerted. They've already proven they're willing to take draconian measures to cover their tracks, and we need to ensure agency personnel don't become additional casualties."

"Agreed," McFarland replied. "I'll ensure our DSV requests are for an innocuous reason."

"What's the second method to figure out which bin Laden scenario we're dealing with?" Christine asked.

"The other approach is to prove bin Laden is *alive*. To do that, we need to track down the prisoner taken from the third floor. The only lead we have takes us to Kuwait, so we should start there."

"I agree," Rolow said. "I recommend we send Harrison and Khalila to Kuwait, to see if they can ferret out where the prisoner is located."

Christine nodded her agreement. "Start fleshing out the details, and let's reconvene tomorrow. Anything else we need to discuss tonight?"

No comments were offered, so Christine said, "I think we know what we need to do: if Osama is dead, verify the body we buried is his. If he's alive, find him."

Christine departed the conference room, as did the others except for Bryant and Rolow.

Once they were alone, Bryant turned to Rolow. "Assigning Khalila to this mission is a mistake. You should reconsider."

"Her contacts in the region are already the best in the agency," Rolow replied. "If we manage this issue properly, we can improve those contacts dramatically."

"I agree with you on that. It's the contacts she'll need to engage that

I'm worried about—they're too dangerous. Khalila is a crown jewel for both sides, and getting her involved in this issue puts her too much at risk. If they get their hooks into her, we might not get her back."

"We were always going to have to risk her at some point," Rolow replied. "This is it."

28

USS *MICHIGAN*

Lieutenant Karen Bass leaned over the navigation table in the Control Room, studying *Michigan*'s operating area outlined on the electronic chart, deciding where to search next. They were approaching shallow water and needed to turn either north or south. Inside the Sonar Room, the sonar technicians were likewise studying their displays, searching for a sign of either the UUV or the mother ship that had retrieved it two days ago.

Captain Wilson's trip to periscope depth for a videocon with the secretary of the Navy had been swift, but the mother ship and its UUV, operating beneath the thermocline, had vanished by the time *Michigan*'s acoustic sensors had dipped below the layer of warm water. They had spent the last two days scouring the surrounding area, focused primarily on the mother ship, since it emitted significantly louder tonals than the UUV. When they detected either contact, *Michigan*'s crew would be ready.

Torpedoes were loaded in all four tubes, with the outer doors open. Wilson had decided to keep *Michigan* in a ready-to-shoot posture, avoiding the noise transients caused by opening the torpedo tube muzzle and outer hull doors. The first sound the UUV or mother ship could detect would be the launch itself and not the torpedo doors opening.

"Conn, Sonar." The Sonar Supervisor's voice came across the Conn speakers. "Hold a new contact on the towed array, designated Sierra three-four, ambiguous bearings two-four-two and two-nine-eight. Analyzing."

Bass glanced at the navigation display. Whatever they had detected was behind them, in either the port or starboard quarter. That was okay for the moment. She would keep *Michigan* steady on course until the contact's bearing rate had been determined, which would feed the necessary information to the algorithms in the submarine's combat control system.

A few minutes later, after sufficient data had been accumulated, Bass decided to turn south, to a course that put both bearings on the starboard side. The maneuver would resolve which of the two bearings was the real one and which was the false, mirror image.

"Helm, right twenty degrees rudder, steady course one-eight-zero."

The former ballistic missile submarine, almost two football fields long, turned slowly to the south.

The Helmsman steadied the submarine on its new course, and the towed array eventually stopped snaking back and forth behind them, stretching back out into a straight line.

"Conn, Sonar. Bearing ambiguity has been resolved. Sierra three-four bears three-zero-one."

Bass analyzed the new information. The bearing to the contact had shifted only slightly during the maneuver, indicating the contact was on a narrow aspect course—pointed almost directly toward *Michigan*. She checked the tentative solution on the active combat control console; the fire control technician had come to the same conclusion.

Sonar's next report came over the speakers. "Conn, Sonar. Sierra three-four is classified submerged, with Seawolf tonals."

Stepping onto the Conn, Lieutenant Bass acknowledged the report and selected the Captain's stateroom on the 27-MC control box, then pulled the microphone from its holder.

"Captain, Officer of the Deck."

The submarine's Commanding Officer answered. "Captain."

"Sir, hold a new submerged contact with Seawolf tonals on the towed array, designated Sierra three-four, bearing three-zero-one."

Wilson arrived in Control a moment later and stepped onto the Conn, stopping beside Bass. After examining the sonar display, he turned to his Officer of the Deck.

"Man Battle Stations Torpedo silently."

Without adequate intelligence on the acoustic capabilities of the mother submarine, Wilson had decided it was wise to man battle stations silently, without sounding *Michigan*'s general alarm. Depending on how close the contact was, which was currently unknown, and its acoustic-detection capabilities, it might be able to detect the loud *gong, gong, gong* reverberating through *Michigan*'s hull into the water.

Personnel streamed into Control, energizing dormant consoles. The Executive Officer, Lieutenant Commander Tom Montgomery, arrived, as did Lieutenant Ryan Jescovitch, the submarine's Weapons Officer. Lieutenant Brian Resor entered Control, relieving Bass as the battle stations Officer of the Deck, and Bass then manned the third combat control console, joining the two fire control technicians focused on developing the target solution—its estimated course, speed, and range.

"Attention in Control," Wilson announced. "Sierra three-four appears to be a regain of the automated mother submarine. Classify Sierra three-four as Master one. Track Master one."

Montgomery hovered behind the three combat control consoles, monitoring the two fire control technicians and Lieutenant Bass as they refined their solutions to Master one. The contact maintained a steady course and speed, apparently oblivious to the impending danger, which simplified the evaluation.

It didn't take long for Montgomery to announce, "I have a firing solution."

Wilson called out, "Firing Point Procedures, Master one, tube Two."

With the target on *Michigan*'s starboard side, Wilson had decided to shoot from a port-side tube, using the submarine's hull to partially mask the launch transient.

Montgomery stopped briefly behind each of the combat control consoles, examining the target solution on each. He tapped one of the fire control technicians, who pressed a button on his console, sending an updated target solution to the torpedo.

"Solution ready!" Montgomery reported.

"Weapon ready!" Jescovitch called out.

"Ship ready!" Resor announced.

"Shoot on generated bearings!" Wilson ordered.

The firing signal was sent to the Torpedo Room, initiating the launch sequence for the torpedo in tube Two. Wilson listened to the whirr of the submarine's torpedo ejection pump and the characteristic sound of the four-thousand-pound weapon being ejected from the torpedo tube, accelerating from rest to thirty knots in less than a second.

Inside the Sonar Room, Petty Officer Andrew Bubb and the other sonar technicians monitored their outgoing unit while searching for any indication the mother ship had either been alerted to the incoming torpedo or counterfired. Sonar referred to their torpedo as *own ship's unit* so their reports wouldn't be confused with information about an incoming torpedo.

"Own ship's unit is in the water, running normally.

"Fuel crossover achieved.

"Steady on preset gyro course, medium speed."

Wilson's eyes shifted to the Weapon Launch Console, depicting their torpedo as a green inverted V heading toward a red semicircle representing Master one, which remained steady on course and speed, giving no indication it had detected the incoming torpedo.

Once *Michigan's* torpedo went active, however, the situation changed dramatically.

"Conn, Sonar. Burst of cavitation from Master one—increasing speed. Down doppler on target—she's turning away, commencing torpedo evasion. Ejecting countermeasures."

The mother ship had detected the incoming torpedo and commenced a standard torpedo evasion. However, if *Michigan's* target solution for Master one was accurate enough, the mother ship wouldn't get away.

Wilson watched as the bearing to their torpedo began to merge with Master one's.

"Detect!" Jescovitch called out.

A few seconds later, he followed up. "Homing! Increasing speed."

Their torpedo had detected a potential target, then after verifying the detection met the required parameters, had classified it as a valid target and was now homing to detonation.

"Conn, Sonar. Multiple transients from Master one. Several contacts appearing on the same bearing. Whatever they are, they're moving fast!"

Wilson examined the sonar display on the Conn. Two new traces had appeared. But they weren't headed toward *Michigan*.

Sonar confirmed Wilson's assessment. "Contacts are heading toward own-ship's unit."

Wilson suddenly realized what they were: small, anti-torpedo torpedoes.

Navies throughout the world had been developing anti-torpedo torpedoes, the undersea version of missile defense, designed to destroy incoming torpedoes instead of missiles. The German Navy had developed
the SeaSpider interceptor torpedo, while the Russians had fielded the
Paket-NK, a dual-use torpedo that could be fired against submarines
and incoming torpedoes. Turkish defense contractor Aselsan had even
explored the concept, successfully developing the Tork hard-kill torpedo.

The U.S. Navy had developed their own anti-torpedo torpedo, deployed aboard several aircraft carriers. But the system had been plagued
with false detections and eventually removed from service. To Wilson's
knowledge, anti-torpedo torpedoes hadn't been deployed aboard U.S.
submarines—until now. It seemed that the mother ship was a test bed
for new technology of various types.

The two new objects launched by the mother ship swiftly closed on
Michigan's torpedo. When the range between them decreased to zero, a
faint explosion echoed through the submarine's hull.

"Loss of wire, tube Two," Jescovitch reported.

The torpedo they had fired from tube Two was no longer communicating with *Michigan*. The reason was obvious. It had been destroyed by
one of the mother ship's defensive torpedoes.

Before Wilson had a chance to react, Sonar called out, "Torpedo
launch transient, bearing three-zero-five!" Seconds later, a report blared
from the speakers, "Torpedo in the water! Bearing three-zero-five!"

A red line appeared on the geographic display on the Conn.

"Ahead flank!" Wilson ordered, accelerating *Michigan* to maximum
speed. He then evaluated what course to turn his ship to.

The incoming torpedo was approaching from the starboard quarter,
which meant *Michigan* was already on an optimal evasion course. Wilson
monitored the bearings to the torpedo, which drew steadily aft, indicating
the torpedo would pass well behind them.

Michigan was safe.

Things changed, however, upon the next announcement.

"Second torpedo in the water, bearing three-one-zero!"

A purple line appeared on the Control Room displays, representing
the new torpedo.

The new bearings remained steady, indicating the torpedo was traveling on a corrected intercept course, which took into account *Michigan*'s course and speed.

After evaluating both torpedoes, Wilson turned to a course that would prevent either weapon from gaining contact. There was a narrow window that would let one torpedo pass by on *Michigan*'s port side and the other on starboard.

"Helm, left ten degrees rudder, steady course one-five-zero." To the Officer of the Deck, Wilson ordered, "Launch countermeasures!"

Michigan ejected a torpedo decoy and broadband jammer, then completed its turn to the ordered evasion course. One torpedo began drawing aft and the other forward, exactly as Wilson had hoped. As best he could tell, each torpedo would remain outside of its target acquisition range, oblivious to the submarine between them.

With *Michigan* on a good evasion course, Wilson's attention shifted to putting a second torpedo in the water against their adversary, the surprisingly capable mother ship. Sonar's next report, however, threw a wrench into that plan.

"Conn, Sonar. Loss of Master one."

Michigan was traveling at maximum speed, and the rush of water past the submarine's acoustic sensors blunted their detection range. *Michigan*'s crew no longer held Master one. That meant Wilson would be shooting in the dark to some extent, using their last estimated target solution. If the mother ship maneuvered, Wilson's crew would have no way of knowing.

Ultimately, what mattered most was putting another torpedo into the water, something for the mother ship to worry about and hopefully distract it from further attacks. Wilson was about to order Firing Point Procedures when Sonar's report demanded his full attention.

"Conn, Sonar. Up doppler on first torpedo!"

The first torpedo had turned toward *Michigan*.

"Conn, Sonar. Up doppler on second torpedo!"

The second torpedo had also turned toward them.

It appeared that the mother ship still held *Michigan* on its sensors and had calculated its new course, sending steer commands to both torpedoes. The weapons were now closing in from each side in a rapidly constricting choke hold.

Wilson realized they were in a serious predicament. Both torpedoes were closing fast, and he couldn't outrun them. They were MK 48 heavyweight versions, carrying much more fuel than lightweight torpedoes. He also couldn't turn away, as either a left or right maneuver would turn into the path of one of the torpedoes.

Sonar announced, "Torpedo to starboard is range-gating. Torpedo is homing!"

One of the mother ship's torpedoes had detected *Michigan* and verified it was a valid target, increasing the frequency of its sonar pings. It was now refining its target solution, adjusting its course and increasing speed as it closed the remaining distance.

"Conn, Sonar. Second torpedo is range-gating!"

The second torpedo was also homing.

"Eject countermeasures!" Wilson ordered.

Lieutenant Resor ejected a torpedo decoy, which would hopefully distract both torpedoes, plus a broadband jammer, which would mask *Michigan*'s sonar signature as it sped away. White scalloped icons appeared on the Control Room displays.

Wilson watched the bearings to both torpedoes intently as they approached *Michigan*'s countermeasures. Both torpedoes blew past them without even circling for a sniff. These torpedoes clearly had the most advanced version of the MK 48 operational software, able to discern between the large submarines they were designed to sink and the small decoys that emulated them.

He glanced at the nautical chart. Thankfully, they were in relatively shallow water—above crush depth—so his crew could survive if *Michigan* was sunk, assuming a rescue submersible arrived in time. At the moment, it looked like that was the likeliest scenario.

"Conn, Sonar. Both torpedoes are at one thousand yards and closing!"

Things looked hopeless for *Michigan*, but Wilson decided to order Firing Point Procedures. If *Michigan* was going down, they'd take the mother ship with them. The next several reports, however, delayed his plan.

"Conn. Sonar. Torpedo to port has turned away." A few seconds later, Sonar followed up. "Torpedo to starboard has turned away."

As Wilson contemplated the unexpected reports, another announcement emanated from the speakers.

"Conn, Sonar. Both torpedoes have shut down."

The behavior of the two torpedoes was puzzling. Both had gained contact on *Michigan* and were homing to detonation. Outrunning a torpedo was always a strategy, but it appeared they hadn't run out of fuel; they had turned away for some reason, then shut down. Perhaps there was a bug in the mother ship's artificial intelligence or in the software loaded into the torpedoes it carried. Either issue was quite fortuitous, and *Michigan* had benefited.

As Wilson pondered the unusual torpedo behavior and a plan to reengage the mother ship, the next Sonar report added to Wilson's confusion.

"Conn, Sonar. Regain of Master one on the towed array, bearing three-four-five. Contact is closing."

Wilson checked the speed display in the Control Room. *Michigan* was still traveling at maximum speed, and not only had the mother ship maintained contact, tracking *Michigan*'s movements, but it had closed the distance. Built from leftover Seawolf propulsion components, the mother ship clearly had Seawolf speed.

The mother ship hadn't fired additional torpedoes, so Wilson wondered what it was up to. Why would it close on *Michigan*? Typically, in submarine fights, a goal was to remain as far away as possible while still maintaining contact, providing valuable distance—and time—to respond to counterfire, and also reduce the probability the target would alert upon torpedo launch.

Perhaps the mother ship wasn't as smart as Wilson initially thought. Its bizarre behavior had presented an unexpected opportunity.

Wilson announced, "Firing Point Procedures, Master one, tube One."

As *Michigan*'s crew prepared to launch another torpedo, Sonar made another perplexing report.

"Conn, Sonar. Receiving underwater comms from Master one."

The mother ship was attempting to communicate acoustically with another vehicle nearby.

"Sonar, Conn. Report all contacts."

"Conn, Sonar. Hold only Master one."

Wilson checked the nearest combat control console display. The mother ship was still gaining ground, paralleling *Michigan*'s track, and there was no indication that one of its UUVs was in the area. Was it possible the mother ship was attempting to communicate with *Michigan*? Did it think Wilson's submarine was one of its UUVs or perhaps another mother ship?

Wilson ordered, "Sonar, Conn. Put the underwater comms on speaker."

The warbly sound of verbal underwater communications emanated from the Control Room speakers, but the words were unintelligible. *Michigan* was traveling too fast, and the flow noise past the submarine's sensors was distorting the sound.

After another glance at one of the combat control console displays— the mother ship kept closing while matching *Michigan*'s course—Wilson verified that the mother ship hadn't displayed additional aggressive behavior. Now that Wilson thought about it, he realized that the mother ship had fired only in self-defense. Perhaps its protocols were functioning properly and it would attack only if fired upon.

Wilson decided to take a gamble. "Helm, ahead two-thirds."

He slowed his submarine so the acoustic communications could be understood.

As *Michigan*'s speed decayed, the words became clear.

"Ohio class submarine. Identify yourself and the reason for your attack."

What also became clear was that the mother submarine was quite capable, identifying *Michigan* as an Ohio class submarine from the tonals it emitted into the water. However, it had asked two questions that Wilson would normally not be able to answer.

During underwater communications between U.S. submarines, the vessels used code names to prevent anyone in the area who might intercept the communications from identifying which U.S. submarines were nearby. Wilson figured the mother ship likely didn't have the codebook loaded into its memory banks, so he decided to answer the first question in plain English. The second question, however, couldn't be answered, at least not truthfully. Wilson couldn't tell the mother ship that *Michigan* was bent on destroying it. Perhaps he could strike up a dialog with the mother ship's artificial intelligence and see where it led.

Wilson pulled the WQC microphone from its holster, then spoke slowly and distinctly. His voice would be transmitted by sonar hydrophones and would be difficult to understand.

"This is Captain Wilson aboard USS *Michigan*. Repeat. This is Captain Wilson aboard USS *Michigan*. Do you have a name?"

The response from the mother ship was quick and direct.

"You're damn right I've got a name! This is Dennis Gallagher aboard USS *Jimmy Carter*. Murray, what the hell are you doing, shooting at us?"

29

PERSIAN GULF

A full moon shone down upon the Persian Gulf as USS *Michigan* cruised slowly on the surface, not far from the silhouette of another black submarine paralleling *Michigan*'s course. Murray Wilson, standing in *Michigan*'s Bridge atop the sail, monitored the activity on the Missile Deck below as several SEALs pulled one of their RHIBs—rigid-hulled inflatable boats—from the starboard Dry Deck Shelter, inflated it, and attached the outboard motor.

As they lowered it into the water, Wilson climbed down the side of the sail, then joined two SEALs aboard the RHIB. The barely audible engine was started, and the RHIB skimmed across the water's surface toward its destination: USS *Jimmy Carter*.

Less than an hour ago, Wilson had stood stunned in *Michigan*'s Control Room after hearing the mother submarine's response to his question—*Do you have a name?* It had taken a while to convince him that the submarine following them was indeed USS *Jimmy Carter* and not an automated mother ship's artificial intelligence attempting to impersonate a U.S. submarine and its captain.

Fortunately, Wilson knew Dennis Gallagher. He was one of the prospective Commanding Officers he had trained during his last shore tour, and he had worked out with him at the gym during lunch, showering afterward. Only when the mother ship had correctly answered Wilson's question—what did Gallagher have tattooed on his right butt cheek—did Wilson become convinced that the mother ship was actually USS *Jimmy Carter*, a Seawolf class submarine manned by an elite crew and modified with a one-hundred-foot-long hull extension outfitted with the most advanced technology in the U.S. Navy.

A conversation had followed, and both Commanding Officers had quickly agreed that a face-to-face discussion was required to sort out what had happened and its implications. Although Wilson was senior and could have requested Gallagher board *Michigan*, Wilson was already thinking ahead. *Jimmy Carter* was outfitted not only with advanced weapon technology but with enhanced communication capabilities, something he might want to tap into depending on where their conversation led. That the secretary of the Navy had lied to him on several occasions, even ordering him to sink another U.S. submarine, was clear. What wasn't yet clear was why and who Wilson could trust.

The SEAL piloting the RHIB eased up on the motor, matching *Jimmy Carter's* speed as the boat pulled alongside. A rope ladder had been draped down the rounded hull, which Wilson climbed as the RHIB loitered alongside. He descended through the nearest topside hatch, where Commander Gallagher was waiting at the bottom of the ladder. After Gallagher welcomed him aboard, they proceeded to Gallagher's stateroom, where they sat at a small fold-down table.

"This entire situation is incredibly screwed up, sir," Gallagher said. "You're going to have to take me back to the beginning."

Wilson couldn't agree more.

He began with *Michigan's* surprise port call in Bahrain, when the secretary of the Navy and her senior military aide had briefed him on his mission: track down and sink a rogue UUV that had sunk USS *Stethem*. Gallagher listened intently, confusion gathering on his face as Wilson recounted that he had detected the UUV being retrieved by a mother ship, which Brenda Verbeck subsequently explained was an artificially intelligent mother submarine built from spare Seawolf parts.

"Wow," Gallagher said when Wilson finished. "That's some story, and wrong on both parts. First, there's no automated mother ship out here. Just *Jimmy Carter*. We pick up our UUVs on occasion for recharging and maintenance, plus we download whatever information the UUVs have intercepted in case their transmissions were corrupted or incomplete. Second, our UUVs couldn't have sunk *Stethem*. They can't launch their torpedoes."

Gallagher explained that *Jimmy Carter's* fleet of UUVs had been developed and deployed quickly under a UON—Urgent Operational Need.

Due to the accelerated development and limited testing, the UUVs had not been equipped with the software necessary to launch their torpedoes. What the United States primarily needed was the ability to intercept otherwise secure communications, which the UUVs could do at little risk. Weaponizing the UUVs without extensive testing and full confidence in their artificial intelligence, however, was another matter.

After Gallagher's explanation, Wilson realized that Secretary Verbeck, or someone supporting her, had fabricated the armed-UUV scenario to justify the destruction of the UUV, along with the supposed mother ship—*Jimmy Carter*—both of which now contained sensitive data that someone desperately wanted destroyed. Not knowing whether Verbeck was corrupt or an innocent pawn in this conspiracy, Wilson wasn't sure how to proceed. Then an idea came to him.

"What do you and your UUVs do with the data they collect? Where is it sent?"

"To a black cell in the Pentagon. It gets screened there, and relevant information is forwarded to the CIA for evaluation."

The CIA.

Wilson wondered to what extent the conspiracy ran; who was involved. But the real question was—who could he trust to divulge what he knew, so that the information shared would spark an investigation and not the elimination of Wilson and his crew? If the wrong people learned that Wilson had discovered the mother submarine he had been ordered to sink was actually *Jimmy Carter*, they wouldn't flinch about adding *Michigan* to the list.

When Gallagher mentioned the CIA, Wilson realized there was one person he could trust without doubt: Christine O'Connor.

"Do you have a communication channel with the CIA?"

Gallagher nodded. "We occasionally pass data to them and get queries."

"Can you establish a videocon with the CIA director?"

"Director O'Connor?"

"I've worked with her several times. She's someone we can trust with this information."

"I can request an urgent videocon. You want it with the director only, correct?"

Wilson nodded.

Gallagher picked up the phone and requested the presence of *Jimmy Carter*'s Communicator, and a lieutenant soon arrived. Instructions were provided and the junior officer left to draft the outgoing transmission. While they awaited the Communicator's return, the two Commanding Officers discussed their unique situation.

"Until we sort this out, I suggest we stick together," Wilson said, "working as a team in case another submarine is sent to sink either or both of us."

Gallagher nodded his agreement. "What's your waterspace assignment?" he asked, inquiring about *Michigan*'s operating area.

Wilson provided the details.

"Same as mine," Gallagher replied, shaking his head.

Waterspace management was a sensitive issue for submarines, with operations centers in Norfolk and Pearl Harbor controlling the movements of every U.S. submarine, ensuring that no two submarines were in the same water at the same time without special safeguards. It was a safety issue: detecting and avoiding other submarines wasn't nearly as easy as it was for surface ships, which used radar to quickly determine the solutions to other surface craft.

Submarines typically used passive sonar only, which meant they knew only the bearing to the contact, with no easy way of determining whether the contact was a few hundred yards away or several miles. Determining a contact's course, speed, and range took time, during which a contact could approach dangerously close. It was not uncommon for submarines, particularly during the Cold War, to collide as one trailed the other in a high-tech game of cat and mouse, guessing wrong at what new course and speed the lead submarine had maneuvered to before the crew sorted it out.

As a result, waterspace assignments were controlled so that if two submarines needed to pass nearby or operate together, one would be restricted shallow and the other deep, with the deep submarine provided with stovepipes—circular areas—where it could come up to periscope depth for communications. That *Michigan* and *Jimmy Carter* had been assigned the same waterspace without these safeguards meant the Pearl

Harbor operations center had no idea that *Michigan* had been sent into *Jimmy Carter*'s operating area. Someone high up had circumvented the normal operating procedures.

"Why don't I go shallow and you go deep?" Gallagher proposed. "I'll need to operate shallow to retrieve and launch the UUVs."

Wilson agreed, and the two men worked out a construct for *Michigan*'s stovepipes, which *Jimmy Carter* would stay out of, so Wilson could come up to periscope depth and communicate at the required intervals.

The Communicator returned shortly thereafter with the message to the CIA, which Gallagher approved for transmission.

"This ought to get their attention," he said.

30

LANGLEY, VIRGINIA

It was almost quitting time on the seventh floor of the Original Head-quarters Building at Langley when Deputy Director for Support Becky Rock, holding a folder in one hand, knocked on the open door to the director's office. Christine looked up from the computer display on her desk and motioned for Becky to enter.

"We received an unusual message a few minutes ago," Becky said, "from the submarine *Jimmy Carter*. The Commanding Officer is request-ing an immediate secure VTC with you, with no one else present."

"Why would the Commanding Officer of *Jimmy Carter* contact the CIA, and me specifically?"

Becky explained the role the submarine played in the communica-tion intercepts by a fleet of UUVs operating in the Persian Gulf, with the data eventually fed to the CIA.

"Do we receive this type of communication request from *Jimmy Carter* often?"

"This is the first time."

"Do you have the message?"

Becky pulled a single sheet of paper from the folder and handed it to Christine, who read the transmission. It was short and direct, with no indication of the subject to be discussed. The last line of the message, however, caught Christine's attention.

CAPT Wilson, aboard USS Jimmy Carter, *sends.*

"Do you know why Captain Wilson is aboard *Jimmy Carter*?"

Becky shook her head. "I assumed he was the Commanding Officer."

"He's not," Christine said. "He's the Captain of *Michigan* BLUE, or at least he was a few months ago."

Christine read the message again, searching for clues to why Wilson was aboard *Jimmy Carter* or why he had requested an urgent videoconference. She found nothing, then told Becky, "Set up a secure VTC immediately. I'll be right down."

Christine entered one of the secure VTC rooms in the communications center, taking a seat in the front row. A moment later, a technician's voice came over the intercom, informing Christine that a connection had been established with *Jimmy Carter*.

The wide-screen display flickered to life, revealing two naval officers seated in a submarine stateroom: Captain Murray Wilson and a commander Christine didn't recognize. Pleasantries were exchanged—Captain Wilson thanked Christine for the quick response and also introduced Commander Dennis Gallagher, Commanding Officer of USS *Jimmy Carter*.

"What's this about, Murray?" Christine asked.

Wilson started at the beginning, explaining how the secretary of the Navy had personally briefed him in Bahrain on a sensitive mission: to destroy the UUV that had gone rogue and sunk USS *Stethem*.

"I'm aware of the issue," Christine said. "I was at the White House when the plan was discussed. How is the mission proceeding?"

"Not as planned," Wilson replied.

He went on to explain how the UUV had docked with a full-size submarine before he could destroy it and that Secretary Verbeck had explained that the submarine was an artificially intelligent, unmanned mother ship herding the UUVs in the Persian Gulf. Verbeck had instructed him to sink the mother ship in addition to the UUV, since it had likely been infected with whatever had caused the UUV to go rogue.

"The problem is," Wilson said, "Secretary Verbeck is either lying to me or someone is lying to her. There is no automated mother ship. The submarine she directed me to sink is *Jimmy Carter*. Additionally, Commander Gallagher has informed me that the UUV could not possibly have sunk *Stethem*. None of the UUVs have their weapon systems activated."

Christine leaned back in her chair as she recalled the Situation Room meeting. Secretary Verbeck had been almost positive that the UUV had sunk *Stethem*. If it hadn't, the alternative was that *Stethem* had been attacked by Iran. It was possible that Verbeck's assessment had simply been wrong, but why didn't she know the UUV was unarmed and that the mother ship was actually *Jimmy Carter*?

"I have to agree," Christine said. "Someone is either incredibly misinformed or lying. The question is, which scenario are we dealing with? If someone is lying, that's an investigation-worthy issue. And if Verbeck is the one doing the lying, the implications are immense."

"Gallaher and I agree completely. The issue appears to be that the UUV in question may have intercepted sensitive data that someone wants destroyed. Now that it's docked with its mother ship, *Jimmy Carter* has been added to the hit list."

"I concur with your assessment," Christine said. "Regarding this data, can you send it directly to the CIA, bypassing the Pentagon?"

Wilson turned to Gallagher, who nodded. "We can," he said. "It's a backup data-transmission method, so we already have the protocols."

"Do that right away, and we'll examine the information. How long will it take to transmit the data?"

"Not long," Gallagher replied. "You'll have everything that was collected by the UUV during its last run by midnight, your time."

"Regarding the SecNav," Wilson said, "we were hoping you could look into the matter. The bottom line is that we don't know if we can trust Secretary Verbeck, and we need that issue resolved as soon as possible."

"I understand," Christine said. "I'll see what I can do and get back to you. What are your plans in the meantime?"

"I'll return to *Michigan* and inform Verbeck that I'm still searching for the UUV and mother ship. I'll stay in that holding pattern until I hear from you, and coordinate with Commander Gallagher once the way forward becomes clear."

The videocon wrapped up shortly thereafter and the display went black.

Christine stared at the blank screen as she evaluated the unusual revelations and their portent. Determining whether Verbeck was innocent or complicit would be a delicate issue. The CIA would be investigating one of the president's cabinet members. This was something she would have to discuss with the president before proceeding.

But first, there was something else she wanted to look into. The issue of what—and who—had sunk *Stethem*.

After returning to the seventh floor, Christine stopped by Tracey McFarland's office.

She informed McFarland, "I just had a secure VTC with the Commanding Officer of USS *Jimmy Carter*. There's an issue we need to look into, most likely pertaining to communication intercepts made by one of its UUVs. I'm having the data sent directly here instead of to the Pentagon. I want you to get working on it right away. Identify any sensitive information someone would want deleted, enough to sink one of our own submarines to do so."

A perplexed look formed on McFarland's face. "Sink one of our own submarines?"

Christine quickly explained things, then provided instructions. "Review the UUV data *Jimmy Carter* is transmitting tonight; look for anything that might spur the SecNav or someone close to her to delete that data. Set up a meeting tomorrow afternoon to review whatever you find, and we'll pull Bryant and Rolow into the loop.

"Also, what's the status of ONI's investigation into the *Stethem* sinking?"

McFarland replied, "They sent a submersible down to examine the damage and look for pieces of the torpedo on the ocean floor. They're analyzing the information now."

Christine checked her watch. It was too late today, but first thing tomorrow on her agenda would be a trip to the Office of Naval Intelligence.

31

SUITLAND, MARYLAND

Located on the forty-two-acre compound of the National Maritime Intelligence Center, a short drive from the White House, is the headquarters of the Office of Naval Intelligence, the United States' oldest intelligence agency. Tasked with maintaining a decisive information advantage over America's potential adversaries, ONI's focus on naval weapons and technology was why Christine O'Connor had scheduled this morning's meeting.

Christine entered the ONI headquarters building, where she was greeted in the lobby by Elizabeth Gherlone, a senior supervisor in the three-thousand-member organization. Gherlone escorted Christine to a third-floor conference room occupied by a half dozen men and women seated around the table. Gherlone made the introductions, informing Christine that today's brief would be led by Sara Inman, who was ONI's senior expert on domestic and foreign torpedoes.

"Sara will brief you on what we know so far."

A large display on the wall was already energized, and Inman commenced her brief.

"The *Stethem* incident is essentially a forensics investigation," she said, "where the victim is the destroyer. We examine its wounds and look for evidence of the weapon employed, as well as the perpetrator. We're still looking for remnants of the torpedo on the ocean floor; thus far, we've found nothing. However, we do have an acoustic recording from which we can discern much, plus we have the damage to *Stethem* to examine."

Inman flipped through several pictures of the destroyer, which had been sheared in half by the torpedo explosion, lying on the ocean bottom.

"You can see that the torpedo detonated beneath the ship, instead of beside it. Notice how the keel on both halves of the ship bends upward, which indicates a bubble explosion from below." She pointed to the sharp, jagged edges where the ship split in half. "You can see what happened when the bubble collapsed, concentrating the energy from the explosion into a water jet shooting upward, driven by the higher pressure beneath the bubble compared to above.

"What we have here is a classic example of a heavyweight torpedo detonation."

Christine keyed on the term—*heavyweight*. She recalled from the Situation Room briefing given by Secretary Verbeck that the supposed rogue UUV carried lightweight torpedoes.

"Are you sure *Stethem* was sunk by a heavyweight and not a lightweight torpedo?"

"Absolutely," Inman replied. "This type of damage, shearing a destroyer in half, can't be inflicted by a lightweight torpedo. Its warhead is too small, typically only about fifteen percent compared to a heavyweight. Against a large surface combatant like *Stethem*, a lightweight torpedo could have punched a hole into the ship, but it wouldn't have been able to break its keel and split the ship in half."

"I see," Christine said.

She wondered why ONI hadn't keyed on this critical issue—that a heavyweight torpedo, not a lightweight torpedo, had sunk *Stethem*—then recalled that no ONI representatives had attended the Situation Room briefing. ONI had been brought into the investigation per standard procedure and had apparently not been briefed about Secretary Verbeck's opinion that a lightweight torpedo fired by a rogue UUV had sunk *Stethem*.

If Verbeck were truly involved, as Wilson suspected, that had probably been done on purpose. Keeping ONI in the dark about the lightweight torpedo supposition had likely been deliberate, since ONI would have been able to quickly debunk Verbeck's claim. However, ONI's conclusion led to a more critical question.

"Do you have an idea of which country is responsible for the attack?"

Inman replied, "We believe *Stethem* was sunk by an Iranian torpedo."

"What makes you think that?"

"The acoustic signature, recorded by underwater SOSUS arrays in the Gulf. Every torpedo produces a unique explosion, based on the size of the charge and type of explosive. The acoustic signature of the explosion that sunk *Stethem* correlates to the Valfajr Iranian torpedo."

"You're saying that Iran sank *Stethem*?"

"That's our assessment at the moment. Of course, it won't become official until all evidence has been analyzed."

Christine tried to piece things together. That *Stethem* hadn't been sunk by a rogue U.S. UUV was welcome news. On the other hand . . .

"Do you know why Iran would attack *Stethem*?"

Inman looked to Gherlone. "That's the most perplexing part," Gherlone answered. "Relations between the U.S. and Iran were no more strained at the time than normal, and *Stethem* was operating in international waters. The attack appears to be politically motivated, but for what reason, we don't know. That's out of our realm."

Christine quickly reviewed what she had learned thus far. Iran attacked *Stethem*. Verbeck claimed it was a rogue UUV, then ordered the UUV and *Jimmy Carter* sunk.

The data collected by the UUV seemed to be the critical issue. But if so, that meant Iran and Secretary Verbeck were somehow connected, with Iran providing the excuse for Verbeck to hunt down the UUV and its mother ship.

Christine took a deep breath. Things weren't adding up. Perhaps the data collected by the UUV, once analyzed, would shed light on the matter.

32

LANGLEY, VIRGINIA

Silence gripped the seventh-floor conference room after Christine explained the situation. Bryant, Rolow, and McFarland wore grim expressions as they processed the information—that Wilson had been ordered to sink *Jimmy Carter*, an Iranian torpedo had sunk *Stethem*, and that Secretary Verbeck was involved in an effort to destroy the data collected by the UUV.

The communications intercepted by the UUV seemed to be the critical issue, so Christine turned to McFarland. "What have you discovered so far?"

"Nothing has triggered any trip wires so far. But there's a ton of data—in the terabytes—which is usually screened first by Pentagon personnel, with only the pertinent information forwarded to us. It's going to take time to sift through it all. However, on a related topic, we've discovered some noteworthy events related to the SecNav and UUV program staff.

"The first is that Secretary Verbeck's senior military aide died of a suspected heart attack a few days ago while hiking with his daughter. We checked the SecNav's travel records and confirmed that her aide accompanied Verbeck on her trip to Bahrain, where they briefed Captain Wilson on his UUV mission.

"The second notable event is that the senior enlisted person overseeing the UUV data screen at the Pentagon was mugged and killed a few days before that."

"Assuming the aide's heart attack was induced," Rolow said, "I think we can conclude that someone is deliberately attempting to delete the UUV data and is also covering their tracks, eliminating those who know what's going on or could piece the information together."

"That leads to a central question," Christine said. "Is the SecNav part of the conspiracy, or somehow being manipulated?"

She said to Rolow, "Put together a task force to investigate Secretary Verbeck. Look into her friends and business partners, potential ties to Iran, or any other reason she might be motivated to destroy the UUV data."

Rolow objected. "You're talking about the CIA investigating one of the president's cabinet members. Our authority to operate on domestic soil is limited, and investigating a political appointee this high up treads on dangerous ground."

"I agree," Christine replied. "I've already scheduled a meeting with the president to brief him on what we know and request permission to investigate Secretary Verbeck. In the meantime, put together a task force and lay out a plan."

"Understood."

Christine turned to McFarland. "Find the critical UUV data, and we should be able to identify the link between Iran and whoever is desperately trying to destroy the data."

"We're working on it," McFarland said, "around the clock."

33

WASHINGTON, D.C.

It was dark by the time Christine arrived at the White House, her SUV stopping beside the West Wing entrance. Most of the White House staff had left for the day, enabling a discreet meeting between the president and the CIA director.

Christine had contacted the president directly, requesting a *snow-blind* meeting. After working on the president's staff for three years, she was well-versed in the protocols surrounding sensitive issues. A snow-blind meeting was one where attendance was limited, with only the participating individuals able to see the appointment on the president's calendar. The president himself had entered tonight's private meeting, meaning that only he—and the two Marines Christine was walking past—were aware of his late-night conversation with the CIA director.

After traversing the hallway to the Oval Office, not spotting anyone along the way, Christine knocked on the president's door. He acknowledged and she entered, finding the president at his desk as expected. She took the center of three chairs facing him.

"What's this about?" he asked, skipping the small talk he had engaged in during her previous visits.

Christine filled the president in on the UUV, *Jimmy Carter*, and *Stethem* issues, with the president voicing his concern over ONI's preliminary assessment that Iran was responsible for sinking the destroyer. When Christine brought up the issue of Secretary Verbeck's potential involvement in the matter, he listened intently.

When she finished, the president sat silently, evaluating the issue. While she awaited the president's response, Christine used the opportunity to assess the situation as well, particularly with regard to the president's relationship to Secretary Verbeck. He had nominated her for the position and she was also a close friend, dating back to his early days as a nascent politician, drawing on the support of rich and influential donors.

The president finally spoke. "You may proceed with an investigation into Secretary Verbeck. However, minimize the number of people at the agency who are involved in this, and when it comes to my administration, report directly, and only, to me."

"I understand," Christine replied. "I've already limited this topic to my DD, DDO, and DDA, and the personnel required to analyze the UUV information."

"Excellent," the president said. He offered an encouraging smile, in light of the upcoming presidential election and the potentially devastating effect a scandal involving his secretary of the Navy could have on the outcome. His thoughts then shifted to the other potential dark cloud hanging over his administration.

"How about the bin Laden issue?" he asked. "Have you made any progress?"

"Not yet," Christine replied. "But we have a team about to land in Kuwait to pursue the matter."

34

FARWANIYA, KUWAIT

Jake Harrison reclined in his leather seat as the Dassault Falcon executive jet began its descent toward Kuwait International Airport. Twelve hours earlier, the jet had lifted off from Ronald Reagan Washington National Airport, banking east toward the Atlantic Ocean. Configured to transport a dozen passengers, it carried only Khalila and Harrison today, along with a CIA case officer named Asad Durrani, a naturalized citizen from Pakistan. This was only the second time Harrison had met the man, but it was obvious that Khalila had worked with him many times before.

Durrani pulled three manila envelopes from his briefcase and handed one to Harrison. "This contains your alias identification documents. Same as last time."

Harrison examined the contents: a birth certificate, Social Security card, driver's license, passport, and credit cards issued under his alias, the same one he had used in Damascus and Sochi.

Dan Connolly.

Durrani handed an empty envelope for Harrison to deposit his true identification and credit cards in, which Durrani then sealed and placed in his briefcase.

The second packet he provided was labeled *Background*, which contained a thick printout of Harrison's fake personal history: hometown, friends, education, employment history, and residences. The third packet was labeled *Cover*, which contained information on his employment in Bluestone Security, a CIA-owned company engaged in legitimate business dealings as well as government-funded weapon sales to approved organizations and countries. Harrison was the assistant director of procurement, en route to Kuwait in search of a supply of cheap and untraceable weapons from various foreign manufacturers—whatever suited Bluestone's customers' desires.

Regarding Khalila's cover, nothing had changed. She was a translator contracted to Bluestone Security and other companies in need of a Middle Eastern or South/Central Asian linguist. Her supposed employment by a CIA-owned company was crucial to her cover, since she often stopped by Langley without any attempt to conceal her visits. During their trip to Syria a few months earlier, Khalila had explained that her ties to the CIA were highlighted instead of hidden.

Many of Khalila's contacts in the Middle East lived in societies that considered women property. In some of those countries, women weren't even allowed to drive and needed a man's permission to get married, travel abroad, apply for a passport, or even to open a bank account. As an ordinary woman in those societies, she'd have no chance of attending the high-level meetings necessary to obtain the sensitive information the CIA desired.

Working for the CIA opened doors for Khalila. She had valuable information—insight into who the CIA sources were, both prisoners and agents, and what information had been divulged. That made her a valuable asset for numerous Middle Eastern organizations and governments. Of course, the information she was allowed to divulge was carefully selected by the Directorate of Analysis; enough to prove her bona fides without jeopardizing American interests.

Harrison had found Khalila's explanation both interesting and alarming. She had essentially admitted that she was a double agent, feeding sensitive information to both sides. Although the CIA believed her allegiance was to the U.S., how did they know for sure? When it really mattered, would Khalila protect America or enable a devastating terrorist plot against it?

As Harrison finished reviewing his alias and background material, he wondered what the plan was this time once they landed in Kuwait. Unlike in Damascus, they weren't attempting to track down a weapon procurement Mixell had made, where Harrison's weapon expertise might help. They were searching for information about a prisoner taken from the Abbottabad compound years ago. How, exactly, was he supposed to assist?

Khalila was far from the friendliest woman he had met, but she had been unusually quiet since they had been assigned to the Kuwait mission, barely saying a word to him since they left the conference room at Langley. During their flight to Damascus a few months ago, Khalila had explained the plan. On this flight, however, she hadn't spoken to him at all, even though she was sitting beside him in the window seat.

Harrison decided to strike up a conversation, find out what was going on.

"What's the plan once we land in Kuwait?"

"I have a contact with ties to Kuwaiti intelligence," Khalila answered, "which is part of the country's security service. I'd rather not deal directly with the Kuwait Security Service, because if they have the information we're looking for, they're not going to provide it to two CIA agents poking around. A query for information this sensitive could spark a draconian response—to eliminate those asking the question."

Harrison wondered if that was the issue—the risky nature of this assignment. But that didn't seem to fit Khalila's personality. He had learned in Syria that she was fearless to a fault, an adrenaline junkie when it came to danger. However, there was one way to find out, and he chose his words pointedly.

"So, that's what you're worried about? You're afraid we might get killed? In my previous line of work, that was a given. You should get used to it."

Khalila's eyes flashed in anger. When she replied, there was a hard edge to her words.

"I'm not afraid. I'm angry."

"About what?"

"I've been forced to let you tag along on this mission. Unlike Damascus, you're not an asset this time. I need to have sensitive conversations with people who won't speak in your presence, no matter how much I vouch for you. I'd rather leave you at the hotel the whole time, and I just might."

"You spoke to Rolow about this?"

"I did. He said we're a team and to stop bitching about it."

"Maybe he wants me to tag along to keep you out of trouble."

"I can take care of myself," she said. "Now I've also got to babysit you."

Harrison smiled. "Let's see where the leads take us before you conclude I'm a liability."

Khalila didn't respond, turning away instead to stare out the Falcon's window as the aircraft dropped below the clouds toward their destination.

With her eyes still gazing out the window, she said, "We'll talk more once we check into our hotel in Kuwait City."

35

KUWAIT CITY

The Dassault Falcon completed its descent, landing at Kuwait International Airport, ten miles south of Kuwait's capital. As the jet taxied toward the terminal under the midday sun, Harrison reviewed what he had learned while reading the third packet Durrani had provided—his cover as a Bluestone Security executive visiting Kuwait to arrange a procurement of untraceable weapons.

Ruled by the Al-Sabah royal family since the eighteenth century, Kuwait was one of the smallest countries in the world. Located at the tip of the Persian Gulf, it encompassed only 330 square miles, with only 4.7 million inhabitants. However, it contained the world's sixth-largest oil reserves.

Its neighbors to the north and south, Iraq and Saudi Arabia, respectively, had often aimed to conquer the tiny but rich emirate, with Saddam Hussein's 1990 invasion the latest attempt. Not having armed forces capable of repulsing attacks from its much larger neighbors, Kuwait had relied on alliances with more powerful countries, particularly the U.S., France, and Great Britain, and had been a British protectorate from 1899 until its independence in 1961.

Following the first Gulf War, the U.S. and Kuwait signed a formal defense cooperation agreement. The small country was subsequently designated as a United States major non-NATO ally, and it now contained the largest U.S. military presence in the Middle East. The alliance included a close collaboration in the intelligence sector, with American forces using Kuwaiti military bases for logistical support, training activities, and staging points for regional military and anti-terrorism operations.

The Falcon coasted to a halt not far from a man leaning against a black sedan. Harrison, Khalila, and Durrani descended the steps to the tarmac where they met Nizar Mussan, a CIA officer serving as an executive assistant for Bluestone Security, who had also met them in Syria. After placing their luggage in the trunk and joining Mussan in the car, they pulled away from the Falcon as its engines spun down to a stop.

Kuwait City was only a few miles away, and shortly after entering the city, Mussan stopped by a side street. Durrani pulled two thick envelopes of money from his briefcase and handed them to Khalila, then informed her and Harrison that he'd be only a phone call away to provide any assistance they needed. He stepped from the vehicle and disappeared into an alley as Mussan pulled back into traffic.

A short while later, Mussan stopped near a small boutique hotel in the center of the city. Harrison and Khalila entered the hotel lobby while Mussan waited in the car, since Khalila had informed him their first meeting was in less than an hour. They were greeted at the lobby counter by an elderly Arab who appeared to be meeting Khalila and Harrison for the first time, although Harrison noticed a flicker of recognition in the man's eyes when he addressed Khalila.

The hotel was a small establishment with only a dozen rooms, arranged in a square surrounding a central courtyard, with the hotel offices and lobby facing the street. They were given keys to a room on the second floor, which contained a terrace overlooking the courtyard.

"Welcome to Kuwait City, Mr. Connolly and Ms. Dufour," he said. "I hope you enjoy your stay."

It took Harrison a second for his alias to register.

Upon entering the room, Khalila tossed her luggage onto the single queen-sized bed. Similar to their previous trips abroad, they would share a room, and although they would sleep in the same bed, Khalila had made it clear that the arrangement was a hands-off one.

Khalila approached the window and pulled the curtain back slightly, examining the courtyard and adjacent terraces. Once she finished her surveillance, she shed her business suit and blouse, stripping down to her bra and panties. She pulled two knives from her suitcase, each set within a spring-loaded housing, then strapped one to each forearm.

She donned a pair of slacks, plus a short-sleeved blouse instead of the long-sleeve one she had removed, then put her black suit jacket on again.

After assessing herself in a full-length mirror, she rotated her wrists outward and flexed her hands sideways, and a knife popped down into each palm.

Khalila wrapped a black scarf around her head and neck, adding a matching niqab that left only her eyes exposed. She slipped her pistol into her purse, plus one of the envelopes of money Durrani had provided. Harrison, meanwhile, had unpacked his luggage and changed into a suit, minus the tie, also donning a shoulder holster and pistol. They were both soon ready to depart.

"During the meeting," Khalila said, "stay alert, looking for any sign of trouble. Once I begin the conversation, my contact will realize I'm there for a different reason than what I had originally expressed; otherwise, he would not have agreed to see me. I cannot predict his reaction once he learns he has been deceived, other than it will be unfavorable. Any questions?"

"Not at the moment."

Mussan was still waiting in the car outside the hotel, and Khalila provided the address for the meeting. He pulled into traffic and headed for the older part of the city, eventually stopping by the curb on a street lined with narrow, two-level storefronts on each side. He waited in the car while Khalila and Harrison entered a small Persian rug store.

There were several customers perusing the selection, plus a male clerk whom Khalila approached and asked a question in Arabic. The clerk didn't respond, but glanced at a small, dark doorway at the back of the store.

Harrison followed Khalila as she passed through the opening and climbed a set of stairs leading to a closed door on the second floor, upon which Khalila knocked.

"Who is it?" a muffled voice asked in Arabic; Harrison knew enough from his tours in the Middle East to understand the man's question.

"Khalila. I'm here to see Ayman."

The door cracked open, and a man wearing a white dishdasha studied Khalila and Harrison before opening the door wider.

"As-salaam alaykum," Khalila said, offering the common Arabic greeting—*Peace be upon you*—as she placed her hand over her heart.

The man replied with a challenge of some sort, although Harrison couldn't quite make out the full translation.

Khalila pulled down the niqab veil covering her face.

His eyes widened slightly, then he replied, "Wa alaykum as-salaam"—*And also with you*—as he placed his hand over his heart and bowed his head.

Ayman beckoned them into a small foyer, where he and Khalila exchanged the standard pleasantries, inquiring how each was doing and how her journey to Kuwait had gone. Khalila then introduced Harrison, whom Ayman eyed suspiciously. Nonetheless, he placed his hand over his heart and greeted Harrison politely.

He led the way into a well-appointed study, where they took their seats at a small table with several chairs set atop a plush Persian rug.

The conversation turned to business, with Khalila beginning the dialogue. An unpleasant look soon formed on Ayman's face, and his voice took on an agitated tone. Harrison couldn't follow the conversation but figured Khalila had just revealed that their meeting was for a different topic than advertised.

Khalila's tone turned conciliatory, attempting to persuade Ayman to provide the desired information. He made a clicking sound with his tongue—an Arab gesture for *no*—as his facial expression turned resolute.

She opened her purse, her hand moving past her pistol, retrieving instead the envelope of money, which she placed on the table midway between them.

Ayman eyed the money, uncertainty creeping into his expression.

Khalila repeated her request, finishing her verbal plea with a finger pointed to the sky. She was invoking *God's will* for some reason.

The man studied Khalila and the money for a moment, then slowly retrieved the envelope. After assessing the amount inside, he tilted his head slightly to the side and smiled.

Then he answered Khalila's question.

36

KUWAIT CITY

As the sun slipped beneath the horizon, Harrison watched as Khalila stood before the mirror in their hotel room, testing both knives concealed in the sleeves of her business jacket again. She seemed nervous, responding to Harrison's questions even more curtly than usual as they prepared for a meeting with an intelligence officer in the Kuwait Security Service.

Khalila had hoped Ayman's tip would lead elsewhere. That she didn't trust the security service was clear, and she had requested a meeting on official Kuwaiti government ground, hoping the location would deter aggressive behavior. Tonight's meeting would take place at the seat of Al-Diwan Al-Amiri, commonly referred to as the Seif Palace due to its location overlooking the sea.

She was dressed similarly to earlier in the day, except she wore no niqab this time, just a hijab wrapped around her hair and neck, leaving her face exposed. When she finished testing her knives, she caught Harrison's eyes in the mirror.

"We're going to use a code phrase tonight. If I say, 'We must take what Allah provides and be grateful,' it means we're in danger and I'm about to engage." She repeated the phrase in Arabic. "Understand?"

Harrison nodded.

Darkness had descended by the time they left their hotel, and it was silent in the car as Mussan drove through the city toward the Seif Palace; Khalila seemed lost in her thoughts, as was Harrison, who wondered why Khalila was so worried. She'd clearly had dealings with the Kuwait Security Service in the past.

When the palace appeared in the distance, Khalila pulled the second envelope of money from her purse and handed it to her partner.

"Put this in your jacket and leave your weapon in the car. We're going to be searched at the entrance, and we'll have to leave our pistols behind, either at the entrance or in the car."

"I thought you picked this location to increase our safety," Harrison replied. "How does meeting in a place where we have to leave our weapons behind do that?"

"Not all weapons will be left behind. My knives and their housings are nonmetallic," she said, reminding him of her revelation in Syria. "They won't set off a metal detector. If anyone has nefarious intentions tonight, they'll be careless, thinking we're unarmed."

"I *will* be unarmed," Harrison pointed out.

"I'm not the one who insisted you accompany me," she said with attitude. "This strategy improves my odds of survival. You can either join me or stay in the car."

Harrison cursed under his breath, then quickly decided as Mussan stopped by the palace entrance. Despite the circumstances, Khalila's odds would be better if he accompanied her. Plus, he doubted the Kuwaiti agents were as well trained as he was in close-combat situations.

"Fine," he said as he placed the envelope in his jacket and pulled his pistol from its shoulder holster, placing it on the seat beside him.

Khalila and Harrison emerged from the car and headed toward the palace entrance, taking in its grandeur. The original seat of Kuwait's government comprised an artificial lake, manicured gardens, a marina, and several helicopter landing pads. The clock tower, covered in blue tiles and capped with a gold-clad dome, was a magnificent example of Islamic architecture, and the Seif Palace's most well-known feature.

They were met near the palace entrance by a man who introduced himself as Basim Iqbal, who wore a dark gray suit with a slight bulge under his left shoulder. Harrison concluded he was armed, his suspicion confirmed when they reached the metal detectors at the entrance. Iqbal pulled a pistol from a shoulder holster and placed it in a basket before proceeding through the detector. He retrieved his weapon, returning it to its holster while Harrison and Khalila passed through the detector without incident.

Iqbal led them down a long outdoor concourse with parallel walkways framing a series of pools and fountains. Although Arabic was the official language of Kuwait, English was a compulsory second language in Kuwaiti schools and was used by Kuwaiti businesses. Khalila conversed with Iqbal in English, more for Harrison's benefit, he assumed, so he could listen in.

Their conversation was of little import to the issue at hand—who was the prisoner taken from the Abbottabad compound and what had happened to him—until they reached the seawall overlooking Kuwait Bay, the palace's perimeter lights shimmering atop the water's black surface. There, Khalila made the query.

Iqbal placed both hands on the seawall railing, staring into the darkness. Khalila turned around, leaning back against the seawall as she searched left and right for evidence of others in the distance. Harrison stood a few paces away, also monitoring the area, spotting no one. However, he noticed a small transmitter in Iqbal's right ear. Someone was likely monitoring their conversation.

"You ask a sensitive question," Iqbal said.

Khalila signaled for Harrison to approach. When he reached her, she held her hand out for the envelope of money in his jacket pocket, which he handed to her. She extended the thick envelope to Iqbal.

He eyed the envelope, then took it and ran his thumb along the edge of the bills. He slipped the envelope into his jacket pocket.

Khalila repeated her question. "Who was sent to Kuwait from the Abbottabad compound?"

"I don't know."

"Who does?"

"Malik al-Rashidi. He would have been the one who made the arrangements when the prisoner arrived."

"Do you know where the prisoner was sent?"

Iqbal shook his head.

"Is there anything else you'd like to share?"

"One thing," he said. "You should not have asked these questions."

"Why not?"

"I now have conflicting guidance. On one hand, I have a mandate that says you're untouchable. On the other hand, I have an edict that requires me to eliminate anyone who asks the questions you just posed."

"That's quite the dilemma," Khalila said. "I recommend instead that you pretend this conversation never happened."

"Unfortunately, I cannot. The edict to eliminate you outweighs the mandate to protect you."

"I see," Khalila replied. "I suppose you're the one who will execute this edict?"

Iqbal nodded.

Harrison noticed movement in the distance. Two men had appeared on the left, walking briskly toward them. To the right, he spotted two more men approaching, weapons drawn.

Iqbal turned and pulled his pistol on Khalila.

Khalila folded her arms across her chest. "This is very unwise of you, Basim. If any harm comes to me, you will not live long. Your wife and children will not live long."

Harrison noticed the indecision in the man's eyes. But his resolve hardened as the four men reached them, stopping a few feet away, two facing Khalila while two focused on Harrison.

"You've placed me in an untenable position," Iqbal said, anger gathering in his voice. "You should have stayed in America and let them send someone else. But no. *You* come to ask these questions!"

"It wasn't my decision."

"You didn't have to follow through. You could have stayed in your hotel room and arranged a mishap for your partner, then returned safely home."

Khalila nodded. "Yes, I could have killed him like the others, but it wouldn't have addressed the issue." She stepped closer to Iqbal. "I came because I *want* the information."

"Well, then," Iqbal said, "you have chosen your fate."

"If this is to be my last night," Khalila said, "perhaps you can satisfy my curiosity. Did this edict to terminate any who inquire about this matter come from Rashidi?"

Iqbal nodded.

There was a tense silence between them until Iqbal spoke. "I'm begging you, Khalila. Walk away and return to America. Pretend this conversation never happened and that whatever clue brought you to Kuwait led to a dead end. I'll take care of your partner."

Khalila stared Iqbal down. When she didn't immediately reply, he said, "For the sake of my wife and children. Don't make me do this. *Walk away!*"

She considered the man's words at length, then turned to Harrison, her eyes meeting his.

"I'm sorry, Jake," she said. "Basim is right. I need to live to fight another day."

Harrison couldn't argue with her logic. It was five men, each armed, against two, with only Khalila wielding weapons. Still, with the element of surprise, as Khalila had explained in the car, they had a chance.

He wasn't about to give up without a fight, even if Khalila chose not to assist. If there was any hope of survival, he had to act now. If he could wrest the weapon from the nearest agent, he'd have a chance. But he was too far away. He needed to get a step closer without the man suspecting anything.

Time was running out.

Harrison was about to spring into action, despite the unlikely prospect of success, when he noticed something odd about Khalila's gaze. Her eyes shifted periodically between Harrison and the Kuwaiti agent nearest him.

He could have misinterpreted her eye movements, but he chose to believe Khalila was about to attack and that she was signaling—*be ready*.

He stalled for time, searching for a way to move closer to the nearest agent.

"You're just going to walk away? You said I could trust you completely unless I learned your identity."

"The current situation is hopeless," she said as her eyes canvassed the five men arrayed against them. "It calls for a reassessment of our partnership."

Turning back to Iqbal, she lowered her hands, palms outward in supplication as she looked to the sky, then spoke in Arabic.

"We must take what Allah provides and be grateful."

The code phrase.

Harrison had little time to analyze why Khalila had chosen to engage rather than walk away. He stepped closer to the Kuwaiti agent nearest him. "What did she say?" he asked, since Khalila had spoken in Arabic.

Before the man could respond, Khalila flexed both wrists and a knife slid down into each hand. She swung one upward, driving it beneath Iqbal's chin into his brain as she threw the other knife at the next closest Kuwaiti agent, impaling him in the center of his chest.

As the man fell to his knees, Khalila used Iqbal as a shield, pulling her knife from his head as a spray of bullets peppered his back. Then she let her remaining knife fly, hitting a third man in the throat. She dropped down, retrieving Iqbal's pistol as a burst of bullets from the third man passed overhead, then finished off both wounded Kuwaiti agents with a shot to each man's head.

Khalila had caught the Kuwaiti agents by surprise, as had Harrison. After obtaining a hold of the nearest man's pistol, Harrison had twisted the agent's hand upward and pulled the trigger, sending a bullet through his skull. Harrison kept the man's body between himself and the last agent as he pulled the pistol from the dead man's hand. Three more bullets, and the last Kuwaiti dropped to the ground.

As the final man fell, joining the other agent sprawled at Harrison's feet, Harrison turned toward Khalila, assessing whether she needed assistance. She had done excellent work.

She retrieved her knives, then said, "We must leave, quickly."

37

SALMIYA, KUWAIT

"This mess isn't going to be easy to clean up," Asad Durrani said.

Harrison and Khalila were sitting around a table with their case management officer in a CIA safe house in Salmiya, a city several miles southeast of Kuwait City. They were on the fourth level of a nondescript, eight-story building owned in its entirety by the CIA, in a flat that had been transformed into the safe house headquarters: the living room was missing the typical furnishings, filled instead with several men at computer workstations, monitoring displays mounted on the walls. Joining them at the table was Marzouq Ashour, a specialized skills officer responsible for managing the CIA safe house. Also at the table was their driver, Nizar Mussan.

An hour earlier, Harrison and Khalila had scaled the outer wall of the Seif Palace, rather than risk heading out through the entrance manned by security personnel, and had been picked up by Mussan. They had swung by their hotel and collected their belongings, then hastily departed. The Kuwait Security Service would quickly deduce who had killed their five compatriots and would undoubtedly determine where they were staying, so new accommodations were required. For the time being, the CIA safe house in Salmiya would suffice. How to deal with tonight's event was the current topic of discussion.

"The seventh floor at Langley is going to have to handle this," Ashour said. "This isn't something I can resolve."

"That's understandable," Khalila replied. "Does the DDO know yet?"

Ashour shook his head. "Not from us, at least. We got your call shortly after we picked up the chatter about something going down at the palace, so I decided to wait until you arrived and we had all the details."

He glanced at the notes he had taken moments earlier. Khalila had taken the lead explaining what happened, although Harrison noted that she had left out several details: the question that had triggered the elimination edict and the part about her being untouchable. Actually, the entire story Khalila had fed Ashour had been a complete fabrication.

"We need to get to Rashidi," Khalila said. "What paramilitary resources do you have available tonight?"

"Hold on a minute," Ashour said. "You two are in hot water and about to be flayed by headquarters for killing five Kuwaiti agents on government grounds. And now you want to go after the head of the Kuwait Security Service?"

"We need to move fast," Khalila said. "It's doubtful he'll realize we're going after him next, but the longer we wait, the more likely he'll make the connection and beef up his security."

"I'm sorry," Ashour said. "The political fallout of an operation against Rashidi would be extreme. Unless the seventh floor authorizes it, I can't help you with this."

Khalila folded her arms across her chest, contemplating the matter. She turned to Harrison, searching for ideas.

Harrison asked Ashour, "What kind of assistance can you provide *unofficially*? For example, could we borrow a few items from your armory?"

Ashour nodded. "I can provide equipment. Just no personnel."

"What about recon? Can we get a look at the security at Rashidi's residence?"

"We have satellite images you can examine. Nothing at ground level at the moment."

"Satellite should be fine," Harrison said.

Ashour had one of the technicians pull up satellite imagery of the area on a wall-mounted display and zoom in to Rashidi's residence, a narrow beachfront estate in Sabah Al-Salem, a city a few miles to the south. Rashidi's house was nestled against Kuwait Bay, protected by a wall that ran across the front of the estate, then down both sides into the bay. Four men could be seen patrolling the perimeter, one in the vicinity of each corner of the estate, plus a fifth stationed at the entrance gate.

"Does he have additional security inside the house?"

"Unlikely. He has a five-man security detail, and those five are accounted for outside the house, as you can see."

Harrison studied the scenario, quickly devising an ingress plan. The fourth side opened to Kuwait Bay. The perfect entry point for a former SEAL. He looked at Khalila.

"Care to go for a swim with me?" He pointed to the back of Rashidi's estate.

"Not necessary," Khalila said. "I'll be entering through the front door."

"How are you going to do that?"

"Leave that to me. But getting into his house is the easy part. Getting out is where you come in."

To Ashour, she said, "As I mentioned, we need to do this tonight, before Rashidi figures things out and increases his security. Can you provide whatever Jake needs for his waterfront entry?"

"Depends on what he needs."

Harrison wrote out a list, which Ashour reviewed.

"I'll have what you need in two hours."

38

SABAH AL-SALEM, KUWAIT

Jake Harrison's head gradually emerged from the black water near the shore of Kuwait Bay. As he moved slowly toward Malik al-Rashidi's estate, he kept his eyes just above the water's surface, creeping lower and lower until he came to a halt, lying on his stomach fifteen feet from the sandy beach, his body still beneath the water, with his head now fully above the surface.

He pushed his face mask up and pulled the rebreather from his mouth, then brought his Heckler & Koch MP7 submachine gun to bear, examining the back of Rashidi's estate through the MP7 sight. Two guards were in view, positioned as expected based on the satellite imagery he had reviewed at the CIA safe house. He turned on his waterproof earpiece, then contacted Khalila, informing her that he was at the desired spot—and properly equipped—to execute his phase of the plan.

Two hours earlier, Marzouq Ashour had returned to the CIA safe house with the items Harrison had requested: a black wet suit in Harrison's size, dive boots and fins, diving mask, and a Dräger LAR rebreather, which was a small, closed-circuit breathing system using pure oxygen, with the unit filtering carbon dioxide from exhaled air. Unlike scuba gear, the rebreather emitted no air bubbles, making it ideal for clandestine operations.

While they waited for Ashour's return, Harrison and Khalila had devised a plan for tonight's meeting with Rashidi and had also visited the safe house armory, where Harrison had selected a bullet-resistant vest, the MP7 with an optical sight and a suppressor, plus a waterproof rucksack containing a cell phone jammer, a security alarm neutralizer, and two sets of C-4 explosive and detonators in case he had to blast his way through a door or two. Only the first item in the rucksack would likely be needed, but he had brought the others along, just in case.

Harrison had passed on night vision goggles since Rashidi's estate was lit well enough from nearby streetlights. As he surveyed the bay side of Rashidi's estate, he noted that despite the late hour, there was a light on in an upstairs room. Ashour would be monitoring their communications from the safe house, and Harrison had talked him into cutting Rashidi's telephone landline once Khalila entered his house. Harrison would then jam the cell phones, preventing any calls for assistance.

For Khalila's part, she had selected no additional equipment aside from a thin, soft-armor, bullet-resistant vest she had donned. Aside from that, she had left the safe house dressed and armed as she had been for the meeting at the Seif Palace, with only the two knives strapped to her forearms beneath her business suit.

Two blocks from Rashidi's estate, Khalila had been sitting in her car, waiting for Harrison's signal through her earpiece. Now that he was in place, she started the car and drove toward the estate. She stopped a short distance from the entrance and walked to the gate, guarded by an armed man who eyed her suspiciously, given the late hour.

"I'm here to see Malik al-Rashidi."

"He's asleep," the man said.

"I didn't ask you what he was doing," Khalila said. "Besides, he doesn't look asleep to me." She motioned toward the house, with the upstairs room illuminated. "Tell him that his friend Khalila Dufour is here to see him."

The guard was about to respond when a sedan with four men drove up, stopping beside Khalila. As the gate slid aside to let the vehicle pass, Khalila examined the men inside the car. They were armed Kuwait Security Service personnel. Rashidi had either figured things out or was simply taking additional precautions.

"Four more guards," Khalila said for Harrison's benefit, who was monitoring her progress through his earpiece. "Having a party tonight, or is this just a shift change?"

The man ignored her question as the car passed by and stopped near the front door, where the agents exited the vehicle and entered the house. Khalila considered abandoning tonight's operation, given the four extra agents. There were now nine armed men to contend with. However, the front gate remained open, and the guard had his phone to his ear, calling Rashidi.

Khalila decided to proceed.

"There's a woman at the gate who says she's a friend of yours," the guard said. "Her name is Khalila Dufour."

Khalila heard Rashidi's voice through the cell phone speaker.

Let me see her face.

The man switched his phone to a video call and held it before Khalila.

Ensure she's unarmed, then let her in.

The guard pulled a handheld metal detector from the gatehouse and surveyed Khalila's body. No alarm went off. He gestured toward the house entrance as the gate closed behind her.

She made her way down the sidewalk, then climbed the steps to Rashidi's residence. She knocked, and the door was opened by one of the four men who had just arrived. Two of them escorted her to the second floor and into a study with built-in bookcases and an antique desk.

Malik al-Rashidi rose from his chair and circled around to the front of his desk, leaning back against the edge as he examined his guest.

"So, you go by Khalila now?"

Moments earlier, Khalila had entered Rashidi's house, which was Harrison's signal to begin. She had accurately forecasted the first phase of tonight's mission—getting inside wouldn't be a problem. The getting-out part, however, required Harrison's assistance.

With his elbow on the sandy bottom supporting his MP7, he centered the optical sight on the man to the right, then pulled the trigger.

The round hit him in the head, and Harrison shifted to the man on the left, who was thus far oblivious of his pending fate. Another squeeze, and both men were sprawled on the ground.

He rose from the water and moved to the back of the residence, then pulled the cell phone jammer from his rucksack and activated it. He peered around the left side of the house. In the distance, he spotted the guard manning the left-front corner of the estate. His back was to Harrison as he monitored the front of the residence.

Harrison moved quietly along the side of the house, his MP7 sighted on the third man as he approached the front corner, contemplating his next move. Once he dropped the next man, the fourth might notice, which meant he had to be in position to take him out quickly, before he could alert the gate guard or the four men inside the house.

He stopped at the corner and peered around, locating the next man, who was positioned as Harrison had expected based on the satellite imagery. The gate guard was partially blocked by a tall hedgerow, and Harrison hoped the guard's focus was outside the estate, not within.

Satisfied he could proceed effectively, Harrison put two bullets in the front-left guard, then immediately turned the corner toward the fourth, drilling two rounds into him. He moved swiftly toward the gate guard, and once he cleared the hedgerow, he put a bullet in the man's head.

He reached the front door, then paused to reassess. There was supposed to be only the five men posted in the estate exterior, not four more inside the house, their whereabouts unknown. However, he figured one or two of the men were near the front door.

Blowing the door open with C-4 was an option, but that would give away his presence. He'd likely be able to take out whoever was near the front door due to the dual effect of surprise and the blast itself, but the others would be warned. A stealthy ingress was preferred.

Harrison reached for the door handle and slowly tried to turn it. The door was locked.

There was one other, fairly stealthy option. Khalila had knocked on the door, and the guard had opened it without any challenge. It was worth a try.

He searched for door cameras mounted nearby and found none, so with his MP7 held ready in one hand, he knocked with the other. A few seconds later, the door opened.

Harrison shot the man at the door twice, then surged past him into the foyer as he fell, spotting a second agent, reaching for his gun. Two more bullets, followed by a third to the head, sent him to the floor as well. After another round to the head of the first guard inside, Harrison moved quietly up the stairs.

Standing before Rashidi in his study, Khalila was keenly aware of the two armed agents behind her.

"Yes, I go by Khalila now. For the time being."

"I assume you're responsible for the incident at the Seif tonight?" Rashidi asked.

"I am."

"Why would you do such a thing? Kill five of my men?"

"Iqbal was about to kill me. I had no choice."

"That's absurd. Iqbal would never harm you."

"He said there was an edict that required my elimination. It had to do with a question I asked."

"What was that?"

"About a prisoner the Americans handed over to Kuwaiti officials several years ago."

"Can you be more specific about this prisoner?"

"The man from bin Laden's Abbottabad compound."

Rashidi's eyes widened, finally understanding what this was about. He looked at the two men behind her. "Wait outside."

The two agents departed, closing the study door.

Rashidi began pacing back and forth. "This edict was handed down years ago, before you started working for the Americans. It was not crafted with you in mind. If Basim had called me, I would have clarified that you are exempt."

"It would have been helpful if you had done so earlier."

Rashidi stopped pacing and faced her, clearly agitated. "Why now? After all these years, why is this question asked?"

Khalila wasn't sure how much she could reveal to Rashidi. But considering how she expected things to play out tonight, she figured it was okay to divulge whatever was necessary.

"Are you aware that the existence of this prisoner was kept secret from the CIA?"

Rashidi started pacing again. Khalila could tell his mind was racing through various scenarios; what information could be divulged, where it would lead, and what the repercussions might be. But he hadn't answered her question, so she repeated it.

"Malik, are you aware that the existence of this prisoner was kept secret from the CIA?"

"Yes!" he hissed as he spun toward her. "It was kept secret from everyone! That was the reason for the edict. No one was to learn the truth."

"What truth was that?"

"You already know. That the Americans took a prisoner from Abbottabad."

She had finally brought Rashid to the point where she could ask the question that really mattered.

"Who was the prisoner?"

"I don't know. I never saw him, and I didn't dare ask who he was. Not that they would have told me."

Khalila pondered whether Rashidi was telling the truth. Her gut told her he was. But what else did he know?

"Where was the prisoner sent?"

"I can't tell you."

Khalila heard the faint sound of several suppressed MP7 shots, followed by two thuds in the hallway outside the study. Rashidi's eyes went to the door as a questioning look formed on his face, but Khalila continued.

"Actually, you *should* tell me," she said. "There are nine dead men on your estate tonight. Let's not make it ten."

"What?"

The study door burst open, revealing Harrison wielding his MP7, which he quickly brought to bear on Rashidi.

"As I was saying," Khalila said, "let's not make it ten dead men on your estate tonight. Where is the prisoner?"

Rashidi eyed Harrison, then the two agents lying on the floor outside the study. Rashidi's facial expression said it all; his resolve crumbled.

"He was sent to Failaka Island," he said. "There's a hidden detention facility on the eastern side, built and run by the Americans after 9/11."

"Is it still active?"

"I don't know. The Abbottabad prisoner was the last man we sent there. All others went elsewhere after that."

"Was there any paperwork for this arrangement?"

"Nothing. All verbal."

"One last question," Khalila said. "Who directed you to keep this a secret from the CIA?"

"I don't know who the men were. I hadn't interfaced with them before, but they knew the code words."

Khalila approached Rashidi and placed a hand on his shoulder. "Thank you, Malik. I know how difficult this was for you."

Then she lowered her other arm and flexed her wrist, ejecting a knife into her hand.

She jammed the knife into Rashidi's right kidney, inflicting an excruciating stab wound. His legs went weak from the pain and he dropped to his knees. Then she slit his throat.

He fell to the ground, clamping his hands around his neck in a futile attempt to stop the bleeding. Blood pulsed through his fingers until his body went still.

"What the hell, Khalila. Why did you kill him?"

"Because the moment we left tonight, he would have made a call, letting whoever orchestrated this cover-up know what we'd been told. We can't get to Failaka Island tonight, and I don't want whoever's there warned so they can pack up and scurry away. If whoever was taken from Abbottabad is still at that facility, I don't want him to slip through our fingers."

LANGLEY, VIRGINIA

PJ Rolow was furious.

Sitting beside Christine, the DDO's face had turned flush, his skin taking on a red hue. But Christine didn't have to look at him to know he was upset. He was doing an excellent job expressing it.

"I can defend your actions at the Seif," he said to Khalila's image on the conference room display. "They planned to kill you, and you defended yourself. But the outright murder of the head of a foreign intelligence agency—an ally to boot—was way out of bounds, even for you!"

They were seated in the director's conference room on the seventh floor, joined by Monroe Bryant and Tracey McFarland, with Khalila and Harrison on the other end of the VTC. Christine had kept the number of participants small due to the underlying topic—who had been taken prisoner at Abbottabad?

"We needed the information," Khalila replied calmly. "If I had left Rashidi alive, it would have been worthless. They could have evacuated the facility at Failaka Island before we got there."

"I don't disagree with your assessment," Rolow said. "But you should have asked first!"

"You would have said no."

"That's why you should have asked! There are other ways this could have been handled. We could have put a team in place before you met with Rashidi, to immediately follow whatever lead he provided. We could have avoided his death."

"It wouldn't have worked," Khalila said. "While we put together a team, whoever is orchestrating this deception would have relocated the prisoner."

"That's supposition," Rolow replied. "They would have had to infer the reason for your meeting with Iqbal at the Seif. After all these years, it's unlikely they would have made the connection."

"I disagree," she replied.

Rolow slammed his fist on the table. "You did *not* have authorization to kill Rashidi! You knew what my answer would be, so you deliberately didn't ask!"

"This isn't the first time I've bent the rules. You knew what you were dealing with when you sent me. Shall we discuss the issue in more detail at this meeting, starting with my true identity?"

If Khalila's question was meant to intimidate Rolow, it had the opposite effect.

Rolow's voice dropped a notch. "Let me make this crystal clear for you. If you ever do anything like this again, you will be dealt with appropriately. Do you understand?"

Khalila was about to offer a retort, but she clamped her mouth shut instead.

He glared at her for a moment, then leaned back in his chair, the color slowly fading from his face.

"I should probably recall both of you to Langley, but considering what you've learned, I think it's prudent to push forward immediately. We're already making arrangements for an insertion onto Failaka Island in two days. *Michigan* is in the area on a CIA-related mission and is being tasked to support."

Christine noticed Harrison's face brighten at the mention of the submarine carrying his former unit, a detachment of two SEAL platoons.

"You'll both participate in the insertion," Rolow said, "Harrison for obvious reasons and you for linguistic purposes. The SEAL detachment has some linguistic ability, but nothing as expansive as yours. Rendezvous information will be provided once the details are ironed out.

"Any questions?"

There were none, and Rolow turned to Christine to see if she had anything to add, which she didn't. Rolow had handled the matter fairly well, and she decided not to engage until after the delicate matter was further discussed, which was next on the agenda.

"That's all for now," Rolow said, then terminated the VTC.

After the display went black, Christine focused on damage control; how to deal with the repercussions of last night's events: killing the head of the Kuwait Security Service and fourteen other Kuwaiti agents.

"As you mentioned," she said as she looked at Rolow, "we have some grounds to work with. Khalila and Harrison were about to be eliminated by the first five agents. Those can be easily justified. Rashidi is the problem. Any ideas?"

Bryant answered, "I recommend we tie them together. We can paint Rashidi's death as revenge for issuing the order to kill Khalila and Harrison."

"It was a years-old latent order that got triggered," Rolow said, "but no one will know that. Everything points back to Rashidi, and we could take the stance that we made an example of him. Anyone who tries to eliminate agency officers will suffer the same fate."

"It's a good start," Christine agreed, "but I'm going to have to brief the administration today, without mentioning the real reason Khalila and Harrison were targeted. We'll have to carefully manage who learns that we're searching for a prisoner taken from Abbottabad."

"To ensure we're on the same page," McFarland said, "that list is just the four of us, Khalila and Harrison, plus the president and his chief of staff, correct?" Khalila had confirmed that no agency personnel in Kuwait had learned the true reason for their meeting at the Seif Palace or with Rashidi.

There was agreement around the table.

"Bring the other deputy directors and public affairs into the loop as required," Christine said, "under a cover story. Does self-defense at the Seif and revenge for Rashidi's death cover all the bases?"

"It should hold up," McFarland said.

"Good," Christine said. "What about Failaka Island? How do we keep *Michigan*'s involvement secure?"

"That's been taken care of," Rolow said. "We tasked them directly through the UUV communication channel. No one else knows. Failaka

Island is within their assigned waterspace, so they can execute the mission without additional Navy authorization or suspicion. The SEALs won't know the real reason for their operation, although we'll have to manage things if the Abbottabad prisoner is actually at Failaka Island."

Rolow glanced at Bryant. "Monroe and I will plan the mission details ourselves. We'll need to lay things out carefully, including how to handle the critical issue—what do we do if the prisoner is there? Does the team simply verify that fact and leave, or do they extract him? If we extract him, what do we do with him?"

"There are several sticky issues we need to work through," Bryant added. "We'll brief you on the plan and get your concurrence to proceed by tomorrow evening."

Christine nodded her understanding.

McFarland spoke next. "There are two issues I have updates on. The first is related to the effort to verify the body buried in the Arabian Sea is Osama bin Laden's. Arrangements have been made for a deep submergence vessel and its support ship. In two days, it should be on station above the location where bin Laden was supposedly buried. A portable DNA analysis kit and technician will be aboard the ship, so the analysis of the sample can take place immediately and under direct CIA control. That brings up the question—who's going to be there?"

Christine canvassed the three other persons at the table. Rolow and Bryant would be tied up preparing for and then executing the Failaka Island mission, as would McFarland, providing analysis support. It appeared that Christine had the least pressurized schedule. After briefing the president tomorrow morning, she could board a flight to the Persian Gulf.

She hadn't really thought about the issue until this moment, then realized it was the right answer. She wanted to be there when the DNA sample results were displayed on the machine. No secondhand reports.

"I'll go," she said.

"I'll have Becky," McFarland said, referring to Deputy Director for Support Becky Rock, "make your travel arrangements."

McFarland added, "I have one more update, this one concerning the investigation into Secretary Verbeck. We're analyzing the UUV data but have found nothing of interest to date. Of particular relevance, however, is that her maiden name is Snyder. Her brother is billionaire Dan Snyder."

McFarland paused to let the information sink in. Christine knew that Brenda came from a rich and influential family but hadn't realized that she and Dan Snyder were siblings.

"We've looked into Dan Snyder's business dealings, and there are several lucrative ones in the Persian Gulf, our area of interest. No smoking gun yet, but we're digging into the details."

"Good work, Tracey. Hopefully, we can make sense of the SecNav-UUV issue soon."

"That's all I've got for now," McFarland said.

As their meeting neared the end, Christine's thoughts returned to their VTC and the fiery exchange between Rolow and Khalila. Until a few minutes ago, Christine hadn't known that Khalila Dufour wasn't the woman's real name. Rolow had withheld that information. But that probably wasn't all that unusual within the agency. Still, she was curious.

"What is Khalila's true identity?"

Rolow replied, "That discussion will take a while. I'll put an appointment on your calendar."

After Christine agreed, Rolow asked, "Is there anything else you need?"

Christine shook her head, then Rolow departed, along with Bryant.

When only the two women remained in the conference room, McFarland said, "He's not going to tell you who Khalila is. You're not the first director who's asked, and he's avoided answering all these years."

"Do *you* know who she is?" Christine asked.

"Nope. I can't access her file."

Christine was surprised at the admission. "Not even the deputy director for analysis can crack the file open?"

"I don't know where it is. It's not with the other personnel files. It's hidden somewhere, and it doesn't come up under a search for Khalila Dufour."

"You've been snooping?"

McFarland nodded. "Rolow treats her differently from the other field officers, so I wondered why. Not being able to locate her file adds to the intrigue."

She leaned back in her chair, eyeing Christine. "There's one more topic I need to discuss with you," she said. "It's about the SecNav investigation. We've discovered one other rather interesting fact about Brenda Verbeck." She leaned toward Christine. "She dated Rolow for five years."

"You've got to be kidding."

"Not at all. You think he would have mentioned it."

"I agree. Have you discussed this with him yet?"

McFarland shook her head. "I wanted to talk with you first, see how you wanted to proceed."

"What's the normal protocol for something like this?"

"Technically, nothing is required. Rolow's not under suspicion for anything; it's more of an oddity at this point. But someone is going to have to pop the question to him—ask him why he hasn't mentioned the relationship and find out what he knows about her. Do you want me to handle it, or do you want to talk with him?"

Christine considered the issue, then replied, "I'll talk with him." She stood. "Right now, as a matter of fact."

"That might not be a good idea," McFarland said. "He's in a mood."

Christine smiled. "That's the best time to engage."

She walked down the hallway to Rolow's office. His door was closed, so she knocked, then entered after his acknowledgment. He was typing on his computer keyboard, his eyes fixed on the display.

"Can you wait a second?" he asked. "I'm dealing with something urgent."

"That'll work," Christine replied sarcastically. "I'll start talking, and you can pay more attention when I say something important."

Rolow glanced at her before returning his attention to the display. He hadn't picked up on her tone.

"After you left, Tracey provided an additional update on the SecNav investigation . . ."

"Uh-huh," Rolow said as he kept typing.

"It was an interesting discovery concerning one of Verbeck's previous romantic relationships."

Rolow's fingers stopped typing. He looked up at her. "And?"

"Why haven't you mentioned that you dated Brenda for five years?"

He leaned back in his chair. "Because it's not relevant."

"That's not how this is supposed to work. You provide the data, and we do the assessment."

"So, now I'm guilty in some way because I dated Brenda? Does that mean that anyone who's had a past relationship with a suspect is guilty by association?"

Before Christine could answer, he asked, "What about you and Mixell? You, Harrison, and Mixell are childhood chums. Best buddies. Given your previous relationship with Mixell, why aren't you under suspicion every time he pops onto our radar?"

Rolow had a point. Her close friendship with Mixell was a delicate issue, considering current events. But she decided to ignore Rolow's question.

"What happened between you?"

Rolow smiled, recognizing Christine's deflection of his question. "I found her to be a bit too . . . conniving."

Christine laughed. "Too conniving for the CIA's deputy director for operations?"

"Brenda is a brilliant woman, her intellect overshadowed only by her ambition. She's bent on climbing the rungs of power, always working on one scheme or another. To Brenda, relationships are merely a means to an end. She was more interested in what I could do for her professionally than what I had to offer as a boyfriend or husband. Regarding our relationship, there's nothing noteworthy that I can recall. But if you must know the details, her favorite color is pink and she loves strawberry ice cream. She's really good in bed, and her favorite position is—"

"Okay, you can stop," Christine interjected.

There was a tense moment between them before Christine asked, "Is there anything *noteworthy* that you recall about Brenda?"

"Not at the moment."

"If you do, let us know."

"Of course. That was always the plan." Rolow smiled again. "Is there anything else?"

"Not at the moment," Christine replied.

40

SALMIYA, KUWAIT

Harrison stepped from the bathroom into the small bedroom, his hair still damp from his shower. It was warm in the room—it was still over a hundred degrees in the city even though night had fallen—and he wore only a pair of shorts. Khalila was likewise skimpily dressed after her shower, wearing a thin white spaghetti-strap shirt that contrasted with her olive skin, plus a matching pair of cotton gym shorts. She was sitting on a wide window ledge, her long legs drawn up to her chest and her arms wrapped around her shins, staring at the nightlife traversing the busy street below.

Khalila had been unusually quiet after her confrontation with Rolow during their VTC with Langley. As she stared at the city lights, she seemed lost in her thoughts.

"You should move away from the window," Harrison said.

"I'm fine," Khalila said. "It's bullet-resistant glass."

They were in a flat on the sixth floor of the safe house. Tonight, the facility was packed with every paramilitary operations officer that Ashour could get his hands on, and Khalila and Harrison had agreed to share a room, as they typically did while traveling. Things appeared calm at the moment, with both intelligence organizations—the CIA and Kuwait Security Service—taking a pause from the previous night's bloodshed, assessing how best to proceed. Not taking any chances, Ashour had reinforced the safe house, in case the KSS had discovered its location and decided to take retribution.

Harrison sat opposite her on the window ledge, checking out the scene below before focusing on Khalila. He had to admit, as his eyes followed her long black hair falling across her shoulders and chest to the thin cotton shirt and shorts clinging to her body, that she was quite attractive. If only her personality were as pleasant as her physique.

Before he turned in for the night, he wanted to thank Khalila for what she had done. Even though he didn't fully trust her, she had come through for him—twice. In the warehouse in Alexandria a few months ago, Mixell had him pinned down, preparing for the kill shot. Khalila had moved into the open, drawing Mixell's fire while Harrison regrouped, and she had taken two bullets. The previous night, she had helped him again. As Iqbal had stated, she could have walked away, leaving Harrison to his fate. But she had engaged instead, taking on five armed men.

Khalila must have felt his eyes on her because she shifted her gaze to him.

"I want to thank you for what you did at the Seif," he said. "You didn't have to."

"Actually," she replied, "I did. Once it became clear that Rashidi had the information we needed, you became indispensable. There was no way Rolow was going to authorize an operation involving Rashidi and assign additional personnel, so you were all I had."

Harrison suddenly realized that Khalila had planned to kill Rashidi all along. Gaining an audience with him had been easy, as she had predicted. But after slashing his throat, there was no way she could have fought her way out. That's where he had come in, clearing the path for her.

"Well, I'm glad you clarified that. For a moment, I thought you were a genuinely caring person looking out for your partner."

"Not really," she said as she turned away, staring out the window again.

Harrison wasn't sure what to make of the situation or of Khalila—whether she had simply used him or they made a great team. Either way, her ruthless nature left him uneasy.

Fatigue was setting in—they'd been up most of the previous night and all day—and Khalila must have been exhausted as well, but something was keeping her up.

"You should get some sleep," he said.

"It's difficult for me," she said as she stared out the window, "especially in places and times like this." She turned back to Harrison. "I envy you. Sometimes I watch you while you sleep. You don't wrestle with demons. You go to sleep each night knowing you have done the right thing: fighting to protect your country."

Demons. Khalila had provided an opening. An opportunity to learn more about her—how she ended up working for the CIA, or even a clue to who she really was.

"Tell me about your demons."

"They do not concern you."

"You're my partner, so I'd say they *do* concern me."

She stared at him for a long moment, and he saw the same glint in her eyes that he had noticed in Sochi, when they had struck their original deal to work together—that she wouldn't kill him if he learned too much about her, as long as he kept it to himself.

"Sometimes," she said, "I don't know if it's revenge I seek or atonement."

Harrison often wondered what motivated Khalila. She was a driven woman—that was clear. But for what purpose?

"Did you lose someone important, and that's the reason you work for the CIA?"

"You could say that."

Harrison examined her hands. She wore no rings, no medallion around her neck, no token from a loved one she had lost.

Before he had a chance to inquire further, she said, "This conversation ends now."

41

SALMIYA, KUWAIT

Jake Harrison returned to the safe house room after having breakfast with Marzouq Ashour in the common area, expecting to find Khalila still asleep. Instead, she was almost fully dressed, wearing a purple blouse—short-sleeved again, since knives were strapped to both forearms—and a dark gray business suit, with the jacket lying on the bed beside a coordinating gray-and-purple headscarf.

"Where are we going today?" Harrison asked.

"*We* aren't going anywhere. I have a meeting today with individuals who would not take kindly to your presence."

"Is that because I'm American, Caucasian, or a former Navy SEAL?"

"Yes, on all counts."

"Who's the meeting with?"

"None of your business. I have critical contacts to maintain, and an opportunity presented itself."

"How long will the meeting take?"

"Why do you care?" she asked as she slipped into her suit jacket.

"I just got word about the Failaka mission. We're taking a helicopter ride to *Michigan* tonight. We head out from the safe house at 7 p.m."

"I'll be back by then," she said as she wrapped the hijab around her hair and neck, leaving her face exposed.

"Is this a risky meeting?" he asked, noting that Khalila hadn't yet tested the knives strapped to her forearms, as she usually did after donning her suit jacket. She also lacked the tension she had exuded prior to meeting with the Kuwait Security Service agents and Rashidi.

"There is always risk in these types of meetings, considering the people I deal with."

Harrison's curiosity was piqued. That Khalila was well connected was obvious, and it made sense that she had to nurture those relationships, instead of engaging only when she needed assistance. Harrison's thoughts went to the conversation they'd had on the flight to Syria, where she had admitted that she was essentially a double agent, providing information to both sides. He wondered, who—or what—was the other side?

Perhaps, if he could get a look at whoever she was meeting . . .

"Need a ride, or is Mussan driving you?"

"Neither. I'm on my own today," she said as she tucked the scarf under her blouse collar.

"Be careful," he said, adding a grin. "If anything goes wrong, I won't be there to save you this time."

Khalila smiled. "I'll keep that in mind."

As she moved toward the door, Harrison surveyed her preparations. She carried a purse, but had left her pistol behind; she was armed with only the two knives.

He wished her luck as she left. After the bedroom door closed, he threw on his shoulder harness and pistol and a light sport jacket, then hurried to the stairs, descending to the ground floor. He cracked the door open as Khalila stepped from the lobby onto the sidewalk.

He moved to the front door, watching through a sidelight as she hailed a cab passing by. As the cab pulled back into traffic, Harrison exited the safe house, immediately raising his hand to flag down one of the other cabs passing by. One stopped and Harrison jumped in, providing a movie-worthy quote.

"Follow that cab!"

The driver didn't bat an eye, as if this were an everyday occurrence, pulling quickly back into traffic, matching the speed and turns of the lead car.

They were soon back in the center of Kuwait City, following Khalila until her cab pulled into the entrance concourse of the Al Hamra Tower, the tallest curved concrete skyscraper in the world, rising over 1,300 feet. Khalila waited in the taxi, and Harrison instructed his driver to pull over to the other side of the street.

A few minutes later, a black limousine stopped at the tower entrance and four Arab men emerged, each wearing the white dishdasha robe traditionally worn by many Middle Eastern men. Harrison recognized one of the men immediately—Abdallah bin Laden, Osama's eldest son.

Khalila emerged from her taxi and walked toward the four men. Harrison pulled his cell phone from his jacket pocket and started a video recording, capturing the occurrence and the four men's faces.

When Khalila reached them, she extended her hand to Abdallah, and they shook and exchanged greetings. Abdallah smiled and seemed pleased to see her. Khalila turned to greet the other three men, but didn't extend her hand. Each man placed a hand over his heart and bowed his head slightly in respect.

Abdallah and Khalila headed into the Al Hamra Tower lobby, walking side by side as they talked, while the three other men followed. Harrison recorded the interaction until they disappeared into the lobby interior.

As Harrison slid his cell phone back into his jacket pocket, he wondered whether the meeting with Abdallah was coincidental or somehow related to their mission to Kuwait. That Khalila seemed driven to determine who was taken prisoner at Abbottabad was obvious. But now, he wondered why.

If the prisoner turned out to be Osama bin Laden, that information would be incredibly valuable. In the wrong hands, it would also be quite dangerous.

42

ARABIAN SEA

Christine O'Connor's hair fluttered in the brisk wind as the forty-meter-long ship sped through the choppy water. She was seated in the flying bridge of a CIA-owned, Spanish-built superyacht capable of sixty-plus knots. Joining her on the bridge was her four-man security detail, doubled from its normal size due to her overseas journey.

After departing Reagan National Airport, her flight had landed in Mumbai, India, where she had boarded the high-tech and speedy CIA boat waiting at a nearby pier. The yacht was now on an intercept course for another ship in the Arabian Sea, and it wasn't long before their target appeared on the horizon: the black-hulled research vessel *Atlantis*.

Atlantis was an oceanographic research ship operated by the Woods Hole Oceanographic Institution. More important, she was the host vessel of DSV *Alvin*, a deep-ocean research submersible owned by the U.S. Navy. *Atlantis* and *Alvin* had been chartered by the CIA for the critically sensitive and challenging effort to obtain a sample of Osama bin Laden's body for DNA analysis.

The CIA yacht eased off on its speed as it angled into a parallel course with the 274-foot-long research ship, preparing to transfer Christine and her protective detail aboard. They were escorted to a transfer boat, which made the short trip across the water, and she was soon in the research vessel's wardroom, where she was greeted by the ship's captain and *Alvin*'s operations officer.

After the introductory pleasantries, they got down to business, beginning with a high-level review of *Alvin*'s upcoming mission. It was classified at the highest level, and no one aboard *Atlantis* knew what they were sending the deep-submergence vehicle down to take a sample of. However, *Alvin*'s team seemed prepared for a rather straightforward dive, sample collection, and return to the surface. Then *Alvin*'s operations officer, Brian Humm, provided a dose of bad news.

"A storm is moving in," he said, "which means we're not going to be able to launch tomorrow morning as planned. If we don't go tonight, we'll have to wait several days. Do you have a preference?"

"Sooner would be better," Christine replied.

"We'll plan for tonight, then, as soon as we're ready."

"Also," he said, "we have an issue with your stipulation that only the pilot be aboard for the mission."

Langley had requested that only the DSV pilot, and not a full three-member team, descend with *Alvin*, to minimize the number of people involved who could piece together what was being sampled.

"We normally have two other personnel aboard to handle ancillary issues or if the pilot is incapacitated for some reason. At a minimum, one person must accompany the pilot during the dive."

As Christine considered the request, Humm offered, "One option, Miss O'Connor, is you could do the dive."

Humm went on to explain that the pilot was typically accompanied by scientists, not DSV copilots, and with a short walkthrough of emergency procedures, she would know enough to bring *Alvin* to the surface in an emergency. Also, as far as how dangerous the dive was, Humm assured her there was little to worry about. *Alvin* had made hundreds of dives, many to deeper depths than they'd be going down to tonight.

After contemplating the matter, Christine agreed. The dive would certainly be more interesting than waiting aboard *Atlantis*. Plus, how often would she get a chance to dive to almost ten thousand feet beneath the ocean's surface?

"Great," Humm said. "We'll arrive at the specified location and be ready to dive shortly after sunset."

43

PERSIAN GULF

A deep red glow was fading from the horizon as a helicopter beat a steady path east across the Persian Gulf. Beneath the Sikorsky MH-60R Seahawk, the vast expanse of black water was filled with intermittent white dots, marking the presence of merchant ships transiting the vital waterway. Inside the helicopter cabin, Jake Harrison sat beside Khalila Dufour as she stared out the side window, her eyes fixed on the gradually dwindling lights as the helicopter headed toward a dark patch in the ocean.

Three hours earlier, Khalila had emerged from her daylong meeting at the Al Hamra Tower. Harrison had decided to hang out nearby before returning to the safe house, grabbing lunch across the street, keeping an eye on the tower exit. It had taken all day, but Khalila finally exited the building, again walking beside Abdallah bin Laden, whom she bade farewell beside his awaiting limousine. Once again, she extended her hand and Abdallah shook it, although it seemed to Harrison that he let his touch linger, which was unusual given the general prohibition against men touching women in public in Kuwait and other Muslim countries. Men would shake hands with a woman only if she initiated the handshake; otherwise, the greeting between opposite sexes was hands-off.

Harrison wondered about Khalila's personal life, about which he knew nothing. Was there something going on between Khalila and Abdallah? Abdallah seemed interested, and Khalila was a good match for the tall and influential bin Laden: beautiful, self-assured, and almost the same height as he was. It wouldn't have been the first time a woman had used her looks to gain an advantage, and from a CIA officer perspective, there was no better group in the Middle East to weasel one's way into than the bin Laden family.

The critical question, Harrison considered, was which side did Khalila truly work for? Did she sit in the meeting all day and simply absorb information, or had she provided data that Abdallah and his companions found interesting? Perhaps information on the potential survival of Abdallah's father?

Harrison finally understood the issues the DDO must be dealing with regarding Khalila. Whose side was she truly on? Without knowing for sure, he couldn't afford to cut her loose. She had excellent contacts in the Middle East, plus, with direct access to the bin Laden family, she was an incredibly potent asset.

A change to the beat of the helicopter's rotors and the aircraft's sudden descent announced their arrival at the transfer point. Harrison peered through the window, as did Khalila, searching the ocean for the silhouette of a submarine against the dark water, eventually spotting the hazy outline on the surface.

The Seahawk slowed to a hover fifty feet above the submarine, the downdraft from its blades sending circular ripples across the ocean surface. Two crewmen in the cabin helped Harrison and Khalila each don a harness. Khalila went first, attaching to a cable, accompanied by her duffle bag of personal items and clothes.

Khalila was lowered from the side of the helicopter, the metal cable paying out slowly, the duffle bag swaying in the downdraft as the helicopter crew aimed to land her in the submarine's small Bridge cockpit atop the sail. The submarine's Lookout grabbed the duffle bag as it swung by, then pulled hard on the lanyard, guiding Khalila into the Bridge. Harrison went next, joining Khalila and two officers, one of whom was the submarine's Commanding Officer.

"Welcome aboard *Michigan*," Captain Murray Wilson shouted over the roar of the helicopter rotor.

As the helicopter pulled up and veered back toward the coast, Wilson dropped down into the Bridge trunk and descended the ladder into the Control Room. Khalila and Harrison followed.

The submarine's Control Room was rigged for black, illuminated only by the small indicating lights on the various panels. Wilson led the way around the Conn, where an officer was turning slowly on the periscope, into the submarine's Battle Management Center, where his crew conducted Tomahawk mission planning and coordinated SEAL operations. The BMC was rigged for low-level light and transitioned to normal lighting once Wilson arrived with the two CIA officers.

Although *Michigan* was built as a ballistic missile submarine, it was a far different ship today from when it was launched in the last century. With the implementation of the Strategic Offensive Reductions Treaty, the Navy had converted the four oldest Ohio class submarines into guided missile and special warfare platforms. Twenty-two of *Michigan*'s twenty-four missile tubes had been outfitted with seven-pack Tomahawk launchers for a total of 154 missiles, with the remaining two tubes providing access to two Dry Deck Shelters attached to the submarine's Missile Deck.

For this deployment, one shelter carried a SEAL Delivery Vehicle—a minisub used to transport Navy SEALs miles underwater for clandestine operations—while the other shelter contained two rigid-hull inflatable boats. Also aboard *Michigan* were two platoons of Navy SEALs, ready should their services be required, along with sixty tons of munitions stored in two of *Michigan*'s missile tubes: small arms, grenade launchers, limpet mines . . . anything a SEAL team might need.

The Battle Management Center was crammed with twenty-five tactical consoles, with twelve on starboard arranged in four rows facing aft. Mounted on the aft bulkhead was a sixty-inch display. Waiting in the BMC, in addition to several members of *Michigan*'s crew, were a dozen SEALs. Harrison was greeted by the men; he knew almost all of them since this had been his last unit before retiring only six months ago.

One man he didn't know was the unit's new commanding officer, replacing John McNeil, who had retired a month after Harrison.

Murray Wilson introduced Commander Jon Peters.

"I'm sorry to hear about McNeil," Peters said. "We served together in Afghanistan. He was a good man." He stepped closer. "If you catch the guy who did this, make it painful."

The SEAL commander's attention turned to Khalila, who had already received plenty of stares from the guys in the BMC. Introductions were exchanged, and everyone took a seat on the starboard side of the room, facing the display mounted on the wall.

As they waited for the operations brief to begin, Harrison felt the deck tilt downward as *Michigan* submerged, returning to the ocean depths. Lieutenant Tracey Noviello, the Officer-in-Charge of one of the two platoons, moved to the display.

Noviello kicked off the mission brief. "As you're aware, we've been tasked with infiltrating a compound on Failaka Island. The mission is to gain access and determine who is being held in the facility. If one of the detainees is the target of interest, we'll extract him. Jake Harrison or his partner will identify the high-value target if he's there."

Upon returning to the safe house after surveilling Khalila at the Al Hamra Tower, Harrison had been handed a communication from Langley. It was intentionally vague, instructing Harrison and Khalila to extract the man at the facility if he was the high-value target. If he was anyone else, they were to simply make note of his identity and return to *Michigan*. If the captive was, in fact, the HVT, Harrison was directed to take all possible measures to conceal his identity while aboard *Michigan*, and additional instructions would be provided regarding where to take him.

Noviello energized the bulkhead display with a remote in his hand. A nautical chart of the Persian Gulf appeared, zooming in on the northern tip.

"The launch point is five nautical miles east of Failaka Island. Two four-man teams will head ashore, one per RHIB, with Harrison joining one team and his partner, Khalila Dufour, joining the other. I'll lead one team, while Senior Chief Burkhardt will lead the other. The mission will occur tonight, as soon as *Michigan* is in position."

Noviello pressed the remote control, and a satellite image of Failaka Island appeared on the display. He started with a basic background of the island.

"Failaka Island is Kuwaiti territory, located twelve miles from the mainland. Prior to the 1990 Iraqi invasion, Failaka Island was populated with over two thousand residents, located primarily in the village of Az Zawr on the northwest side of the island. When the Iraqis invaded, they expelled the island's residents and used Failaka's buildings for target practice. The island's infrastructure was significantly damaged and has not yet been fully repaired. Although some residents have returned, many of the homes remain empty. The west side of the island has regained some of its vitality, with the establishment of a beach resort. The east side of the island remains abandoned, except for one location."

Noviello increased the magnification of the satellite image. "There's an active facility, built mostly underground, on the east side of the island. Due to this being a short-fused mission, we don't have much recon on the island—only two days' worth of satellite images.

"What we do know is that it's a guarded facility." A red circle appeared around the end of a road that disappeared into the landscape as it headed underground. "As far as we can tell, there is only one access point, with ingress and egress occurring only at night. A single van arrives at about 2 a.m. each day, departing before sunrise, originating from and returning to Az Zawr near the ferry docks. This is most likely a supply run. As I mentioned, we have only two days' worth of intel, so we don't know if this is a consistent daily routine."

Another click of the remote control and the display shifted from the satellite image to a low-level, daytime view of the island, showing a road angling downward, dead-ending before two large metal doors leading to an underground facility.

"We were able to get some drone footage of the facility entrance. You can see a guard posted on each side of the road, with a small guardhouse on the left containing the door controls.

"Regarding ingress, Failaka Island is surrounded mostly by a sandy beach, so ingress won't be difficult. Once ashore, we'll have a half-mile trek to the facility. The goal is to be in position by 2 a.m., when the van arrives and the entrance doors are opened."

Noviello looked to Commander Peters to see if he had anything to add.

"As Lieutenant Noviello stated," Peters said, "we haven't had much time to plan this mission. Sheakoski, Keller, Hacker, and Harrison will join Noviello in the first fire team, while Senior Chief Burkhardt will lead Pickering, Narehood, Meyer, and Dufour. You've got two hours to work out the details."

44

RESEARCH VESSEL *ATLANTIS*

Bright white lights illuminated the aft deck of *Atlantis* as Christine O'Connor climbed down through the circular hatch into *Alvin*'s seven-foot-diameter titanium sphere. Already inside was Ken Hillsley, *Alvin*'s pilot for tonight's mission, conducting prelaunch checks. There wasn't much for Christine to do as she examined the components inside the small sphere she would call home for the next few hours. Packed with electronic equipment and five porthole windows, the visibility in the recently refurbished submersible was an improvement over the three windows in *Alvin*'s previous sphere, Hillsley explained.

With its new, slightly larger, three-inch-thick titanium sphere, *Alvin* could dive for up to ten hours to a depth of 6,500 meters—over four miles—and, most famously, had been used to explore the wreckage of RMS *Titanic* in 1986. Launched from *Atlantis*, the DSV had carried Dr. Robert Ballard and two others down to the remnants of the ship that had sunk in 1912 after striking an iceberg on her maiden voyage across the North Atlantic Ocean.

Equipped with an array of sensors, including four video cameras and several sonars, *Alvin* also sported a sophisticated navigation system using a fiber-optic gyrocompass, which would prove critical to guiding *Alvin* to the location where bin Laden's body was expected. The submersible featured two robotic arms that could be fitted with mission-specific sampling and experimental gear. The modifications required for tonight's task had already been completed.

As Hillsley prepared for launch, Christine reviewed the emergency procedures she had been briefed on, which weren't very challenging. If *Alvin* became disabled, the outer cladding of the submersible could be discarded via controls inside the vessel. The titanium sphere, containing Christine and Hillsley, would then rise to the surface.

The prelaunch checks were completed satisfactorily, and the sphere's hatch was shut and sealed. Christine felt the lurch as the hydraulic piston attached to the top of *Alvin* lifted it from the ship's deck. The DSV rose slowly in the air, toward the top of the A-frame Launch and Recovery System (LARS)—massive metal arms rising from each side of *Atlantis*, connected together at the top.

Once *Alvin* completed its ascent, it was locked into place. The DSV was now suspended above the ship, ready for the next phase. Brian Humm gave the order, and two massive pistons on each side of the LARS tilted the A-frame outboard, swinging *Alvin* into position over the ocean. The hydraulic ram above them reversed, lowering *Alvin* into the water where it was released from the piston. The DSV bobbed on the surface while the cable to *Atlantis* was detached.

When the tether was disconnected, Hillsley turned to Christine. It would take ninety minutes, he explained, to reach the ocean bottom. With no connection to *Atlantis*, they would be on their own until they returned to the surface.

He opened the ballast tank vents, and *Alvin* began its descent.

45

USS *MICHIGAN*

Three hours after their operations brief, as *Michigan* hovered at periscope depth five miles off the coast of Failaka Island, Harrison and Khalila stood on the second deck in the submarine's Missile Compartment, each with their SEAL team. Harrison was outside Missile Tube Two with Lieutenant Tracey Noviello and the other three SEALs in his fire team—Sheakoski, Keller, and Hacker—while Khalila waited beside tube One with Senior Chief Russ Burkhardt and the other SEALs in his fire team: Pickering, Narehood, and Meyer.

Each wore a black dive suit and rubber booties and was outfitted with fins and a face mask, plus a rebreather instead of scuba tanks since they'd be underwater only a short time until they were aboard the RHIBs. Each SEAL and CIA officer also carried a waterproof rucksack, containing the weapons and other equipment they'd need for the mission.

Although both RHIBs were stored in the Dry Deck Shelter attached to Missile Tube Two, Senior Chief Burkhardt's team would enter tube One. With two RHIBs in one shelter, there was insufficient room for all eight SEALs, plus Harrison and Khalila. Harrison's team would extract one RHIB while Burkhardt's team exited the other shelter, then grabbed the second boat.

Harrison and his fire team stepped through the circular hatch in the side of Missile Tube Two. Noviello shut the hatch, sealing the five men inside the seven-foot-diameter tube. Harrison led the way, climbing a steel ladder into the Dry Deck Shelter, bathed in diffuse red light.

The Dry Deck Shelter was a conglomeration of three chambers: a spherical hyperbaric chamber at the forward end to treat injured divers, a spherical transfer trunk in the middle, which Harrison had just entered, and a cylindrical hangar section where the two RHIBs were stowed. The hangar was divided into two sections by a Plexiglas shield dropping halfway down from the top, with the RHIBs on one side and hangar controls on the other.

The five men donned their fins, masks, and rebreathers, and Noviello rendered the *okay* hand signal to the Navy diver, already stationed in the DDS, who operated the controls.

Dark water surged into the shelter from vents beneath them, pooling at their feet and rising rapidly. The hangar was soon flooded down, except for an air pocket on the other side of the Plexiglas shield, where the diver operated the shelter. There was a low rumbling sound as the circular hatch at the end of the hangar moved slowly open to the latched position. Harrison and the SEALs hauled one of the RHIBs from the shelter onto the submarine's Missile Deck, then connected a tether to it from a shelter rail and activated the first compressed air cartridge.

As the RHIB expanded, Sheakoski and Keller swam aft along the Missile Deck and opened the hatch to a locker in the submarine's superstructure. They retrieved an outboard motor and attached it to the RHIB, then activated the second air cartridge. The RHIB fully inflated, rising toward the surface. Sheakoski and Keller followed the boat up while Senior Chief Burkhardt's team pulled the second RHIB from the shelter and duplicated the process.

Sheakoski returned a few moments later, rendering the *okay* hand signal, as did Pickering from Burkhardt's team. The two SEALs disconnected the RHIB tether lines from the shelter and swam toward the surface.

Harrison was the last to climb aboard his RHIB, as was Khalila into hers. The outboard engines were already running, but barely audible. Their position updated on Keller's handheld GPS display, then he shifted the outboard into gear and pointed the RHIB toward their insertion point on Failaka Island. Senior Chief Burkhardt's RHIB followed.

46

ALVIN

Alvin descended through the darkness, continuing its trek toward the ocean floor nine thousand feet below the water's surface. Inside the submersible, it was quiet at first, the only sound being the hum of the carbon dioxide scrubbers purifying the air, until Hillsley turned on music, which was now playing softly in the background. The external lights were kept off during the descent, saving the vehicle's battery power until they reached the bottom. What they were searching for hadn't been fully explained to Hillsley—and wasn't going to be—although Christine wondered if he had deduced the reason for their mission. After all, bin Laden's burial in the Arabian Sea was public knowledge.

If Hillsley suspected, he didn't let on, spending the time instead monitoring *Alvin*'s equipment, including its scrubbers and oxygen bleed, ensuring the air inside the sphere was properly maintained. Everything was functioning properly, and Hillsley eventually struck up a conversation, during which Christine learned a great deal about *Alvin* and the fascinating sea life surrounding them.

The first two hundred meters of their descent was through the euphotic zone, also called the sunlight layer, where enough light penetrated the water to support photosynthesis and where the majority of aquatic organisms lived. The light outside faded, becoming greenish at first, gradually transitioning to dark blue. After ten minutes, they entered the dysphotic or twilight zone, where only a small amount of light penetrated, and Christine watched as numerous glowing bioluminescent animals floated past *Alvin*'s portholes.

Darkness then closed in as *Alvin* entered the aphotic—or midnight—zone, devoid of natural light. Inside the submersible, the only light came from blinking LEDs built into the sophisticated electronics. Outside the submersible, occasional greenish flashes were emitted by small fluorescent marine animals disturbed by *Alvin*'s descent through their realm.

It was cold inside the sphere; the temperature had plummeted due to the near-freezing seawater surrounding them. A chill set in, and Christine put on a sweater and pair of jogging pants she had borrowed from one of the crew members aboard *Atlantis*, following the advice of *Alvin*'s operations officer.

As they descended, Hillsley monitored *Alvin*'s sonar display for the sonic beacon in bin Laden's body bag. To conserve power, the beacon emitted a pulse only once every hour. The pulse had been detected by the sonar equipment aboard *Atlantis*, so they knew it was functioning and they were in the right spot. Still, even a small angular error in a nine-thousand-foot descent could place *Alvin* far from their objective once it reached the ocean bottom.

About halfway down, Hillsley picked up a pulse from the beacon and made a slight adjustment in their downward trajectory, energizing one of *Alvin*'s seven thrusters for a few seconds.

As predicted, it took ninety minutes to complete the descent. As they approached the ocean bottom, Hillsley turned off the music and energized additional equipment, including its external lights, illuminating a flat, featureless, sediment-covered bottom out to a range of about thirty feet.

Christine peered out one of the five viewports; there were three in the forward portion of the sphere, each about seventeen inches in diameter, with a smaller, twelve-inch-diameter portal on each side. Additionally, there were three small displays mounted to the equipment racks, connected to cameras mounted to *Alvin*'s exterior.

Hillsley set *Alvin* to hover ten feet above the ocean floor. While they awaited the next sonic pulse from bin Laden's body bag, they searched the immediate area, doing a slow spin at their current location. Hillsley examined the results from three different sonars: two seafloor profilers, plus a dual-frequency scanner that could detect objects buried down to forty feet beneath the ocean floor.

About the time they finished searching their current location, *Alvin* received another ping from the sonic beacon, coming from a bearing of zero-one-one. Hillsley set *Alvin* to the northerly course, proceeding slowly. Although the submersible was capable of a speedy two knots, Hillsley explained that they typically cruised along the bottom at only one-half knot to preserve battery power. As they traveled toward the object, Christine directed Hillsley to de-energize *Alvin's* cameras. She wanted no recording of what was about to occur.

They crept slowly above the ocean floor, with Hillsley monitoring the three sonar displays, until an object was located almost directly ahead—a small, gently sloping protuberance on the otherwise flat bottom. Hillsley shifted the fore-aft thrusters to reverse, stopping *Alvin* just before the bump.

Alvin was well equipped for tonight's task, with a tube corer in one of the submersible's claws, although it was much smaller than the standard corers used by Hillsley in the past, since its purpose was to take a small tissue sample once it pierced the body bag. But first, they had to clear a path to whatever lay beneath the ocean sediment.

Hillsley activated a suction tube used for taking sediment or organic samples, set to discharge instead of suction. In its current configuration, it worked like an underwater blower, clearing the sediment away as Hillsley moved it back and forth with *Alvin's* other manipulator. A black speck beneath the sediment appeared, growing larger as more material was blown away. The intense sea pressure had compressed the plastic bag around its contents, and the outline of a body became evident, lying atop a set of chains and beside a spherical object that must have been the sonic beacon.

Hillsley asked no questions as he prepared the corer in the manipulator's right claw. He turned to Christine, who simply nodded. He inserted the corer through the bag into the corpse, then withdrew the corer with its sample and placed it into a bio box staged in the submersible's storage bin.

Once the bin was secured, Hillsley dropped several hundred pounds of iron weights from the DSV to begin the ascent. As they rose, *Alvin's* lights illuminated the body bag until it faded into the darkness.

47

FAILAKA ISLAND, KUWAIT

The two RHIBs headed toward shore, with Harrison's boat in the lead. As he scanned the dark horizon, the beach appeared in the distance. Keller identified their insertion point—a dark strip of sand—and adjusted course.

The SEALs in both RHIBs, along with Harrison, had shed their swim gear and donned bullet-resistant tactical vests, plus helmets with built-in communications and attached night vision goggles, arming themselves with MP7s with attached suppressors. Khalila had also shed her swim gear, but instead of donning tactical gear, she wore the same pants, shirt, and headscarf she had worn when she boarded *Michigan*, but with soft armor beneath her blouse.

After the mission brief aboard *Michigan* earlier, Harrison and Khalila had joined the squad of SEALs in the Battle Management Center while the submarine moved into position, devising a plan incorporating Harrison's and Khalila's participation. While reviewing the reconnaissance in more detail, it had become evident that although the east side of the island was unpopulated aside from the facility in question, a half dozen or so bright yellow lights had appeared on the beach each night.

Zooming in on the satellite imagery had revealed the details—groups of men and women gathered around bonfires, partying, most likely consuming drugs, alcohol, or both. Technically, drinking alcohol wasn't illegal in Kuwait, but buying, selling, or carrying alcohol, or being drunk in public, was, which made consuming alcohol a challenge. Drugs, on the other hand, were strictly forbidden, but they were still prevalent among the younger population.

Taking into account the presence of these small groups along the shoreline, the SEALs had selected a long stretch of beach devoid of any visitors. Additionally, Khalila had proposed a plan to infiltrate the facility, which the SEALs had accepted.

The plan required the SEALs to get their hands on tonight's supply van, without peppering it with bullet holes. Although Hacker spoke Arabic, providing an opportunity to engage the van driver once the vehicle was stopped, Khalila had suggested she pose as a drugged or intoxicated woman walking along the road, supposedly from one of the nearby parties. Hopefully, the driver would stop to inquire with less suspicion than if a man approached, which would provide Khalila an opportunity to neutralize the driver without damage to the van. If anything went wrong, the SEALs would be positioned nearby to intervene.

Just before reaching shore, the RHIB drivers shifted the engines to neutral, and the boats coasted to a halt as they grounded onto the beach. The SEALs hauled the boats across the beach and hid them in the foliage. Noviello then led the squad into the island interior.

The two fire teams spread out, remaining within visual distance of each other, with Noviello leading one team and Senior Chief Burkhardt the other. After a half-mile trek, they reached the road leading to the facility.

The two teams took positions on opposite sides of the road, hidden in the brush. They waited for thirty-five minutes, until Narehood announced, "Movement."

Harrison examined the road through his night vision goggles. Approaching in the distance was a van containing only the driver; no passenger. When the vehicle's headlights became visible, Khalila moved onto the road and started walking, pretending to be in a doped-up stupor, toward the van. Once her figure was illuminated by the van's headlights, the vehicle slowed, stopping a few feet before her.

Khalila continued toward the van, babbling as the driver lowered his window. When she reached the driver's door, she pulled her pistol from the small of her back and aimed it at the man's head.

She opened the door, then pulled the man from the van, where he was met by Meyer and Narehood, who searched him for weapons and any special access cards that might assist with gaining entry to the facility. They found none. After Khalila checked his wallet for his name,

Narehood zip-tied his hands behind his back and gagged his mouth. Khalila explained the plan to the man: he would wait in the bushes by the road until morning, then head to the beach.

The van's rear doors were opened, revealing several pallets of food and other items, which were unloaded to make room for all eight SEALs and Harrison. The SEALs and Harrison climbed into the back of the van while Khalila hopped into the driver's seat. Kuwait was one of the least restrictive Muslim countries when it came to gender, with women being allowed to drive since 1979, so the team had decided that Khalila should be the driver, since her mastery of the region's languages was superior to Hacker's.

They were also concerned that the same driver, or set of drivers, made the facility's nightly supply run, and a strange Caucasian driver would cast suspicion. An attractive Arab woman would have better odds of talking her way into the facility without raising suspicion.

Once the SEALs were inside the van and the rear doors closed, Khalila put the vehicle in gear and started down the road.

In the distance, the van's headlights illuminated the road sloping down toward the facility entrance, guarded by two men, one on each side of the road. As Khalila approached, the man to the left stepped from the guardhouse and waited. An uneasy feeling settled over her as she examined both men. It was the way they carried their weapons. These men weren't paramilitary professionals. They were run-of-the-mill thugs for hire. Not what she was expecting.

She stopped the van beside the man.

"Who are *you*?" he asked in Arabic.

"Khalila," she said, "Omar's girlfriend. He couldn't make it tonight, so he asked me to make the run."

The man pulled a flashlight from his pocket and turned it on, examining Khalila's face. The van was a commercial vehicle with the front sealed off from the back, so none of the SEALs or Harrison were visible. If the man checked the back, he'd be in for a surprise, but Khalila hoped that surprise would be delayed until they gained access. Otherwise, they'd have to blast their way in, giving away the element of surprise.

The man shone the light in Khalila's face again. "Omar's married."

Khalila shielded her eyes from the light with her left hand, moving her right hand down to within easy reach of her pistol, which was slid inside the waistband of her pants behind her back again.

"Well," she said, "let's not tell Omar's wife."

The man grinned and turned off the flashlight, then stepped back into the guardhouse. He made a call, informing someone that tonight's supply van had arrived, then the entrance doors opened with a rumble, pulling slowly apart.

Once the doors opened wide enough, Khalila pulled forward into a loading dock illuminated by bright white lights, containing several pallets of boxes that would almost fill the entire van. It looked like the nightly van run didn't just drop off supplies; it picked up material as well. She parked the vehicle as the entrance doors closed behind her.

No one else was present in the loading dock, so Khalila tapped the metal partition behind her, providing the all-clear signal. The SEALs and Harrison emerged from the back of the van and moved forward as a metal roll-up door in the middle of the far wall began rising. The SEALs reached the wall just in time, taking position on each side of the door as four men armed with submachine guns appeared in the opening.

Khalila stepped from the van, hoping the keep the men's eyes on her and not on the periphery as they entered the loading dock. The SEALs on both sides, weapons aimed at the men, surged forward as Hacker shouted in Arabic to drop their weapons. Khalila drew her pistol as well. Faced with ten armed opponents, the four men wisely dropped their firearms.

Their hands and feet were quickly tie-wrapped, and Khalila stopped beside them, probing them for information. When all four men refused to answer, she put a bullet in the head of the nearest man.

The other three started talking.

There were six other armed men in the facility, but all were off duty and sleeping, and the locations of their rooms were provided. When Khalila asked where the prisoners were held, she got blank looks. There were no prisoners or detainees in the facility, they said, only workers.

She relayed the information to the SEALs, then stopped by Harrison. "Something's not right."

"Yeah," he said. "I'm getting the same feeling."

Noviello also seemed concerned, but decided to press on, leaving Meyer behind to guard the men and their exit route.

The rest of the team continued in single file, passing a small cafeteria and kitchen, then entered a large common area with several long tables, each lined on both sides with men and women wearing white surgical gowns, face masks, and gloves, processing a white powdery substance on the table. Interspersed throughout were several unarmed supervisors overseeing the work.

When eight armed men in tactical gear and Khalila burst into the room, activity stopped as the men and women stared at them. It was silent in the room as the supervisors slowly raised their hands.

A quick search of the area produced no weapons, and Khalila and Hacker interrogated the supervisors while four of the SEALs rounded up the six off-duty armed men.

When queried about the location of prisoners or detainees, there were more blank stares. However, one of the supervisors said there was a section in the facility containing cells, but they were empty. The entire facility had been abandoned by its previous owners five years ago, taken over by its current occupants due to its isolated and secure location.

Noviello sent several SEALs to search the entire facility, confirming what the supervisor stated. There were no prisoners or detainees, only empty cells and interrogation rooms.

It soon became clear that the men and women were processing cocaine, preparing and packaging it for shipment to the mainland. The facility where the prisoner from Abbottabad had been sent was now nothing more than a drug lab.

48

RESEARCH VESSEL *ATLANTIS*

Alvin bobbed on the surface, illuminated by bright white lights from *Atlantis* as the LARS A-frame was pivoted above the submersible. Inside the DSV, Christine waited in anticipation; it wouldn't be long before the DNA sample was analyzed. Two portable DNA-scanning machines had been loaded aboard *Atlantis* before it had left port for tonight's mission. McFarland had hand-selected the accompanying DNA technician and supervisor, both chosen not only because of their proficiency with the portable scanners but also their clearances, having been read into the most sensitive CIA programs.

Neither technician had been briefed about Neptune Spear, but that wasn't necessary. They just had to determine how closely the sample taken from the body on the ocean floor matched the two samples in their possession: one of Osama bin Laden taken from CIA archives, and another one from bin Laden's sister, who had been treated for cancer in the U.S., with the latter provided as a backup sample in case there was an issue with Osama bin Laden's.

Both men were waiting topside on *Atlantis* as *Alvin* mated to the LARS and was lifted from the water. The A-frame then pivoted the DSV over the ship's stern, where it was lowered to the deck. Christine climbed through the hatch as the DNA sample was provided to an awaiting CIA technician, and she joined him as they headed toward one of the labs aboard *Atlantis*, which had been set aside for their use.

Inside the laboratory were two IntegenX portable DNA scanners—a primary and a backup—each the size of a laser copier. Christine shed her borrowed sweater and sweatpants as the technician prepared the sample and added the refrigerated reactive agents, then began the analysis simultaneously on both machines.

The DNA taken from the corpse on the ocean bottom was being compared to the two sample profiles loaded into the scanners, identified only as Sample #1 and Sample #2. Both machines processed the DNA strands until they finished their analysis an hour later. Christine joined the men as they read the information on a color screen built into each scanner. Each machine displayed identical results, which the supervisor explained.

"A comparison with sample one," he began, "indicates the two individuals are siblings."

Christine nodded. Sample one was from Osama bin Laden's sister.

"Sample two," he said, "matches the sample just obtained."

The remains on the ocean floor were Osama bin Laden's.

"Are you sure?" Christine asked. "What's the probability the two samples are from different men and the machines improperly correlated them?"

"There's always a possibility without full DNA sequencing, but the odds in this case are extremely slim."

"How slim?"

"Based on the DNA site matches identified, the odds of these two samples being from different men is about one in a hundred million."

Christine thanked both men as relief washed over her. The thought that bin Laden was still alive and his existence concealed by a rogue intelligence organization had weighed heavily on her. At worst, the man taken prisoner at Abbottabad was a courier, and keeping his capture secret while information was extracted from him made perfect sense.

At this point, it probably wasn't all that important to find the courier. He had likely been disposed of years ago, once he had exhausted his usefulness.

49

LANGLEY, VIRGINIA

Inside the director's seventh-floor conference room, it was silent after Harrison and Khalila finished reviewing their trip report with Christine, Bryant, Rolow, and McFarland. It seemed that everyone around the table had prematurely concluded that the prisoner taken from the third floor of the Abbottabad house was Osama bin Laden. The confirmation that the corpse on the bottom of the Arabian Sea was Osama seemed conclusive proof that bin Laden had, in fact, been killed during the Abbottabad raid.

McFarland broke the silence. "It looks like we misinterpreted Mc-Neil's note. Let's start over, back at the beginning." There was murmured agreement around the table, so she continued. "What kicked this issue off were the deaths of Nagle and McNeil, which we associated with the Abbottabad assault. We initially had two theories: the first was that bin Laden had been taken prisoner and those who knew were being silenced, and the second being that the assault team deaths were the work of al-Qaeda, exacting revenge for bin Laden's death.

"Now that we've ruled out bin Laden's capture, the elimination of the assault team by al-Qaeda is the only theory that makes sense. But there's a peculiarity. The SEAL deaths occurred at a steady pace for several years following the Abbottabad raid and abruptly stopped a few years ago. Then they picked back up with Nagle and McNeil a month ago. Why?"

Christine answered, "It may have to do with Zawahiri's death. Al-Qaeda needs a new leader. Perhaps they've chosen one, and he's decided to finish what Zawahiri began. Or maybe there's a struggle for leadership and one of the contenders is attempting to garner support by terminating the last few assault team members."

McFarland opened her laptop and pulled up a summary of the potential successors to Zawahiri, which had been prepared for Christine's briefing at the White House the morning after the attempted assassination of Secretary Verbeck, and displayed it on the conference room monitor on the far wall.

McFarland went quickly through the list, one slide per man.

"Our assessment is that the leading contender for the new leader of al-Qaeda is Saif al-Adel. He would have the resources and connections, plus a strong motive, to complete the elimination of the Abbottabad assault team members."

Harrison glanced at Khalila, wondering if she had any information to offer. She had just spent an entire day with Osama's eldest son and had no information worth mentioning? Not even that she had met with him two days ago?

He decided to stay quiet, evaluating how best to proceed with what he knew. As he considered his options, McFarland continued.

"We're already working the angle that al-Qaeda is responsible for the assault team deaths," she said. "We'll keep everyone apprised as we learn more. In the meantime, however, that conclusion doesn't explain McNeil's note—*3rd floor desk. Find him.* If he wasn't referring to Osama bin Laden, then who?"

"It looks like we jumped to the incorrect conclusion that McNeil was referring to the reflection in the computer display," Christine offered. "We should take another look at the video."

"My thought exactly," McFarland replied.

She brought the video up on the conference room display and advanced the file until McNeil reached the third floor. Against the back wall of the room was a desk crowded with various items: a computer tower, display, keyboard, several thumb drives, a handheld radio-transceiver in a charger, a cup holding several pens and pencils, three stacks of manila folders, and a few books standing beside each other.

McFarland paused the video, letting everyone study the desk's contents. Harrison decided to check out the book titles in case they offered a clue, but nothing registered. It was silent in the conference room until McFarland blurted out an observation.

"The radio!"

Harrison focused on the handheld transceiver in its charging stand as McFarland expounded. "That's a standard-issue CIA radio from the early 2000s. What is a CIA radio doing on bin Laden's desk?"

"Perhaps it's a souvenir from a dead agency officer," Bryant offered. "Bin Laden had a souvenir AK-47 assault rifle in his bedroom, but no bullets were loaded. Maybe the radio is something similar."

McFarland shook her head. "Look at the charging stand. The green light is on. You don't keep a souvenir radio charged."

Christine replied, "Maybe this explains how bin Laden avoided capture those first few years. He didn't move into the Abbottabad compound until 2006. He evaded capture for five years despite several promising leads, but each fizzled out. Perhaps he was being tipped off."

"I don't like it," Rolow said. "That implies we had a traitor on the inside. Someone feeding information to bin Laden. For what reason?"

"We employ a lot of foreign nationals," McFarland countered, "especially in that region. This wouldn't be the first time we assessed their allegiance incorrectly."

"Where do we go from here?" Bryant asked.

"Let me pull up the operation records," McFarland replied.

She opened the mission report on her computer and scrolled to an appendix containing a list of items taken from the compound. She read a few of them aloud: five computers, ten hard drives, over one hundred thumb drives and computer disks . . ." She kept going through the list.

"Bingo!" she said. "Transceiver and charger." She looked up from her laptop. "It was one of the items taken from the third floor."

"Why wasn't the presence of this radio picked up during the analysis of the material harvested from the compound?" Rolow asked.

"The material was collected somewhat haphazardly due to the time crunch, with the assault team having only a few minutes to collect material before Pakistani forces arrived. Anything of interest was shoved into garbage bags, then sorted once the team returned to Afghanistan. I suspect that whoever reviewed the material assumed that a radio from one of the assault team members had accidently been caught up in the compound's contents. That'd be my guess."

"So, we have the radio," Bryant said. "What does that do for us?"

"Every transceiver has a serial number. Find the transceiver, and we'll know who it was issued to. We can then have a conversation with that person, asking how it ended up on bin Laden's desk."

"Where is it now?" Rolow asked.

McFarland perused the report. "Doesn't say. I'll have to go through subsequent records. The material from the compound initially came here for analysis, but it's since been dispersed to various locations. Bin Laden's AK-47 that Monroe mentioned, for example, is in the agency museum here at Langley. Most of the rest is likely locked in a vault somewhere. I'll track the radio down as soon as possible."

She leaned back in her chair, pleased at what she had deduced.

"Great job, Tracey," Christine said. To Rolow, she asked, "What's next?" He had scheduled the meeting to discuss several topics.

"Tracey has an update on the SecNav issue. Nothing on Mixell yet, but the review of the UUV data turned up something interesting." He turned to McFarland.

"It's not a lot to go on," she replied, "but we found an Iranian communication referencing a pending receipt of a priority shipment from SI. There are a lot of companies with the initials *SI*, but given that the UUV and SecNav appear to be linked, and that her brother is Dan Snyder, a reasonable conclusion is that Iran is expecting a shipment from Snyder Industries. However, we've searched all ship manifests leaving the U.S. mainland for the last six months, and nothing from SI to Iran has been logged."

"You think it's off the books?" Bryant asked.

"That's what we're going with for now. It'll take a while, but we might be able to discover what was shipped, or at least verify a shipment occurred. Once we know more, we can discuss how to proceed."

"Anything else?" Christine asked.

"I think we've covered everything," Rolow said. "We've got three leads to follow: assess whether al-Qaeda leadership is responsible for the assault team deaths, locate the radio on bin Laden's desk, and figure out what SI shipped to Iran. Harrison and Khalila will resume their original task of tracking Mixell down; perhaps we'll get some useful information out of him if we can take him alive.

"In the meantime, Jake and Khalila will have a few days off. They did some good work in Kuwait, despite their disregard for clearly established protocols."

He lent a hard stare toward Khalila, who hadn't said much during today's briefing. She'd met with Rolow before this meeting; Harrison had spotted her leaving the DDO's office, a glowering look on her face.

As far as a few days off went, the timing was excellent. Maddy had a gymnastics competition this weekend in Maryland, one of a half dozen national meets her team participated in each year, and she and Angie were flying in early to see the sights in D.C. He'd be able to spend a few days with them.

"Thanks for the room at the Intercontinental," Harrison said to Rolow. Upon accepting the agency's job offer a second time, the DDO had arranged a room for him at the upscale hotel in southwest D.C., where the agency kept a block of rooms reserved for its use, until Harrison rented a place somewhere.

As the meeting wrapped up, Harrison's thoughts returned to Khalila's meeting with Abdallah bin Laden and his three companions, which she had failed to mention. It was a delicate issue. He had promised Khalila that anything he learned about her would be kept to himself. But his concern about her loyalty to the CIA was growing. He needed to put his doubt to rest, determining whether or not he could trust her with more certainty. If she really was working more with al-Qaeda than the CIA, the agency needed to know.

Christine stood, signaling the meeting was over. Khalila was the first to depart, striding down the hallway toward the elevator. She was clearly in a mood following her meeting with the DDO.

Harrison took advantage of Khalila's departure and approached Christine as the others filed from the room.

"Do you have a moment?" he asked.

"A few," she said.

Harrison closed Christine's door after following her into her office. She noticed the precaution, but kept quiet as she settled into the chair behind her desk. As he stood before her, searching for the best way to start, she gestured to the chairs before her desk. He took a seat, then began.

"I'm not really sure about Khalila," he said, "regarding where her loyalty lies."

He went on to relay what Khalila had told him on their trip to Syria, when she explained how she moved freely about Langley without drawing suspicion from her Middle East contacts; that she provided information to both sides, although the information she was allowed to provide to the other side was screened and approved by McFarland.

Christine listened intently until he reached the salient part. "Khalila met with Osama's eldest son, Abdallah, two days ago in Kuwait."

"Really," Christine said. "You think she would have mentioned that."

"Exactly."

"That's not damning information, though," Christine added. "That's her job—to cultivate relationships beneficial to the agency, and gaining access to the bin Laden family and their associates would be pretty high on the list of agency desires. Perhaps they discussed nothing of relevance to our meeting today."

"That's possible," Harrison said. "But I also got the feeling there's something going on between Khalila and Abdallah. When they met, they seemed a bit . . . chummy."

Christine smiled. "That's not an indictment either. Khalila is a beautiful woman, and men tend to be a bit . . . *chummy* with women as attractive as she is."

Harrison had to admit that Christine was right, and she would certainly know firsthand. She had fended off guys interested in her the entire time they dated.

He assessed Christine's responses thus far. The conversation wasn't unfolding as he had expected, with Christine pointing out the lack of concrete evidence that Khalila shouldn't be trusted.

"However," Christine said, "I have my doubts about Khalila as well. There's definitely something about her that the DDO is hiding. But unless you've got something else, there's nothing specific for me to look into."

Harrison recalled the video he had recorded outside the Al Hamra Tower, when Khalila introduced herself to Abdallah and the three men, then talked for a short while before heading into the building. He was too far away for the recording to pick up the conversation, but the agency might have the tools to determine what was said.

"I have a short video of when she met with Abdallah and three other men. It's from across the street, but perhaps you can decipher what they discussed."

"Send me the video," Christine replied, then picked up her phone and dialed Tracey McFarland.

When Tracey answered, Christine said, "I'll be sending a short video over with a meeting between Khalila and four men in Kuwait. I'd like you to identify the men and augment the audio, if possible, to determine what was discussed."

"No problem," McFarland said. "How urgent is this?"

"Sooner rather than later," Christine replied. "But don't bump anything critical."

"I'll get someone working on it as soon as I have an opening."

ARLINGTON, VIRGINIA

An hour after the meeting at Langley, as Jake Harrison waited outside Terminal C of Reagan National Airport, he checked his watch. The flight with Angie and Maddy aboard had landed, and he was expecting a text message anytime now. A short while later, Maddy contacted him, letting him know they were almost at the gate. Her text was followed by one from Angie on a separate chat.

We're here. Looking forward to some time alone.

Harrison was too, but he'd been so busy at Langley with debriefs from his trip to Kuwait, plus catching up on potential leads the team had on Mixell, that he hadn't planned ahead. He had only the single room at the Intercontinental, with a pullout bed for Maddy. Although a silent jaunt in the bathroom might suffice, it wasn't his idea of a romantic evening together.

He had a few SEAL friends in the area, but having Maddy hang out with a burly SEAL for an evening probably wasn't her idea of a good time, plus he'd have to come up with a cover story explaining why they were pawning her off on a stranger. Nothing came to mind.

Another stream of passengers began exiting Terminal C, and he spotted Angie and Maddy in the crowd. His daughter ran and jumped into his arms. He'd been away from home for only a short while, but Maddy took after her mother when it came to impulsiveness and exuberance. He recalled their last meeting in D.C., when Angie had done the same thing; she'd sprinted across the lobby of the Hotel Washington and leaped into his arms, straddling his waist with her legs as she locked her lips onto his. The lobby occupants—distinguished guests wearing suits and elegant dresses—had stared at the couple, but Angie seemed not to notice or care, her eyes locked on to his, an infectious grin on her face.

Angie was more reserved in Maddy's presence, giving him a short but passionate kiss. They collected their luggage and headed to the car.

"What would you like for lunch?" Harrison asked as they pulled onto the George Washington Memorial Parkway.

Angie didn't care and Maddy wanted a cheeseburger, so Harrison chose a sandwich shop near the hotel, which also served pizza and burgers.

After dropping off their luggage in their room, they went to lunch, slipping into a booth with Angie and Maddy facing Harrison. While they waited for the server, Harrison asked whether Maddy was ready for her meet.

"Not really," Maddy said. "I'm still having trouble with my beam routine. I can't consistently hit my back handsprings."

Harrison had no idea how to help, so he offered some encouraging words. "Just do your best."

After placing their order, they reviewed their plans for the day: a few hours of sightseeing near the National Mall. After confirming the details, Maddy excused herself to go to the bathroom.

He couldn't talk with Angie over the phone about how the search for Mixell was going, so she took the opportunity to inquire.

"Have any leads?"

"Nothing solid at the moment."

"What took you to Kuwait?"

Angie had no idea about the Abbottabad prisoner issue, so Harrison sloughed off her question. "Just a bad lead. Potential ties to an organization in the Middle East."

"You need to find Mixell," she said. "The longer he's on the loose, the higher the odds he'll find you first."

Harrison noticed the concerned look on Angie's face, which somehow made her seem more beautiful. Even in regular clothes, she was quite sexy. She wasn't wearing anything fancy today, just a pair of tight jeans and a formfitting halter top. As they entered the restaurant, he had watched heads turn to follow Angie's passage through the crowded deli.

"So," Angie asked, her thoughts aligning with his, "what's the plan for tonight? Just one room?" She smiled mischievously as she slipped a foot from its shoe, then ran it up along the inside of his thighs. "I imagine it's going to be really *hard* for you this week, not being able to spend any time alone."

Harrison admitted that he'd done a poor job of planning ahead, then an idea came to him. One that had the potential to address two issues.

He pulled his cell phone out and called Christine O'Connor's work number. Her executive assistant put the call through.

"Hey, Chris, it's Jake," he said when she answered. "Do you still work out? Gymnastics, I mean."

"Hi, Jake. I'm fine," she said. "How about you?" He noticed the tone in her voice.

"Sorry. I'm in a pickle and was wondering if you could help out."

"Yeah, I still do the gymnastics thing sometimes. Why do you ask?"

"Maddy has a meet on Saturday and is having problems on the beam. Do you think you can give her some pointers before the meet? I know she'd appreciate it. I'd appreciate it too." He lowered his voice. "I could use some time alone with Angie, with someone keeping Maddy occupied."

"Let me get this straight," Christine said. "You want the director of the CIA to babysit your daughter so you can get laid?"

"I'll owe you."

"You already owe me."

The image of him holding on to Christine and the Russian president overhanging a cliff immediately registered. With his grip on each slipping in the rain, he'd been forced to choose and had pulled President Kalinin to safety. However, he figured the score still tilted in his favor, since he had saved Christine's life twice. But arguing that fact was clearly not the best strategy. He decided to concede her point.

"I'll owe you more," he said.

"Don't you have any friends in the area?"

"Only one who can help Maddy with her beam routine."

After a moment of silence, Christine replied, "Fine. I should make you wait the whole week, but how about tonight? I can modify my plans and pick Maddy up around seven thirty, and we can spend an hour or two at the gym."

"That'd be perfect. Thanks, Chris."

Maddy returned from the bathroom as the waiter delivered their food.

Harrison checked to make sure she wasn't watching him as she tried to handle her oversized burger, then he winked at Angie. She wiggled her toes and smiled.

51

LANHAM, MARYLAND

Seated at the desk in his hotel room a block from the Capital Beltway surrounding Washington, D.C., Lonnie Mixell took a break from planning the next al-Qaeda-sponsored terrorist attack on U.S. soil, an event that, if executed successfully, would exceed 9/11 in its impact. In the interim, another effort paid the bills, and he pulled up a status report on the shipment from Snyder Industries to Iran. Everything was proceeding as planned, and the equipment should offload at its destination port in two days.

He was about to return to the complicated but rather enjoyable al-Qaeda plot when a notification appeared on his computer display, indicating he'd received an encrypted transmission. He clicked on the note, which launched a portal to a secure messaging site.

Good work on the first four men. But you need to finish the job. Your friend Harrison is back in the U.S., staying at the Intercontinental in southwest D.C. You should pay him a visit. Sooner rather than later.

Mixell typed a response: "Understand. But I was hoping for something more dramatic, requiring the presence of his wife. Harrison working solo on the East Coast complicates things."

His wife is with him at the hotel for the next few days.

Mixell took a moment to reconsider his plans, then replied: "Would tonight make you happy?"

Very.

"What's his room number?"

Don't know.

"Do you have any other helpful information?"

No.

Mixell signed off from the app, and the messages disappeared from his computer. He pulled up a map of Washington, D.C., zoomed in to the vicinity of the Intercontinental and shifted to satellite view, then studied the area.

It didn't take long to devise a plan.

52

ARLINGTON, VIRGINIA

Christine O'Connor entered the Carlyle restaurant in Shirlington fifteen minutes late for her 6 p.m. dinner date, reaching the second floor as a waiter brought Tracey McFarland and her husband another round of drinks. One of Christine's protective agents took a seat at the bar, while another positioned himself at a two-person table reserved ahead of time, offering a clear view of the director and her dinner companions.

This was her third outing with Tracey, who had talked Christine into a double date this time. Christine had initially declined, with so much going on at work, then had reluctantly agreed to tonight's date with a guy Tracey had highly recommended. Christine hadn't let on, but Jake's call today was fortuitous, since Christine had reconsidered and wasn't looking forward to the event, giving her an excuse to cancel the date but still meet up with Tracey.

Tracey introduced her husband, Mike, who was an older but handsome guy.

"Sorry I'm late," Christine said. "Got held up at the office. I also can't stay too long. I'm taking Jake's daughter to the gym tonight. She's got a meet on Saturday and is having trouble with her beam routine."

Tracy filled her husband in on Christine's gymnastics pedigree.

"You certainly look the part," Mike said.

His comment elicited a wry look from Tracey—commenting on Christine's looks with the first sentence out of his mouth.

"What? I'm just offering a compliment. Christine looks great, especially for a woman her age."

This time, his comment earned him an elbow in the side, since Tracey was a few years older than Christine.

The waiter returned with a cosmopolitan for Christine, and Tracey and Mike ordered dinner while Christine ordered just an appetizer, since she'd be heading to the gym soon. After the waiter took their orders, Mike headed to the bathroom.

"So, how are things going with double-O-seven?" Christine asked.

Tracey had found herself divorced a few years ago and, as an attractive woman in her forties, had enjoyed her newfound freedom, going through men like fashion accessories. Her friends had stopped learning their names and started giving them numbers. Tracey had eventually settled down and married number seven, and with Tracey being a CIA employee, it hadn't taken long for her friends to nickname her husband 007. The moniker somewhat fit, since Mike was a retired CIA field officer, having spent twenty years in the Middle East.

"Things are good," Tracey replied. "I'm jealous of his retirement. He's staying busy, though, working forty-plus hours a week. But at least he's doing something he enjoys instead of the daily slog at the agency. He's building us a new house. General contractor and all that. Slow going, since he's a perfectionist, but it's almost done.

"How about you?" Tracey asked. "You clearly didn't like the guy I picked out for tonight. But I've got a long list of men who'd look perfect on the CIA director's arm. And a list of guys who wouldn't." She offered a mischievous smile. "Depends on what you're looking for."

Christine laughed. "I'll take 'em clean-cut for now."

"Or I could find you a good Russian," Tracey replied.

Tracey's comment caught Christine off guard, unsure whether she was referring to her heritage—Christine was half-Russian—or her previous relationship with Russian President Yuri Kalinin. But one thing was clear—Tracey knew more than she should have.

"You've been snooping in my file?"

"I couldn't help myself," she said. "It's that thing you've got going with Harrison. It's not often that a director goes out of her way to hire someone, and not just once but twice."

"Is it that obvious?"

Tracey nodded. "But only on the seventh floor. We're pretty tight-lipped about stuff up there, so I wouldn't worry about the underlings learning that you've got the hots for a married man."

"I wouldn't exactly say that," Christine replied. "I respect his marriage and would never come on to him. It's just that—I waited too long."

"I'll say," Tracey replied. "You turned him down twice."

"That's in my file?"

"You bet. When you have a clearance as high as ours, they go all the way back to where you grew up. Interview your neighbors and friends, people you went to school with."

Despite the security clearance investigations over the years, Christine had never seen the actual files—what they had gleaned and the corresponding assessments.

Tracey continued, "Jake even hung around a few years after you said no the second time. That's dedication on his part, and stupidity on yours, if you don't mind me saying so."

Christine swirled her drink, then took a sip. "I can't argue there."

Mike returned from the bathroom as the food was served.

The ensuing conversation with Tracey and her husband delved into numerous topics, and Christine lost track of time. She finally remembered her babysitting/gymnastics-training appointment and checked her watch. She should have left five minutes ago.

"I need to run," Christine said. "I've got to pick Maddy up."

As Christine reached into her purse, Tracey said, "We've got the check. Get going."

53

WASHINGTON, D.C.

Christine's black SUV pulled up to the entrance of the Intercontinental a few minutes past seven. Harrison was waiting in the lobby with Maddy, who was dressed in her gymnastics leotard and carried a small gym bag filled with hand grips and other assorted gear. Christine apologized for being late, informing Harrison they'd be back in about two hours. The gym was only a few miles away.

Maddy climbed into the back of the SUV with Christine, and the vehicle pulled out into traffic. It was obvious that Maddy was excited to work out with Christine, but she also seemed nervous. She clutched the gym bag in her lap and examined the two men in the front seats. She leaned toward Christine and whispered, "Who are those men?"

Not wanting to get into a discussion about why she needed protective agents, Christine whispered back. "They're coworkers. We sometimes go out to dinner together."

Maddy squinted, studying the two men a bit closer.

"They don't seem very friendly."

"They're very nice," Christine said. "It's been a long day. They're just tired."

They soon arrived at the gym where Christine worked out on occasion. It was partially full tonight, with the higher levels working late, as usual. Once reaching level nine, it was standard practice at elite gyms to start the girls on split-shift practices: two hours before school and four hours afterward during the week, plus six hours on Saturdays. By the time the girls reached high school, if they had the talent to compete at the national level, they were practicing thirty-six hours a week.

Caitlin Johnson, one of the upper-level coaches, broke off from the girls, greeting Christine and Maddy when they entered, while Christine's *coworkers* remained in the SUV. Christine had hoped Caitlin would be available to help with Maddy's beam routine. But she was tied up with practice until nine thirty, when the gym closed. Still, Christine had trained for seventeen years, from the age of five until she graduated from college. Back handsprings weren't terribly complicated, and Christine hoped she'd be able to diagnose Maddy's issue.

"It is good to see you again, Christine," Caitlin said. "We're done with the beams tonight. They're yours until we close."

Maddy joined Christine in the locker room while Christine changed into her gymnastics leotard in case she needed to demonstrate the correct way to execute the move. It was one of the rare times she wore clothes that revealed her blemishes: bullet wounds in her right biceps and thigh, plus her left shoulder. Maddy's eyes went to the scars.

"Everything works fine," Christine said, declining to explain how she had received the wounds.

They returned to the beam section of the gym, containing eight full-height beams, each four feet off the ground, plus several floor beams, which were only a few inches high and used as stepping stones to the normal-height beams when learning new, complex moves.

Christine had Maddy warm up on one of the floor beams.

54

WASHINGTON, D.C.

Lonnie Mixell stood on the wharf across the street from the Intercontinental, examining the twelve-story building, with its penthouse terrace and bar. He wore a light windbreaker, beneath which was a shoulder holster containing his SIG Sauer P226 with attached suppressor, plus a sheath containing a six-inch knife. As he prepared to step across the street, his mind went to a night a few months earlier, at a location not far away, just across the Potomac River. To the last time he saw Trish alive, with the coward Harrison holding her hostage, shielding himself with a woman.

He had waited months for this day as his wounds from his encounter with Harrison healed, lying awake at night as he imagined the various ways he might take from Harrison what his former best friend had taken from him. He even considered letting Harrison live, to spend the rest of his days with the memory of his wife dying in his arms.

But first, he needed to determine what room Harrison and Angie were in. The Intercontinental at the wharf, where the CIA booked rooms for their officers, wasn't the kind of place that gave out that information. Any visitor or devious attempt to gain access, such as an individual posing as a food delivery guy, would be told to wait in the lobby while the resident was contacted, confirming it was okay to send him up. This wouldn't do. He needed the element of surprise.

Mixell had a plan, of course, and he walked across the street and into the alley beside the hotel. There was a service door for personnel, which was shut, plus a loading dock entrance in the side of the building, and the metal roll-up door was also closed. He leaned against the wall not far from the service door and pulled a pack of cigarettes from his pocket, even though he didn't smoke. He had planned ahead, stopping by a convenience store along the way.

He lit a cigarette and took a puff.

It was only a matter of time.

55

WASHINGTON, D.C.

After Jake handed Maddy off to Christine in the lobby, he headed back to his hotel room. After traipsing around D.C. all afternoon, followed by dinner at the Capital Grille, Angie had initially kicked off her shoes and collapsed onto the bed. When he returned to the room, however, he realized she hadn't wasted any time. She lay on the bed propped up against the headboard among the pillows, her body covered by a white bedsheet. The bottle of pinot noir he had ordered up to the room had been opened and two glasses poured, with one in Angie's hand, and soft music was playing in the background. After verifying he had returned without Maddy, she pulled the sheet away, revealing her luscious body scantily clad in a black-lace teddy.

He took the glass of wine from her and leaned in for a kiss. She pulled him into bed, and he began exploring her body, his hands running slowly up her thighs. As his lips grazed her neck, he slid the straps of her teddy over her shoulders, then pulled it down over her breasts, the material catching for an instant on her hard nipples. She pulled his shirt over his head and threw it on the floor, then moved her hands down the lean muscles in his back. He kissed her breasts, and she moaned softly as she tugged on his pants. He got the idea and kicked them off.

A sound penetrated the waves of pleasure, and it took Jake a second to realize it was his cell phone. He glanced at the screen and recognized the number. It was from Langley.

"I've got to take this," he said.

Angie cursed under her breath as he retrieved his phone and answered the call.

"Harrison here."

It was Khalila. "You might be taking the week off," she said, "but I'm working the issue. That shipment from SI to Iran that McFarland mentioned this morning? Analysis tunneled into the Snyder Industry transportation logs and found a shipment that went to the Port of Baltimore in the middle of the night."

"And?" Harrison said. "I imagine there are a lot of late-night shipments to the port."

"There's no record of the shipment arriving." She paused, then added, "I think Mixell's involved."

"What makes you think that?"

"The timing. The shipment left a Snyder Industry dock in Maryland two days before he killed McNeil. He just happens to be in the area? Plus, he smuggled Russian weaponry into the Port of Baltimore a few months ago—he's got contacts there. This has Mixell's fingerprints all over it."

Khalila had a point. A clandestine shipment to Iran certainly smelled of Mixell. "What next?"

"Analysis is working the shipment end. Trying to figure out what ship the containers were loaded onto and what's inside. Rolow sends his regrets, but he wants you to come in and review what we've got, first thing tomorrow. The meeting is at eight."

"All right. I'll see you in the morning," he said, then hung up the phone.

Angie was sitting up in bed, the sheet pulled around her body as she stared at him.

"We might have a lead on Mixell," he said. "A shipment he might be involved in. I need to head in to Langley tomorrow."

"To meet with Christine?"

Harrison sighed. *How many times do we have to go over this?* "You really need to stop thinking about Christine."

"*I* have to stop thinking about her? What about *you*? I asked you about a plan for tonight—spending time alone together—and the first thing that comes to your mind is Christine!"

Angie had a point, but he hadn't been thinking about spending time with Christine. He'd been searching for a way to keep Maddy occupied and had devised an ingenious plan, if he said so himself, creating some romantic time for them while helping Maddy with her beam routine. He should be commended for his effort, not demonized.

"I thought it might help Maddy," he said. "Nothing more."

He leaned in to kiss her, but she turned away.

Frustrated at not getting through to her—about how much he truly loved her—he went to the sliding glass doors that opened to the balcony. Pulling them aside, he stepped into the cool night air wearing only his boxers. The view was spectacular, overlooking the Potomac River, the boats cruising the waterway, and the Alexandria skyline in the distance.

The scenery, however, was lost on him. Instead, he remembered something that had occurred more than ten years earlier. It was a month after he proposed to Angie. Christine had called—unaware of his proposal—letting him know she was ready to settle down. The next day, he had returned home from work to find Angie in a gloomy mood. When he pressed her for the reason, she had blurted out—*I can't compete with her!*

Angie had never met Christine and had spent the day researching her on the internet. By then, Christine was an analyst for the House Appropriations Committee, leading the reviews of Pentagon weapon programs, and was well connected in D.C. Angie had come across a picture of Christine at a White House state dinner wearing a formal evening gown that hugged her body. Her hair had been pulled up, highlighting her glittering blue eyes, high cheekbones, and the sleek lines of her neck. Several other men and women stood nearby, most of them staring at Christine.

He had tried to explain to Angie that she had nothing to worry about—that she simply didn't know how beautiful she was, largely because she didn't put the effort into it that most women did. She was happy to pull on a pair of jeans and tie her hair in a ponytail, and head out to dinner without any makeup. Angie was as beautiful as Christine and just as smart. They both had college degrees, but Angie had done it the hard way, working nights to put herself through school, the first in her family to graduate from college. He repeatedly told her to stop worrying about Christine—that Angie was everything he ever wanted in a woman. But no matter how many times he told her so, she just scowled and told him to quit lying.

He returned to the room to find Angie still in bed, the sheet wrapped around her body and tucked under her arms. She was still turned away from him, but it didn't matter; she was beautiful from any angle. He sat beside her and kissed her shoulder. When she turned her head toward him, he gently tugged on the sheet. But she held it firmly against her body.

Harrison sighed and lay on his back, staring at the ceiling, searching for the right words, something he hadn't already told her a dozen times or more.

A moment later, Angie's face was above his, looking down at him.

"Well, come on," she said with a grin, the sheet still tucked under her arms. "You're not going to give up that easily, are you?"

He ripped the sheet away and pounced on her, and she shrieked with laughter until his attention moved from her lips to more erogenous zones, and it wasn't long before her cries of ecstasy spilled out into the night.

56

ARLINGTON, VIRGINIA

Earlier in the evening, Maddy had finished warming up on the low beam, and Christine had noted that her back handsprings looked fine. But that wasn't unexpected. Once girls moved to the normal beam, their fear sometimes kicked in and affected the move. Performing blind backward moves on the four-inch-wide beam was terrifying for some girls. Even on a basic back handspring, a girl's feet would leave the beam before the hands were planted behind her. If the hands didn't land where they were supposed to, the move could end in disaster.

Christine had Maddy move to the normal beam, and she noticed the girl's body tense before the move. She executed it fairly well, but lost her balance at the end and fell off. She tried a few more times, unable to stabilize herself after completing the move, falling off the beam each time. The first thing Christine noticed was that Maddy was landing the move with her first leg straight.

"You're peg-legging the landing," Christine said, hoping Maddy understood the term. "You need to land with your first knee slightly bent, to absorb some of the rotation before your back foot lands. If you don't, then your back foot has to hit perfectly to stop the rotation without losing your balance."

Maddy understood the issue and practiced landing with her first knee slightly bent. It helped, keeping her on the beam after she landed, but she was still quite wobbly, which would result in a major point deduction.

Christine watched her more carefully now that her leg landing was fixed and noticed that her hips were twisting a few degrees while she was upside down during the move, which Maddy had to compensate for after the landing.

"You're not keeping your hips square," Christine said, explaining that Maddy was introducing a slight twist as she bent her knees to begin the back flip. While preparing to execute the move, gymnasts stood with one foot in front of the other on the beam, so it was difficult to keep hips square during the bend, but it was a crucial element of the move. Twisted hips resulted in an off-center flip through the air, which made the landing wobbly as Maddy tried to right herself.

Maddy understood and spent the next thirty minutes trying to fix the problem, to no avail. The twist was ingrained into her muscle memory, and it would likely take a few days or even weeks of practice to correct the issue. Maddy didn't have that much time—her meet was on Saturday—and Christine could see the emotion gathering on the girl's face as she repeatedly failed to land the move properly.

She was about to burst into tears when Christine had an idea, watching Maddy's hand placement during the move. She used a standard side-by-side placement, providing an inch or two of margin in case the hands didn't come down centered on the beam. But some girls used an alternate technique, which might correct Maddy's hip twist.

"Have you ever tried a staggered hand placement?" Christine asked.

Maddy shook her head, so Christine held her hands in front of her, demonstrating the technique, placing one hand two inches forward of the lead hand, in the curve between the thumb and index finger of the first hand. Maddy seemed skeptical, so Christine climbed onto the beam to demonstrate, taking a moment to think through her normal technique, adjusting it to match Maddy's.

She executed the move at normal speed, showing how a staggered hand placement could work just fine, landing the move perfectly. She then executed the beginning of the move at half speed, showing how she began with a slight twist in her hips, like Maddy. She commenced the back flip, halting her rotation as her legs went vertical, her toes pointed to the ceiling. She held her pose on the beam, essentially a handstand, pointing out to Maddy how her shoulders were slightly twisted due to the staggered hand placement but that her hips were now square.

Maddy nodded her understanding, and Christine finished the move, landing solidly on the beam without a single wobble.

Christine had Maddy practice the staggered hand placement on the low beam for a dozen back handsprings until Maddy consistently planted them correctly. She then had Maddy move to the high beam, and Christine noticed her body tense again.

"Just like the low beam," Christine said. "No different. Relax and think about each element of the move in sequence, then execute."

Maddy stared ahead and focused, then took a deep breath and went for it.

Her hands hit the beam on target, one slightly ahead of the other, and by the time her legs landed, her body was perfectly aligned. She finished the rotation without even the slightest wobble. Maddy extended her arms to finish the move as her face beamed with excitement.

"Again," Christine said. "Do it nine more times in a row, correctly, and we'll be done for the night."

Maddy executed the move perfectly nine more times, then she jumped down from the beam and rushed over to give Christine a hug, squeezing her tightly.

Christine checked the clock on the wall, assessing whether they had spent enough time at the gym for Harrison and his wife to have a proper romantic evening. It seemed that they had.

She thanked Caitlin for the use of the beams, then changed back into her work clothes and returned to the SUV with Maddy. They were soon on their way back to the hotel.

57

WASHINGTON, D.C.

The service door on the side of the Intercontinental opened, and two women wearing housekeeping outfits emerged. They ignored the man smoking nearby as they engaged in conversation and turned away, headed toward the main street. As the door swung closed, Mixell moved swiftly, grabbing it before it latched.

He moved into the hotel's service area and wandered around casually, passing a few workers until he was spotted by a supervisor, a woman in her fifties with gray hair and the required equipment: a handheld radio clipped to her waist. She examined the man wearing jeans and a gray windbreaker, then approached him.

"Excuse me, sir. You're not supposed to be back here. Do you need help getting to the lobby, or is there something I can help you with?"

Mixell quickly scanned the area; it was just the two of them in a long hallway with several intersections in the distance. He glanced at the woman's name tag.

"Yes, Adelle, there's something you can help me with." He pulled the knife from its sheath and pressed it against her abdomen. "Stay quiet, and let's talk somewhere private."

Adelle's eyes went wide, but to her credit, she kept her mouth shut and led Mixell into a nearby supply room. She turned to face him as he closed the door behind them.

"I need assistance," Mixell said. "The room number where a man named Jake Harrison is staying."

"I have no idea," Adelle replied. "You'll have to ask one of the lobby assistants."

Mixell smiled. "Let's pretend your life is at stake and you have to obtain the answer. How would you do that?" He already knew the answer and glanced at the radio clipped to her waist to provide a hint.

Her face clouded in uncertainty for a moment, but then it cleared as she reached for her radio and brought it to her lips.

"This is Adelle in housekeeping. I received a request for fresh towels for a guest, but there's an issue with the registry display, and I didn't get his room number before the guest hung up. Can you provide the room number for a Jake Harrison?"

"One moment," was the response, followed by, "1051."

"Thanks," Adelle replied.

Mixell held his hand out and she handed him the radio. He turned it off and slipped it into a pocket in his windbreaker. Now came the delicate part. He needed Adelle to stay silent until the deed was done. There were a few ways that could be accomplished, but he required one that was quiet and wouldn't risk getting blood on his clothes. One way in particular stood out.

He spun Adelle around and covered her mouth with one hand as he pressed his body against hers, pinning her against the wall. With his hand firmly around her mouth and chin, he gripped the back of her head with his other hand and twisted, turning Adelle's face around toward his. Her body squirmed as she tried to break free, her neck muscles straining as she fought the rotation. She tried to speak, but the force on her jaw from Mixell's hands prevented her from talking. He could tell she was pleading for her life, but the only thing he heard was a desperate whimper.

To Mixell, there was something tantalizing about this type of death. The thought of physically overpowering an opponent, even if it was a fifty-year-old woman, brought immense pleasure.

As her head twisted slowly toward him, he saw the pain on her face and the panic in her eyes. He paused for a moment and smiled warmly, offering Adelle a glimmer of hope. Then he twisted her head with all his strength until her neck gave way with a sickening sound of shredding tendons and cartilage.

He released her and she fell to the floor, and he knelt beside her as she stared at him. She was paralyzed but still conscious, and she opened her mouth to scream, but no sound came out. Mixell placed a hand over her mouth and nose until her eyes stopped moving.

Mixell found a service elevator and pressed the button for the tenth floor, emerging in the middle of a long hallway not far from the guest elevators. After a quick glance at the room number directions on the wall, Mixell headed to his left, passing several rooms until he reached 1051. He placed his ear to the door; he heard only the sound of soft music.

He examined the doorframe. It looked solidly built, but a forceful enough ram by a man of his size and strength should be enough to splinter the frame. If not, a few bullets into the door lock mechanism should sufficiently weaken the frame to gain access. In the latter case, he'd lose a few seconds of surprise, but he figured Harrison was probably undressed without quick access to his firearm.

He stepped back from the door and was reaching inside his jacket to retrieve his pistol when one of the guest elevators dinged, announcing its arrival on the tenth floor.

Two men in suits emerged, followed by Christine O'Connor and a young girl. The issue required a split-second decision, and Mixell turned away immediately and headed down the hallway, quickly analyzing the situation and his next move. Surprise was still on his side, but not nearly as much facing two armed protective agents. Harrison would also join the fray after hearing the shots.

Plus, there was the issue of the young girl, apparently Harrison's daughter. His contact who provided the information about Angie's visit had left out the fact that his daughter was with them as well. Although Mixell had no aversion to killing children if they deserved it, Jake's daughter was an innocent bystander in his dispute with her father. So was Angie, but she was quid pro quo for Trish.

Approaching an intersection, he resolved to take one final look behind him before deciding whether to engage or not. As he turned the corner, he glanced over his shoulder. The young girl was in the lead now, running down the hallway toward her room.

Mixell continued on.

Jake Harrison and his wife would live another day.

58

LANGLEY, VIRGINIA

In the director's seventh-floor conference room the next morning, they were already into the second hour of their meeting as Harrison and Khalila, along with Christine and three of her deputies—Bryant, Rolow, and McFarland—reviewed the information discovered by the directorate for analysis, along with the implications.

The shipment from Snyder Industries to Iran had been identified. Ten CONEX boxes with a fake manifest number—one that didn't match anything issued by the Port of Baltimore—had been identified aboard a cargo ship that departed the port the day after a similar-sized shipment left the Snyder Industry loading docks in Lanham, Maryland. Personnel in the directorate for analysis had tunneled further into the Snyder Industry databases, identifying the items transferred into the CONEX boxes that night: over one hundred high-speed gas centrifuges.

"These types of gas centrifuges," McFarland explained, "are used predominantly to separate uranium-235 from uranium-238 by applying centrifugal force upon uranium hexafluoride. These centrifuges—banned for sale to Iran by U.S. sanctions—are far more advanced than the ones currently in use by Iran, which would allow them to take the final step toward manufacturing weapon-grade uranium.

"The goal in previous negotiations with Iran has been to limit the breakout time—the time it would take for Iran to produce enough weapon-grade uranium for a single nuclear weapon—to twelve months. Limiting the breakout time to twelve months is no longer possible, since Iran has improved their uranium-enrichment capabilities over the last few years. However, the highest enrichment Iran has achieved to date is sixty percent, lower than the ninety percent required for weapon-grade uranium.

"With Iran's current centrifuges, it would still take several months for Iran to complete the enrichment of sixty percent–enriched uranium to weapon grade. But the advanced centrifuges from Snyder Industries would shorten that time to days. That means, assuming Iran has sufficient stockpiles of uranium, enough weapon-grade material for a nuclear bomb could be produced every few days."

"I thought sixty percent–enriched uranium could be used for nuclear weapons," Bryant posited.

"It can," McFarland replied, "but it takes a lot more uranium at sixty percent enrichment for the same weapon yield. Using sixty percent–enriched uranium also complicates the weapon design and delivery to its target. We don't expect Iran to move forward with nuclear weapons until they have weapon-grade uranium."

"We can't afford to let these centrifuges make it into Iranian hands," Christine said. "Where is the ship carrying the centrifuges?"

McFarland pulled up a map of the Persian Gulf on her computer and presented it on the conference room display. A yellow symbol representing a neutral surface ship appeared on the display, having just passed through the Strait of Hormuz, headed northwest.

"As you can see," McFarland said, "the ship carrying the centrifuges is already in the Persian Gulf, destined for the Iranian port of Imam Khomeini, scheduled to dock in seventeen hours—first thing tomorrow morning, Gulf time."

"That doesn't give us much time to come up with a plan," Rolow said. "Can we coordinate with the U.S. Navy and have them interdict the merchant, then board and confiscate the centrifuges?"

"We could under normal circumstances, but there's a complication." McFarland tapped her computer, and four red symbols appeared on the display, surrounding the yellow one. "The merchant is being escorted by four Russian surface combatants. I don't think a simple interdiction is in the cards."

"Why don't we destroy the centrifuges once they're offloaded in the port?" Khalila asked.

"Not a good plan," McFarland replied. "Without getting our hands on ship manifests, we can't figure out which containers the centrifuges are stored in."

"What about the uranium-enrichment facility?" Harrison asked. "Can that be destroyed instead, once the centrifuges reach their destination?"

McFarland shook her head. "Their primary uranium-enrichment plant is at Natanz, deep underground in a hardened complex beneath the Karkas Mountains. There's no assurance we can destroy the facility with conventional weapons. Plus, we'd be talking about a strike against a target on Iranian soil, rather than at sea in international waters. If we want to prevent the centrifuges from reaching their intended destination, it looks like our best option is to sink the merchant."

"How do we do that without engaging the Russian ships, or is that even possible?" Bryant asked.

"That'll be up to the president and secretary of defense," Christine answered. "I'll have to brief them right away." She turned to McFarland. "Pull a presentation together—I'll need something in an hour."

As Christine rose to leave the conference room, McFarland spoke.

"There's one more issue. I located the radio taken from the third floor of the Abbottabad house. It's in an agency storage facility in Leesburg, Virginia." McFarland pulled up a slide with the facility name and storage container ID. "I can send someone over to get it, but it might be a good idea to keep the issue between the six of us."

"I agree," Christine said. "I'll pick it up after I brief the president today. Send me the location address."

59

WASHINGTON, D.C.

The desired cast of participants for this afternoon's meeting had been hastily assembled, with Christine about to begin her brief in the Situation Room in the West Wing. The president and Christine were joined by Secretary of Defense Tom Glass, Secretary of the Navy Brenda Verbeck, Secretary of State Marcy Perini, Chief of Naval Operations Admiral Joe Sites, Captain Glen McGlothin—the president's senior military advisor—plus Thom Parham, the president's national security advisor. The first slide of Christine's presentation was displayed on the video screen on the wall opposite the president, and he signaled for Christine to begin.

The first few slides briefed the participants on the basic issue: over one hundred advanced gas centrifuges had been sold by Snyder Industries to Iran, in violation of U.S. sanctions against the country. The centrifuges were currently in transit, scheduled to arrive in an Iranian port in fourteen hours. Verbeck hadn't been pre-briefed on the details, and when Christine revealed that the centrifuges had been linked to Snyder Industries, Verbeck's face paled.

Christine didn't delve into the issue of Secretary Verbeck's relationship with the CEO of Snyder Industries; it was far too sensitive of an issue to discuss in the present forum. Plus, the SecNav-UUV-gas-centrifuge investigation was incomplete. There was no direct link yet between Verbeck and the gas centrifuges, although her relationship with Dan Snyder, the suspicious deaths of her military aide and senior Pentagon supervisor, and the fabricated UUV stories she had told to Murray Wilson were highly suspect. Whether she was an innocent pawn, master puppeteer, or something in between had not yet become clear.

After the problem was articulated, the brief shifted to the U.S. response: Should action be taken, and if so—what and when? It quickly became clear that those around the table held the same opinion as Christine and her agency colleagues: they could not allow Iran to take custody of the gas centrifuges. The topic then turned to the options available, with intervention while the centrifuges were still aboard the merchant being the preferred alternative, to avoid a sensitive military attack or clandestine operation on Iranian soil. Once an attack at sea had been settled upon, Secretary of Defense Tom Glass took the lead.

Satellite imagery of the Persian Gulf appeared on the Situation Room display, with the image zooming in to the merchant in question, *Vayenga Maersk*, being escorted by four Russian frigates. In addition, a red symbol appeared ahead of the five-ship convoy, in the shape indicating a submerged contact.

"In addition to the four Russian surface combatants, the merchant is being escorted by a Russian nuclear-powered attack submarine. Its exact location is currently unknown, but we do know it's in the Persian Gulf. It was detected by our SOSUS arrays on the ocean floor, passing through the Strait of Hormuz a few miles ahead of *Vayenga Maersk* and the four Russian surface warships.

"As far as military options go, they boil down to an attack by aircraft, surface warships, or submarines. We have sufficient assets of all three to implement any of these options. However, air and surface attack carry a higher risk of bringing Russia into this conflict, which we'd like to avoid. A missile attack against the merchant, from either aircraft or surface ships, would provoke an immediate response from the Russian surface combatants, since they won't be able to tell which ship has been targeted. Plus, there's always the possibility that one or more of our missiles could lock on to the wrong ship. A submerged attack, on the other hand, offers the opportunity for a more surgical strike, launching a surprise attack at a much closer range and with a higher probability of avoiding collateral damage to the Russian escorts."

Glass turned to Secretary of the Navy Brenda Verbeck, who continued where Glass left off.

"We have two submarines in the Persian Gulf: *Jimmy Carter* and *Michigan*, and both can reposition in time to sink the merchant before it reaches port. The plan would be to employ both submarines in tandem, with one used to distract the Russian submarine while the other moves in for the attack."

Verbeck looked to the Chief of Naval Operations, who provided additional details.

"There's still the risk of collateral damage to the Russian ships; our torpedo could lock on to the wrong contact, or we might have to sink the Russian submarine if it engages. But overall, an attack using submarines offers the highest probability of sinking the merchant without damaging any of the Russian warships."

"Seems like a solid plan," the president said, "if everything goes well. What are the cons? What's the worst-case scenario?"

Sites replied, "It could be disastrous. We could accidentally sink one or more Russian warships, they could sink one or both of our submarines, or both sides could take losses. And in the end, the merchant might escape and make it to port."

The president went around the table, soliciting input from everyone in attendance, then made his decision.

"Let's go with the attack by *Jimmy Carter* and *Michigan*. Plus, I'd like a backup plan in case the merchant makes it to port."

Sites replied, "We'll get orders sent to our submarines right away."

After the meeting ended, Christine got the president's attention. "I'd like to get on your calendar today or tomorrow to update you on some of the issues we've recently discussed. Do you have any availability?"

"Tomorrow at three, or this evening if it's critical," he replied.

"I'll set something up with your secretary."

Christine's conversation with the president didn't go unnoticed. Brenda Verbeck's eyes followed Christine until she left the conference room.

60

USS *MICHIGAN*

Standing on the Conn of the Ohio class guided missile submarine, Lieutenant Brittany Kern surveyed the watchstanders on duty in the Control Room, pausing to examine the navigation parameters:

Course: 340
Speed: 10 knots
Depth: 600 feet

Above *Michigan*, restricted to a depth of four hundred feet, *Jimmy Carter* matched *Michigan*'s course and speed as the two submarines operated in tandem. *Michigan* would soon come shallow, however, venturing into *Jimmy Carter*'s realm. *Michigan* had just entered one of its stovepipes, a circular area that *Jimmy Carter* was prohibited from entering, letting *Michigan* rise toward the surface without any risk of running into the attack submarine.

Just outside the stovepipe, *Jimmy Carter* was also preparing to head to periscope depth, with the submarine crews syncing their trips to copy the radio broadcast so both would receive message updates at the same time.

Kern's eyes shifted to the red digital clock. It was 8:40 p.m., and with the Captain's night orders directing her to download the broadcast at 9 p.m., it was time to begin preparations. The sun had set an hour earlier over the Middle East, and it would take time for Kern's eyes to adjust to the darkness.

"Quartermaster, rig Control for gray."

The bright Control Room lights were extinguished, leaving only a few low-level lights. Kern reached up, activating the microphone on the Conn.

"All stations, Conn. Make preparations to proceed to periscope depth."

Sonar, Radio, and the Quartermaster acknowledged, and the Electronic Surveillance Measures watch was manned.

After waiting several minutes, giving Sonar time to adjust their equipment lineup and complete a detailed search, Kern ordered, "Sonar, Conn. Report all contacts."

Sonar acknowledged and reported several contacts, none within ten thousand yards.

Kern called out, "Rig Control for black."

The lights in the Control Room were extinguished, leaving only the faint multicolor indications on the submarine's control panels and the red digital navigation repeaters glowing in the darkness. Kern adjusted the sonar display on the Conn, reducing its brightness to the minimum. Reaching up, she pulled the microphone from its holder and punched the button for the Captain's stateroom. "Captain, Officer of the Deck."

Murray Wilson answered, "Captain."

Kern delivered the required report, to which Wilson replied, "I'll be right there."

Wilson entered the Control Room and joined Kern on the Conn, settling into the Captain's chair on the starboard side. After reviewing the sonar display and the submarine's parameters, Wilson said, "Proceed to periscope depth."

Kern reached up in the darkness and twisted the port periscope locking ring. The barrel slid silently up through the submarine's sail, and Kern folded the periscope handles down as the scope emerged from its well, then placed her right eye against the eyepiece.

"Helm, ahead one-third. Dive, make your depth eight-zero feet. All stations, Conn. Proceeding to periscope depth."

The Helm rang up ahead one-third on the Engine Order Telegraph as the Diving Officer directed his planesmen, "Ten up. Full rise, fairwater planes."

As *Michigan* rose toward the surface, silence descended on Control aside from the occasional depth reports from the Diving Officer.

"Passing one hundred feet."

The Diving Officer reported the submarine's depth change in ten-foot increments until the periscope broke the ocean's surface. Kern began circling, completing a revolution every eight seconds, scanning the darkness for nearby ships. She spotted only two faint white lights to the west.

"No close contacts!"

Conversation in Control resumed, now that *Michigan* was safely at periscope depth, and Kern slowed her rotation, periodically shifting the scope to high power for long-range scans.

The Quartermaster announced, "Conn, Nav. GPS fix obtained."

A moment later, Radio followed up. "Conn, Radio. Download complete."

Kern announced, "All stations, Conn. Going deep. Helm, ahead two-thirds. Dive, make your depth one-eight-zero feet."

The Helm and Diving Officer acknowledged, and *Michigan* tilted downward. After the periscope slid beneath the ocean waves, Kern lowered the scope back into its well.

"Rig Control for gray," she announced, and the low-level lights flicked on.

A few minutes later, as Kern ordered the Control Room rigged for white, a radioman entered with a message clipboard in hand. Captain Wilson flipped through the messages: all but two were routine traffic. *Michigan* had received a new waterspace management message, along with new operational orders.

Wilson studied the OPORD, noting the complexity and urgency of the mission: eleven hours to get into position and sink a merchant escorted by Russian warships. Additional information would arrive SEPCOR—via separate correspondence. Wilson also noted the unique tandem arrangement with *Jimmy Carter*, which Wilson assumed had just received new orders as well. Sonar's next report confirmed his assessment.

"Conn, Sonar. Detect burst of cavitation from *Jimmy Carter*. Down doppler. She's increasing speed and turning to the northeast."

Wilson called the Messenger of the Watch over to the Conn.

"Round up all officers. There will be a meeting in the Wardroom in fifteen minutes."

To his Officer of the Deck, Wilson ordered, "Come down to six hundred feet, course zero-seven-zero. Increase speed to ahead flank."

61

LEESBURG, VIRGINIA

It was after 5 p.m. when Christine emerged from the Pentagon, having stopped by the Navy's operations center coordinating the merchant ship attack, ensuring the CIA had provided all relevant information about the ship and its contents. As a former Pentagon weapons program analyst and national security advisor, she was interested in the planning—it was a part of her previous job that she missed.

By the time she departed the secure spaces in the Pentagon and retrieved her cell phone, a message from McFarland awaited: the address of the CIA facility in nearby Leesburg, Virginia, where the radio taken from the Abbottabad compound was stored.

It was rush hour on the Capital Beltway and its arteries, and the ninety-minute trip to Leesburg in the back of her SUV provided an opportunity for her thoughts to wander: the pending attack on the merchant ship transporting the gas centrifuges, Secretary Verbeck's potential involvement in the scheme and its cover-up, the prisoner taken from Abbottabad and what had happened to him, and Khalila's true identity.

Her driver followed the GPS directions to the agency facility, turning from a main highway onto a two-lane road delving into a heavily forested area in the Virginia wilderness, with trees leaning over a poorly maintained road. After a ten-minute trip, the vegetation gave way to a several-acre clearing containing a three-story building surrounded by an electric fence topped by barbed wire.

Christine's SUV stopped by the single entry point, guarded by two armed men, and the driver showed his agency ID. The gate slid aside and after entering the compound, the driver parked near the entrance. There were only a dozen cars in the parking lot.

Christine left her protective agents behind in the vehicle, and after another ID check in the building lobby, she was directed to the basement, where a single person manned a large warehouse of row upon row of containers stacked forty feet high. Upon closer examination, she realized it was a sophisticated filing system with built-in drawers.

Following a third ID check and an entry into the visitor log, the man looked up with a surprised expression after realizing who she was. Christine provided the drawer ID and the man typed it into the computer. A robotic forklift nearby started moving, turning in to one of the corridors, stopping midway down the row. Its arms rose, then slid into grooves where they clicked into place, and a drawer was extracted.

The forklift returned to the front of the warehouse, where it deposited the drawer on a table off to the side.

"Let me know when you're done, ma'am," the man said as he handed Christine a printout with the container combination.

Christine punched the numbers into the drawer's electronic lock and lifted the lid. She sorted through the container's contents, which appeared to be all of the electronic equipment taken from the third floor of the Abbottabad house. However, there was no radio. She searched the contents again and located the charger, but no radio.

She spotted a sheet of paper in a holder inside the container, which was an itemized list of the drawer's contents. Christine went down the list, her finger stopping when it came across the desired item—*handheld transceiver.*

Christine turned to the warehouse attendant. "Do you know what happened to the transceiver that's supposed to be in this drawer?"

"I can check the logs to see if it's been checked out." He began typing on his computer. "By the way," he said, "why all the sudden interest in that drawer?"

Christine was surprised by the man's question. "What do you mean, *all* the sudden interest?"

"You're the second person who's searched through its contents today."

"What?" Christine said reflexively. There were only five others who knew about the drawer. "Who was the other person?"

The man pulled up the visitor log. "Khalila Dufour."

Christine wondered why Khalila would want the radio, if she'd even taken it in the first place. Perhaps it wasn't there to begin with.

"Did she take the radio?"

"She didn't check anything out, but I can't say for sure that she didn't pocket the radio while she was here. I didn't watch her the whole time. That's not my job," he added defensively. "I just retrieve and store the drawers."

Beads of sweat formed on his brow as he spoke with the director of the CIA, who seemed upset with the performance of his duties.

Christine gave a terse nod, determined not to take her anger out on the man standing before her. By the time she exited the facility, however, the sun had begun to set, and the darkening skies matched her mood. She was fuming. Why would Khalila have taken the transceiver? Christine had no answers because she knew too little about Khalila. She'd had enough of the DDO's secrecy concerning Khalila's identity. He was going to come clean about who she was—tonight.

She called Rolow's office phone in case he was still at work, but it went to voice mail. When she called his home phone, he answered.

"PJ here."

"This is Christine," she said, tamping down on her anger for the moment. "We need to talk—tonight."

"About what?"

"We'll discuss it when I get there."

She checked his address in her phone, filed under an alias since the DDO's residence was a closely guarded secret, even within the agency. He lived near Fairfax, Virginia, not far away.

"I'll be there in a half hour."

Christine hung up, and as she walked to her car, she decided she wanted the entire cast of characters present tonight, especially Khalila. She dialed Harrison.

When he answered, she asked, "Do you know where Khalila is?"

"She's sitting beside me in the car. We just left the NCTC," he said, referring to the National Counterterrorism Center in McLean, Virginia. "We've been running down potential leads on Mixell."

"Bring Khalila to the DDO's house, now. There are a few things we need to discuss."

Harrison must have noticed Christine's tone, because he didn't inquire about the details. His only question was a simple one.

"What's the address?"

62

FAIRFAX, VIRGINIA

PJ Rolow, the deputy director for operations, lived alone in a two-story colonial on a secluded ten-acre plot monitored by a sophisticated security system, with a four-man protective agent detail stationed less than a minute away. Christine's SUV pulled into Rolow's driveway and Christine emerged from the vehicle, leaving her protective agents behind. As she moved up the walkway, her simmering anger and frustration regarding Khalila reached the boiling point.

When Rolow answered the door, Christine barged into his foyer.

"Who is she? Khalila!"

Rolow backed up as she advanced, his eyes going wide in the presence of the enraged director. He said nothing as Christine glared at him.

He finally nodded, then moved past her, closing the front door. "Let's talk in my study."

Rolow led Christine upstairs, where he turned off his cell phone and placed it on a small table in the hallway before entering the study. Christine did the same; they were clearly going to discuss classified matters.

Once inside the study, Rolow closed the door and went to a credenza, where he poured a drink into a crystal glass. He offered her one, but she declined.

"Who is she?" Christine asked again.

"I can't tell you."

"What do you mean, you can't tell me? I'm the director of the CIA."

"Doesn't matter," he said. "Khalila's file is sealed."

"On whose authority?"

"The president's."

Christine was taken aback, wondering why the president would withhold this information from her. But Rolow hadn't specified *which* president.

"The current president?"

"No. A previous one."

"Fine. I'll have the current president authorize it."

"He won't. Once he sees her file, he'll seal it just like the last two presidents."

"We'll see about that," Christine retorted. She had an excellent relationship with the president. He had been the one who had nominated her for CIA director in the first place.

She moved toward the door to retrieve her phone, but Rolow took her gently by the arm.

"It'd be better if you didn't know."

"Who else knows?"

"Only Bryant and me," he said as he released her.

"That's what the presidential decree says?"

Rolow nodded. "Only two persons at the agency are authorized to know: the DD and DDO."

Christine contemplated Rolow's assertion—that it'd be better if she didn't know—then decided to shift topics.

"I have concerns about Khalila, and what I want to know is whether she can be trusted."

Rolow considered her question at length, and when he didn't immediately respond, Christine blurted, "Damn it, PJ, it's a simple question! Can she be trusted?"

"I don't know!"

Christine was stunned by Rolow's admission.

"What do you mean, *you don't know*? She's a CIA field officer with access to classified information, and she's currently involved in two incredibly sensitive investigations: a potentially corrupt secretary of the Navy and that bin Laden might have been captured instead of killed."

"I know, I know," Rolow replied.

"What the hell, Rolow? Why did you let someone you don't fully trust into this position?"

"Her access to critical individuals and organizations in the Middle East outweighs the risk."

Christine glared at him for a moment. When she spoke, her voice lowered a notch. "I should be the one who makes that assessment." Then she moved toward the door.

"Where are you going?"

"To get my phone. I'm calling the president."

This time, Rolow didn't stop her.

She called the president on his cell phone—knowing his number was one of the perks of being on his staff as his national security advisor. When he answered, she put him on speaker.

"Good evening, Mr. President. This is Christine O'Connor. I apologize for bothering you tonight, but there's a critical CIA file sealed by a previous president, and I need your permission to access that information."

"What file is that?"

Rolow intervened. "Mr. President, this is Director for Operations PJ Rolow. The file concerns the background of one of our field officers. It contains highly sensitive information, and the file was sealed by the last two presidents, accessible only by myself and the deputy director. I strongly recommend you sustain that precedent."

"You're asking me to withhold critical information from the director of the CIA?" the president asked. "Information that you and the deputy director have access to? That sounds a bit backward, if you ask me."

Rolow expounded on what he had discussed earlier with Christine. "The thought process is that CIA directors are political appointees who typically don't stay in the job very long. They're also affiliated by party, and the information in this file could be weaponized against administrations of the opposite party for political gain."

"You realize, PJ, that Christine is from the opposite party of my administration? Yet I appointed her as CIA director anyway?"

"Yes, Mr. President, I do realize that. It's just that—"

The president interjected, "You have my authorization to provide whatever information is in that file to Christine. She has my complete confidence. Is that understood?"

"Yes, Mr. President."

"Christine," the president added, "brief me on the contents of the file at the earliest opportunity."

"Yes, sir."

The president hung up and Christine placed the phone on the hallway table. After returning to the study, Rolow closed the door again and gestured toward a chair.

"I'll tell you what I know."

Christine refused the proffered chair, standing with her arms folded across her chest.

"I'm waiting."

63

LANGLEY, VIRGINIA

Tracey McFarland, working late in her office, was wrapping things up for the evening when she noticed an email arrive in her in-box. It was from the translation section of the CIA Office of Terrorism Analysis, where she had sent Harrison's video of Khalila meeting Abdallah bin Laden and his three companions outside the Al Hamra Tower in Kuwait City.

She opened the email and reviewed the identity of the four men: Harrison had been correct—one of them was Abdallah bin Laden, Osama's son. She then reviewed the transcript of the conversation between Abdallah and Khalila, derived from audio they were able to pull from the video. She read the transcript, confused from the outset, then returned to the beginning.

This can't be right.

The audio must have been of poor quality and misunderstood. Her thoughts went in several directions as she debated how to proceed, then she picked up the phone and called the linguist who had translated the audio and sent the email.

When he answered, she said, "This is McFarland. I'd like a backup translation of the audio file you just sent me."

"I'm confident it's correct," the man said.

"I didn't ask if you thought it was correct!" Tracey yelled. "I said I want a backup translation! And I want it in the next five minutes!"

"Yes, ma'am."

"I also want you to lock that file down, with my authority or higher to access."

Tracey slammed the phone down, then debated what to do next.

Christine needed to know. She picked up the phone again and dialed the director, but the call went directly to voice mail. Her phone must be off.

She tapped her desk, waiting for the second translation to come in. She'd given the man five minutes, but she had no idea how long it would really take. She then decided to call the person who *really* needed to know.

Jake Harrison was driving west on Interstate 66 with Khalila sitting beside him, headed to the DDO's home outside Fairfax, when his cell phone rang. When he brought it to his ear, it was McFarland on the other end.

"Jake, this is Tracey," she said. Her voice seemed unsettled. "I received the report on the video you took of Khalila meeting bin Laden's son. I know who she is."

Harrison glanced at Khalila, then replied, "Please, share the news."

"I need to discuss this with the DDO and Christine first. But what I can say for now is—do *not* trust her."

"I see," Harrison said, answering succinctly to conceal the topic of his conversation with McFarland. "Anything else?"

"I'll get back to you soon, but be careful," McFarland said, then hung up.

"Who was that?" Khalila asked.

She had noticed the glance in her direction, followed by his cryptic response to McFarland. Despite his best attempt, her suspicion had been raised. After a moment of hesitation, he decided to reveal a portion of their conversation.

"McFarland," Harrison replied. "She says not to trust you. Should I be worried?"

Khalila laughed. "Hardly."

Earlier in the day, Khalila had left on an errand, and after she had returned, she'd been in a dark mood the rest of the afternoon. For some reason, it felt good to hear her laugh.

Harrison grinned, then returned his focus to the road.

He caught a flash of movement in the corner of his eye, then felt cold metal against the side of his head. He glanced at Khalila; her pistol was pressed against his temple.

Harrison clenched his hands on the steering wheel as he assessed his options. There weren't many, and they were all bad. They continued down the road in silence, with Khalila neither pulling the trigger nor putting her weapon down.

He sensed her indecision, then asked again, adding more emphasis to his words.

"Should I be worried?"

"That depends on what else McFarland told you."

Another email from the Office of Terrorism Analysis appeared in Mc-Farland's in-box, followed immediately by her phone ringing.

She picked up the phone. "McFarland."

"I've obtained an independent translation," the man said. "The original translation is correct."

"Thank you," McFarland said, then hung up the phone, her mind going numb for a moment.

She reread the audio translation, focusing on Abdallah's greeting when he had met Khalila.

Welcome, sister.

If Abdallah was bin Laden's son, that meant Khalila was—Osama bin Laden's *daughter.*

64

FAIRFAX, VIRGINIA

When Rolow finished explaining, Christine stared at him in stunned silence for a moment, then sank into a chair.

"I'll take that drink now."

Rolow poured one in a crystal glass and handed it to her.

She took a sip, then asked, "How the hell did you get your hooks into her?"

"She came to us."

"Oh, that's a red flag."

"Agreed. It took a while to sort through things, and we're still not sure what to make of it. We ended up keeping her at the farm for two training cycles as we tried to convince ourselves she'd come forth with a genuine aim to help us, rather than to work her way into a position where she could feed information to al-Qaeda and other terrorist organizations."

Rolow explained, "To exploit her connections, Khalila pretends to be a double agent, providing screened information to Middle Eastern contacts in exchange for actionable information for us."

"What's your assessment? Do you think she's truly working for us or someone else?"

Rolow shrugged. "She's always obtained the information we desired and has never revealed anything unauthorized as far as we can tell, but she's also lost a few partners in the process. We're not sure if it's a string of bad luck or she's covering her tracks, eliminating anyone who learns too much."

"And you teamed her up with Harrison?"

"The president said to pull out all the stops on the SecNav assassination attempt, so that meant we assigned Khalila. Harrison's not an irreplaceable asset like she is; his loss wouldn't be significant."

Christine didn't agree with Rolow's assessment. Harrison *would* be a significant loss, at least to her. But she had to keep her personal interests from interfering with her job. Rolow was correct; compared to Khalila, Harrison was disposable.

"If any of our political enemies find out who we've let into the agency . . ." she said.

"As you can see," he said, "this is a sensitive issue from several angles. The maximum secrecy regarding her identity is required."

Christine agreed, then considered what she had learned today, suddenly realizing that Rolow didn't know about bin Laden's radio. In her mind, what Khalila had done was a telltale. She was protecting whoever had been aiding her father while he was on the run. She explained to Rolow that the radio was missing and that Khalila had visited the facility earlier in the day.

"That tells me," she said, "that she's not on our side."

The revelation created a concerned look on Rolow's face.

65

MERRIFIELD, VIRGINIA

With the cold metal barrel of Khalila's pistol pressed against his temple, Harrison decided his best chance of survival was to talk his way out. He'd been there before, in Syria, when Khalila had her pistol aimed at him from across the room.

"We have an agreement," he said. "I keep whatever I learn about you to myself. I haven't violated that agreement, which means you need to hold up your end of the bargain."

"I included a caveat," Khalila replied. "Our agreement holds as long as you don't learn who I am. So . . . what did McFarland tell you?"

"You've got a pistol pointed at my head. What do you think my answer's going to be? Plus, I'm driving down the interstate at seventy miles per hour. Do you really want to put a bullet in my head right now?"

He let his question sink in, then continued, "At this point, all I can do is reiterate our agreement—whatever your secret is, it's safe with me. Put your pistol down and let's talk."

He pressed harder on the gas, accelerating the car.

Khalila glanced at the speedometer, then at the traffic they were speeding past.

Slowly, she lowered her weapon.

The pistol was still in her hand, but it was resting in her lap now instead of aimed at his head. There was a vacant look in her eyes as she stared directly ahead. It was quiet in the car as it sped down the interstate, until Khalila finally spoke.

"I was thirteen at the time," she began. "I remember sitting in front of the TV, watching the replays of the aircraft crashing into the Twin Towers in New York City, staring in horror as the buildings collapsed. I remember being amazed at the destruction wrought by two aircraft and terrified by what the victims must have endured. The men and women crushed inside the buildings, and others trapped by the fires on the higher floors, choosing to leap to their deaths instead of being burned alive. In my dreams, I still hear the sound of their bodies hitting the pavement.

"After learning my father was responsible, I was overwhelmed with guilt and shame. Arabs value family honor, and my family has been dishonored by the murder of three thousand innocent men, women, and children. While some cheered what my father had accomplished, I vowed to do what I could to restore that honor. To repay America in some way for what my family had done.

"After I graduated from university, I joined al-Qaeda, using my status as Osama's daughter to work my way into a leadership position, where I eventually proposed the plan I'd been plotting all along. I would offer my services to the CIA using the rationale I just explained—the shame and sorrow for what my father had done—hoping to make amends in some way. Al-Qaeda leadership approved, and I've been feeding them information ever since I became a CIA officer."

Harrison pondered Khalila's stunning revelation—that she was Osama bin Laden's daughter—along with her backstory of shame and atonement. The rationale for her joining the CIA could be either true or false, depending on which side she was truly working for.

Khalila seemed to read his mind, or perhaps the issue was never far from hers. "Only I know my true motivation. But what matters is that both al-Qaeda and the CIA believe I'm working for them. Within that construct, I can achieve what I desire."

"What if one side determines you're really working for the other side?"

Khalila shrugged. "There's a phrase for that—*It's been good knowing you*. But I've already achieved much, saving the lives of hundreds, if not thousands. I can go to my grave knowing that I accomplished my goal."

"So," Harrison said, "how does this work out? Our agreement is—I stay alive as long as I don't learn your true identity—but you're the one who revealed it."

"It doesn't matter," she said, glancing at the pistol in her lap. "You know who I am now."

66

USS *MICHIGAN*

"Helm, ahead two-thirds."

Murray Wilson observed from the Captain's chair on the Conn as the Officer of the Deck, Lieutenant Brian Resor, slowed *Michigan* from ahead flank. Based on the Common Operational Picture—a fused sensor display incorporating worldwide assets, including satellites—the merchant ship and its Russian warship escort should be just within sensor range.

It was 3 a.m. and quiet on the mid-watch as *Michigan's* crew prepared to engage. Wilson would have preferred to wait until daylight, when periscope observations provided valuable information, helping *Michigan's* crew quickly determine the contact's course and range. However, the merchant ship, *Vayenga Maersk*, was scheduled to dock at 8 a.m. and would soon enter water too shallow for *Michigan* and *Jimmy Carter* to operate effectively.

Jimmy Carter, *Michigan's* sister ship in this endeavor, would attempt to capture the Russian submarine crew's attention, letting *Michigan* slip within range of its MK 48 torpedoes. It was unlikely that the Russian submarine would fire unless it or one of the surface ships were attacked, so Gallaher's goal aboard *Jimmy Carter* was to simply distract the Russian crew. If the Russian submarine fired, however, Gallagher was authorized to sink it.

Gallagher's submarine was supposedly several thousand yards off the port beam, but *Jimmy Carter* had been too quiet to track during the high-speed transit as both submarines repositioned to sink the merchant before it reached port. While traveling at ahead flank, the turbulent flow of water across the submarine's acoustic sensors reduced their effective range. But now, as *Michigan* slowed to ten knots, her sensors could search farther out.

Sonar reported, "Conn, Sonar. Gained one submerged and five surface contacts, designated Sierra three-one through three-six. Sierra three-one, on the port beam, is *Jimmy Carter* based on tonals. Sierra three-two, to the east, is classified merchant, and Sierra three-three through three-six, also to the east, are classified surface warships. Analyzing."

Wilson, who overheard the report, ordered the Officer of the Deck, "Man Battle Stations Torpedo silently."

The Messenger and the LAN Technician of the Watch spread the word throughout the bunk rooms and common areas of the Operations Compartment, while the Chief of the Watch informed personnel in the Engine Room. Personnel streamed into Control, taking their seats at dormant consoles, bringing them to life as they donned their sound-powered phone headsets, while supervisors gathered behind their respective stations.

After receiving reports from each station, the Chief of the Watch announced, "Battle Stations Torpedo is manned with the exception of the Conning Officer."

Wilson announced, "This is the Captain. I have the Conn. Lieutenant Resor retains the Deck. Designate Sierra three-two as Master one and Sierra three-three through three-six as Master two through five. Master one is the target of interest, while we must avoid sinking Master two through five if possible."

He followed up, "Make preparations to proceed to periscope depth. Rig Control for gray."

The Control Room lights shifted to gray, helping Wilson's eyes prepare for periscope observations at night.

A moment later, Sonar reported, "Conn, Sonar. Surface warships are classified Russian Admiral Grigorovich and Admiral Gorshkov class, two of each."

Wilson acknowledged the report, then studied the sonar display on the Conn. The merchant and Russian warship bearings were clumped closely together, which indicated they were a fair distance away. It would take time for the combat control system algorithms to discern their range. In the meantime, Wilson needed to be sure that Master one was indeed the merchant, by examining her navigation and deck lighting arrangement through the periscope.

"Rig Control for black."

The lights flicked off, enveloping the Control Room watchstanders in darkness, aside from the faint illuminations of their displays and control panel indications. Not long thereafter, Wilson received the report he'd been hoping for.

"Conn, Sonar. Have a new contact designated Sierra three-seven, bearing zero-eight-five, classified submerged. Analyzing."

They had found the Russian submarine, which was out in front of the merchant and surface warship convoy. He now knew which area to avoid.

Wilson announced, "Designate Sierra three-seven as Master six. Track Master six."

"Conn, Sonar. *Jimmy Carter* is increasing speed."

It seemed Gallagher's crew had also detected the Russian submarine and were moving out to distract their adversary. It was time for *Michigan* to engage.

Wilson twisted the periscope ring above his head, then announced, "Raising number two scope." As it rose from its well, he flipped the handles down and adjusted the optics for his eye prescription.

"All stations, Conn. Proceeding to periscope depth. Dive, make your depth eight-zero feet."

The Diving Officer complied, and *Michigan* tilted upward.

67

FAIRFAX, VIRGINIA

As Christine and Rolow mapped the way ahead regarding Khalila, Christine heard Rolow's front door open and close, followed by footsteps on the stairs. Christine turned to confront Khalila once she arrived with Harrison, but another woman appeared instead. Secretary of the Navy Brenda Verbeck stopped in the study's doorway.

The two women locked eyes for a moment before Brenda turned to Rolow.

"What's the plan?"

McFarland's revelation that Rolow had dated Brenda for five years flashed in Christine's mind, and she suddenly realized that their relationship had endured in some capacity. A capacity that didn't bode well for her tonight.

The realization must have been evident on her face, because Brenda said, "So, you finally get it now. This was never going to turn out the way you imagined, Christine. You live in an imaginary world of right and wrong, good and bad, innocent and guilty. A world where I go to jail and you live."

From a nearby table drawer, Rolow pulled a pistol with an attached suppressor, then leveled it at Christine.

"I misinterpreted the reason for your visit," he said. "I figured you had come across definitive proof that Brenda was involved in the death of her aide and Pentagon supervisor or that she had deliberately misled Captain Wilson regarding the UUV. That being the case, and with you being the only person who knew all the elements of the plan—you were the only one at the agency who had talked with Wilson—we figured it was time you were removed from the equation."

"This is unfortunate," Brenda said. "I've tried to keep those affected to the minimum, and I hate to see a woman as accomplished as you meet her demise, but I really don't have a choice. The others—Bryant, McFarland, and your two field officers—have incomplete information and can be managed, and whatever Wilson has discovered can be concealed with the right security classifications and nondisclosure agreements.

"Plus, there's nothing linking me to the murders of my aide and the Pentagon chief." Brenda moved beside Rolow and draped an arm on his shoulder. "PJ was kind enough to make the arrangements.

"Unfortunately," Brenda said, "you have the necessary information to put it all together. That's something we can't allow."

68

USS *MICHIGAN*

"Passing one-five-zero feet," the Diving Officer announced.

Through the periscope, the moon's blue-white reflection became visible, wavering on the water's surface, growing slowly larger as *Michigan* rose from the ocean depths.

"Eight-zero feet."

When the scope optics broke the surface, Wilson began rotating the periscope, scanning the darkness for nearby ships.

"No close contacts!"

There were several white lights in the distance to the east, and Wilson steadied up on the contacts, shifting the periscope to high power, then squeezing the doubler on the periscope handle. There were five ships headed north, based on Wilson seeing their port running lights. Four were warships, evident by their clean navigation profile—a red port running light and single white masthead light—while the fifth ship, in the middle of the four warships, was a merchant, its deck lights partially energized.

"Stand by for initial observations, Victor one through five," Wilson announced.

Lieutenant Commander Tom Montgomery, *Michigan*'s Fire Control Coordinator, divided the five contacts among the three operators manning the combat control consoles, and each watchstander called out, "Ready."

After aligning the periscope on the first contact, Wilson announced, "Victor one, designated merchant. Bearing, mark." He pressed the red button on the right periscope handle, sending the contact bearing to the combat control system, then shifted to the next contact. "Victor two, designated surface warship. Bearing, mark." He pressed the red button again.

Wilson repeated the process for the next three warships, then flipped the periscope handles up as the Periscope Assistant, standing beside him, reached up and rotated the periscope locking ring. The scope descended into its well, minimizing the potential that *Michigan*'s approach would be discovered by one of the Russian warships' periscope detection radars.

Montgomery evaluated the bearings to the five visual contacts, comparing them to the sonar bearings to Masters one through five, then announced, "Victor one correlates to Master one, the target of interest."

Now that Wilson had confirmed Master one was indeed the merchant, he evaluated the quality of their target solutions. He stopped by the three combat control consoles, joining Montgomery. All three operators had similar solutions, with the merchant traveling at a typical twenty-knot speed, headed toward its reported destination of Imam Khomeini. Wilson concluded that the merchant's estimated course, speed, and range were accurate enough to engage.

The final question was—were they within range of *Michigan*'s torpedoes?

"Weapons Control Coordinator." Wilson addressed the submarine's Weapons Officer, overseeing torpedo employment. "Assign Master one to tube One. Report fuel remaining."

Lieutenant Ryan Jescovitch complied, reporting, "Fuel remaining, twenty-one percent."

The combat control system algorithms had calculated that after the torpedo completed its mission—detecting the target and homing to detonation—it would still have twenty-one percent of its fuel remaining. More than enough, Wilson concluded, to catch the merchant, even if it was alerted by the Russian warship crews and attempted to evade.

Wilson evaluated the five surface ships on the geographic display on the nearest console. The five ships were packed tightly together, with two Russian warships on each side and the merchant in the middle. It was a difficult scenario, ensuring their torpedo sank the merchant and not a nearby warship.

World War II–era torpedoes were straight runners, launched from close range and aimed ahead of the target so the torpedo simply ran into the ship. But modern torpedoes were artificially intelligent weapons with their own sonars and computerized brains. Launched from much farther distances, they would travel most of the way with their sonars off to delay alerting their target, turning on the sonar in their nose at a predetermined point.

Michigan's torpedo would have to pass beneath both warships on the near side of the formation before going active, when its independent processing would take over, attacking the first valid target identified, which would hopefully be the merchant. While it was a scenario Wilson and his crew had trained for, it would have to be carefully managed.

"Firing Point Procedures," Wilson announced, "Master one, tube One primary, tube Two backup. Use standard surface presets, except enable each weapon one thousand yards from Master one."

Montgomery stopped briefly behind each of the combat control consoles, examining the target solution on each one, tapping one of the fire control technicians. The technician pressed a button on his console and Montgomery called out, "Solution ready."

The operator at the Weapon Launch Console sent the course, speed, and range of their target to the torpedoes in tubes One and Two, along with applicable search presets, then announced, "Weapon ready."

"Ship ready," Lieutenant Resor announced, informing Wilson that the submarine's torpedo countermeasures—their decoys and jammers—were ready to deploy.

"Match Sonar bearing and shoot!" Wilson ordered.

The torpedo was ejected from its tube, then turned to an intercept course with Master one.

Under normal circumstances, it was unlikely the Russian warship crews would detect the incoming MK 48 torpedo. It was fired from long range, so the launch transient would have been undetectable. The torpedo's sonar would be dormant during the inbound transit, programmed to turn on after it passed beneath both warships. The torpedo's engine noise was also unlikely to alert anyone of the attack, given the warships' own propulsion-related noise and the proximity of the loud merchant.

However, Wilson was attacking at night, and the bioluminescent trail of the incoming torpedo would be detectable. The two Russian warships on this side of the formation would likely counterfire.

Wilson waited tensely as their torpedo sped toward the five-ship convoy. When it was several thousand yards away, Sonar made the report Wilson feared.

"Torpedo in the water, bearing one-zero-five! Correlates to launch from Master two." A few seconds later, Sonar followed up. "Second torpedo in the water, bearing one-zero-eight! Correlates to launch from Master four."

Wilson responded immediately, "Helm, ahead full. Dive, make your depth four hundred feet."

Two lightweight torpedoes were headed *Michigan*'s way, launched from the Russian warships' deck-mounted torpedo tubes. Sonar confirmed Wilson's assessment.

"Sonar, Conn. Incoming torpedoes are classified as Paket-NK lightweight torpedoes."

As *Michigan* tilted downward and accelerated, Wilson evaluated the nearest tactical display, selecting the optimal evasion course.

"Helm, left full rudder, steady course three-four-zero."

The Helm complied and *Michigan* turned to port.

Normally, evading a lightweight torpedo fired from this distance wouldn't be difficult, but these two were traveling side by side, sweeping a large swath of the ocean with their sonars. The torpedo to the north might approach close enough to detect *Michigan*. Wilson decided to give it something to focus on besides his submarine.

"Officer of the Deck, launch countermeasures."

Lieutenant Resor complied, launching a torpedo decoy, followed by an acoustic jammer.

FAIRFAX, VIRGINIA

Christine tried to talk her way out of Rolow's madness—killing a CIA director in his study—but he had an answer for everything. Christine had two protective agents in her SUV parked outside, who would know she had been killed in the DDO's home, but Rolow pointed out that neither man would be threatened as he emerged from his home and approached the vehicle, stopping by the driver's side. The window would be rolled down to speak with the DDO, and it would be over in seconds, both agents dead. Their bodies would be disposed of, along with Christine's, in a suitable location, and one of America's enemies would be blamed.

Their conversation seemed to be coming to an end when the doorbell rang.

Rolow handed his pistol to Brenda and went to his computer, pulling up a nine-panel grid of security cameras. On one of them, Harrison and Khalila stood at the front door. Harrison pressed the doorbell again.

Christine capitalized on the unexpected arrival of the two agency officers.

"They know I'm here," she said. "Before I arrived, I called Harrison and told him to meet me here. Plus, my SUV is out front. You can't kill me now, unless you plan to kill Khalila and Harrison, along with my protective agents. You can't surprise all four of them at once."

"Leave that up to me," Rolow growled.

Christine had no idea how Khalila would factor into all of this, but she left that for Rolow to worry about.

He took the pistol back from Brenda, then told her to wait in his bedroom, so her presence in the study wouldn't alert Harrison or Khalila to the ongoing foul play.

After she left, Rolow approached Christine, placing the pistol barrel against her head.

"When Harrison and Khalila arrive," he said, "play along and you'll live. We'll work something out afterward."

Christine knew Rolow was lying. His only way out was to kill all three of them, then lay the blame on Khalila, an al-Qaeda agent who had infiltrated the CIA. Still, at least there was a glimmer of hope when there had been none before. Both Harrison and Khalila were armed, which gave them a chance.

In the meantime, Christine nodded her understanding—she'd play along, for now.

Rolow placed the weapon in the pants waistband behind his back, then pressed a key on his computer, unlatching the front door.

"Come in," he said to the computer display. "We're upstairs in the study."

Christine watched Harrison and Khalila enter the foyer, then head upstairs.

Jake Harrison climbed the stairs to the second floor of Rolow's house, spotting two cell phones on a small table beside a door. He knocked, and when Rolow acknowledged, he entered the DDO's study, followed by Khalila.

He immediately sensed that something was wrong. Christine and Rolow were standing opposite each other, and there was something unnatural about Christine's posture. She stood stiffly and seemed worried, maybe even afraid. He tried not to let on as he greeted Rolow and moved toward Christine, keeping the DDO in front of him.

Khalila hung back near the door. She'd been in a dark mood since their conversation in the car, when she had agreed to abide by their agreement—she would take no action against Harrison as long as he kept her identity a secret. The situation had become more complicated now that McFarland and likely others in the CIA knew who she was.

As he studied the DDO, Harrison came to the conclusion that something was definitely wrong. Rolow was tense as well. Harrison's instincts told him—*act now*!

He pulled his pistol from his shoulder harness and leveled it at Rolow. He saw Rolow's right hand twitch—he had started going for something behind his back, then decided otherwise.

"He's armed," Christine said. "He's got a pistol behind his back. He was going to kill me."

"Really," Harrison said, his eyes narrowing as he remained focused on Rolow. "Put your hands in the air and turn around slowly."

He could see the rage on Rolow's face as he followed the instructions. Khalila moved forward and pulled the pistol from his back, then joined Harrison.

When Rolow turned to face them again, Harrison kept his eyes on him, then asked Christine, "What's going on?"

"He's in league with Secretary Verbeck. Rolow is the one who arranged the deaths of Verbeck's military aide and Pentagon supervisor. Verbeck is in his bedroom right now."

"Is she armed?" Harrison asked.

"Not when she left the study."

Harrison motioned to Khalila to round up Verbeck, and she moved into the hallway and disappeared. She returned a moment later, with Secretary Verbeck leading the way. Verbeck stopped beside Rolow while Khalila stayed near the door, keeping both pairs—Rolow and Verbeck, and Harrison and Christine—in view.

"Where do we go from here?" Harrison asked Christine. "We've got a complicated situation, with a renegade DDO and corrupt SecNav. Who do we call—the FBI?"

"I think you're going to have a problem doing that," Rolow said.

"Why is that?" Harrison asked.

Rolow gestured toward Khalila.

She had a pistol in each hand: her own, plus Rolow's. One was pointed at the DDO while the other was aimed at Harrison.

"Drop your weapon, Jake," she said.

"What the hell, Khalila? What are you doing?"

"Drop your weapon!"

Harrison realized too late that Khalila had played them all, her true colors emerging now that she had stumbled into an absolute coup for al-Qaeda: the execution of the CIA director and DDO in one swoop.

She had been absolutely brilliant, worming her way into the CIA and playing along until the perfect opportunity presented itself.

He considered whether to take his chances in a shootout. The odds weren't in his favor, however. Khalila's eyes and a pistol were locked onto him, while Harrison had his firearm pointed at Rolow. He'd have to swing his pistol toward Khalila and shoot before she squeezed the trigger. The odds of him firing first were nil.

Harrison briefly entertained the thought of diving into a roll, giving her a moving target as he brought his weapon to bear, but she'd shoot the instant she detected sudden movement.

It took a few seconds, but Harrison finally conceded.

He dropped his pistol onto the floor.

"Kick it to me," she said, and he complied. The pistol slid to a stop at her feet.

Rolow turned to Harrison and Christine. "Looks like we're back on the same team."

70

USS *MICHIGAN*

"First torpedo bears one-one-five. Second torpedo bears one-two-zero."

Wilson acknowledged Sonar's report and evaluated the situation—both torpedoes were approaching from *Michigan*'s starboard aft quarter—then reassessed his submarine's evasion speed. He had ordered ahead full instead of flank in an attempt to retain the thin copper wire attached to their torpedo. The ship convoy would likely change course, and Wilson's crew would need to send an update to their torpedo. It was still traveling blind, with its sonar off, and would need a course correction if the merchant maneuvered before the torpedo gained contact.

Until the torpedo enabled and detected its target, it was Wilson's responsibility to keep it on the proper path. He glanced at the Weapon Control Console. Thus far, they had retained the wire.

He returned his attention to the incoming torpedoes. They remained on a steady course with an aft bearing rate, indicating they had been fired on a line-of-bearing solution—back up the path of the incoming MK 48 torpedo—rather than on a corrected intercept solution toward *Michigan*, which meant they would pass behind the evading submarine. Wilson evaluated the distance between the nearest torpedo and *Michigan* at the closest point of approach, concluding they would be far enough away from it to avoid detection.

Montgomery announced, "Target zig, Master one through Master five. Contacts are turning away and increasing speed."

It appeared that the Russian warships had communicated with the merchant, then turned in unison away from the incoming torpedo. The maneuver itself wasn't a problem as long as the Russian warships were burdened with the slower merchant; *Michigan* could remain within engagement range. The more important issue, however, was that their MK 48 torpedo was no longer traveling on a course that would intercept the merchant.

As Montgomery and the rest of the Fire Control Tracking Party attempted to discern the convoy's new course and speed, their torpedo went active.

"Tube One has enabled," Jescovitch called out. He followed up a moment later with, "Detect!" indicating their torpedo had detected an object that required further evaluation. Several seconds later, Jescovitch announced, "Homing!"

Wilson stopped by the Weapon Launch Console, evaluating the tactical picture. The torpedo couldn't discern which of the five surface ships it was homing on, but Wilson's crew could. The symbol representing their MK 48 torpedo was closing rapidly on Master four. It was homing on one of the Russian warships.

"Pre-enable tube One," Wilson announced.

Jescovitch complied, turning their torpedo's sonar off. Their weapon would now continue traveling directly ahead, with homing and detonation disabled.

After evaluating the course the convoy had turned to and its new speed—twenty-eight knots—Wilson directed, "Insert torpedo steer, right sixty."

The steer was sent to the torpedo over its guidance wire and the torpedo executed the order, turning back onto an intercept course with the convoy. Wilson monitored the torpedo's journey until it passed beneath the two nearest Russian warships. It now had a clear path toward the merchant.

"Command enable tube One," Wilson ordered.

Lieutenant Jescovitch complied, sending the command to the torpedo, turning on its sonar and handing decision-making over to the torpedo again.

It immediately detected the merchant ship looming ahead, then transitioned to homing. It closed the remaining distance, and the first indication their torpedo had detonated was Jescovitch's report.

"Loss of guidance wire, tube One!"

A few seconds later, Wilson heard the deep rumbling of a torpedo explosion traveling through the water and *Michigan*'s hull.

Shortly thereafter, Sonar announced, "Breaking-up noises from Master one."

Tension in the Control Room began to fade now that they had evaded both lightweight torpedoes and sunk their target of interest. Then another report from Sonar blared across the speakers.

"Torpedo launch transients, correlating to Master six." The report was followed shortly by, "Torpedo in the water, bearing zero-four-zero!"

Wilson had temporarily ignored the Russian nuclear attack submarine, supposedly being distracted by *Jimmy Carter*. However, the sinking merchant ship had garnered the attention of the Russian crew; they had realized the convoy was under attack and had counterfired. Whether *Jimmy Carter* or *Michigan* was the target, Wilson didn't know.

There wasn't time to determine which submarine had been targeted. That could be sorted out later. They were dealing with a heavyweight torpedo this time, which was much faster and could travel significantly farther than a lightweight.

"Helm, ahead flank! Left full rudder, steady course two-eight-zero. Launch countermeasures!"

71

FAIRFAX, VIRGINIA

With her eyes still focused on Harrison, Khalila said, "I know how this looks, but I'm on your side."

"You have a strange way of showing it," he replied.

"I have to do it this way. I need you to stay out of this."

"Stay out of what?"

"Remember the conversation we had in Sochi, about how you intervened in the Mixell issue in Afghanistan, making things worse?"

Harrison nodded.

"I need you to stay out of this," she said again as she turned her attention to Rolow. "This is between me and the DDO."

Harrison stared at Khalila, trying to make sense of what she was saying.

"Do you agree?" she asked.

"All right. I'll stay out of it."

Khalila holstered the pistol she had pointed at Harrison, keeping the other weapon aimed at the DDO.

Rolow put his hands on his hips. "What's this about, Khalila?"

She reached behind her back and pulled out a transceiver that had been clipped to her skirt. She tossed it to the DDO, who caught it in both hands.

"Recognize this?" she asked.

Rolow examined it for a few seconds. "Looks like an older-model agency field radio."

"Correct. Did you misplace it?"

"What do you mean?"

"It's the radio that was on bin Laden's desk. I took it from the agency storage facility today and ran the serial number. It's *your* radio. Care to explain?"

"There must be a mistake. It's not my radio."

"It's your radio, all right. Let me theorize how it got onto bin Laden's desk; perhaps it will jog your memory. You had an exceptional record as a Middle East field officer, isn't that right?"

Rolow nodded. "I did well."

"You did better than well. You were the best-performing field officer in the history of the agency, single-handedly responsible for thwarting over a dozen al-Qaeda and ISIS terrorist attacks. You were appropriately recognized, rising through the agency ranks to become the youngest DDO ever, correct?"

"That's right."

"So, about your uncanny ability to obtain intelligence leads that disrupted terrorist attacks—were you good or just lucky?"

"I suppose—"

Khalila cut him off. "I'll answer that question. It's neither. Instead, you had help. An inside source you struck a deal with. Someone high up who fed you information in return for tips that kept him safe. Except, by the time of the Abbottabad raid, you had been promoted from a Middle East field officer into another section of the agency and could no longer feed him the vital information that would have kept him alive. Isn't that right?"

Rolow gave her a long stare, then finally responded, "What I did was for America's benefit, not just mine."

"You're going to have to explain that," Khalila replied.

"Osama bin Laden was a coward. He was willing to provide whatever information I needed in return for his safety. That information saved thousands of American lives. Would it have been better to forfeit the lives of those men, women, and children—to capture one man? Yes, I helped your father stay alive, but I saved thousands of Americans in the process."

"It wasn't your decision to make! If my father had been captured or killed earlier, perhaps the al-Qaeda network could have been destroyed entirely, saving even more lives!"

"There's no way to know," Rolow argued. "But I do know the path I chose saved lives."

Harrison was about to join the conversation, then remembered he had agreed to stay out of it. Then Khalila asked the question he'd been about to pose.

"What about the Abbottabad assault team members? The men who risked their lives taking down Osama. Did you feed their names to al-Qaeda, helping to eliminate them?"

"I hate to disappoint you, but I don't work with al-Qaeda."

"Oh, so when it comes to betraying your country, you have standards?"

"State it however you want. But that was *my* work, eliminating anyone who could have made the connection between the radio on bin Laden's desk and me. Unfortunately, I didn't factor you into the equation."

Rolow's words touched on a sensitive topic, because Khalila exploded with rage.

"You took advantage of me! You knew why I joined the agency, to right the wrongs my father committed. To restore my family's honor! And all along, I was working with the devil who helped my father escape justice!"

"What did you expect from me?" Rolow said, his voice going stern. "For me to come clean so I can have an honest relationship with a woman that *no one* in this agency trusts? I'm the only one who had your back, putting you into situations where you could help atone for your father's sins. You should be thanking me!"

"I will not thank you!" she said, her voice rising as her hand began trembling in anger. "Your twisted logic may have justified your actions in your mind, but it doesn't in mine!"

The emotion suddenly vanished from her face. Her hand stilled, and when she spoke again, her voice was calm.

"You were faced with a decision and made a choice. I've made mine."

She pulled the trigger, putting a bullet into Rolow's forehead.

Verbeck stared in disbelief as her former lover collapsed at her feet, blood spreading slowly across the floor.

Khalila turned to Christine and Harrison. "I've taken care of this mess for you. You're welcome."

Then she swung her pistol toward the secretary of the Navy.

Verbeck held her hands up before her, palms out in a supplicating manner.

"And you," Khalila said to Brenda. "Rolow must have really been in love with you, because he confided in you, told you what he'd done. You've used it as leverage against him ever since."

"What can I say," Brenda said, "other than—we must take what Allah provides and be grateful."

"Do you mock me?" Khalila asked. "Because that's a really bad plan when the pistol is in my hand."

Harrison sensed Khalila's rage building again. "Put the gun down," he said.

Khalila ignored him, so he stepped in front of her. "You're not the judge, jury, and executioner."

Her eyes went to Rolow, his body sprawled on the floor, then back to Harrison. "You clearly haven't been paying attention."

"That's enough," he said. "Let the legal system take care of Verbeck."

"She was in a position of trust and betrayed America! She deserves the same fate as Rolow."

"I did not betray my country!"

Harrison turned to Verbeck as she continued, "I sacrificed a few people to protect my brother, but I did not betray my country."

"What about the centrifuges?" Harrison asked.

"They are of no concern. Once they are received and my brother paid, appropriate intelligence would have fallen into our hands, and we would have located and destroyed them. My brother makes a buck, and the United States remains safe."

"They're likely headed to Natanz. That facility is practically indestructible without a nuclear strike."

"I'll admit, I didn't think everything through all the way. But I'm sure we would have found a way to destroy the centrifuges. I'm not a traitor to my country."

Harrison turned back to Khalila, his eyes locking with hers.

She shook her head in disgust, then lowered her pistol.

"Fine. Do with her as you please."

72

USS *MICHIGAN*

"Torpedo launch transients, bearing zero-four-zero! Correlates to Master six."

Sonar's report was quickly followed by another. "Second torpedo in the water, bearing zero-four-zero!"

Wilson examined the tactical display on the Conn. The Russian submarine had fired two torpedoes, that much was clear. But had its crew fired a salvo against one of the American submarines, or had it fired one torpedo at each?

As *Michigan* finished turning to its evasion course, Wilson studied the torpedo bearings. They were diverging, which meant one torpedo had been fired at *Jimmy Carter* and the other at *Michigan*.

Another report from Sonar blared across the Control Room speakers. "Torpedo launch transient, bearing zero-two-zero. Correlates to *Jimmy Carter*."

Commander Gallagher had counterfired, which would keep the Russian submarine crew preoccupied for a while. The task now, for each of the three submarines, was to evade the incoming torpedoes.

Wilson studied the torpedo bearings on the Conn display. They were drawing slowly aft, which was a good sign, but no guarantee the torpedo would pass by without detecting *Michigan*.

"Multiple mechanical transients, bearing zero-two-two! Correlates to *Jimmy Carter*."

Four more red bearing lines appeared on the Conn display.

"Conn, Sonar. Detect four additional torpedo launches from *Jimmy Carter*. They appear to be the same type of torpedo that destroyed our MK 48 when we fired at *Jimmy Carter* a few weeks ago."

Wilson acknowledged the report. Gallagher had launched four anti-torpedo torpedoes, most likely two at the heavyweight headed toward *Jimmy Carter* and two toward the torpedo chasing *Michigan*. The four new bearing lines began to diverge, two slanting toward the torpedo pursuing *Michigan* and the other two merging with the torpedo chasing *Jimmy Carter*.

Not long thereafter, Sonar reported, "Conn, Sonar. Explosion bearing zero-two-four."

A faint explosion, not nearly as powerful as a heavyweight torpedo detonation, echoed through *Michigan*'s hull. It had likely been one of *Jimmy Carter*'s ATTs. Confirming Wilson's assessment, three torpedo bearing lines disappeared from the Conn display: the Russian torpedo headed toward the Seawolf class submarine, plus two of the ATTs.

Four torpedo bearing lines remained: the heavyweight torpedo chasing *Michigan* and the two ATTs chasing it, plus the MK 48 *Jimmy Carter* had fired at the Russian submarine.

"Heavyweight torpedo detonation! Bearing correlates with Master six. Loss of Master six."

Sonar had lost the propulsion-related tonals from the Russian submarine, which meant its engine room had been severely damaged. Whether it was going to the bottom, however, Wilson didn't know. Russian submarines, typically built with nine or ten compartments, could withstand the flooding of a single compartment. The crew's fate would be determined by how many compartments the MK 48 explosion had breached.

A moment later, Sonar reported, "Breaking-up noises on the last bearing to Master six."

The Russian submarine was headed to the bottom, its compartments beginning to implode. Wilson hoped *Michigan* didn't share the same fate.

He examined the remaining three bearing lines. The bearing to the lead ATT had merged with the incoming Russian torpedo. The ATT was closing on its target.

Sonar reported, "Explosion, bearing zero-six-five! Loss of Russian heavyweight and one of the ATTs." Sonar followed up. "Last ATT has shut down."

Wilson examined the display. There were no more torpedoes in the water, and the four Russian surface warships were hightailing it away from the area.

Michigan and *Jimmy Carter*'s mission had been accomplished. The merchant had been sunk, with the Russian submarine destroyed in self-defense.

73

BANGOR, WASHINGTON

ONE MONTH LATER

Christine's SUV coasted to a halt beside USS *Michigan*, moored to the Delta Pier at Naval Base Kitsap. Waiting at the submarine's brow was Lieutenant Commander Tom Montgomery, who greeted Christine and escorted her onto the submarine and down a hatch into the Operations Compartment, arriving at Captain Wilson's stateroom.

After *Michigan* sank the merchant carrying the gas centrifuges to Iran, the guided missile submarine had returned to its home port for refit and crew change-out. Inside the black leather satchel Christine carried was a citation and medal. She'd be presenting Wilson with the CIA Intelligence Star for his effort in sinking the merchant, plus the numerous other issues he'd helped with over the years.

A private meeting with Wilson had been arranged, avoiding the sensitive nature of awarding the submarine's Captain, but not each crew member whose support was vital, the CIA medal. For the Navy's part, however, each member of *Michigan*'s BLUE crew was being recognized with a Navy Meritorious Unit Commendation. Wilson was unaware, however, of the pending CIA honor.

Wilson rose from his desk to greet Christine, then gestured to a small table as he closed his stateroom door.

They engaged in small talk, eventually segueing to *Michigan*'s mission in the Persian Gulf and the crew's excellent performance. They had sunk the merchant while preventing the inadvertent attack against all four Russian surface warships, which would have compounded the problem created when *Jimmy Carter* sank the Russian submarine.

Now that the subject had turned to *Michigan* sinking the merchant ship, Christine reached into her satchel and retrieved a palm-sized medal case, which she placed on the table along with a certificate folder.

"I believe standing at attention during an award presentation is proper protocol."

Wilson eyed the contents on the table, then smiled. "It is."

Both rose from their seats, then Christine opened the folder and read the citation, handing it to Wilson afterward. The CIA Intelligence Star was one in a group of medals referred to within the agency as *jock strap* medals, since they were often awarded secretly due to the classified nature of the respective operation and subsequently couldn't be displayed or even acknowledged publicly. In Wilson's case, however, the medal could be worn proudly with his others, since his involvement in sinking the merchant ship carrying the gas centrifuges was public knowledge.

Christine opened the small case and retrieved the medal, then pinned it to Wilson's uniform as was customary in the Navy. She congratulated Wilson, but instead of shaking his hand, she gave him a hug. They had been through a lot together, and Wilson had come through for her every time.

Christine bade Wilson farewell and was escorted from the submarine, climbing topside as twilight began creeping across the Pacific Northwest. As she approached her SUV, her thoughts turned to Khalila.

How to handle her would be a delicate matter. Part of that management involved Jake Harrison, whom she had arranged to meet later today at his house in Silverdale, not far away. Inside her satchel was another folder, this one containing a nondisclosure agreement involving Khalila's true identity; Harrison's agreement was the only one outstanding.

Mixell's trail had gone cold, and Harrison had headed home for a week to spend time with Angie and Maddy. Although Christine sensed tension in Angie's presence, she looked forward to seeing Maddy, checking up on how her back flips on the beam were going and how she had done at the gymnastics meet a few weeks earlier.

She pulled out her phone and dialed Harrison.

74

SILVERDALE, WASHINGTON

Harrison picked up his cell phone, answering the call he'd been expecting.

"Hi, Jake. This is Chris," the voice said. "I've finished up at the naval base and I'm on my way over. Sorry about running late."

"Not a problem," Harrison replied. He glanced at his watch. Angie was about to start cooking. "What are your dinner plans?"

Angie must have heard him answer his phone and had joined him in the living room. When he asked Christine about dinner plans, Angie caught his attention, mouthing the word *no* as she waved him off with her arms.

"Just a second," Harrison said before Christine replied.

After he put the call on mute, Angie spoke first. "I thought she was just bringing some paperwork for you to sign."

"She's running late, and it's almost dinnertime. She could join us."

Angie frowned. "We've only got two sirloin steaks in the fridge."

"I could run out and pick up another one."

Angie had her hands on her hips, unmoved by his offer.

"She's my boss," Harrison said. "Plus, the time together will help you realize that we're just friends now, nothing more."

Angie hesitated a moment, then acquiesced. "All right. But pick up better steaks. New York Strip. Make it filet mignon. And a bottle of wine. Whatever kind she likes best."

He took the phone off mute. "Hey, Chris. We'd like you to join us for dinner if you have time."

There was a short silence on the line before she replied, "Thanks for the invitation, and I accept. I'll arrive a few minutes later, though. I'll need to stop somewhere to pick up food for my protective agents."

"Sounds good," Harrison replied. "See you in a bit."

Harrison hung up as he grabbed his car keys from the foyer table. "I should be back in thirty minutes."

Twilight was transitioning to dusk, the sky blanketed by dark gray clouds threatening to open up at any moment, as Lonnie Mixell checked the GPS map instructions on his cell phone. His eyes returned to the road, searching for Roundup Lane on the right, spotting the sign as a car pulled out from the road, turning onto the street toward him. The car matched the make and model of Harrison's vehicle, and it took only a few seconds to verify Harrison was the driver. Mixell covered his face as best he could, scratching his forehead as Harrison drove by.

Mixell turned onto Roundup Lane, then traveled down the winding road, pulling off onto a dirt path in the heavily forested area, where he parked the car and assessed the situation. The retribution he had in mind required Harrison at home with his wife. However, it was likely that Jake was running an errand and would be back soon, making Mixell's entry into his home in the interim that much easier. When Harrison returned, he'd be waiting for him.

For tonight's endeavor, Mixell had a pistol in a shoulder holster beneath his gray windbreaker, plus a six-inch-long stainless steel knife in a sheath strapped to his belt. He left the car and worked his way through the brush toward Harrison's home, stopping at the edge of the vegetation bordering Harrison's yard. There was only about twenty or so feet of open space to this side of the house.

He moved to the back for a quick reconnaissance, spotting a single back door to the house and an old barn in the distance. Everything was as he expected. He returned to the front of the house and was about to put his plan into motion when he spotted a black SUV heading down Roundup Lane, turning into the driveway to Harrison's home.

Mixell hid in the brush as the SUV stopped near the walkway to the house. Christine O'Connor emerged from the back seat, joined by a protective agent who stepped from the front passenger side. After accompanying the director to the front door, the agent returned to the vehicle, where he and the driver pulled out burgers and fries from a takeout bag.

Christine's unexpected arrival had thrown a wrench into Mixell's plan; in particular, the unplanned presence of two armed protective agents, sitting in a vehicle behind what was most likely bullet-resistant glass. However, Mixell had been traveling disguised as a hunter in case he was stopped by law enforcement for some reason, who might note his assortment of weapons. In the trunk of his car was a .30-06 rifle, along with a selection of rounds for just about every contingency. Several armor-piercing bullets should do the trick.

He returned to his car and retrieved the rifle and desired rounds, slowing on his return as he neared the edge of the vegetation bordering Harrison's yard. He crept closer until he had a clear view of both protective agents, each finishing his meal. He reviewed the revised plan in his mind: twenty feet to the SUV, plus another twenty to the front door. About thirteen yards. It would take only a few seconds to gain entry into Harrison's home.

As he stood hidden a few feet into the brush, he slowly placed the rifle against his shoulder, taking aim at the nearest protective agent. He pulled the trigger, taking a split second to verify the round had penetrated the vehicle's glass window. The first agent slumped in his seat as Mixell shifted his aim to the second man and squeezed the trigger again, producing the same result.

Mixell dropped the rifle and sprinted past the vehicle toward the front door as he pulled out his pistol. He had no idea if the two women inside had heard the rifle shots or, even if they had, realized what was going on, but he wasn't taking any chances. Speed was of the essence, ensuring neither woman could call for help before he gained control.

When he reached the front door, he fired two bullets into the doorframe near the latch, then kicked the door open, splintering the frame in the process. He surged inside, spotting Angie and Christine emerging from the kitchen to find out what was going on. He leveled his pistol at the two women.

"Stay right where you are."

Mixell heard footsteps on the stairs and looked up to spot Harrison's daughter halfway down, freezing when she saw the armed stranger in her house.

He swung his pistol toward Maddy as Angie cried out, pleading with Mixell to spare her.

"Come down and join your mother," he said.

Angie reiterated Mixell's direction, and the girl quickly descended the remaining steps, joining the two women. Angie pulled her daughter behind her.

Mixell pulled the knife from its sheath.

75

SILVERDALE, WASHINGTON

It was dark by the time Harrison returned from the store. As he pulled up beside Christine's SUV, he spotted the two protective agents slumped in their seats, their heads and headrests splattered with blood, two bullet holes in the windshield. His hand instinctively went for his weapon, but he carried none tonight. He stepped from his car and moved quickly toward the SUV, pulling on the driver's side door handle. The door opened, and Harrison retrieved the agent's pistol, which he verified had a full magazine of bullets, with one round chambered.

Staying close against the house, he moved toward the front door, stopping when he reached the edge of the dining room window. Through the glass, he spotted Angie and Christine sitting at the dining room table across from each other. Angie sat frozen with a terrified look on her face, her eyes filled with tears. Christine was seated with her back to Harrison, but he could see the tension in her shoulders. His pulse quickened when he saw Maddy sitting in Mixell's lap at one end of the table. One of Mixell's arms was wrapped around her waist while his right hand wielded a knife, resting on her shoulder. Maddy was trembling in fear, her eyes focused on a board game on the table before her.

Mixell kept Maddy's head between him and Harrison, so Harrison couldn't get a clear shot; he'd have to enter the house first. He dropped below the window and moved to the front door. It was closed, but the doorframe had been shattered. He pushed the door open as gently as possible, but it made a scraping sound as it freed itself from the frame.

Mixell had likely been alerted, either by the sound of the door opening or Harrison's car coming up the driveway. He was also seated facing

the dining room entrance. The odds of surprising him and getting a clear shot with Maddy in his lap were low, plus he didn't want to risk Mixell's reaction to his sudden entrance, with a knife near his daughter's throat.

Harrison slid the pistol inside his waistband behind his back, then moved slowly into Mixell's view at the dining room entrance. Mixell spotted him immediately.

"Hello, Jake."

Mixell spoke in the same casual tone he had used after Harrison confronted him in Afghanistan after he had killed his second prisoner.

"Lonnie." Harrison kept his voice steady, despite his rising trepidation for his daughter.

"Hands in the air," Mixell said, "and turn around."

Harrison complied, and Mixell noticed the pistol stuck behind him.

"Put your weapon on the floor and kick it over to me."

Slowly, Harrison pulled the pistol out as he faced Mixell again, then placed it on the floor and kicked it across the room.

Mixell smiled and spoke to Maddy. "It's your turn."

She hesitated, her eyes going to her father.

"Go on," Mixell urged. "We need to see who reaches the end first. This car represents you." He touched one of the small plastic cars on the game board with the tip of his knife. "And the other car represents your mom. We need to determine who lives and who dies."

Harrison recognized the board game, one that the three of them—Mixell, Christine, and himself—had played often as children: *The Game of Life*, which Harrison had bought for Maddy a few years ago.

Maddy spun the wheel, then moved her car six spaces.

"You're cheating," Mixell asserted. "You moved an extra space."

"I did not! The wheel says six, and I moved six spaces!"

"You moved seven."

"I did not! I started here"—she pointed toward her original spot—"and moved six spaces!"

"You started *here*," Mixell replied, pointing to a space one spot behind where Maddy had started, "and you cheated, moving an extra space. You know what happens to cheaters, don't you?"

Maddy shook her head, her eyes filling with tears.

"Have you heard of the Code of Hammurabi? It's an ancient code of laws often described as *an eye for an eye, a tooth for a tooth*. When one man takes something important from another man, he gets to do the same." He kissed Maddy on the cheek. "You don't understand what I'm talking about, but your father does."

"I didn't cheat," Maddy said, her words barely audible.

"I'll tell you what," Mixell said. "I'll spin for you."

He moved her game piece back to the space he had pointed out, then turned the wheel slowly, stopping on the number five.

Maddy moved her car five spaces, then looked at Mixell with her hand still on her car. He nodded, and she released her game piece.

"Oh my goodness!" Mixell's voice shifted to a sweet, lilting tone. "This is perfect, since we're running short on time."

Maddy had landed on a stop sign labeled *Safe Route* on top and *Risky Route* on the bottom, with the path to the end splitting into two roads.

"Only we're going to change the options. One route is for Maddy, and the other one is for Angie." He looked at Harrison. "Your father gets to choose."

"That's enough, Lonnie," Christine said as she stared at Mixell with a hateful look. "Let her go. She has nothing to do with this."

Mixell laughed. "Oh, no, Chris. I'm going to hurt Jake the same way he hurt me. I'm going to take away something important from him." He turned to Harrison. "But I'm a compassionate man, so I'll let you choose who dies. Your daughter." He pointed the knife toward Maddy's neck, then slowly toward Angie. "Or your wife."

Maddy burst into tears, no longer able to hold back her fear, her body trembling as sobs escaped between deep breaths.

"Everything's going to be okay," Angie said. "Dad's not going to let anything happen to you."

"Shut up!" Mixell yelled. He placed the knife against Maddy's neck, his focus still on Harrison. "You've got five seconds to decide or your daughter dies."

"Let her go!" Harrison shouted.

"Is that your decision?"

Harrison's eyes met Angie's. It was an impossible decision to make,

choosing between the two persons he loved more than anyone else in the world.

"It's okay, Jake," Angie said, her voice quavering. "Just kill this son of a bitch and take care of Maddy."

"It appears we've reached a decision," Mixell announced. "Of course, it was made by Maddy's mom instead of her cowardly father."

He pushed his chair back and stood with Maddy before him, a firm grip on her left arm and his knife hand resting on her shoulder. After guiding her a few feet, he stopped behind Angie's chair, where he released the girl. She ran to Harrison as Mixell placed his hands on Angie's shoulders, the knife still in his right hand.

"Maddy, go to your room," Mixell said, "and don't come downstairs until morning. If you happen to have a phone upstairs, don't call anyone until tomorrow. If you do, I'll kill your mom and dad, and it'll be *your* fault."

Maddy stood behind her father, her arms wrapped tightly around his waist, the side of her face buried into his back. She was sobbing hysterically now, and Harrison felt her tears soak into his shirt.

"I'm not as heartless as you think," Mixell said.

"Go upstairs," Harrison said gently but firmly, "and wait until your mom or I come for you. Understand?"

He felt Maddy nod as she slowly released her grip around his waist. Then she ran upstairs, crying the whole way until her bedroom door slammed shut.

Mixell grinned and slid the flat side of the blade across Angie's throat. Her tears broke free and streamed down her cheeks. "Jake . . ."

Mixell looked down at Angie, then quickly back to Harrison. "After all these years, she's still quite beautiful. I have to admit that I was jealous. And angry. For the second time, you took the woman I wanted. First Chris, then Angie. Although both are attractive, their personalities are different. Angie is more"—he paused as he searched for the right words, moving the knife in little circles only an inch from her neck—"emotional. So animated and full of life."

"Let her go, Lonnie. Angie has nothing to do with this."

"You still don't get it," Mixell snarled. "She has *everything* to do with this. You brought her into this the moment Trish died."

Harrison had always thought Mixell's revenge was focused on him, payback for reporting him to their superiors and for testifying against him at his court-martial. But things had changed when Trish was killed, after Harrison stood behind her with a pistol to her head. It was Mixell's bullet that had done the deed, but that didn't matter to him.

Mixell had crafted a similar situation tonight, standing behind Angie with a knife to her neck. If he had his way, Angie would end up dead on the floor, just like Trish.

Searching for a way to save Angie's life, Harrison considered charging Mixell, hoping to surprise him. But he concluded it wouldn't work. Mixell would slice her neck open the instant he charged.

His only option was to talk Mixell out of his plan, refocus his anger.

"I'm the one you want," he said. "I'm the one who sent you to prison, not Angie."

"You're clearly not listening," Mixell replied. "So, we'll move on." His grip tightened around Angie, and Harrison could see the rage building in his face.

"Do you understand what you took from me?" he screamed, his face turning red.

The knife danced in rhythm to his words, never straying far from Angie's throat.

Harrison searched for words that would defuse Mixell's anger. "I had a job to do. It was nothing personal."

Mixell stared at Harrison for a long moment. When he replied, his voice dropped low and ominous.

"Well, it's personal now."

He pulled Angie up from her chair and held her tight against his body, his left arm wrapped around her waist. The tip of his knife pierced her neck, drawing blood.

"Don't!" Harrison's heart pounded in his chest. "You don't have to do this!"

"You're right," Mixell said. "I don't. You're going to make me."

As Harrison wondered what he meant, Mixell moved his knife to his left hand, then retrieved his pistol from its shoulder harness. He placed the weapon on the table, then took two steps back, pulling Angie with him.

"I'm giving you an opportunity. Go for it."

He turned to Christine, still seated at the table. The pistol was beyond her reach, but she could get to it if she rose from her chair and lunged for it. "If you so much as move," Mixell said, "I'll slice Angie's throat."

"You sick bastard," Christine replied. "You accuse Harrison of being a coward, yet you stand behind his wife with a knife to her throat. Why don't you show some courage and settle the score directly with Jake? See which one of you is the better man."

"Nice try, Chris," Mixell replied, "but you're not going to talk me out of this. Tonight will end only one way. The unanswered question is whether Jake stands there like a coward or tries to save his beloved wife."

Harrison glanced at the pistol. It was much closer to Mixell. He could slice Angie's neck and still reach the pistol first. He was baiting him.

If he went for the gun and Mixell stabbed Angie as a result, it'd be Harrison's fault she was dead. If he did nothing, with Mixell's pistol only a few feet away, and Angie died, he'd forever blame himself for her death. Regardless of his decision, he would live with guilt for the rest of his life. Exactly what Mixell wanted.

As Harrison struggled to find the words to respond, the silence was broken by thunder as the skies opened up. The raindrops hammered against the windows as tears flowed down Angie's cheeks.

"It's okay, Angie," he managed to choke out. "I'm not going to let anything happen to you."

"That's quite delusional," Mixell replied, "considering the circumstances. But let's continue our conversation. *Was it worth it?* Was the satisfaction of thwarting my plan against the United States worth Angie's life? If you could go back in time and let me win and Angie live, would you do it?"

As Mixell waited for a response, Harrison couldn't focus on anything besides the look of sheer terror and desperation on Angie's face.

Mixell seemed disappointed he couldn't coax the words from his former best friend. "Let's try something different," he said. "Do you remember the first time you saw Angie? Or perhaps the moment you realized you were in love with her?"

An image appeared in Harrison's mind: Angie curled up beside him in a hammock, the warmth of her body as she nestled in the crook of his arm, her head resting on his chest.

"That's it," Mixell said, adding a malevolent smile. "Now hold that thought . . . and watch."

With a single thrust, he pushed the entire blade into Angie's neck.

Her eyes went wide as the knife slid in and the tip of the blade emerged from the other side of her neck. Her mouth opened, but no sound emerged. An anguished scream Harrison barely recognized as his own escaped his throat as he broke across the room toward Mixell.

As he closed the distance, Mixell pulled the knife from Angie's neck, going for the pistol on the table with his other hand. Angie's legs gave out, and she collapsed to the floor as Mixell grabbed the gun. Harrison launched himself toward Mixell, but not before Mixell got off two shots, hitting him in the chest twice.

Harrison slammed into Mixell, knocking him to the floor beneath him. He grabbed Mixell's wrists, keeping the gun and knife away. As they struggled, Harrison was aware of several things: the sharp pain in his chest and the slick warmth spreading from his wounds; his breathing becoming labored as he tried to break Mixell's grip on the pistol and knife; Angie on the floor only a few feet away, her hands clamped around her neck, blood oozing between her fingers and from her mouth; Christine moving toward Angie.

Christine knelt beside Angie, pulling her away from the two men. Angie was kicking frantically, trying to get air through the blood choking her throat. Christine turned her head to the side to drain the blood from her mouth, but it kept coming. Blood was flowing into her throat, clogging her airway.

Angie focused on the woman above her as she tried to breathe, and it was a look Christine would never forget. Angie's eyes were filled with the terror that accompanied the certainty of death; she knew she'd been mortally wounded. Christine remained by her side, searching for a way to help, but could think of nothing that would save Angie's life.

Beside them, the two men were still struggling on the floor. Harrison was on top of Mixell, his legs intertwined beneath him in a wrestling move that kept Mixell from throwing him off. Harrison had his hands clamped around his opponent's wrists, trying to keep Mixell's knife and pistol from doing more damage. Blood from Harrison's gunshot wounds was coating both men, and he was weakening. Mixell was forcing the gun toward him.

There was another pistol, Christine realized—the one Harrison had kicked across the floor. She was about to retrieve it from the other side of the room, but Mixell's gun was only an inch away from a clear shot at Jake's head.

She surged toward Mixell, grabbing the pistol in both hands, attempting to wrest it from his grip. She pulled and twisted the gun with all the strength she could muster, and it finally came free. But the blood-coated pistol slipped from her hands, spiraling in the air across the dining room, landing on the floor where it slid to a halt against the far wall.

Mixell freed his legs and tossed Harrison aside, pushing himself to one knee, the knife still in his hand. His gaze went to the pistol, then to Christine, their eyes locking. She was closer to the gun, halfway between Mixell and where it lay.

Christine leaped toward the gun, landing on her stomach as she grabbed the pistol. She twisted onto her back and swung the gun toward Mixell, firing as he sprinted through the dining room opening toward the back door. She got off one round, missing him, putting a bullet into the doorframe instead.

She followed him from the dining room as he rammed into the back door, the frame splintering as the door sprang open. She fired again, hitting him in the shoulder. But Mixell kept going, disappearing into the darkness.

Christine returned to the dining room as Harrison crawled toward Angie, propping her head and shoulders onto his lap. Her eyes were wide and frantic, filled with tears of pain and fear, her legs kicking weakly as she struggled to breathe.

Pulling her phone from her purse, Christine dialed 911. After being informed help was on the way, she called her protective detail, in case Mixell hadn't killed them before entering the house. There was no answer.

As Angie looked up at her husband, she tried to speak, but the only thing that came out was a rivulet of blood that ran down the side of her face. Christine sensed the despair in Harrison's voice as he talked softly to her. He had undoubtedly seen many wounds in combat and knew her fate.

Christine turned her attention to Harrison. His shirt was saturated with blood from the two gunshot wounds. His face had turned pale and his breathing was labored. He'd been seriously wounded, with one or both lungs likely punctured.

Angie's legs stopped moving and her body went still, and the light slowly faded from her eyes. Harrison kept consoling her until she died in his arms. He pulled her close and held her tightly as tears streamed down his face.

Harrison looked slowly up at Christine, who was kneeling beside them with Mixell's pistol in her hand. He had a look she would always remember; of indescribable anguish.

He placed Angie's body on the floor beside him, then tried to push himself to his feet.

"What are you doing?" Christine asked.

"Going after Lonnie."

"You're in no condition to pursue him. You'll be lucky to survive just sitting here."

Christine could see the emotions playing on his face—anguish, rage, and hate—along with the realization that she was right.

"I'll go after him," she said.

He grabbed her arm. "You're no match for him."

"He's wounded and only has a knife, while I've got a pistol. I *can* kill him, and I *will*."

She pulled from Harrison's grip, then, without further debating the wisdom of chasing down a former Navy SEAL, moved swiftly to the back door, stopping to peer into the backyard. The light from the house illuminated a barn in the distance, the door swinging slowly shut in the rain. As she prepared to sprint across the grass, she removed her high heels, then glanced at Harrison one last time. He had pulled Angie onto his lap again, cradling her head against his chest, tears running down his face as he rocked her gently back and forth.

Christine's resolve hardened, and she slipped through the doorway into the cold night rain.

76

SILVERDALE, WASHINGTON

Mixell stood just inside the barn door, peering back toward the house as he assessed his wound. He had taken a bullet in his shoulder, but the injury wasn't serious. He moved his arm around. It was painful, but he had full mobility.

As he tried to figure out how to get to his car without getting shot again, he spotted Christine emerging from the house, armed with a pistol, moving swiftly toward the barn. He still had his knife, but after noticing a flat-bladed shovel nearby as his eyes adjusted to the darkness, he sheathed the knife, picking up the shovel instead.

Christine stopped by the corner of the barn, then worked her way toward the entrance. She hesitated near the door and questioned again the wisdom of chasing down a trained killer. Then the images of Mixell thrusting the knife into Angie's neck and of Harrison holding his dying wife in his arms erased all doubt. Tightening her grip on the pistol, she slowly entered the barn.

There was a flash of movement, which Christine noticed too late. The flat side of a shovel slammed into her head, knocking her to the ground.

She had no idea how long she lay there as her senses gradually returned. She was lying facedown on the cold dirt. The right side of her head was throbbing, and she felt warm blood running down the side of her face. The pistol was gone, and she had the vague recollection of it tumbling from her hand, lost in the darkness somewhere.

Christine rolled onto her back, spotting Mixell standing above her, holding a shovel. He knelt beside her, pinning her to the ground with a knee.

"You stupid bitch. You thought you could hunt me down?"

Christine offered no response as she assessed her predicament. She now had no weapon, while Mixell had a knife and shovel.

"Hopefully, Jake will live," Mixell said, his voice tinged with amusement. "At least for a while, tormented by the memory of his wife dying in his arms. Knowing that she's dead because of him."

He paused and surveyed Christine. "Now, what to do about you? Killing the director of the CIA is going to bring a lot of heat on me. But no more than I've already got, I suspect. That's bad news for you."

Mixell placed one foot on Christine's chest as he stood, then placed his other foot on her right wrist, immobilizing her arm.

"There's a nursery rhyme about five little piggies," he said, "about one going to the market and another one staying home. But the reality is, all piggies go to the market." He examined Christine again. "Let's see. Two arms, two legs, and one head. That's five little piggies. I'm going to take them off, one by one." He grabbed the shovel with both hands, holding the blade directly over Christine's right arm. The light from the house glistened off the shovel's sharp blade.

"This little piggy went to the market."

He raised the shovel, preparing for a vicious thrust downward. When the shovel reached its highest point, Christine pivoted at her waist, raising her hips and legs off the ground in a reverse handstand move. She kept her legs together, slamming both feet into Mixell's shoulder as he drove the shovel downward.

The impact knocked the shovel off course, and it sank into the dirt a few inches from her arm. Christine's blow also knocked Mixell forward, and he staggered two steps before regaining his balance. He no longer had a foot on her chest.

She rolled to her feet and faced Mixell. He left the shovel stuck in the ground, pulling his knife out instead. She froze for a second, scanning the ground for the pistol, but it was nowhere to be found. They were a few feet inside the barn, with Mixell between her and the exit. She was trapped.

He moved toward her and Christine bolted toward the back of the barn, searching frantically for a weapon or means of escape. She saw nothing useful along the way, realizing to her dismay that there was no rear exit to the barn.

As Mixell strode confidently toward her, Christine spotted a ladder to the loft and leaped onto the rungs, scrambling upward. Mixell sprinted toward her and grabbed one ankle, pulling her downward as he stabbed the knife into her left calf. She kicked him in the head with her other foot, jamming it down into his face.

Her ankle pulled free and she finished climbing to the loft, but Mixell was close behind. There was a railing on the far side of the loft she could jump over, and perhaps she could land without sustaining any serious injuries. Or perhaps she could go up, climbing onto the beams supporting the roof.

She ran toward the nearest vertical beam, which had several hanging hooks screwed into it. Using the hooks as footholds, she climbed upward, disappearing into the darkness. She froze as Mixell walked below, the knife in his hand.

"Christine, where are you? Come out, come out, wherever you are," he said in a singsong voice.

Christine was shrouded in darkness atop a center beam that ran the length of the barn. It was an easy jump down onto the loft, but a thirty-foot drop to the main floor on each end of the barn. Blood trickled down her left calf onto the beam, and pain sliced through her leg with each step, but the blood loss didn't seem severe and the pain was manageable. With Lonnie on the loft below her, the only option for escape was to make the long jump to the main floor.

As she debated the odds of landing without breaking any bones, an idea came to her. Mixell was moving slowly down the loft, scouring the area above him. Christine followed quietly, matching his pace, staying several feet behind him, hoping he'd keep moving down the entire length of the loft. Her hope rose as he approached the railing. He was almost close enough to it, and he just needed to step a few feet to either side of the center beam.

He reached the railing and turned around, moving to one side as she'd hoped. She stepped onto a side beam and leaped toward the next one, grabbing onto it as if it were a gymnastics parallel bar, and her body swung down toward Mixell.

She slammed into him with both feet, hitting him in the chest, sending him staggering back toward the railing. He weighed over two hundred pounds, and the railing splintered under his weight and momentum, and he fell backward onto the ground below.

Christine released the beam and dropped onto the loft, then peered over the damaged railing. Mixell was lying on his back, his eyes closed, motionless.

After descending the ladder, she grabbed the shovel Mixell had left behind, then slowly approached him. He hadn't moved, but in the dim lighting, it was hard to tell if he was dead or just unconscious. She stopped above him, the shovel in both hands, debating whether she should wait for law enforcement or take the matter into her own hands as Khalila had done with Rolow.

As she contemplated the matter, Mixell opened his eyes, and she realized to her dismay that he still had the knife in one hand.

He drove it into her left thigh, then grabbed the shovel with his other hand, ripping it from her grasp.

When the knife sliced into her thigh, Christine's knees went weak from the pain, and she collapsed onto the ground as Mixell stood. She crawled away, clambering to her feet as Mixell whacked her in the back with the shovel, knocking her to the ground again.

He stood over her and tossed the shovel aside, switching the knife between hands, then knelt with one knee on her back, pinning her down with her face turned to the side.

"You're a tough broad to kill. But you're going to die tonight. Slowly, just like Harrison."

He placed the end of the knife on the back of her shoulder, in the same spot she had shot him, then drove it into her flesh.

Christine cried out in pain as he twisted the knife inside her, then pulled it out.

"How's that feel? An eye for an eye, right?"

She was now bleeding from her calf, thigh, and shoulder.

"Now, where shall we cut next?"

"Lonnie, stop," Christine pleaded. "You don't have to do this. If there's anything good left inside you, please stop."

"If there's anything good left inside me," he mused. "That implies I might be pure evil." He placed the blade on the back of her neck, directly over her spine. "You aren't a very good negotiator."

"Everyone can be redeemed. You just have to want it."

"I guess that's the problem, Chris. I don't *want* redemption. I wanted Jake to pay for what he did to me and Trish, and now it's time for you to pay, for siding with Jake against me."

He leaned closer as he pressed the knife harder against her skin. "Goodbye, Chris. As the saying goes, it's time for—lights out."

Christine heard a twang as something slammed into Mixell, knocking him off her back. She rolled over, spotting Maddy with the shovel in her hands.

Mixell lumbered to his feet as he searched for the knife, which had been knocked from his hand when he'd been hit with the shovel. Maddy swung again, missing him as he backed up. She swung once more, but this time Mixell blocked the shovel with one arm and grabbed the shaft with the other, then yanked it from her.

His face lit up in rage as he swung the shovel toward Maddy, striking her on the side of her head. Christine heard a sharp crack as Maddy flew through the air, her body falling lifelessly to the barn floor, a red stain spreading out from her head.

Mixell pointed at her as he shook in anger. "I told you not to come out of your room!" He turned to Christine. "Look at what she made me do!"

Still enraged, he moved toward Christine, tightening his grip on the shovel. He swung, but Christine avoided it, backing up quickly. He swung and she avoided the blade again, but barely this time. She was running out of room as she retreated, and her back hit the wall.

There was nowhere else to go.

Mixell twisted the shovel, lining the blade up to slice through her. As he pulled back into his swing, Christine spotted the knife on the ground a few feet behind him and to the right. When the shovel started moving forward, she ducked into a roll, the blade swishing through the air above her, regaining her feet for two steps before pretending to stumble to the ground.

As she turned to face Mixell, she held the knife, now in her right hand, with the blade facing up alongside her forearm, hidden from view.

Christine waited, balanced on her haunches, as Mixell approached.

This time, when he pulled the shovel back, she launched herself toward him, driving the knife into his abdomen.

Mixell stumbled backward, the shovel still in one hand, dragging its blade along the ground. She charged him again, jamming the knife into his chest as she fell on top of him.

He grabbed Christine's right wrist, immobilizing the knife with one hand and her throat with his other, cutting off her airway. But Mixell was now bleeding from his shoulder, abdomen, and chest, and was slowly weakening. Christine tried to pry his grip on her neck loose with her left hand, and eventually, his fingers relaxed enough for her to breathe again. Not long thereafter, his body went limp, both arms falling to the ground.

She placed both hands on Mixell's chest as she caught her breath, staring at the man who was once her childhood friend. A man who had turned into something pure evil, slaying Jake's wife and maybe even Harrison and his daughter as well.

Her thoughts turned to Maddy and she hurried to the girl, checking for a pulse. She was unconscious and bleeding, but alive.

As she wondered how long it would take for help to arrive, she heard the faint sound of sirens growing steadily louder. It would take a while before they searched the barn, so she carried Maddy to the house through the heavy rain as paramedics and law enforcement arrived.

77

BREMERTON, WASHINGTON

The sound of conversation roused Christine from her slumber. She was curled on a couch in Jake Harrison's room in Naval Hospital Bremerton, where he and Maddy had been taken the previous night. Two nurses were attending to Harrison, who had regained consciousness after his surgery. Technically, she wasn't allowed in the intensive care unit, but an exception had been made for the CIA director.

She pushed herself upright, wincing as pain sliced through her left shoulder, where Mixell had driven his knife. The wound had been cleaned and bandaged, as had the injuries to her calf and thigh. But her physical pain was nothing compared to the emotional pain Harrison would endure once he became lucid and his thoughts turned to Angie.

Thankfully, Maddy had survived and was doing well. Mixell had fractured her skull, but brain scans had detected no swelling or damage beyond a severe concussion. She would remain in the hospital for a few more days, however, in case there were complications. Harrison's parents were on their way; Harrison would be in no condition to care for Maddy following his hours-long surgery, repairing the damage from Mixell's bullets.

The nurses left the room, and Christine stood and stopped beside Harrison's bed. When his eyes focused on her, they had a strange look. She pushed the thought aside as she took his hand in hers.

"How are you doing?"

He didn't answer, so she asked, "Do you understand what I'm saying?"

Harrison nodded. "How's Maddy?" he asked weakly.

Christine explained what happened. Just as Mixell was about to kill Christine, Maddy had shown up in the barn, whacking him in the head with a shovel, saving Christine's life. She chose not to mention Maddy's fractured skull. She was going to be all right, and there was no need to alarm him.

"Mixell?"

"He's dead."

When she used the word *dead*, her thoughts went to Angie, and Harrison's must have as well. His eyes clouded in pain, and he turned away as tears rolled down his cheeks. She held his hand as he worked through the emotion. When he turned back toward her, there was a hardness in his features, and he pulled his hand away from hers.

"It's your fault," he said. "If you hadn't talked me into joining the agency, Angie would still be alive."

Christine was momentarily at a loss for words. Technically, he was correct. But she couldn't have foreseen last night's outcome months ago. Enlisting Jake's assistance had been the right thing to do. At least, that's what she had told herself. In the deep recess of her mind, though, doubt crept in. Had she talked him into joining the CIA for the right reason?

"I'm done," he said. "I'm done with the agency, and I'm done with you."

"You don't mean that, Jake."

"I do," he said. "I don't ever want to see or hear from you again."

He closed his eyes and ignored additional attempts at conversation.

After a while, Christine resolved herself to the situation, which was only temporary, she told herself. Jake would stop blaming her; it was only a matter of time.

She went to the bathroom and splashed cold water on her face, then examined herself in the mirror. She wore no makeup and her face looked pale and drawn out, last night's events seemingly adding years to her appearance.

As she stared at her image in the mirror, she couldn't shake Harrison's words, blaming her for Angie's death. After contemplating his accusation for a while, she reluctantly agreed. If she hadn't dragged him into the first Mixell case, resulting in Trish's death, Angie would still be alive.

Harrison was right.

It was all her fault.

78

WASHINGTON, D.C.

It was unusually warm and stuffy in the West Wing basement, with the Situation Room packed with personnel gathered for this afternoon's meeting. The president sat at the head of the table, joined by Kevin Hardison and Christine O'Connor, a host of other staff and cabinet members, plus the three individuals who would lead this afternoon's briefs: Secretary of Defense Tom Glass, Secretary of State Marcy Perini, and FBI Director Bill Guisewhite.

Notably absent from today's meeting was Brenda Verbeck, who was under investigation by the FBI. However, the matter had been withheld from the public and even the rest of the president's cabinet and staff. Only the president and Hardison, a handful at the CIA, and a small cell at the FBI knew what Verbeck had done.

First up was Director Guisewhite, with an update on the simplest of the three issues on today's agenda—the gas centrifuges.

"Good afternoon, Mr. President. The investigation into the illegal sale of gas centrifuges by Snyder Industries to Iran is proceeding well. We've collected enough information to charge Dan Snyder and two others within Snyder Industries with a violation of U.S. sanctions. The case is ironclad, in my opinion, with the only question being—how many years will Snyder and his accomplices spend behind bars. The CIA deserves significant credit in this matter for discovering the sale of the centrifuges from the UUV communication intercepts, plus locating the equipment aboard the merchant ship en route to Iran."

"Good work, Bill and Christine," the president said.

Following Guisewhite's update, the topic shifted to the impact of the

U.S. Navy's intervention in the Persian Gulf. Secretary of State Perini continued the afternoon's brief.

"As you're aware, our engagement with the Russian warships escorting the merchant achieved its primary objective—preventing the centrifuges from being delivered to Iran. There's been no significant blowback from sinking the merchant, partly because we revealed that the ship was carrying equipment that would have dramatically improved Iran's ability to manufacture nuclear weapons and that the late identification of the merchant's cargo and imminent arrival at an Iranian port required quick and drastic action. Another factor in our favor was that the merchant crew safely abandoned the sinking ship; no civilian lives were lost.

"Unfortunately, the secondary goal of preventing conflict with Russia wasn't completely realized. While we avoided collateral damage to the surface warships, we sank one of Russia's nuclear-powered submarines. Your firm stance with Russia on this matter—that if a country puts its warships in harm's way, it has to accept that harm might occur—has proved effective. Additionally, the Russian submarine fired first, justifying *Jimmy Carter*'s response, counterfiring in self-defense.

"Regarding the incident, Yuri Kalinin has acquiesced. The Russian president remains indebted to America for our support during the military coup that temporarily deposed him, and while he's posturing angrily in public, he has accepted the outcome privately. Helping matters, their submarine sank in shallow enough waters—above crush depth—and we assisted with the crew's rescue. To summarize the issue, President Kalinin has assured us that there will be no Russian retaliation."

After Perini finished her brief, the president turned to Secretary of Defense Glass, who was prepared to discuss the most delicate of the three issues—Iran's sinking of *Stethem*.

"The evidence is clear," Glass began. "Based on ONI's analysis of the explosion's acoustic signature and inspection of the damage inflicted, we know an Iranian heavyweight torpedo sunk *Stethem*. You've asked for a payback plan, and we think one of Iran's new frigates would make an excellent man-made reef in the Persian Gulf."

The president nodded. "A superb suggestion."

Glass continued, "The plan is strictly quid pro quo. The frigate will be sunk by one of *our* heavyweight torpedoes. I was hoping to assign the honor to Captain Wilson and his BLUE crew aboard *Michigan*, but they've returned to their home port and the GOLD crew is now manning the submarine. However, *Jimmy Carter* is still in the Gulf, and pending your concurrence, orders will be sent to its crew."

The president canvassed the men and women around the table for their thoughts on the matter, and after no one voiced an objection to the plan, the president announced, "Make it so."

The meeting wrapped up, and as the president left the Situation Room, Hardison locked eyes with Christine. This had been the first of two meetings scheduled for this afternoon. In a few minutes, a second meeting would begin, between only the president, Hardison, and Christine.

79

WASHINGTON, D.C.

Inside the Oval Office, Christine took a chair facing the president at his desk, while Hardison selected a seat beside her. They had just spent an hour in the Situation Room discussing issues the public was aware of, and the president was now turning to the more delicate, confidential matters: Rolow, Khalila, and Verbeck. Each was a complicated affair with profound implications, especially with a presidential election only months away. Christine and Hardison had spent the last month hammering out plans to deal with each problem, with the president approving the way forward for two of the three issues thus far.

Regarding Khalila's execution of PJ Rolow, the matter was being swept under the rug. Much explaining would be necessary if the public learned that the CIA's deputy director for operations had been slain by one of the agency's own officers. The questions would likely lead to the revelation that Rolow had been killed by Osama bin Laden's daughter. The president's enemies would weaponize that information, painting the administration and CIA as incompetent bunglers, allowing al-Qaeda to infiltrate the agency. As far as the public was concerned, Rolow had died of a heart attack. His funeral had been closed-coffin, hiding the true cause of his death.

The next issue that had been resolved was the CIA's employment of Osama bin Laden's daughter. Only eight persons knew Khalila's true identity: the three of them in the Oval Office, plus Bryant, McFarland, Harrison, and the two linguists who had translated the video clip of Khalila greeting her brother in Kuwait. Everyone aside from the president had signed nondisclosure agreements preventing the release of Khalila's true identity.

"To follow up on Khalila," the president said, "keep her file sealed, and take measures to ensure her identity isn't revealed to anyone else aside from your new DDO, once he or she is selected. Regarding Khalila's disposition, I leave that to you. As long as you trust her, keep her in the family. The last thing we need is for her to end up on the outside—or even worse, the other side—where she might reveal CIA secrets or that the agency was idiotic enough to employ Osama's daughter. That's a mess that neither we, nor our successors, will want to deal with."

"I understand," Christine replied. "For now, she's continuing with the agency with the same measured trust Rolow exhibited. In my opinion, his instincts regarding her were correct. Khalila is an extremely valuable asset, as long as she can be trusted."

"I concur," the president replied.

The conversation then moved to the final, unresolved matter—what to do about Brenda Verbeck. The way ahead was obvious to Christine, but Hardison had opposed her recommendation. Technically, the matter was out of her swim lane—it was a domestic law enforcement issue—but the president had requested her input, given that she was the only one with firsthand knowledge of what Verbeck had done.

"I've come to a decision," the president said. "The only direct link to the murders Verbeck ordered was Rolow, and Khalila eliminated that lead. Without Rolow and Mixell, whom Rolow hired, the FBI has been unable to obtain any evidence that Verbeck is connected to the Pentagon deaths aside from her verbal admission to you, Christine.

"If the matter goes to trial, there's a high probability Verbeck will be acquitted. Additionally, I prefer to not drag my administration into a public scandal months before the election. Given the above, an acceptable solution has been devised. Verbeck has tendered her resignation as secretary of the Navy, citing personal reasons, and I've accepted."

Christine's hands clenched the end of her chair armrests. "You've got to be kidding. She orders the executions of two men and gets away with it?"

"I share your distaste for the solution," the president replied. "But if we press charges against Verbeck, the only thing we will accomplish is damaging my reelection chances. I might add, your jobs are tied to mine. If I lose, both of you will be replaced by the new president."

"I don't give a damn about my job," Christine replied, "if losing it is what it takes to put Verbeck behind bars."

The president smiled. "That's what I've always liked about you. A woman of conviction and moral clarity, regardless of the consequences. However, the odds of Verbeck's conviction are too low to suffer the consequences of her indictment."

Christine fumed as she considered the president's decision. She knew he was right, though. If Verbeck went to trial, it'd be Christine's word against Verbeck's, and without corroborating evidence, a good defense team would likely get Verbeck acquitted. It was an age-old paradigm: the rich and powerful get away with murder.

The president wrapped things up, addressing Christine. "You've done great work since you took over as CIA director, handling several difficult issues, including the recent Mixell incident. I must say, however—trouble seems to follow you."

Christine nodded. "It appears so."

"By the way," the president said, "great job on the Osama bin Laden issue, verifying he was indeed killed during the Abbottabad raid."

"Thank you, sir. I'm glad we were able to put that issue to bed."

EPILOGUE

"That was a close one."

"Yeah, too close."

The two men were sitting beside each other at a metal table in a ten-by-ten-foot room with a smooth concrete floor and no windows, surrounded by roughly hewn granite walls. It was cold in the complex, and it had an antiseptic *new facility* smell.

"Fortunately," the first man said, "the issue was contained. We'll need to do a better job on operational security going forward."

"The boss is already working on it."

The man on the left checked his watch. "It's almost time."

His eyes went to the blue folder before him on the table, then to the bookcase of thick three-inch binders, containing the notes from the many years of daily *conversations*.

He opened and perused the contents of the folder, looking up as a tall, elderly Arab with a long gray beard and wearing a white dishdasha was escorted into the room by a security guard. The man ambled toward the table, his slippered feet shuffling across the smooth concrete floor. The guard left, and the interrogation room door automatically locked when it closed.

The Arab sat down in a chair opposite the two men.

"How are your new accommodations?" one of the men asked.

"Adequate," the Arab replied. "We moved suddenly. Has someone discovered your deception?"

"Not at all," the man replied. "This lovely facility became available, so we decided to move."

"Why were you moving drugs into the facility as we left?"

"That's none of your concern."

The Arab smiled. "What shall we discuss today?"

One of the men pulled a picture from the blue folder and pushed it toward the Arab. "Do you recognize this woman? She goes by Khalila, but we were wondering if you could identify her for us."

The elderly man examined the photograph, then looked up. "It has been many years, but of course I recognize her. She's one of Najwa's daughters."

Both men scribbled a note about Najwa, Osama bin Laden's first wife, confirming what they already knew.

"Do you know why she'd be working for the CIA?"

The Arab's eyes widened slightly, then his gaze dropped to the picture again. When he looked up, his dark eyes had the expression of someone who knew far more than he was letting on.

"I doubt she is truly working for the Americans. But if she is and you'd like to know why, you'll have to ask *her*."

AUTHOR'S NOTE

I hope you enjoyed reading *The Bin Laden Plot*!

As I mentioned in the author's note of the previous novel, Book 6 (*Deep Strike*) was a mini-reboot to the Trident Deception series, moving Christine from the White House to Langley and pulling Harrison from the Navy so he could play a larger role in the series. Book 6 was also the beginning of a secondary plot involving Mixell and his childhood friends Jake and Christine. As detailed at the end of *Deep Strike*, there was a debt to be paid, which Mixell took out on Angie.

I telegraphed her demise in a previous author's note, mentioning that Angie stood between Jake and Christine, which needed to be resolved, and that I'm a thriller writer—I don't write divorce court scenes. If you were upset upon Angie's death, that's a good thing. It means that even though she appeared in only a few chapters, you connected with the character, which is what I was hoping for.

The next novel completes the Mixell/Christine/Jake storyline with a twist. Hopefully you'll enjoy that novel as well.

Disclaimer #1: The Dan Snyder character in *The Bin Laden Plot* is not the Dan Snyder who owned the Washington Commanders. I use real people's names for most of my characters—individuals who have helped me as a writer or who have won the option to be a major character at one of my book release parties. Brenda Verbeck is one of them, and Dan Snyder is her brother, both in real life and in the book. Another example is Jason Johnson, the Pentagon Navy chief who Mixell killed. He's my son-in-law, who wanted to be a character in the book, and I obliged. ☺

Disclaimer #2: The details of the raid on Osama bin Laden's Abbottabad compound in this novel have been simplified to avoid bogging down the story and to avoid areas where there are conflicting accounts of what happened. Additionally, the retelling in this novel blends fact with fiction to support the storyline. For those interested in the details, there are several unclassified and slightly different versions of the raid available via open-source documents.

Finally, the usual disclaimer: Some of the submarine tactics described in *The Bin Laden Plot* are generic and not accurate. For example, torpedo employment and evasion tactics are classified and cannot be accurately represented in this novel. The dialogue also isn't 100 percent accurate. If it were, much of it would be unintelligible to the average reader. To help the story move along without getting bogged down in acronyms, technical details, and other military jargon, I simplified the dialogue and description of operations and weapon systems.

I did my best to keep everything as close to real life as possible while attempting to develop a suspenseful (and unclassified), page-turning novel. Hopefully, it all worked out and you enjoyed reading *The Bin Laden Plot*!